FLIGHT
OF
SHADOWS

SIGMUND BROUWER

A NOVEL

FLIGHT OF SHADOWS

BRO

WaterBrook
PRESS

FLIGHT OF SHADOWS
PUBLISHED BY WATERBROOK PRESS
12265 Oracle Boulevard, Suite 200
Colorado Springs, Colorado 80921

ISBN 978-1-4000-7033-6
ISBN 978-0-307-44636-7 (electronic)

Published in the United States by WaterBrook Multnomah, an imprint of the
Crown Publishing Group, a division of Random House Inc., New York.

WATERBROOK and its deer colophon are registered trademarks of Random
House Inc.

Library of Congress Cataloging-in-Publication Data
Brouwer, Sigmund, 1959–
    Flight of shadows : a novel / Sigmund Brouwer.—1st ed.
        p. cm.
Sequel to: Broken angel.
Summary: In a future world where the fundamentalist government distorts
true Christianity, a winged girl named Caitlyn escapes to the Outside but soon
finds herself on the run again from an organization seeking her body's genetic
information.
    ISBN 978-1-4000-7033-6—ISBN 978-0-307-44636-7 (electronic)
    [1. Science fiction. 2. Christian life—Fiction. 3. Genetic engineering—Fiction.
4. Survival—Fiction.] I. Title.
    PZ7.B79984Fk 2010
    [Fic]—dc22

                                            2009048011

Printed in the United States of America
2010—First Edition

10 9 8 7 6 5 4 3 2 1

Other novels by Sigmund Brouwer

Broken Angel
Fuse of Armageddon
The Last Sacrifice
The Last Disciple
The Weeping Chamber
Out of the Shadows
Crown of Thorns
The Lies of Saints
The Leper
Wings of Dawn
Blood Ties
Double Helix
Evening Star
Silver Moon
Sun Dance
Thunder Voice
Degrees of Guilt

Caitlyn,

We had agreed—the woman I loved and I—that
as soon as you were born, we would perform an act of
mercy and decency and wrap you in a towel to drown
you in a nearby sink of water, like a kitten in a sack
dropped into a river.

But in the motel room that was our home, the
woman I loved died while giving birth. You were a tiny
bundle of silent and alert vulnerability and all that
remained to remind me of the woman.

I was nearly blind with tears in that lonely motel
room. With the selfishness typical of my entire life to
that point, I delayed the mercy and decency we had
promised you. I used the towel not to wrap and drown
you, but to clean and dry you.

As I lifted your twisted hands and gently wiped the
terrible hunch in the center of your back—where your
arms connected to a ridge of bone that pushed against
your translucent skin—I heard God speak to me for the
first time in my life.

God did not speak in the loud and terrible way as
claimed by the preachers of Appalachia, where I fled
with you. Instead God spoke in the way I believe God
most often speaks to humans—through the heart,
when circumstances have stripped away our obstinate
self-focus.

Holding you in your first moments outside the womb, I was overwhelmed by protective love. Even in the circumstances you face now, believe that my love has only strengthened since then.

I do not regret the price I paid for my love for you. But I do regret what it has cost you, all your life. And I have never stopped regretting all that I kept hidden from you.

Outside, wind and rain and darkness. On the main floor, rattling of the big windows that took the brunt of the storm.

But below, in the hidden rooms, where there was usually hushed silence, Jessica Charmaine approached a glass wall to a sound that she dreaded. Groaning.

Charmaine had learned that her hybrids on the other side of the glass had a wide range of sounds, and it wasn't difficult to read emotions into those sounds.

Sometimes, for example, she would enter and hear soft mewling. She would know in an instant that one had rolled away from the other. And that each would grope and roll until they were united again. She would help them back together and watch their faces contort in joy at the touch of the other.

Other times, their sounds expressed curiosity. Fear. Puzzlement. Sorrow. Frustration. She was convinced that they were trying to speak.

She knew why they were incapable of it.

Charmaine had two doctorates. The first was in genetic science, and the second, by necessity for this long-term experiment, was as an uncertified surgeon. She prided herself on her medical skills and her specialized knowledge. As required, using the equipment behind her in this large, partitioned room, she'd long ago mapped out the genomes for these creatures. She still spent hours and hours puzzling over their gene sequences; if she could unlock the mystery, no longer would this experiment need to remain hidden from the world. In her studies, she'd learned early by comparing the genetic mutations of the hybrids to *Homo sapiens,* that the FOXP2 gene of the hybrids had been altered by three specific amino acid differences.

She could have written a fascinating paper on this, definitively answering a long-disputed theory on why humans could speak and chimpanzees could not. The paper—and the existence and characteristics of her hybrids—would establish her reputation as a world-class scientist at the top of her game.

The irony, of course, was that the same existence and characteristics demanded the secrecy that would doom her as a scientist to perpetual obscurity. Unless she cracked the mysteries behind the genetic code of the hybrids and their near miraculous powers. To say the payoff would be enormous gave no idea of what was at stake. Without doubt, it would be the physics equivalent of generating an antigravity device.

She'd been close once. Oh, so very close. Decades earlier, as a co-director in the Genesis Project. But as the experiments neared the brink of final discovery, a scientist named Jordan Brown had unleashed a near-perfect storm of destruction upon the project. Along with the total deletion of irreplaceable computer data and all backups, he'd triggered a laboratory explosion and an official loss of all the cataloged embryos. Even so, Charmaine might have had a chance of rebuilding her research, but funding for the crippled project had been swept away by much larger events: the Water Wars that forced government focus on survival, not experiments.

All would have been lost, except for three embryos not listed in the official report. Two of the three embryos belonged to these hybrids, serialized embryos she'd managed to rescue just before the explosion and over the years had secretly nurtured to maturity. For these two hybrids, she'd sacrificed her personal life in search of her holy grail, and her ambitions had slowly evolved. Charmaine had accepted this evolution so completely that she took a different satisfaction from her long hours with the hybrids. When she first spoke to them, it had been merely experimental, trying to learn whether they had the required motor and mental skills for speech. Now it was different, reflective of her emotional commitment to them. Always the detached observer, Charmaine guessed that part of her bond to them was maternal, a subconscious reaction to her deliberate choice to put career—and this long-term experiment—ahead of anything else in her life. It could even be said that her affair had been dictated by the hybrids. She was single and attractive, but with her need for secrecy, she had limited her suitors in a practical way to serve her quest. Except for Jordan Brown, who had been a fugitive since the lab explosion, the man she'd chosen for a prolonged affair was the one and only other person who had knowledge of the hybrids.

Because of her maternal bond, when entering the glass cage, she would often lean over them, utter soothing words, or help each find the other if they had separated. They were adolescents, still growing. She knew they loved her. This gave her joy. Not enough perhaps to make up for the irony that such an incredible scientific achievement had to be hidden so carefully until someday she learned their secret. But enough that she did not resent all the time they needed from her. Their world had become her world.

Tonight, the groaning told her that for the next many days and nights, there would be no joy. This sound from their partition was a unique tone for them, like unarticulated words of resigned anguish. It told her that one or the other was feeling pressure again from unrestrained muscular growth.

One of the many alterations in their genetic makeup had left the hybrids without the ability to produce myostatins—molecules that fit into receptors on the membranes of muscle cells and blocked growth. Even without their deformities, their skeletal structures were incapable of withstanding strain exerted when their muscle growth bloomed past a certain point. Without the operations to pare those muscles back, they would have died years earlier.

She sighed. Yet once more, the looming collapse of their ribs would make the next weeks sheer hell for the hybrids.

The partition was lit softly and well padded on the floor, separated from the remainder of this laboratory by the glass wall that allowed her to observe them at any and all hours. Charmaine's side was equipped so that she could perform surgery in one area and indulge in her pursuit of genetic knowledge in the other.

Their side was almost like a nursery for babies. The difference was the lack of simple toys. The hybrids were blind and had only grotesquely short-ened legs and stumps for arms, born with stubs of fingers and toes at the end of their appendages. Their faces seemed to have smudged features, as if they constantly rubbed their faces against the glass.

She did not find their appearance hideous. At least not anymore.

As she touched a hand to the glass, their groaning stopped briefly.

She didn't know if they could hear her, or feel the movement of air through the circular holes at the top of the glass wall, or perhaps smell her skin. But she'd never been able to catch them unaware of her watching them. This awareness would be reflected by a stillness when she was nearby. Even when separated and mewling, each would pause in its search for the other, turning their deformed faces in her direction with the instinctive searching of visual cortexes that had never developed.

Charmaine sighed again as the groaning resumed, a sound that pierced her with sadness.

This cycle had hit both hybrids at the same time.

Charmaine hated it. One would have to suffer while the other received the operation that provided relief. There was no other way. They were too valuable to risk simultaneous operations; doing it separately meant if one died, the other would still be alive.

At her renewed sigh, despite their obvious pain, both hybrids wiggled their arms stumps in her direction. Waving, like small children. It didn't surprise her anymore. Too much of their genetic makeup belonged to *Homo sapiens*. This, too, pierced her with sadness, that they had the instinct to love her.

Now, however, for the first time in years, to help her endure this sadness, she had a renewed strength and sense of purpose.

Much as Jordan Brown had tried to stop it, the Genesis Project was on the verge of total resurrection. All these years later, she had just learned of his single mistake—in the aftermath of the long-ago lab explosion, he had not destroyed the third embryo. Charmaine now knew that the last embryo, like her hybrids, had survived to maturity and, unlike the hybrids, carried the genetic material that could unlock everything.

This embryo no longer had a serialized catalog number. But a name, given by Jordan Brown.

Caitlyn.

ONE

Tuesday night

Although the claustrophobia of the city oppressed her, Caitlyn felt most like a caged bird when she pushed her cart down the perfumed corridors of the Pavilion luxury hotel, her longing for the Appalachian hills of a childhood of innocent trust exacerbated by the endless walls gilded with artificial light.

It had been weeks since she escaped Appalachia, and sustained by anger, she'd learned that she had to blend in to survive. But she couldn't escape her longings. Finished cleaning one room, she'd hurry the short, shadowed distance of the corridor to the next, hoping the drapes would be wide apart so that when she stepped inside, she would immediately be able to look through the floor-to-ceiling glass at the far end of the suite to see the sky above the city and ignore, if only for a moment, the invariable crumpled bed linens, lipstick-stained cigarette butts, partially full wine glasses, and the other detritus of sybaritic living that marked the Influentials who moved through this building.

If the curtains were closed and the room was in darkness, Caitlyn would ignore the light switch and instead fling the drapes apart to give herself the rush of freedom that came with sudden brightness. For Caitlyn, the openness of the sky was a balm, allowing her to imagine she was above the clutter and noise and greediness of the city. Even then, there was cruelty in the transparency of her prison, for this brief joy also brought the need to feel the winds that had given her shivers of pleasure when, as a girl in Appalachia, before she'd understood what she would become, she and her father would perch on a rocky ledge to overlook a valley and hawks on the updrafts.

Despite the sheets of glass that blocked the wind from her, she would pause frequently from sorting wet towels or from wiping stains and hair off porcelain to look out again and let the view brighten her soul, letting her mind drift to those memories, wishing she could step out through the glass and into the void, wishing that wind was pushing against her face again. Like the first time she'd discovered the reason for her instinctive yearning for height.

When her drudgery in the soiled carelessness of the rich was too much and her yearning became too great to endure, she would flee to the flat roof of the hotel to stand on the hot, sticky graveled tar among the hissing vents. She would renew her cold anger by thinking about her papa—Jordan—and how he had betrayed and hurt her.

To draw on hope for strength and determination, she would turn her mind to Billy and Theo, her only friends, from Appalachia, who had escaped Outside when she did. They'd planned, the three of them, to escape to the west, through the lawless lands that bordered the city-states to reach wild, desolate territories largely unpeopled after the Wars. But she wasn't ready yet. She would tell herself that Billy and Theo would wait and that she could go another day without visiting the surgeon it had been arranged for her to meet Outside. Day by day, she would push aside those plans because it was easier simply to exist, and she would take what pleasure she could in this caged existence by closing her eyes to the wind and dreaming of flight.

Of soaring.

Again.

Standing on pebbled rooftop tar, she almost didn't hear the faint crunching of gravel behind her, but she heard the voice.

"I know things about you. But all I will tell you about me is my name. Everett. So you can shout my name as you beg for mercy."

Caitlyn whirled at the closeness of the voice. It was dusk now, and she was standing near the edge of the roof, forty stories above the city. She had been soaking in the glowing filaments of orange and red among the streaked clouds to the western horizon, letting her unfocused gaze take her thoughts beyond the silhouettes of the other tall buildings of the city. Occasional currents of slight wind had swirled upward from the sun-heated city concrete, and she'd tingled each time at the sense of moving air.

"It was I who arranged for you to work the penthouse floors," he said. "You fascinate me. I know things about you, but I want to know more."

He was only a few steps away. There was just enough light to see a smile on his face, as if he'd deliberately engineered her startled response. A half-empty bottle of red wine held low in one hand. A glass of it in the other.

One glass. Just for him. He paused and took a casual drink before speaking again.

"At the end of every day, you come here before leaving. And you come up here during the day. Sneaking away from your work. Often. What is it? For me, it would be the enjoyable sensation of knowing I'm above all of them."

Everett lifted his bottle and pointed beyond the city wall. "Illegals and Industrials. Living in shanties and soovies, among the discards of their previous generation. Serving me and those like me. Even with a work permit, you're just an Invisible. Not above them in any sense except when you stand up here. Is that why you come here, to pretend your life is more than cleaning up after us?"

She hadn't known his name, but his voice was as polished as she'd imagined, for she had seen him many times, most often accompanied by a beautiful woman as he passed her and her cleaning cart in the hallway, never the same woman twice. Caitlyn found it mesmerizing: his polished appearance and the easy way he bore the accruements of wealth, the discreet jewelry, the sheen of his clothing, the thick silvering hair rumpled by design, the rimless glasses, the sheer handsomeness of a face that had lost no confidence even as the first wrinkles began to tug at the sides of his eyes.

He was a separate species from her. A prince unaware of the silent servant girl. Or so she'd believed until now.

As he stared at her, she could not find her voice.

"No answer?" Everett asked.

Something inside her began to recoil at the secretive charm at the edges of his smile. He was standing between her and the rooftop door back into the hotel.

"I know things about you," he said, "because I watch you all the time."

Another smile. Control and pleasure. He gestured at a shiny black globe on a pole at the edge of the roof. "I have an arrangement with security. Surveillance cameras. Everywhere. Right now, recording the two of us. Something I'll watch again and again when I have finished with you."

When I have finished with you.

As Everett sipped at his wine and watched over the edge of his glass for her reaction, there was a narrowing of his eyes, obvious even in the last light of dusk, perhaps to see if she understood the implied threat.

"Where do you live?" he said. "Where do you go after you leave this roof and walk out the front lobby? What's your name? What do you dream of? I want to know everything about you. I want to possess you."

A broader smile. "What will I find when we unwrap the loose clothing that you wear like a cloak? I think that's what I want to know most. All those hours watching you on camera as you clean rooms, wondering what you hide."

Everett savored another sip of wine. "We have all night, you know."

Caitlyn stepped sideways, to go around him. He stepped sideways too, chuckling.

"You don't understand," he said. "The door is locked. There is no way back into the building without the key in my pocket. I have the leisure to indulge in my desires. Here. Now."

"Security," she said, pointing to the surveillance cameras. "Someone will know."

"You truly don't understand. That's part of what will make this satisfying. Especially after all these weeks of watching you, waiting for this. I own those cameras. After, there will be many, many more who will enjoy watching what I do to you."

Everett shook his head. "Don't you realize how special you are? For those of us with jaded tastes, the prospect of degradation with someone as freakish as you must be shared."

Freakish. Her recoil must have been obvious.

"When you work," he said, "there are times your clothing clings tight to your back. It must be hideous, what you so carefully hide. Most women are plastic perfection. To unveil you will be extraordinary…"

More wine before he continued. "In a way, I'm a director. From hours and hours of surveillance film in various places of the hotel, I've put together a montage of your life as a maid. Your innocence and unawareness is so mundane that it cannot help but build an appetite for how it will end. I've had practice, of course. You're not the first. But I think you'll be the most delightful. None of the others in my films have been freaks."

His turn to take a step. Toward her. "It will be nicer if you don't fight. Try to find enjoyment in this. Think of yourself as a star, about to debut."

She backed away. Until the abutment of the roof's edge pressed against her. With a forty-story drop to the streets that she hated.

"Don't spoil this," he said. "Don't jump. If you are compliant enough, this won't end the way it did with the others. I'll let you live. You're special enough, and I have a suite in the hotel to keep you in. Who knows? Perhaps you will learn to look forward to nights on the rooftop with me."

She couldn't jump. Not with him so close.

Everett was on her with a swiftness that made her gasp, dropping the wine bottle and glass, showering her with shards. Then wrenching her away from the edge, pulling at her cloak, fumbling at the horrible hunch on her back.

Caitlyn hated the Outside. She hated the danger it seemed to hold for her. She hated that every morning she had to find a way to force herself to walk along the streets, ever watchful that someone might step out from the crowd. She hated the sensation of being pursued, although she told herself again and again that Mason Lee, the bounty hunter who had forced her out of Appalachia, was well behind her, left for dead. She hated that every morning as she dressed, she needed to strap a small, sharp knife inside a sheath at the back of a belt around her waist.

Her premonition had been correct, however. A hunter had shown up with the unexpectedness she'd dreaded. But not the hunter she'd expected. Still, there was only one way to respond.

Pinned by his arms, she was still able to reach behind and pull the knife from its sheath.

He was grunting in unnatural passion, lost in his hunger, arms pinning her, hands pulling at the terrible hunch on her back. His fingers found the skintight black microfabric and began to spread open the gap at the back. Pressed against him, with the wine on his hot breath washing over her, all she could manage was a small upward thrust with the knife.

Everett screamed, fell backward.

It was dark now. It took him several moments to realize what had happened. She watched him reach down with his hands and feel the hilt of the knife.

He struggled to sit up.

"You freak," he said.

His calmness was unnerving. He pulled out a cell from one pocket and snapped it open, eyes on her as he spoke. "Send someone up. She had a knife."

Pause. "I know because it's in me."

Another pause. "Of course I know the bleeding will be worse if I pull it out. Get someone here quickly. Take care of me first. Then her. Like the others. Make her disappear."

He snapped the phone shut. In the darkness, she imagined she could feel his glare. "Freak. It didn't have to be this way."

More fumbling at his pocket. "You can't see this, but it's the key to the door."

Sudden movement of his arm. A small tinkling sound farther away. He'd thrown it into the dark.

"No escape now," Everett said with a harsh laugh interrupted by a groan. When it passed, he said, "You've probably got enough time to beg me not to have you killed. At least let me enjoy that."

Caitlyn adjusted her cloak so that it covered her body again, hanging from where it was secured around her neck. She reached beneath the cloak and pulled an outer layer of microfabric downward, rolling it until it reached her waist so that the hunch of her back was now exposed. The inner layer was skintight, and with the breeze, it felt like her upper body was naked beneath the cloak. Then she moved to him and squatted.

"Back off," he said. "Don't make it worse on yourself. Freak."

She reached for him. He tried to push her arms away, but she was far, far stronger than she looked.

"I want my knife back," she said. And pulled it loose.

Then she whirled away. To the edge of the roof.

Freak.

She let the gusting wind calm her. The door behind her opened. Shouts. Two men. Maybe three. She didn't look back.

She spread her wings beneath the cloak. Pushed off the ledge into the open sky.

And flew.

TWO

At the sound of voices in the moist, cool air, Mason Lee stopped pacing on the rocky ground at the bottom of the underground waterfall. Because of the sheer blackness of the interior of the cave, Mason Lee had long ago lost any rational ability to sense the movement of time. He could only guess by his count of rat tails that it had been nearly six weeks since he had heard any voice but his own, an isolation so long that his right arm, broken and put into a cast in the days before entering the cave, had fully healed and he'd been able to strip the cast away.

Mason should have died from dehydration, far above on one of the ledges of the giant shaft above him and the river.

A stab of brightness in his right eye had saved his life. He'd been fading in and out of consciousness on a stone ledge near the top of the water, mouth torn and bloody from chewing on rope, delirious with thirst, maddened by the sound of water that was so close, yet so far, and sent even closer to absolute insanity by his fear of the dark.

The intensity of the sudden pain in his eye had clarified his conscious thoughts, and in that instant he realized that one of the rats he'd listlessly allowed to explore his body and lick at the blood on his mouth had bitten into the softness of his eye. Reflexes that made Mason such a good hunter served him, weak as he was, and he'd snatched the rat off his face and, in rage, snapped its head off with his own teeth.

Without thinking about it, he'd sucked greedily at the copper of the rat's blood. Instead of flinging the rat's body into the giant shaft that the waterfall had carved downward in the cave throughout millennia, Mason held on to the rat, feeling power return to his body as its warm liquid renewed him.

Complete insanity, brought on by the darkness, had retreated at the stimuli of the rat's actions and his own. Rational thought began again, and Mason's cunning had returned.

The presence of rats told him that he wasn't as completely buried inside the mountain as he had feared. Somehow, somewhere, they were able to enter and exit at will. The rats, then, gave him hope.

And nourishment.

Mason didn't eat the entire body of that first rat, but saved enough as bait to catch another. And, when needed, another. He saved the tails, guessing that he was eating one rat every day.

In those first few hours of his return from the dead, he'd also begun to apply rational thought to escape. He knew he was on one of a series of ledges that led to the bottom of the waterfall. Before she'd eluded him, he'd been in pursuit of the girl, aware that the series of ledges was part of an escape route. Metal hooks at the edge of the uppermost ledge supported a rope ladder that hung down to the next ledge. But climbing down was useless because the second rope ladder, leading to the third ledge, was missing.

There was a solution though. If Mason could find a way to split the rope ladder lengthways, he'd be able to use one half of its length to drop to the next ledge and take the other half with him to drop to the ledge below it. From there, he'd be able to descend the other rope ladders already in place. He knew at the bottom there was a way out. She had taken it. *She*. Caitlyn. The freak who had humiliated him and left him to die this horrible death.

In his few days trapped on the uppermost ledge, overwhelmed by panic because of his fear of the dark, he'd been uselessly chewing like an unreasoning animal on the rungs of a rope ladder coiled beside him, hoping to split the ladder.

But with the rat that had attacked his right eye safely digesting, Mason had searched for a better way. He'd felt around in the dark until he found a rock with a sharp edge. Then he'd patiently hammered at the center of the first rung with that rock, imagining with each blow that he was driving granite splinters into the skull of Caitlyn, for hate sustained him as much as the protein and liquid he drew from the rats.

Once that had succeeded in cutting through the rope, Mason knew he'd survive. There were plenty of other sharp rocks in this cave, and with rats to hunt, he'd have all the time he needed. Three weeks later, an estimate based on the count of rat tails and the length of his shaggy beard, he'd hung one length of rope from the metal hook at the edge of the ledge, and with the other half coiled around his waist and tied securely in place, he'd slid down to the second ledge, then repeated the drop to the third ledge with the uncoiled rope.

All had gone as expected. Until he reached the bottom of the huge vertical cavern, where the final rope ladder had dropped him onto a small semicircular landing area carved into the rock beside the water.

Sound, not sight, told him that the flow of the waterfall disappeared via an underground river. He couldn't cross the river; the flow was too fast. With no way of seeing how the water exited, he could not evaluate his chances of survival by holding his breath and going into the river, especially because he did not know how to swim.

Yet Mason Lee was too angry and too filled with hatred to give up on life. Caitlyn was Outside, somewhere. Fueled by fantasies of how he would exact revenge before drinking her blood just as he did from rats, he'd paced the semicircle, stopping only to kneel at the edge of the fast-flowing water when the pacing made him thirsty, grateful that he'd had the foresight to take with him as many dead rats as he could knot together by their tails. If this had been how the girl escaped, sooner or later others would come. His energy did not diminish, but rose with each day. *Hatred and anger.*

Now finally, he heard voices.

And saw the glow of flashlights, the first visual stimuli he'd had since being trapped on the ledge. He'd been so long in pitch black that the light was a stabbing pain again, but only in one eye, and it was in this moment he realized the rat had permanently blinded his right eye. His good eye, for his left eye was milky and had a tendency to wander.

He'd lost his good eye. Because of Caitlyn.

He'd deal with that soon enough.

Now he was offered escape. The lights and voices came from two men bobbing in the water with life jackets.

So this was how their kind fled Appalachia to the Outside.

Their flashlights were directed in front of them, showing the end of the cavern, where a small gap existed between the top of the river and the channel into which it flowed. This close to freedom, they would not have expected any more danger.

Mason couldn't swim. But all he needed was a life jacket.

"You smell something?" one man asked as they neared Mason.

"Yeah," the other said. "Some kind of animal."

They began to turn their flashlights toward the edge, where Mason was squatting.

He'd conquered his greatest fear—darkness—and now felt immortal, exultant with life and rage, and as flashlight beams pinned him, he pounced from his squat, throwing himself through the air like a panther.

THREE

Theo heard footsteps, which caused him to anticipate two things.

The first was that Billy's soft snoring would stop. They slept close enough together that when Billy woke to the sound, Theo felt Billy's huge body shift and tighten in response to possible danger.

"It's all right," Theo whispered to his friend. "I'm awake. It sounds like little Phoenix."

It wasn't pitch black in the soovie because it had been cloudless when nightfall arrived to tamp out some of the day's heat, and there had not seemed much of a chance of rain before they'd cocooned themselves for the night. No cardboard cutouts to block the soovie's window openings or the light of the half moon, or to muffle the raucous sounds of the soovie park.

Theirs was a stripped soovie, with a low weekly rental that they paid by working in the nearby glass smelter. No upholstery on the ceiling, no panels on the interior of the doors. Carpet ripped out. All wiring long removed for the value of the copper. Even the seat paddings were gone, springs removed. Theo liked to imagine what it might have been like two generations earlier, humming down a highway. Before gasoline rationing became permanent and before the government realized it could control migration with selective gas coupons. The ubiquitous six- and eight-passenger vehicles had become junk, millions of them, useless—until after the Wars, when families were forced to set their axles on blocks and convert them into homes. The vehicle graveyards became the neighborhoods of a generation whose mobility was limited to these gutted metal shells.

When it came to hearing, Billy Jasper never questioned Theo's judgment. So Theo didn't have to explain that when Phoenix's left foot dragged, he could distinguish the slight rasping contact against the ground from all other noises. She and her mother lived in a soovie down the row and across.

"She shouldn't be out," Billy whispered back. It was an obvious statement, so Theo knew Billy meant it as a question.

Curfew began immediately after dark. In the summer, like now, that meant later at night. Community policing was instant and often brutal. It had to be. A soovie was a fine place to sleep out of the elements, but it was essentially a trap. Few had windows, so makeshift cardboard cutouts were used instead. The wealthier among them had sheet metal windows that could be put into place at night. When the weather was bad, a soovie with blocked windows—cardboard or sheet metal—gave the occupants no chance to see out. In a matter of seconds, an intruder could do a lot of damage to a sleeping occupant.

Then came the second thing that Theo had anticipated.

A tap on the door. The girl always came to them when she needed help.

"Billy? Theo?" Phoenix was only six, but no child survived in the soovie park without street smarts. She was whispering too, hoping not to wake anyone in the soovies around them. It was a huge risk. There was barely enough room from soovie to soovie to open a door.

Theo didn't hesitate. He was sitting upright and had slipped his glasses on at the sound of her footsteps, at least a full minute before she'd arrived. Theo leaned across Billy, who was still on his back, and cracked open the door.

"Inside," Theo said.

With the lightness that only a child could possess, Phoenix scrambled over Billy. She didn't giggle the way she usually did around Billy. The man was a giant, but children sensed his gentleness with far greater acumen than adults.

Theo liked the soovie for the most part. The two front bucket seats provided a place to sit on afternoons when the soovie's interior wasn't too hot. Just pull out the cardboard window cutouts and let a breeze go through. Steering column was gone, so Theo found it roomy. Billy, on the other hand, would have felt crowded anywhere, so he didn't complain either. Plenty of interior storage for their meager possessions and, where the engine block had been removed, a storage area that was securely padlocked.

The back two-thirds served as a sleeping area. Theo had the driver's side because he wasn't nearly as large as Billy, who needed to fold down the front passenger seat to be able to stretch out completely.

With the upholstery and padding gone, not many places for rats or mice to hide, so no scratching or chewing sounds to distract him as he fell asleep. With the wiring gone, it meant no possibility for light supplied by electricity from the central circuits. But Theo was fine with candles. He was also fine with showering and sewage arrangements—none. Billy and Theo were required to walk about a hundred yards among the rows of soovies to reach the communal outhouse. Because of curfew and intense embarrassment at using a chamber pot with Billy close by, Theo simply avoided drinking water any time after four in the afternoon. It left him parched, but that was better than the alternative.

As for the metered showers near the communal outhouse, neither could afford them. This was good too. If Theo were clean, then he'd smell Billy at night in the soovie. Or vice versa. Both had to be clean, or both had to carry the sooty stink of their jobs, and then one didn't notice the other.

All in all, when they hunkered in for the night, Theo didn't mind living in a soovie. His prison dorm at the Factory in Appalachia hadn't been much larger. And for all that it lacked, he now had the one essential he'd risked his life for when he'd escaped the Factory. Freedom.

Theo savored this every day, even if the freedom came with a price— accepting the leadership of the soovie park's authorized gang. As long as he followed the rules, he didn't have to answer to anybody.

But little Phoenix had broken the rules. Theo didn't have to wait long to find out why she'd risked so much trouble.

"Billy," she said, breaking into a sob that she must have fought hard to muffle as she snuck past the other soovies. "You need to help. The death doctor is coming."

FOUR

A gang of boys, up from the sewers, had found Caitlyn. Distracted her from hunger. Last food she'd had was hours earlier, during a break from cleaning rooms in the Pavilion. Vegetables and crackers and luncheon meat from a barely touched room service tray.

"What is it?" The boys pointed upward.

Although one of the small boys below her had whispered, his question reached Caitlyn clearly. She was a gargoyle, hunched on a building ledge a couple of stories off the ground. She remained in a squat, arms around her knees, the hunch of her back against the wall, head tucked down for protection. She'd never felt this alone. Nor this lonely. Not even in the days after her father had first abandoned her in Appalachia. But she did not feel sorry for herself. Loneliness was something to be endured, no different than rain or wind. Or yet another attack.

She'd hoped the relative darkness and shadows would protect her until the night was so late the streets would be deserted. But the boys passing through this side street had been too sharp-eyed, the glow of the main streetlights too far-reaching.

When they had gathered below her, she didn't expect mercy. Illegals, whether as adults or as orphaned children of these street canyons, lived by their own rules. No face tattoos for them.

"Let's see if it moves," another one of the boys answered. Seconds later, a stone bounced off the building's concrete, just to her left. Then another. And more, until a few struck her arms.

Caitlyn flinched. No self-pity. But anger. At the boys. At life.

When she moved, the boys began to jeer. Then pelted her with more stones.

"A brick," one of the boys said. "Here's a brick."

Enough, Caitlyn told herself.

She stood. Balanced on the edge. That quieted the boys for a second.

"It's a person!" one laughed. "Get him!"

More stones. A gang mentality, formed in the very young. One boy tried flinging the brick, but he was not strong enough to get it more than halfway up. When it crashed, all the boys laughed.

Amusement and diversion.

She wasn't afraid of the boys. The oldest could not have been more than nine. She found herself grateful for the distraction. Anger at her situation was a better sensation than loneliness. Fighting in the rain took your mind off the rain.

A bigger boy found the brick. She didn't want him throwing it; it could inflict serious injury.

All right, she thought, *I'll give them something to talk about.* Beneath the cloak, she once again pulled the outer layer of her microfabric bodysuit down to her waist. Again, she spread her arms and, in so doing, unfurled the appendages on her back that formed the hideous hunch.

She allowed herself to fall forward.

She became a giant shadow, swooping down on them like a bird of prey.

They scattered, screaming at this supernatural monster. Nothing like this had they seen ever, in or out of the sewers.

As Caitlyn reached the ground, she passed just over one of the boys and gave a loud, hideous growl.

He yelped and somehow managed to increase his speed, then disappeared with the others.

On the ground, she found herself smiling. The growl was a nice touch.

Her smile ended when someone stepped out from a crevice between buildings. Someone taller than she was. Wider at the shoulders. The glow of the distant streetlights didn't allow her to see the person's face. Or even guess at gender. Until he spoke.

"Great trick," the male voice said. "How did you do that?"

"Go away," Caitlyn answered.

She gave her answer no thought, and it surprised her.

In a flash of introspection, she realized that circumstances had changed her. She was not the quiet Caitlyn she'd been as a child, growing up as a freak and an outcast, clinging to the father she adored and to his love, isolated by small communities in the hills of Appalachia in his ultimately futile attempt to hide her existence, and isolated within those small communities because she was so different.

Thinking of the attack on the rooftop, she knew the former Caitlyn would not have calmly rearranged her clothing before yanking a knife out of a man's belly.

What had happened to her?

She'd survived the hunt that had driven her Outside. Endured her solitude in the city. Facing this unknown man in the alley, she realized she'd become strong and unafraid of the unexpected. In learning who she was, she was no longer broken and ashamed of her freakishness, but proud and defiant, choosing to push aside all emotions except cold anger at what Jordan Brown had inflicted upon her.

The man was still standing in front of her. She was keenly aware that beneath her cloak, the microfabric was barely more than an extra layer of skin over her upper body and that the second layer was still pulled down, leaving the hunch of her wings exposed except for the cloak.

"Go away," she repeated. Her right hand was behind her back, on the hilt of the knife in her sheath, sticky with blood that hadn't quite dried. If her life had been reduced to survival, she knew how to face the challenge.

She watched him for a threatening move. After all, he, like the boys, was on the streets past curfew. No facial tattoos. He too was an Illegal. Unlike the boys in the gang she had terrorized into fleeing, he was beyond his teens. His arms and legs seemed odd. Longer than normal. He was thin, like her. Almost, yes, freakish.

"They call me Razor," he said. "I'm fast. I'm sharp. I'm dangerous."

Caitlyn didn't like cocky. Most nights she dreamed of Billy Jasper. Who, in Appalachia, had knocked a man off a horse to save her, had later waded into a raging river to keep her from drowning. Quiet, shy. And smarter than he believed he was. Unaware of how much comfort there was in the contrast of his strength and gentleness. "Add stupid to your list."

"Stupid?"

"Fast. Sharp. Dangerous. Stupid. You don't understand simple English. *Go* means move. *Away* means any direction, as long as you put distance between us." She tightened her grip on the knife. Continued to watch him closely.

Caitlyn had always been an observer, never a participator. She had a keen eye for detail. It struck her that while Razor was slender and handsome, he was off kilter in a way that wasn't obvious. Not only the longer arms and legs. His chest seemed slightly misshapen, as if his body had once been like putty, slightly stretched and twisted.

"I need to know how you did that flying trick," Razor said. "I've got a few of my own. Maybe we can trade. You learn from me. I learn from you."

"Go. Away." She'd just stabbed a man to save her life. She didn't want to find out she was now willing to pull a knife because of irritation.

A sound like scuttling rats made him look over his shoulder. Back toward the streetlights at the end of the alley. The boys had returned. With bigger boys. A mob, maybe twenty of them. Caitlyn didn't have to wait until they were closer to check for facial tattoos. This time of night, they could only be Illegals. But bigger and more dangerous.

"There!" came a cry.

"Don't run," Razor said. "They're like animals. They chase anything that moves. Besides, there's no place to go. You'll only be trapped. Our best chance is here."

The boys fanned out and moved toward them.

Caitlyn ignored the warning and spun on her heels. From her ledge, before swooping over the boys, she'd already planned her escape. Down the alley. To a drainpipe to climb. She was light. Had freakishly strong arms. High enough up, she'd cross over from the drainpipe to a steel fire escape on the exterior wall. And from there, a climb to freedom.

But Razor was faster than she'd expected, almost beside her. "I'm telling you, don't run."

At the drainpipe, she leapt and caught it with both hands.

And felt herself yanked down by her cloak. She barely managed to land on her feet. By then, the pursuing boys had closed the gap. Razor had pulled her down.

"Idiot!" she hissed. No time to make it up the drainpipe.

Razor had turned his back to her. Guarding her against the gang that pressed closer. Maybe four or five steps of space. But now that they had Caitlyn and Razor trapped, the Illegals were leisurely in their caution. Some carried short lengths of pipe. Others, knives.

"Think we've got some Influentials slumming it?" one of the taller boys asked his companions.

"One of them's the one that dropped from the ledge," came a high-pitched voice. "That's all I know."

"Back off," Razor told the tall one. "You'll be the first one hurt."

"Here? We own this place at night."

"Think so?" Razor reached into his pocket. He snapped on a small flashlight and pointed it at his face and grinned wolfishly.

"Razor!" their leader said.

"Fast, sharp, and dangerous," he answered.

"We didn't know. Don't do nothing, all right? We were only having fun."

Razor made a shooing gesture with his hand. They began to move away, without turning their backs on Razor.

Then a strobe of red and blue filled the alley, and the slow movement of the Illegals became full flight again, leaving Caitlyn and Razor trapped in the headlights of a fast-approaching Enforcer vehicle.

It screeched to a stop. The doors were flung open. A cop on each side leaned over the doors, each pointing a shotgun at the two of them.

FIVE

There was no need to worry about being caught breaking curfew—when Billy and Theo and Phoenix arrived at her mother's soovie, about a dozen people had surrounded it. Some carried lanterns, casting eerie shadows on the other soovies in line up and down the row.

"No!" Phoenix wailed. "He's there already!"

She pulled Billy to the back of the crowd.

Billy was taller than anyone and, over the heads of the crowd, saw through the windows of Phoenix's soovie. Her mother had earned money as a prostitute; she could afford glass windows. Inside, the silhouette of a crouched figure.

The death doctor?

"Phoenix," Billy said. Billy felt Theo close at his side. "Are you sure you understand why he's there?"

"Yeah," Theo said. His neck was skinny and made his head look big. The heavy glasses that were wider than his face added to the illusion. "People just don't let other people die."

In Appalachia, anyone who was sick got help from a doctor. Phoenix, half crying, had told them her mother was too sick, and now the doctor was supposed to kill her.

Phoenix tugged on the shirt of a man in front of them. He turned around, his face a scowl. He was middle-aged, a pattern of shadows from the lanterns across a balding forehead. "I was here before you."

But he backed away slightly, seeing Billy's size.

"Tell Billy," Phoenix said, instructing the man. "The death doctor is here to make my mother die, right?"

"Leave me alone." He tried to melt back into the crowd.

Billy was so aware of his bulk that he hated to even raise his voice. Yet Phoenix was more important than self-consciousness. He reached with his right hand and grabbed the middle-aged man by the shoulder and spun him back.

"Tell me about the death doctor." Billy squeezed his fingers on the man's shoulder. "Is Phoenix right?"

"Hey!" The man clutched uselessly at Billy's hand, trying to pull it loose. "This ain't fair. I'm going to bring this to Vore. He'll fix you for getting in the way."

"What is the doctor doing in there?" Billy asked. Other people had turned to watch them. "Why is everybody here after curfew?"

Having others take notice of the conversation seemed to take some of the fear out of the man. "Think we're here for fresh air? Her things are going to be divided up. And don't try to change the order of the line. I was here before you. So you're going to have to wait till I've had a good look at what she's got."

Billy was constantly afraid he misunderstood people. It's why he was usually slow to reply in conversation and why, he knew, people thought he was stupid. If they didn't say something directly, he'd puzzle over the words until he was satisfied that he knew whether they were using an expression or being sarcastic.

Billy didn't have time for that now. He wanted a clear answer. "Is the doctor going to kill her?"

The man screamed, drawing more attention. Billy realized that in his frustration he'd squeezed too hard. He released his grip slightly, and the man jerked away.

"He can't kill her soon enough," the man said, looking around him for support. "And don't think Vore is going to let you get away with pushing us around."

Billy was already knocking his way through the crowd, ignoring cries of complaint. He was aware that Theo and Phoenix had followed.

At the soovie, Billy knocked on the window. The figure inside was holding an extended needle.

"She's not dead yet," the doctor snarled, his voice clear through the closed glass windows. "Give her some respect at least."

"Mommy!" Phoenix cried. "Mommy!"

Whimpering from the woman.

"Leave her alone," Billy said, his face close to the glass.

"You're kidding, right? Or are you an idiot?"

"Open the door."

"Go away."

Howls of protest came from behind Billy. He didn't care. He opened the door and reached inside. Clutched at the doctor's arm. Succeeded in yanking away the arm with the needle. He didn't let go and started to pull the man out of the soovie.

"Here comes Vore!" someone shouted.

Billy kept pulling. He reached in with his second hand to get better traction. He turned the doctor sideways and managed to get the doctor's head and part of his shoulders out of the soovie. Billy felt a pinprick of pain, but ignored it. Until he realized there was a needle in his forearm. Billy dropped his second hand and snapped the needle off at the base.

He resumed pulling. Without anger. He simply needed this man away from Phoenix's mother. Once this fight was finished, he'd turn to the next fight. Even if that meant Vore.

"Billy! Billy! Billy!" It was Theo, with rapid pulls at Billy's shirt. "This is serious."

The silence of the crowd behind him told Billy that something had changed. He still didn't quit until he'd managed to pull the doctor out completely.

Phoenix jumped up and crawled inside. "Mommy. Mommy."

More whimpering, but the sounds changed to comfort. Phoenix pulled the door shut.

Billy turned away from the soovie. Coming through the crowd was a man his size, but with a huge belly. Shaved bald. With five men, nearly as big, in formation behind him, like geese in flight, except much more ponderous and deliberate.

"Lock it," Billy said to Phoenix. "Don't let anyone back in."

Billy shut the soovie door and turned to Vore.

"I've been wondering when you'd try something," Vore said. He held up his hand, commanding his gang to stop. "Guys like you join a soovie park, and sooner or later you think you can take the top position."

Theo stepped forward, between Vore and Billy. "He's just helping the woman."

Vore snorted. "You're the kid who walks around talking to himself all day. How about you get out of here before I snap you like a chicken bone."

"Just listen," Theo said. "He's not here to run a gang. The little girl came to us because—"

Vore slapped at Theo, knocking him down like a mosquito. "Shut up."

Billy reacted. Didn't try to think it through like usual. Just reacted. He took the half step to cover the distance to Vore. He brought his hand back to punch.

Vore smiled. Almost a leer.

Theo wobbled to his feet. He jumped on Billy's arm. Hung on it.

"Don't," Theo said, gasping. "They'll kill us."

At least that's what Billy thought Theo was saying. Theo's voice sounded hollow.

Billy's arm was a solid rock, unwavering with Theo's weight on it.

"Billy," Theo said. "I lost my glasses. But don't worry. I'm not hurt. Don't fight."

Which to Billy was a lie. Theo was hurt. His nose was sideways, red with gore. Billy lowered his arm. He was blinking, trying to figure out what to do. All of this had happened so fast. He was all right with what might happen to him next. He'd been hurt before and wasn't afraid of pain. But it wasn't right that Theo might suffer.

The other five had taken advantage of the distraction to surround them.

"Hey, Vore!" the man Phoenix had first asked to explain the death doctor to Billy was shouting. "Kill them! We get to divide their stuff too, right?"

Vore swung his head sideways and silenced the man simply by staring.

Billy squinted. It actually looked like a second Vore was standing in front of him. A dull roar seemed to fill his ears.

Vore, both of them in his vision, tilted slightly.

Billy realized he was on his knees.

Theo was trying to hold him upright.

The needle, in Billy's forearm. He remembered feeling it earlier. But it was difficult to put that thought into words. Whatever the doctor had been ready to inject into Phoenix's mother was now in Billy.

"Knife out their eyes," Vore instructed his men. "They'll still be able to work for us."

"Won't matter to me," Theo said defiantly. He was fighting to keep Billy upright. "I can hardly see anyway."

"No," Billy said. The noise came from his mouth like a slow vibration. He felt himself sway.

Vore grinned. To Billy, the movement on Vore's face seemed to shimmer.

Without warning, an immense panic overwhelmed Billy. So sharp and powerful that he lurched to his feet again despite the drugs washing through his body. Something terrible! Nearby! Monsters! Danger!

He began to flail.

Theo jumped away screaming. Only for a split second. There was a blue arc, striking Theo like a horizontal lightning bolt.

Theo wasn't the only one who had screamed. The five men surrounding them had first crouched, then bolted with yells of fear. Vore too screamed. He had spun around, lurching away from them, trampling anyone in his way. The crowd had become fluid in mass hysteria, scattering in all directions.

Something horrible was happening. But Billy couldn't leave Phoenix behind. Or Theo.

Billy fought his panic and the death drugs that had been injected into him. He picked Theo up and held him under an arm. Billy dragged himself back toward the soovie, Theo limp in his grasp.

Billy's tongue was dead. He tried to call Phoenix's name but couldn't make a sound, paralyzed by the overwhelming sense of panic he could not shake.

Billy managed to get his fingers on the door handle. He tore at it, and his hand popped loose. He realized he'd pulled the handle off the door.

Billy tried to pull the door from the frame, but the steel was unyielding. The effort drained him, and he found himself on his knees with the roaring in his ears now so loud he couldn't hear Phoenix anymore.

Then, as his consciousness darkened, came nothing.

SIX

Two men with long-handled gaffs stood on the bank of a narrow, fast-moving river, about a half mile from the guarded wall at the base of the mountain, well screened by the terrain and trees. A glow of orange was all they could see to indicate the lights and barbed wire and high electric fence that made for a two-hundred-yard cleared zone on the Appalachian side of this wall, a perimeter that flanked the entirety of the small state that had seceded from the rest of America to form a theocracy.

While the river came from the direction of the wall and flowed from the base of the mountain, it did not pass under the wall. It flowed out from a cave just above the two men. An underground river that surfaced here. They'd been alerted that a couple of Appalachians were about to escape, helped by the Clan. The two men had blankets and ample food waiting for the Appalachians.

Johnny Brannon was here in case either of them needed medical help. As a physician's assistant and a father of two young boys, he had difficulty finding time for much when it came down to it, but he made time for this.

Like Abe Turner, the older man, Brannon lived in Lynchburg. Small towns had all but disappeared after the Wars. Too difficult to protect against roving bands of Illegals. The landscape here in the Carolinas and all along the eastern seaboard was a lot different than it had been a hundred years earlier. After the Wars, the natural evolution of societal living had been a regression to the walled cities of ancient times. Influentials had shifted to city-states, linked by high-speed rail at three hundred miles per hour, where it was possible to protect about thirty thousand in the inner core with twenty-foot-high walls and patrolling soldiers. Generally about a hundred thousand camped outside the walls, the daily migrant workers who were allowed through the guarded checkpoints into the city to supply cheap labor. All open land between the city-states was country without law and structure.

Abe Turner scanned the fast-moving water with his flashlight.

"Matthew 4:18, brother," Abe said. Abe had escaped Appalachia about a decade earlier but refused to talk about the circumstances.

For the sake of God's love, Johnny Brannon, the younger man, told himself, *find the patience to let the old man ramble.*

"Yup, like Jesus said," Abe continued. "I will make you fishers of men."

Matthew 4:19. Johnny internalized the correction. No point making Abe feel bad.

Johnny couldn't spend as much time on the Bible and the history of it as he'd like to but still gave serious effort to learning. His wife was tolerant of his faith but wasn't a believer.

"Who knew it could be so exciting to be a follower?" Abe asked. "We've got gaffs here, not a rod and reel, of course, but we'll still pull them out, like fishers of men."

"Didn't the disciples fish with nets?" Johnny asked. He couldn't help himself after all. But Abe could be so pompous and condescending. Johnny sometimes thought that was the reason Abe liked being a believer. Everyone had to be nice to him.

"Maybe some used nets," Abe said, "but when Jesus is in your heart, he speaks right to a person. I'm no net fisherman, so how could Jesus be speaking to me about net fishing? What I hear is the Lord telling me to use the right kind of bait and to reel in all those unbelievers who need him so bad."

So imposing your modern-day perspective on a manuscript thousands of years old is the best way to understand the Bible? Choose an interpretation that makes you feel good? Johnny was thinking something different. That the fishing Jesus saw involved throwing a net out and dragging it back in, keeping it in constant repair. This took hard work and patience, often with a lack of results. Fishermen of that day had hands scored with scars, sore backs. It wasn't as exciting as reeling in a hard-fighting bass.

Johnny was determined to be respectful of the older man, however, and didn't speak those thoughts.

Johnny took his mind off the minor irritation by thinking how brave these Appalachians were, so determined to get away from the religious prison of their country, wondering what it would be like going through a long underground river, not quite knowing what was waiting Outside or even if you'd make it.

This was just the starting point. Johnny and Abe would get the men from the river onto a train, on the northeast route for a couple hours of high-speed to Lynchburg. The underground railroad rotated city-states that accepted refugees on a six-month basis. Johnny and Abe, as volunteers from Lynchburg, had only made four trips in the last four months; one of the reasons volunteers traveled with the refugees was to form an immediate friendship and bond.

From what Johnny knew about Appalachia, the trip would be an incredible culture shock. Behind the electric perimeter fence that surrounded all of the steep and remote valleys of Appalachia were small towns, heavily policed by the religious leader, Bar Elohim, and all travel, except for religious leaders, was done by horse and buggy. In Lynchburg, the refugees would for the first time see how Industrials and Illegals camped in shantytowns and soovie parks outside the walls, just for the chance to migrate into the city in the mornings to work for minimum wage, only to be forced back out again in the evenings. The alternative was to try to live in the lawless open land between city-states, where the survival rate for any but the savage and strong was too low to make the risk worthwhile.

The refugees at least, while never granted voting rights and doomed to remain among the Invisible, could eventually earn the right to get identity chips in their fingers and a form of citizenship as asylum seekers from the oppression of Appalachia. While unable to vote, they would have the right to legal work and to rent apartment units within the protection of the city walls, largely invisible within the system, unlike the Industrials, who had no citizenship and were forced to accept bar-coded facial tattoos if they wanted to enter the city for each day's employment. Smaller bar codes could have served as a way for computers to keep track of their movements, but facial tattoos were the most effective way of identifying the Industrials at a glance, and this made protecting the Influentials much easier since Industrials composed the bulk of the population. To minimize the chance of riots, Influentials barred them from gathering in groups and made them leave the walled cities before curfew. The lowest class were the Illegals—those who refused facial tattoos for the sake of freedom and were reduced to hiding in the city sewers or prowling in gangs outside the city walls, among the shanties and soovies, with a curiously structured society of their own.

Thinking about the tremendous adjustment these refugees faced took

Johnny back in his memory to the previous time he'd been here along the river. Unfortunately, with Abe.

Six or seven weeks back, they'd waited along the water, expecting only a young woman. Instead, there'd been a National Intelligence man, drugged for short-term memory loss. They'd only been able to figure out his identity from a card in his sodden wallet. Carson Pierce. They'd never heard from him again, of course, nor ever learned what had taken him into Appalachia and then out again like this.

And there'd been an old woman with him—Gloria—and an odd pair of friends. A big, big man, gentle in the face. Billy. With a chatterbox kid who could barely see. Theo. Johnny had gotten the two of them into an apartment in Lynchburg and found them a job, then helped them run away, somewhere into the shanties or soovies.

About a week later, they'd been alerted to come back for the woman. But she hadn't appeared in the river. Instead, she'd walked up behind them. Completely dry. In a dark cloak that hid most of her body. She too had settled into an apartment, only to disappear a little later.

Lightning flashed from a faraway thunderstorm.

"End times are upon us," Abe said to Johnny before the rumbles reached them. "Won't that be great? Just like that lightning. Flash, we'll be taken away. All the sinners who deserve God's wrath will get left behind, and we'll be sitting in heaven, just laughing at all the wrongdoers and the full dose of God's punishment inflicted on them. Plagues. Wars. You name it."

Johnny was rescued from one of Abe's usual end-time rants by the sight of a yellow life jacket in his flashlight beam floating down the current.

"Abe." Johnny pointed.

The life jacket was empty. Abe snagged it with his gaff and dropped it at his feet.

Johnny scanned the river. Then came the second life jacket. Not empty.

"Hold the light for me!" Abe said. Unnecessarily.

Johnny did as directed.

"Hey!" Abe shouted. "Over here. Ready to help!"

The man kicked in the water toward them. As Abe reached out with his gaff, what Johnny saw in his flashlight beam was a snapshot of a man's face that would be burned forever in his mind.

The contrast of wet facial hair and emaciated face showed someone who had been in a prison for weeks, barely fed. And the remnants of the right eye, dark and wrinkled, like a puckered prune.

The man's other eye was milky and, in the brief time that Johnny had the light on it, seemed to wander.

Poor man, Johnny thought. *What kind of hell have the religious zealots in Appalachia put him through?*

SEVEN

H ey, Skinner, this is unbelievable," the first cop said. The fat one. He'd flipped Caitlyn's cloak over her head and had patted her down. He'd quickly discovered two folded pieces of paper beneath her microfabric and her knife in its sheath.

He'd tossed the folded papers into the front seat of the car, along with the knife.

Now her hands were cuffed behind her back. The cop had bent her over the hood on the driver's side of the car, pressed her face sideways against the smooth metal. She could hear the ticking of the engine cooling down. And smell the fat cop's body odor, like soured mustard.

"The knife?" the second cop, Skinner, asked. "Most of them carry something."

"No." Fat One was running his hands along Caitlyn's back. Until this night, no one except her father, and once a doctor when she was a child, had touched the deformity. Now, twice in the space of hours, she'd endured violations that made her shudder with shame and rage.

"She's wearing some kind of tight bodysuit," Fat One said to his partner across the hood. "There's some kind of opening, a vertical slit down the back. And something really weird underneath."

The cop was going to reach inside. It was over then. Her secret exposed. She should have listened to Jordan, gone immediately to the surgeon he had sent her out of Appalachia to find.

"Leave her alone," Razor said, handcuffed too and bent across the other side of the hood. "Unless you want a major civil liability."

Caitlyn was blinded by the cloak over her head but heard a thump on the hood. And a groan from Razor.

"That give you any idea of why you should keep your mouth shut?" Skinner said to Razor.

"Monitor this," Razor said. "I'm clearly saying that you lifted my head and banged it down. That's another civil rights violation."

Another thump. "Illegals don't have civil rights. Even if they did, my partner has a probable cause to search for weapons. He already found a knife."

The fat cop's hands were pulling the microfabric apart where it had been designed to snap open easily.

His hands paused as he reached under the fabric. Then departed. He'd stepped back.

"Hey, Skinner, we need a shotgun on her." His voice was quieter.

"You can't just shoot—" Razor's voice was cut off by a thump, harder than the first two.

"What do you have?" Skinner asked his companion. "I'm busy here. In a civil rights issue."

Another thump.

"Whatever it is," Fat One said, "we need it on digital record."

"So lift the cloak and turn her back to the windshield. Let the monitor get it."

Caitlyn knew what he meant. A wide-angle monitor mounted on the rearview mirror gave an unbroken surveillance of all squad car activities, including their arrest minutes earlier.

"You're going to have to come here with a rifle and a flashlight," Fat One said. "I don't think the monitor will get enough detail."

Every pistol and rifle carried by an Enforcer had a small video camera along the bottom of the barrel to record any situation where a weapon was drawn or fired. The surveillance records were used in postmortems, to justify an Enforcer's actions in court, or analyzed for additional training. But only in situations that involved Influentials.

"Don't think of moving," Skinner told Razor. One more thump on the hood. "Understand?"

Scuffling of leather told Caitlyn that the fat cop was moving around the front of the car.

"Get a good shot of her fingers," Fat One said. "This is some weird crap."

Then the cop's hands again, pulling apart the vertical slit of the micro-fabric. More tugging, oddly gentle, until her deformity was exposed and spread. Flashes of light told her that the cops were scrutinizing what they'd found.

"Insane," the second cop said. "A set of fake wings. What will the Illegals come up with next?"

"Should we find out how this is attached?" Fat One asked.

"Only if you want hours of paperwork to justify our probable cause for why we undressed her. Let's take her in and let one of the females find these...things."

"Good call," Fat One said, still staring at the wings. "Let this one be someone else's problem."

EIGHT

W earing a gas mask to protect himself from any remaining mist from the fear pheromones, Avery Weldon stepped down from the stealth chopper and waved his crew onto the ground with him. There were six new recruits to the National Intelligence agency. They too wore gas masks and carried stretchers.

Knowing they would follow, Avery didn't hesitate as he made his way across open ground to the side of the rusted soovie and the motionless bodies of Billy Jasper and the kid named Theo.

Ten minutes, max, Avery thought, before any of the dispersed crowd returned after the collective panic attack. Plenty of time to load both of the bodies and clear the area.

Avery wasn't looking for a crowd though. He had an undercover agent inside the soovie park. Avery expected the agent any second.

"We're in," Avery said into the microphone inside his gas mask, speaking to the undercover NI man who had called in for a helicopter rescue of Billy and Theo. "Now's the time to get out if your cover is blown."

The gas mask was equipped with internal speakers.

"I'm cool," came the disembodied reply. "Nobody saw me lob the bomb. I ran with the rest of them."

"What about when you Tasered our targets?"

"Only had to Taser Theo, to keep him from dispersing. Here's what you should know. The big one didn't run."

"But he's down," Avery said.

"I didn't put him down," the agent said. "He made it to the soovie before falling. The pheromones didn't scatter him with the rest."

Avery was impressed. Not many had the mental strength to resist the bombardment of senses inflicted by fear pheromones.

But if the undercover agent hadn't put him down, what had?

Avery knelt beside the big one. Frowned at the sight of a broken-off needle in Billy's forearm. The agent who had called them in said it started with a death doctor. Avery made the obvious conclusion. He clicked off his internal microphone to speak to his crew.

"This one goes straight to the paramedic," Avery barked. That fact that Billy Jasper wasn't dead yet was another testament to his strength. "Tell medical staff he was probably pumped with chemicals, likely some kind of euthanasia cocktail."

Four of the men strained to lift Billy and, once they had him on a stretcher, hustled him back to the paramedic on the chopper. The other two loaded Theo.

Avery went back to the internal mike. "You there?"

"Where else?" his agent said, somewhere among the rows of soovies.

"If your cover isn't blown, maintain the operation."

"For as long as you want." The agent sounded cavalier, and Avery guessed there was good reason for it. As long as no one in the soovie park suspected the agent's role, it was relatively easy living in exchange for substantial hardship pay. This agent had been recently divorced. He needed the money.

"Out then." Avery clicked off. He frowned again. This time because he heard sobbing.

It came from the rusted soovie. The girl. She had been protected by the soovie's windows from the fear pheromones dispersed by a lob grenade.

He stood and flashed a beam through the window, catching the small girl in the face. He waited for a scream of terror at the sight of his gas mask but immediately realized the girl was blinded by his flashlight. Could only see the bright whiteness.

"Where's Billy?" she said through tears. "My mother stopped breathing."

Avery knew what had led to their agent risking a blown cover. Avery would not have authorized the stealth chopper to get here otherwise.

The small girl was now at the mercy of the rest of the soovie park inhabitants. There were hardly any children in soovie parks. Of all that might be inflicted on the girl, slavery wasn't out of the realm of possibility.

But she wasn't his business. Soovie parks were soovie parks, outside of city borders, outside of city concerns. If people made a choice to live there, they accepted all the consequences that went with it.

But Avery was a father too. "Come here," he told the girl.

She shrank back at the strange voice and clutched the body of her mother, sobbing louder.

Avery calculated how much time remained of his self-imposed ten-minute deadline before the soovie park inhabitants started drifting back. Some of them, from experience, would realize that fear pheromones had been used to disperse them and would be eager to get at the contents of the soovie of the latest dead among them.

"Come here," he told the girl. "I'll get your mother to a hospital."

The hopeless will cling to the slightest of hopes, and the girl responded to his lie. She unlocked the soovie door and stepped out.

Avery scooped her in his right arm and lifted her off the ground.

"We need this one too," he announced to his crew.

"My mother! My mother!" She began to pound on Avery's shoulder.

Then traces of the remaining fear pheromones, brought by inhalation, reached the olfactory region of the girl's nasal cavities, just below and between her eyes. The smell, faster acting and more powerful than any other sensory cue, caused her mitral cells to fire a message directly to her nervous system. Almost instantly, she was overwhelmed by panic, incapable of rational thought.

Avery had miscalculated. Not about the presence of lingering fear pheromones, nor about her physiological reaction to them. And he knew the dangers of trying to stop adults from fleeing as adrenaline jolted their bodies. He'd been wrong in thinking he was strong enough to contain the girl when the panic hit her.

She exploded in his arms. The flurry of her blows knocked his gas mask askew.

In surprise, he sucked at air and had just enough rationality to swear at himself for his carelessness.

Then the fear hammered him senseless too. With a roar, he blundered and flailed toward his own crew.

NINE

Mason Lee huddled beneath a blanket at the side of the river with only his hands exposed. He'd eaten two sandwiches in a matter of seconds, slightly put off by the strangeness of the taste but too hungry to care. He held a thermos cup of hot chocolate and sipped it, grateful for the warmth that traveled down his ragged throat.

"You're safe," the older man said. "Just want you to know that. I escaped Appalachia myself, and I can tell you it's worth it."

Mason immediately tingled with a sense of danger. For the last five years, Mason had made sure that every single one of his bounty hunter captures went to every vidpod in Appalachia. If the older man had lived there, any second he might recognize Mason. That would be the old man's death sentence.

"How long back?" Mason asked. Casual. As if a man's life didn't depend on the answer.

"Been at least ten years," Abe said.

"Good for you," Mason said. "Real good." His voice cracked. He hadn't spoken much over the last few weeks, except for the mutterings and grunts to remind himself he was still alive.

That didn't mean, though, the old man was safe. Or the other. He'd let this play out before he decided if these two men might be more useful dead than alive.

"Mind if I examine your eye?" This was the younger man, who had introduced himself as Johnny, squatting beside him. "I'm a physician's assistant."

"Go ahead."

Johnny leaned in close. Mason closed his left eye—the wandering one—against the brightness of the flashlight beam. Much as his left eye had always bothered his vanity, it was always fun watching how people reacted to him. Might be more fun just being down to one eye, watching people squirm as they tried not to show they noticed. Mason liked people on edge.

"Punctured," Johnny pronounced judgment on the right eye. "Lost its fluid. I'm afraid nothing can be done. We'll have to remove what's left and stitch your eyelid in place."

Johnny was perched precariously on his heels. Wouldn't take much of a lunge to knock him over. Mason held back his impulse.

"Long term, maybe we can get you a synthetic eye to replace it," Johnny said. "Maybe some surgery to fix the muscles behind the other one."

"You saying something about my wandering eye?" Mason had knifed men for less. The gaff would work just as well once he got it from the older man, who was leaning on it like a cane. Or grab the gaff on the ground, just out of reach, that Johnny had set down.

"I'm saying we're going to help you as much as we can," Johnny answered. "We've got a safe apartment inside the city walls waiting for you. Nothing fancy, but it'll keep you out of the shantytowns and soovie parks. You'll have identity papers. Work permit. A job somewhere in the city. And a savings account with enough money to keep you going a few months. All thanks to the underground railroad that got you out of Appalachia."

Mason shivered as he forced himself to eat his anger. In Appalachia, because of his position, he'd rarely had to impose that kind of discipline on himself. Here, he wanted to get a feel of his surroundings. Like a panther dropped into new territory.

The older one, who called himself Abe, spoke. "There's blood on the other life jacket. The empty one. Just above the water line. Near the neck rest. Just like on yours."

Mason blinked. It was strange having just one eye to blink. He hadn't expected, of course, that Outsiders would be waiting here for the two men escaping Appalachia. When they'd first shone a light on Mason, though, it had not seemed like there would be a problem. Until this.

Now maybe he *would* have to kill them and take his chances. He clicked his teeth together, planning it. Maybe stand up casual and half fall, pretend he needed the gaff on the ground for support. Swing it around, take the older one first. Then take a little extra time and gaff the doctor in the eyes, get him back for the wandering eye insult.

"Let him rest," Johnny told Abe. "Look at him shiver. Who knows what happened on the other side."

This gave Mason enough time to come up with an answer.

"Going through the underground river, he went crazy," Mason said. He coughed a few times, almost like he was relearning to use vocal cords. "He screamed about things pressing in. Started thrashing around, pulling himself out of his life jacket, unzipping it at the front. Hit his head on a rock sticking down from the roof of the tunnel. Knocked him out. Blood everywhere. I tried holding him as good as I could. But he slipped out, and the water was too fast for me."

For a few seconds, although Abe and Johnny didn't know it, their lives balanced on a razor-thin edge. Mason looked from the younger man to the older man to the younger man, trying to gauge whether they believed him. At the slightest sign of distrust, he'd turn savage on them. Their food and hot chocolate had given him back the energy that the water of the river had taken from him.

"Some things I myself don't like remembering about my own escape," Abe said after a respectful silence. "It's why I'm here with Johnny, helping. You're in good hands. All you got to do is follow us, and everything's going to be just fine."

"Appreciate that," Mason said. Then, like an afterthought. "Either of you here when a kid named Billy Jasper made it out?" Mason asked. He wanted Caitlyn but didn't want to reveal it directly. "Strapping big one. Speaks slow but has a good heart."

"Oh yeah," Abe said, enthusiastic to help. "Had a kid with him. Named Theo. Quirky kid. Likes to talk to himself. Does weird stuff with numbers. It's supposed to be a secret from the government, so when they wanted to leave Lynchburg, I put them in touch with a believer in DC."

"Be good to find them," Mason said.

"No problem," Abe said. "We should be able to help you with that too."

TEN

B reathing through her mouth to avoid the smell of stale vomit, Caitlyn sat rigidly in the Enforcer car. She'd been uncuffed briefly before they shoved her into the backseat so the cops could cuff her again, hands in front this time, and the cuffs had been attached to a chain attached to a steel ring in the floor. There was enough slack in the chain to let her lean back, but there was little more she could do. The rear doors had no interior handles. No escape.

She kept trying to force her mind away from speculation at her fate. The cops had been wrong to judge her as an Illegal by her lack of facial tattoos; through the network that helped people escape Appalachia, she had been provided residency papers for a legal apartment and identity papers that allowed her to work. In theory, she had committed no crime, and once that was established, in theory, as an Invisible she had the right to demand to be released. In practice, however, she feared what would happen after she was forced to strip and her deformity was inspected closely enough to raise questions about her true identity.

In Appalachia, an NI agent named Carson Pierce had employed the bounty hunter Mason Lee to find her and her father. While Mason would never escape Appalachia, Caitlyn knew Pierce was here. Outside. Still looking for her. Back in Appalachia, Mason Lee had wanted to cut her apart for her ovarian eggs; would the government do the same once Pierce finally succeeded in what he'd begun with Mason Lee?

The Enforcer car passed beneath streetlights. If the cops in front were talking, Caitlyn couldn't hear. Thick clear plastic was a barrier between the front seat and back, with a two-way microphone and speaker. She knew this because when Razor had told Caitlyn the cops could listen in on their conversation, the second cop had flipped a switch and barked at them to shut up.

Caitlyn had given Razor the same instructions. If it weren't for him, she would have been up the drainpipe and a long way toward freedom.

Now Razor leaned forward to his hands. From Caitlyn's perspective, it appeared that he had bent as far forward as possible to scratch the back of his neck. He straightened.

The car alternated between shadow and light. It revealed that Razor had dark hair that looked like he cut it himself, ragged at the edges. He had even features, cheekbones verging on sharpness. Her guess about his age seemed correct. He was a young man. Who didn't seem too disturbed at his situation.

At the next streetlight, she noticed his fingers moving. Had there been a glint of wire among his fingers?

The car did not reach the next streetlight for her to confirm her guess. Instead it slowed abruptly. To Caitlyn, it sounded like the engine had quit. She saw the driver leaning forward, as if turning the ignition key.

There wasn't much traffic. Never was except for government vehicles. Only the extremely rich could afford gasoline and the taxes. But almost immediately, a black four-door sedan moved up to the left of the cop car. The passenger in the black car had his window down and was holding a badge, his lips moving as he shouted something that Caitlyn could not hear because of the barrier between the front and rear.

Caitlyn rocked forward as the cop hit his brakes.

The black sedan stopped with them. The passenger got out and leaned into the driver's side of the cop car. A man, midthirties. Khaki pants. Black sports coat. Showing his badge again.

Now Caitlyn could hear muffled words as the conversation continued. Nothing about the conversation seemed friendly. Both cops—Skinner and Smitty—were shaking their heads in the negative to whatever was suggested by the man from the black car.

Khaki Pants pointed at his badge emphatically, then gave up. He slipped it inside his sports coat. But his hand didn't come out empty. It was some kind of stubby, pronged weapon, not much bigger than his palm.

There was the flash of a blue arc and a crackling sound that made it through the thick plastic to Caitlyn's ears. Both cops seemed to vibrate, then slumped.

"NI," Razor said. As if this was routine for him. "They're the only ones who don't care what the monitor records. And the only ones with Tasers. At least legal Tasers. They only work if the fingers on the Taser match the fingerprints registered to it."

Khaki Pants hit the electric door unlock but waited for his driver to come around before he opened the back door to Caitlyn.

"Change of venue," he said in a neutral voice. He pointed the Taser at Caitlyn. "Don't fight me on this. I can throw you in the trunk as easily as you can climb in yourself."

The driver was a woman. About the same age as Khaki Pants. Tailored jacket. Dark pants. Dark hair. No smile.

She held a handcuff key.

"Let's get this done," she told her partner. "Pierce is going to love us for this."

"That's probably a big motivation for you, isn't it? Think I can't tell you're hot for him?"

"We're on the monitor," she answered.

"I know. Statement still stands. But come on, the guy's ten years older than you."

"If you weren't gay with a crush on him, what Pierce thinks about any woman wouldn't bother you so much."

"Cold," he said. Then he looked at the monitor and spoke loudly. "Pierce, when you review this, you gotta know she's joking. Really."

"And I'm in a hurry," she said. "So stop trying to impress him."

Khaki Pants stepped back, still gripping the Taser and watching Caitlyn.

No Smile leaned forward to unlock Caitlyn's cuffs. She smelled faintly of shampoo. Not a trace of perfume.

Razor lifted his wrists and rattled the chain that attached his handcuffs to the floor. "What about me? At least cut me loose before you go."

"Be glad you get to stick around for when the cops wake up," No Smile said in a flat voice, working the key into the chain that held Caitlyn's cuffs. "You don't want to be part of this."

Razor spoke softly. "Then I suggest you close your eyes. Caitlyn."

Caitlyn didn't understand. She kept watching Razor. Just as No Smile removed Caitlyn's cuffs from the floor chain, Razor lifted his hands again. This time no rattle of chains. And his hands were free. He tossed something past her, out the open door.

Her eyes followed. So did Caitlyn's. Except suddenly there was Razor's hand over her eyes, pressing her head back against the seat. Even so, an incredible brilliance flashed between the cracks of the fingers.

He dropped his hand from her face.

There was still a ball of white glow on the pavement, enough for Caitlyn to see both agents staggering and frantically rubbing at their eyes.

Razor scrambled over her and, without any hesitation, sprinted behind Khaki Pants. Razor yanked the man's coat off, pulling it backward down his arms so the man couldn't fight. Razor grabbed the agent's gun hand and twisted the Taser toward the agent. He squeezed the man's fingers against the trigger.

Another blue, crackling arc. Khaki Pants dropped, Taser still in his hand. With no emotion on his face, Razor lifted the weapon, pointed at the woman and squeezed the agent's limp fingers to shoot again. He opened the front door of the cop car, dropped the weapon on the floor, and paused to address the monitor attached to the rearview mirror.

"Pierce," Razor said, covering his face with his hands and speaking between his fingers, "whoever you are, better luck next time. That girlfriend of yours. Hot looking. Slow though. Might want to think about that."

Razor backed out and was panting slightly as he reached into the rear seat to help Caitlyn slip out of the car. The final glowing of the white ball showed where the key had fallen from the woman's hands onto the pavement.

Razor moved into the front seat and took back the folded papers and Caitlyn's knife. He returned to the backseat and grabbed Caitlyn's wrists and unlocked the cuffs.

"Told you," he said. He handed her the papers and knife. "Fast. Sharp. Dangerous."

"Told you," Caitlyn said, fighting the impulse to smile as she tucked the papers away and sheathed the knife again. "Go away."

"We're still live on camera," he answered, pointing at the rearview mirror. "They've already got cars on the way. No sirens. No lights. Rule of thumb. Enforcers can get to anywhere in the city in a hundred and twenty seconds. I'm not going to wait and argue. Want to stay alone? Or run and take your chances with me?"

ELEVEN

Wednesday

The doctor dropped this off for you while you were sleeping," Abe said. Mason was in Abe's small kitchen, pouring himself a cup of coffee. His back still to Abe, Mason finished pouring coffee as if he owned the tiny apartment suite and Abe was the guest. Mason's second cup already. In the cave, he'd missed coffee. Badly. The aroma. The taste. The small, satisfying jolt of caffeine. Missing coffee, more than rats crawling over his face, would have been enough to drive a man crazy. Mason thought with some satisfaction that it was a good thing he was mentally strong enough to have survived all of it without slipping into insanity.

He'd heard the padding of Abe's feet on the floor but had not turned. The old man wasn't a threat in any sense, except that Abe talked and talked and talked, irritating enough that Mason wasn't against killing the old man just to make the world a quieter place.

Not yet though. Mason needed access to the old man's knowledge. When Mason had taken a sip of the second cup, he finally leaned on the counter and faced the old man, as if giving Abe permission to speak again.

Abe was dangling an eye patch, holding it out to him by the string. "Your visit to the medical center is this afternoon. They'll x-ray the arm you said was busted, just to make sure the bone healed straight. Maybe today they'll stitch the eyelid over the socket, but it will be temporary, until you get a glass eye. Might be best for now to cover your eye with this."

"Don't need it," Mason said. He'd been vain in Appalachia, doting on his appearance in a place where appearance mattered more than inner self. Keeping his hair long and curly and his mustache neatly waxed. But that was his old self. Time in the cave had been like time in a kiln, burning away the outer self to reveal what was pure inside. He'd learned what was important. Making it through one minute and then the next. He'd gone to the edge and back. Was supreme now. Didn't matter how the world looked at him anymore. He was his own man. Had earned that by finding a way out of Appalachia. On his own terms.

Abe glanced at Mason's face. Then away. "Might help other people though."

"Meaning?"

"Until they got to know you, they'd be nervous. Just looking at you, I mean."

Abe was right about that. Mason had looked in the mirror earlier and noted with satisfaction how monstrous he appeared. That would help him. When he needed to force people to talk—and he could anticipate this happening more than once over the next few days—the more he scared people, the more they talked. He'd wear the patch and pull it off when convenient. Flash them the shriveled eye and stare at them with his milky left one.

Mason finally reached for the eye patch, feeling a twinge of pain in his right arm. Weeks in the cave, with a diet of rat meat, high in protein, low in fat, had knitted the bone. The arm was skinny, needed exercise. But it was serviceable.

He decided he didn't need the medical center. His arm was fine, and he didn't care about stitching the eyelid over his blind eye, or even having the remnants of the eyeball removed. Going to the medical center would just waste time.

Mason first wanted the girl. Then the agent, Pierce—the one who had broken Mason's arm.

"Where'd they end up?" Mason asked. Again, too cagey to reveal he wanted Caitlyn.

Abe was confused at the switch in conversation.

"My friends," Mason said. "Remember? The big slow one. Billy. And his friend."

"You want to get settled first, don't you?"

"I feel fine," Mason said. "Be nice to see familiar faces."

"Don't get me wrong," Abe said. "You'd be better off cutting your hair first. Put on some good clothes. Use the eye patch."

"I feel fine," Mason said.

"You grew up your entire life inside Appalachia. There's things you need to know about Outside, now that you're in it."

Mason savored another cup of coffee. The old man was a useless windbag, but he could at least make good coffee.

"What it comes down to," Abe said, "is that society here has what I call strata. Separate layers. Easy to tell apart."

"I'm listening."

"At the top, you have the Influentials. At the bottom, the Industrials and Illegals. Between, well—as an Invisible, you get ranked according to a lot of things. Not like Appalachia, where everyone pretty well lives the same kind of life. Here people judge you by how you look. If you want to be part of this world and move in it without interference, you need to look like you fit in. Invisible."

Mason grew still. He was, first and foremost, a hunter. He knew there were times when blending in was paramount.

"A person needs papers to move around? Identification?"

"You'll want to keep your papers on you. Just to prove you're not an Illegal in case Enforcers ever ask. Other than that, you have rights that the Illegals and Industrials don't. Go wherever you want. Inside the city walls though. Out in the shantytowns or soovies, it's a different story. Mostly, outside the walls they'll have to leave you alone. But if anything ever happens, they'll make your body disappear. 'Cause they know if you're in a position to report being robbed or assaulted, Influentials will take down their entire neighborhood."

Mason frowned. "GPS doesn't track everyone? A person doesn't have to carry a registered vidpod?"

Abe laughed. "See? Appalachia was your whole life. No, the government doesn't watch your every move. We have vidpods, but they aren't registered to keep track of your movements by GPS."

"A person can move anywhere. Anytime." This thought was intoxicating for Mason. To be a predator with no fences.

"Not quite," Abe said. "There are times I miss Appalachia for how it protected a person. Sure, you lost some freedom. But what you got in return was safety. Here, it's the law of the jungle."

Mason smiled at the thought.

"In the jungle," Abe said. "Might is right. And might comes in your right hand."

"People go around fighting?" Mason's heartbeat rose a little.

"Nope. That would be too uncivilized."

"But you said the law of the—"

"Jungle. You establish your power around here with money. That's why all the strata. Money is power. Power establishes where you fit, which layer is yours. The government doesn't follow your every move. But the banks do."

Mason swished some coffee in his mouth before swallowing. "I don't understand."

Abe held up the fingers of his right hand. Spread them apart. "These put me in a position as far above the Industrials and Illegals as I am below the Influentials."

Mason didn't like it when people made him feel stupid. "Do me a favor. Spell out what you mean."

"Once an Invisible establishes good credit with a bank," Abe said, "you're eligible for implants. Doesn't hurt. They're tiny computer chips injected into your fingertips with a syringe. When you buy something, you wave your fingers over a register, and the computers debit your bank account. You get cash from money machines the same way."

Looking at Abe, he felt the hunter's adrenaline. Like a big cat. Discovering wounded prey.

"Nice to know," Mason said. "Doesn't sound safe to me. Anyone could chop off a person's hand."

Abe laughed again. "You're sharp. That's what Illegals used to do if they managed to get you alone somewhere. Until we put in security measures. For starters, you need a password too."

"Good thing," Mason said, wondering how long it would take to learn Abe's password.

Mason drained his coffee and set the cup on the counter.

"Thanks for explaining things," Mason said. "Maybe you can help me get cleaned up right away for the trip to DC. I'd sure like to find Billy and Theo."

TWELVE

Caitlyn stood in darkness, a prisoner in a long, narrow closet with a high ceiling. She was alone, prepared for the actions she had decided to take when the door finally opened.

The night before, Razor had taken her down a hallway in the basement of one of the downtown skyscrapers, getting access through a side door beside the loading dock.

He had unlocked the bolt on the outside of the door and led her inside the room with exaggerated politeness that Caitlyn guessed was the result of the awkwardness of the two of them entering such a confined area.

Although she was curious as to how he'd gotten the code to the security pad that let them into this building, or how he was able to maintain a secret room inside it, she'd informed him she was not in a mood for conversation. Just in a mood for food. Razor had obliged, giving her bottled water and fresh fruit and cold chicken from a small cooler.

He'd watched in silence as she ate. Then Razor had set up the bed by pulling it like a shelf from the wall and promised she would be safe. Now he was gone.

It was obvious this was where he lived. On one of the long walls was the mattress shelf that folded upward when unused. When out, it filled half the width of the closet. On the wall opposite the mattress shelf, a few pairs of pants and shirts on hooks. At the far end, away from the door, with the small refrigerator tucked into the corner, other shelves had been built across the width of the wall, holding locked rectangular boxes. The lowest shelf served as a desk with a small chair tucked beneath it beside the refrigerator. Candle holders, with white candles burned halfway down, had been screwed in three places on the walls. Not much else. Just earlier, in Razor's absence, she'd explored the small space and found some books on magic. Under the mattress, there were small unmarked vials. With hypodermic needles nearby. And a short length of surgical tubing.

Upon first stepping inside this cubbyhole, Caitlyn hadn't asked about the full-length mirror on the wall opposite the bed shelf. Anyone who called himself fast, sharp, and dangerous obviously had enough vanity to demand the mirror.

With Razor on the floor, Caitlyn had spent the night on the mattress shelf, huddled beneath blankets. All through her childhood in Appalachia, she'd been safe and secure in her solitude with Jordan. As she remembered it, she had spent this innocence on a broad plateau between the past and the future, where little happened on either side to affect their lives. After Mason Lee had begun pursuit, though, she'd been thrust off that plateau into a life where nothing, not even survival, was certain from one hour to the next. Not even her father's love for her.

After her escape from Appalachia, in the weeks of living in the city, miserable as it had been, she'd at least found the plateau of routine again. Predictability. The safety of boredom.

Until the night before, when she'd been forced to leap from the top of a building. Once again, the present had become a knife's edge, where the past on one side seemed beyond existence and the future on the other consisted only of the danger that might arrive in the next hour, the next minute. The next opening of a door.

Like now, waiting and waiting for the outer bolt to scrape, a warning that someone was about to enter. She couldn't even be certain it might be Razor. For all she knew, he'd locked her inside and sent someone else to take her, for any of a number of possible reasons, none of them good.

THIRTEEN

Another hot, cloudless day, and Carson Pierce was well protected by the solar-reflecting glass of his hotel room, giving him a view of mirrored windows of the building across the street.

Pierce rarely presented any vibe except relaxation. It wasn't a pose. Simply an undeliberate result. Part of it was his clothing. He was far enough up the NI food chain to ignore dress code. Never a suit jacket. Today was a black mock turtleneck, short sleeves. Not fitted so tightly as to blatantly show off his work in the gym, but not loose enough to hide the coiled physical strength in his body, even at rest. His face and blondish hair would put him at thirty, but his eyes, a blue so pale they verged on gray, had a hardness that to close observers would add another decade.

When possible, Pierce preferred to be at street level. He needed to be near the action to understand it better, for it to seem real. That's why he was now in the Pavilion hotel, in the downtown core. Able to get onto the street for action in seconds, but in a place that allowed him to be wired for connection.

Otherwise, whenever he was forced to be cocooned in a sound-deadened, sanitized, and air-conditioned office at the big building, Pierce would stare at the computer screen's images as abstractions. He'd watch and make keyboard commands and phone calls, but it felt like a multiplayer warrior game, one without the special effects to compensate for the artificial stakes. Some midlevel agents preferred it that way. If the game didn't seem real, neither would the blood. Easier, then, to sacrifice players.

That's why he avoided the office. Outside of the cocoon, weather and smells and sounds reminded him that operations were flesh and blood and the clumsiness and randomness of people responding to pressure and relationships. It's why he'd gone into Appalachia himself to find the girl instead of sending in a lower-level operative wired for 24/7 audio and video.

It also meant he carried full responsibility for having returned without her weeks earlier. Why he'd wanted to remain responsible for the continued search.

After her escape the night before, Pierce had taken a train from home and checked into this hotel suite at the Pavilion, within a few blocks of where Caitlyn and the Illegal had fled the NI Agents. The suite was still a form of cocoon, but when things broke loose—a certainty sooner or later—he'd be out in the street immediately, in the action. Bean counters might argue the hotel was unnecessary, given that his home was only twenty minutes away, but Pierce wasn't worried. He had no desire to move further up the NI food chain into political territory, so another hand slap added to his docket was one more reason he wouldn't have to face a promotion. He also knew that Daniel Wilson, his immediate boss, who did work at a level where politics were unavoidable, would ensure that the costs were buried.

The reason was simple. This operation was high priority and tightly controlled.

Roughly two decades earlier, just before the Wars, the military genetic experiments that had spawned Caitlyn had been classified with code-ten security. Pierce knew nothing had changed the secrecy level or the urgent need for the code-ten. As Wilson had explained, the discovery of Caitlyn's existence in Appalachia had given the government a chance to recover crucial experimental knowledge that had been lost when a rogue scientist destroyed the laboratory and found a way to melt down all the software and backups. As proof of the politics Pierce would have to face if he couldn't avoid promotion, not even Wilson's higher-ups wanted to know details of how recovery of data would be accomplished. They wanted deniability, and they wanted the experiments resumed, but as before, out of sight. Pierce's small team of operatives understood the goal was to capture the girl; only Wilson and Pierce knew some of the reasons for it.

For Pierce, it had not taken much to transform the Pavilion's hotel room into a base of operations. Just his gym bag with a couple of changes of clothing and a toiletry kit. And his laptop and a vidphone and an encrypted Internet connection.

At a table near the window, with a view of downtown DC, Pierce had his laptop open and was ready for Wilson to come on the line for vidchat. A room service tray was on the floor behind him. Good as the scrambled eggs and croissant had been, he didn't think it was worth what the hotel charged. Coffee, on the other hand, was such a priority for him that the price could have been double and he wouldn't have cared. The Pavilion's coffee was excellent—he didn't spoil the dark richness by adding cream.

With a confirmation ding, Daniel Wilson's head and shoulders filled the computer screen. Wilson had a block of a head, covered with close-shaved hair that had once been deep red but was silvering after his three decades in the agency.

"Forgot to ask," Pierce said. "Did you get my postcard?"

Pierce had spent two weeks in Cuba after returning from his unsuccessful foray into Appalachia.

"I did," Wilson said. "So original. 'Weather is here. Wish you were beautiful.' Shared it with all my friends."

"But I was in Cuba. So that left nobody for you to share it with."

"More idle chitchat?" Wilson asked. "Apparently it's a bad habit that you've obviously passed on to your team. What's her name? Holly? Ten seconds into reviewing last night's mess-up on the Enforcer monitor, and I discover she's hot for you."

"That'll change," Pierce said. "She doesn't know me yet."

"You know I don't like complications anytime. This would be the worst of times for you to be tempted to do something stupid. Maybe she needs to be transferred. And the bigmouthed clown with her."

"I've looked at the tape a few times too," Pierce said. "They couldn't expect what happened, so I don't blame them for the escape. We're trying to keep this under wraps. No sense sending them out and bringing others in. And you know I hate the suits who expect their operatives to act like machines. If Holly and Jeremy go, I'd just bring in a couple more smart asses. More fun to work with."

"Don't make it too fun," Wilson said. Paused. "And thought I already made it clear I was done with idle chitchat."

Pierce rubbed his face with both hands. He looked at Wilson on the screen again. "Yeah. We almost had her. The Illegal knew what he was doing. He knew that everything was recorded."

"All of them do. Nobody lives on the streets long without understanding what happens when Enforcers show up."

"That's not what I meant," Pierce said. "He did a good job of orchestrating it. It's one thing to dodge Enforcers. It's another to be conscious of where the camera is while you're doing it. He's not a run-of-the-mill Illegal."

"We'll get him," Wilson answered. "He kept his face off the camera, but there's enough there. I mean, how many Illegals pull that kind of stunt? Forensics is pulling together the trace elements of what caused the flash. We'll track him backward when we find out how he got the chemicals. And we've got her face locked in with face recognition software. It won't be long. We'll have her."

Pierce had given plenty of thought to the girl's face on the video. He'd tracked and lost her in Appalachia, never once seeing her. If it hadn't been for a set of x-rays leaked from Appalachia showing the unusual bone structure that would support wing development, they would have had no chance of finding her Outside either. All they'd had to go on was the tracking device they'd managed to put into the glasses of a kid named Theo, because Pierce had been with them going out of the underground river and was able to find them later in Lynchburg. When Billy and Theo had fled Lynchburg and moved into the shantytowns outside DC's wall, it helped narrow the search. NI had access to all local Enforcer communications. It had been a simple thing to have computer software monitor for keywords that triggered an alert and to have his team on 24/7 notice. The previous night, all it had taken was the word *wings,* and Pierce had been notified in seconds, with operatives on the way less than a minute after the video feed confirmed the girl in the squad car was likely Caitlyn. Pierce was grateful for the lack of vehicular traffic on the streets—he was aware that a generation or two earlier, his counterparts would never have been able to strike with such swiftness.

"You know, she could have chosen any city other than DC," Pierce said to Wilson's image on the screen. "Isn't it strange she's here? In the lion's den? NI headquarters?"

DC, like New York, had copied the other city-states, ringing the inner city with walls. Clearing the postwar rubble around it with armies of bulldozers. And giving up on fighting the shantytowns and soovie parks that kept returning. Influentials needed cheap help, supplied by desperate Industrials who made no demands for any kind of government infrastructure.

"Stranger that the same night we find her," Wilson answered, "we have to stealth chopper her friends out of a soovie camp right outside DC."

"I've given that a lot of thought," Pierce said. "Can't think of anything else except coincidence. It happens. Not coincidence that they are nearby.

That's why we had them tracked from the Carolinas, and we were in alert mode here in DC. But coincidence that the near-riot happens the same night we finally find her."

"Still don't like it," Wilson growled. "Got the situation with the kid with the glasses under control?"

Theo. But Pierce knew Wilson wasn't a details person.

"Avery's going to try a song and dance on them at the hospital. We'll be able to track them once they leave. If it's not coincidence, we'll find out soon enough."

"In the meantime?" Wilson asked.

"Holly and Jeremy are putting heat on some of the locals. Holly will be here any minute to discuss it. I'll let you know if there's anything new, but I'm confident we'll get her. Soon." Pierce paused, then spoke in a softer tone. "This one seems different, doesn't it?"

Wilson was more cynical. "She can fly. It's not our job to ask anything about that. Find her. Move on to the next job. Keep the wheels turning."

"Got that message loud and clear. Just like every time you've delivered it about this operation."

"We both need to keep our heads down on this one," Wilson said. "This is way bigger than anything you and I want to deal with except on a need-to-know basis. You got *that* loud and clear too. Right?"

Pierce leaned forward to the computer screen, sensing Wilson was finished and about to go. "Got it. You and Elizabeth doing okay?"

Pierce didn't have to explain. He was good enough friends with Wilson. Trouble was, it seemed they didn't get together much these days.

"It's not getting worse," Wilson said. "I suppose that's the best we could ask for at this point."

"Can't imagine what it's like." Pierce danced around the word *leukemia.* "Luke's only eight."

Wilson gave Pierce a grim smile. "What it's like is that you'd take it on yourself if you could take it from your kid. And that there's nothing you wouldn't do to stop his pain, even if it meant putting a noose around your neck and jumping off a building." Wilson stopped himself. "Sorry."

"Let me know what I can do," Pierce said. "Really."

"Get this done; then get yourself over to our place and help me grill some Freddy Flintstone steaks, and make sure you don't leave until there's a couple empty bottles of red."

The screen went black as Wilson clicked off before Pierce could answer.

Pierce could guess why. Wilson didn't want Pierce noticing how hard Wilson had to fight to blink back his tears.

FOURTEEN

H ungry?" the man asked. He pointed to a tray with green gelatin and stale toast. "I can make sure to get you something a little better than the hospital food."

Theo *was* hungry.

"You're from the government," Theo answered, ignoring his hunger. He sat in a chair beside Billy, who was unconscious, his massive body filling the hospital bed completely, drip tubes in arms, breathing steadily. His right bicep was heavily bandaged. "Then tell me what's going on. One second, me and Billy are going to fight Vore. The next, I wake up here."

Theo had his arms crossed, staring at the blur of some big guy across the room who had just introduced himself as Avery from some agency. National Intelligence. Theo was having a hard time concentrating. His nose hurt. Not that he needed the pain as a reminder. Along with the usual blur, white fuzz filled the foreground of his vision. He'd already gingerly run his fingers across it, so he knew it was a wide swath of bandage across the bridge of his nose, pulling tight on the skin of his face. Cotton filled his nostrils. He had to breathe through his mouth, and his upper palate was dry.

"How about thanks?" Avery said. "You notice your nose is fixed."

"But not my glasses." Theo wasn't giving this guy anything. The hospital felt like a prison. Theo knew a lot about prison.

"To your left. On the bed tray."

Theo squinted. He had to resort to feeling around. His fingers bumped glasses frames. He snatched them off the tray. He ran his fingers over the frames and felt some bubbles where glue had dried unevenly. He put them on and winced at the pressure on the bridge of his nose but decided the pain was well worth the cleared vision.

Theo saw that the big man across the room was old enough to have wrinkles around the corners of his eyes. Short, cropped dark hair but bald across the top of a wide head. Sitting relaxed, legs crossed, in a black suit. Brown tie. Same kind of outfit as the men who had come to their apartment in Lynchburg and asked questions about Caitlyn, promising them money if they turned her in. Theo and Billy had done just the opposite—given Caitlyn warning, then run away, abandoning the apartment, the work permits, and becoming Illegals in a soovie park. Even here, this close to DC, they thought they were safe from government. He and Billy had believed that soovie camps were too unstructured and chaotic and had too many other Illegals for the government to track them down.

But somehow the government had.

Theo knew this conversation was about Caitlyn but wasn't going to show it. He studied the government man and pressed his lips together in a subconscious gesture of intended continued silence.

Avery looked amused, as if he understood that Theo was seeing him with fresh eyes. "It was the best we could do during the night to put them back together. By the thickness of those lenses, you must be blind without them."

"Hyperopia. Got it real bad. Means I'm farsighted. Can't count my own fingers without my glasses."

"Yeah. You check out fine otherwise. Doctors examined you same time as they did your friend. That thick scar on your right forearm. How'd you get that?"

"Not your business." In Appalachia, Theo had escaped from a Factory. Only way he could stay free was if he lost the tracking device that was put in every prisoner. He'd been forced to dig it out with a knife. Himself. The subsequent infection and fever had almost killed him.

"The report's got you at five feet four inches," Avery said. "Eighty-two pounds. You better hope you grow some, talking like that. Not always going to have your friend around to protect you."

"He's going to be okay. Right? And what about Phoenix? You didn't leave her there in the soovie park."

"Suddenly we're friends, when you need something."

"He's going to be okay, isn't he? And if you left Phoenix there by herself, you and me got nothing left to talk about, because as soon as Billy can walk, we're going straight back to the soovie park."

"The girl's getting medical attention. Here. And your friend is all right, only because he's bigger than an ox. The death doctor put a chemical soup into him that would have killed anyone else in twenty minutes. As it was, he nearly went anyway. Took a total blood transfusion to clean him out. You have any idea how much that costs?"

Theo had a good idea it meant that Avery and the government wanted something. Theo also had a good idea what that something was. Just like before.

"What do you want?" Theo said. He knew it was about Caitlyn. Like before. He was also wondering how the government had found him and Billy. "People who live in soovie parks don't have much money."

"Tell me about yourself," Avery said. "Not much chance you were born in a soovie park. What're you running from?"

"How about explaining what happened last night?" Theo had no doubt the government man was going to get around to a lot more questions. Once he found out that Theo wasn't going to answer a single one of them, he'd leave. Theo figured he'd better get his own questions in first.

"Sure," Avery said, very relaxed. "We heard things were about to get real ugly in the soovie park. We got there in a chopper. Dispersed the crowd. Took you out of harm's way."

"I could figure that for myself. How? I was so scared that I thought I was going to die."

"Not your business." Avery grinned. "That's a phrase I just learned from someone."

"How'd you know what was happening?" Theo asked. "With the crowd. To come in and fly us away?"

"You're funny," Avery said. "What makes you think you're valuable enough to be rescued?"

"We're here. You spent money cleaning out Billy's blood. You must have thought we were worth it."

Avery grunted.

"How'd you know what was happening?" Theo asked. "Then I want to know what makes us valuable."

"There's always someone in a soovie camp paid to pass on information to the government. Cell phone on a private frequency. Think we ever want some kind of organized uprising surprising the people in the city?"

This didn't sound like a lie to Theo. Influentials worked hard to make sure there weren't any riots. Too many Industrials and Illegals. Not many Influentials.

"And what makes us so valuable to fly us out?"

"Wasn't you we were protecting," Avery said. "It was Phoenix's mother. She, um, knew a lot of men. Heard lots of stuff from all sorts of places. She was someone paid to pass on information."

"Maybe you could have got there before the death doctor."

"Maybe. We didn't know how sick she was until it was too late."

"You went in to rescue a dead woman?" Theo asked. He began to think he shouldn't show too much suspicion in case the government really didn't want something from him or Billy.

"Went in to rescue a memory stick," the government man answered. "Had a bunch of information on it that lets us know who runs things. What they might have planned. You know as well as I do how the scavengers take everything in the first half hour after someone dies."

"Then I guess you're done with us," Theo said.

"How about answering one question then?" Avery said. Pleasant smile.

"Probably not," Theo said. It was going to be about Caitlyn.

"There's a second reason you had value to us." Avery leaned forward. "What you two showed was real moral courage. The government needs people like that. So here's my question. You and your friend want to go back into another soovie park and start passing information to us? Money's good, and we'll make sure you're always protected. Just like last night."

"Nope."

"Too bad. Guess we'll have to turn Phoenix loose. By herself. Outside the city walls. Unless you want to change your mind. Then we'll make sure she gets adopted by a nice family inside the city."

FIFTEEN

The way I remember it, they didn't teach us much history in Appalachia," Abe said. "Doubt that's changed."

In Lynchburg, blinking against sunshine that he just couldn't force himself to accept as real after all his time in the depths of the mountain, Mason had just followed Abe out of a set of steps from an electric train that looped around the city, just inside the walls. Boarding the train, he'd watched Abe swipe his right fingers once, then twice, past a post with sensors to pay for both their fares, explaining that for some items, a password wasn't necessary because the purchase was too small and it was more expedient to let people move through as quickly as possible.

Mason wasn't asking many questions, although he had plenty. Appalachia was a state where the size of towns had been limited to ensure crime rates stayed low. Here, he was in a city with people and streets and buildings crowded into a density that he would not have believed without walking through it.

Not that it frightened him. Or made him wish for Appalachia. He'd dreamed of this. A larger playground for a person of his appetites. No need to bow to religious leaders at every turn. Excitement and anonymity among throngs of people instead of standing out to be stared at in small cloistered communities where every movement was regulated for conformity.

But he needed to become as familiar with the territory as possible. So he tried to soak in what he could, occasionally craning his head awkwardly because his vision was limited to one eye. One thing that distracted him was all the advertisements with writing. Appalachia didn't have advertising. And reading was outlawed.

Not that he cared much. Here, on large posters, scantily clad female bodies advertised products. He didn't need to read to enjoy that. No wonder Appalachia didn't allow this stuff.

As for learning more, on the train, Abe had been a nonstop tour guide anyway, pointing out items of interest to Mason. In this way, it was good that

Abe had escaped Appalachia too. Anyone else would not have had the perspective on what Mason knew and didn't know about the Outside world.

"School shoved too much history down my throat," Mason grumbled in answer to Abe's question. "Hated it."

"That was history from Appalachia's point of view," Abe said, walking at a moderate pace, obviously relishing his role as a tutor. "There's a lot you're going to have to unlearn."

"Not that interested," Mason said. "Is that the apartment ahead?"

They were going to visit another Appalachian refugee. Mason knew he was in danger. Abe had been out of Appalachia too long to know Mason's real identity. No guarantee that would be the same at the apartment.

"Lot of stuff happened in America during and after Water Wars," Abe continued happily. "New national security measures that overrode any civil liberties. Reconstitutions."

"Life is what it is," Mason answered. After listening to nonstop babble on the high-speed from Lynchburg to DC, Mason just wanted the old man to shut up. Mason was irritated anyway. The sensors at the cash-free entrance to the train gates had not required a password. How could Mason get it off the old man until he watched him punch it in? "Knowing how things got the way they did doesn't change the way it is now."

"Doesn't it matter to you how Canada became the new Saudi Arabia when water became worth almost as much as oil? Then lost all power because they didn't have the national will to build an army to protect themselves and their lakes?"

"Nope. Don't even care to know what Saudi Arabia is."

"Destruction of the American economy when the automotive industry crashed because the refineries had been bombed by the Muslim extremists who took control of Great Britain?"

Mason thought if he didn't answer, the old man would get the hint. It didn't work.

"Automobile graveyards when gas got too expensive? Tent cities replaced by soovie parks during the massive depression that followed the Water Wars? The soovie uprisings? The building of the walls around the cities? When I got out of Appalachia, I discovered decades of missing history."

"Just miss my friends," Mason said, determined to shut up the old man. "Be great to find them."

It was a short walk past rows and rows of medium-sized square apartment blocks. Enough to make Mason miss the neat streets and welcoming porches of the houses in the small towns of Appalachia. But only if he were sentimental. Which he wasn't.

"Medium strata," Abe explained as they neared the end of the rows. "Nobody wealthy lives in this area. Just Invisibles like you and me. But the Illegals can't hide here either. Most everyone from Appalachia gets to this area first."

"Who pays?" Mason asked. If Mason ever went back inside Appalachia, all this information would be worth plenty to Bar Elohim, the nation's great religious leader.

"We're like the early church," Abe said. "Each of us gives as much back to the body as possible, easing the transition for whoever else makes it here. Once you're settled in, you'll get your chance to contribute and help other refugees. The important thing is not to dream about becoming an Influential. That's impossible. It's a closed system. Instead, remain grateful that you're part of the invisible middle class."

"Yeah," Mason said. "Everything looks the same here. Which apartment are we visiting?"

Abe pointed at a mark on one of the doors. "Right there, of course. The fish symbol. Just like the early church."

Mason saw a sideways double loop, with one end cut off. He guessed, with enough imagination, it could be a symbol for a fish.

"See," Abe said, "the age of Pisces—that means fish—began around 210 BC, and Jesus took the sign of the fish as his main symbol, and Virgo the Virgin for—"

"Shut up," Mason said. This was the place. He didn't need to be nice to Abe any longer.

"Huh?"

Mason knocked on the door.

A young woman opened it, looked past Abe at Mason, and shrank inside, her mouth open in horror.

"It's all right," Abe said to her. "I know his appearance might throw some off, but—"

Mason knew it was more than his eye patch. He saw it instantly because he'd been looking for it—recognition. But she made the mistake of leaving the door open a second too long.

Mason shoved the old man through the doorway, into the apartment. Abe stumbled, caught his balance, and turned toward Mason. Leading with his left elbow, Mason drove it into Abe's cheekbone. The old man didn't even gasp. Just dropped. Out cold.

Normally Mason would have stopped to admire this. But the woman had fled farther into the apartment. She was his priority.

SIXTEEN

The outer bolt scraped.

Caitlyn had been waiting nearly an hour for the sound, standing on a chair. An extra hour in the dark, wondering who would be there when the door opened.

She sprang upward from the chair. It took her about four seconds to get into place so that she was suspended just below the ceiling. Arms spread. The palm of one hand pressed into one wall, other palm pressed against the opposite wall. Holding herself horizontal. Stomach muscles tight with exertion. Legs unwavering. Facedown, with her back almost touching the ceiling. It was a position called the iron cross; because of her muscular structure and the lightness of her bones, she could hold it for minutes and minutes, far longer than any world-class gymnast.

She'd been stupid to trust Razor. He'd crept out, locked her in behind him. Obviously expecting her to be helpless whenever he returned.

When the door did open, the crack of light briefly revealed that it was Razor, not someone else. He held no weapon.

She said nothing from her perch above him. The element of surprise was, at this point, a better weapon than the knife Razor had returned to her after escaping the Enforcer car.

He shut the door, putting the room in darkness again.

Moments later, directly below her face, Razor struck a match. Lit a candle. Stuck it in a candle holder. The wavering light showed that Caitlyn had folded up the mattress shelf. With the exception of the chair beneath the shelves across the width of the back of the closet, it was essentially a bare room.

"Caitlyn?" His whisper held disbelief that she was gone.

"Impossible," he muttered. He moved to the back of the closet and crouched. As if Caitlyn could be hidden behind the chair. Above him, she was now between Razor and the door.

This was the moment of escape. She would drop, yank open the door, dash outside before he could react. With the bolt on the outside, she'd be able to lock him in the closet the same way he'd locked her in. Then she'd be gone.

But the door opened again before she could act.

"Hey!" Razor spun to face the light that exposed the entire interior.

Below Caitlyn, a skinny man in a wheelchair rolled through the doorway. Pushed by one of the biggest men Caitlyn had seen, even bigger than Billy. His bald dark head was directly below where she braced herself between the walls. The smell of rancid sweat almost made her gag.

"Where is she?" the wheelchair man said quietly. His hair was thinning. He had a blanket across his lap. A knife on top of the blanket. "Melvin sent for you an hour ago. Bad idea, ignoring Melvin. You know Melvin got Jimmy here."

With the light from the hallway spilling past the figures in the doorway, Razor's face was partly in shadow. Still, his expression was easy to read. Even from the ceiling.

Disbelief.

"Melvin?" Razor said.

"Think Melvin is stupid? Think Melvin don't know what's happening in his own quadrant? Think Melvin don't know all your secrets? Your playacting? This is Melvin. He's known about this weasel hole of yours for weeks. Just didn't make sense to let you know Melvin knew until it was worth Melvin's while. Like now. Melvin wants to know where she is."

"Where who is?"

"Wrong answer," Melvin said. He toyed with his knife and spoke without raising his eyes. "Jimmy. Only one. Don't mark him up. Make it the diaphragm."

Below Caitlyn, the big man squeezed between the wheelchair and the wall and advanced on Razor.

"Sorry, man," Jimmy said. "I like you. Just following orders."

Jimmy was wearing a gray T-shirt and gray sweatpants, and he flexed an arm as thick as Caitlyn's thigh and drove his fist into Razor's gut.

Razor fell backward, splayed on his back, his mouth like a gaping fish as he sucked for air.

"You're not dying," Melvin said. Monotone. "Most people start finding oxygen in less than minute. You just don't want Jimmy hitting you more than three times. He's Melvin's because he's the biggest man Melvin could find. Jimmy hits you with four shots like that? Diaphragm explodes. Then breathing just doesn't happen anymore."

Caitlyn felt like her own diaphragm had just exploded. On the floor, looking up, it would be impossible for Razor to miss seeing her across the ceiling. She was watching for it and it came—the flicker of recognition in his eyes as he registered her presence above him.

Razor blinked a few times in surprise. He wheezed as his upper body convulsed with the effort to breathe. And talk.

"Jimmy, help him up."

Caitlyn saw the man's broad, broad back as Jimmy reached down and pulled Razor up by the shirt with as much effort as another man might lift a kitten by the scruff. Jimmy kept hold of Razor, still facing away from Melvin and Caitlyn. If Jimmy turned now, he'd probably see her above him.

"Jimmy," Melvin said. "Shake his arms. You never know what he's got up his sleeves."

Jimmy shifted his grip, his massive hands dwarfing Razor's wrists. He followed Melvin's instructions. A small bouquet of flowers shook loose. Red roses.

"What's this?" Melvin said.

"Magic is who I am." Razor's voice was strangulated. "You know I love tricks. Poisonous fumes in the blossoms. You flip them in a person's face, and it knocks them out."

"Cool," Jimmy said.

"Idiot," Melvin snapped at Jimmy. "No poison in those flowers. Razor made that up. When you going to understand sarcasm?"

"Well . . .," Jimmy began.

"Shut up," Melvin said. "You need to learn rhetorical questions too. Just not now."

Back to Razor, Melvin said, "Melvin wants her. Where is she?"

"Don't. Know." Razor obviously still had difficulty breathing after the punch to his diaphragm.

"Jimmy. Again."

"I don't like this," Jimmy said. He had a weirdly high voice. Still holding Razor with his left hand, he threw another punch. Same place. Razor's body bucked backward.

"Keep him on his feet," Melvin instructed Jimmy. "Melvin hates leaning forward to talk to someone."

Jimmy held Razor upright, his back to Melvin and Caitlyn.

"She was with you last night," Melvin said. "Right? Melvin knows you can't breathe. So just nod."

Razor bobbed his chin down. Then up. Down.

"You had the flowers for her?" Melvin asked. "Means you expected to talk to her soon."

Razor nodded again.

"This is big stuff," Melvin said. "See, Melvin was all comfortable this morning, and Enforcers busted in. Don't matter to them that special arrangements have been in place for years. They're suddenly in Melvin's face, making threats. Melvin asks why, and what they show on a small vidscreen is some guy doing magic tricks and springing this girl from a cop car, and did Melvin know someone like that? Got to say, that was good how you did it. What was it you used to burn their eyeballs like that? Even on the vidscreen it was so bright it hurt."

Razor was back to the point where he could wheeze. But not where he could acknowledge a compliment.

"Any idea what she's worth?" Melvin asked. "Melvin wasn't stupid enough to tell them who you were. Otherwise they'd be here instead of Melvin. And Melvin wouldn't get a piece of the action."

Razor managed to shake his head sideways.

"Melvin turns her in," Melvin said. "Melvin gets about five years of what Melvin makes running the Illegals in this quadrant. Melvin don't turn her in, all those years of special arrangements with Enforcers mean nothing. They'll turf Melvin. Any idea why she's worth that much to them?"

Another sideways shake of Razor's head.

"What Melvin really wants to know," Melvin said, "is why she's worth that much. Maybe Melvin can play this for more than what they're offering. Got the answer?"

"No," Razor gasped.

Caitlyn's arms began to tremble from the exertion of holding herself in place. And from fear. Razor knew she was near the ceiling. How long was he going to protect her by remaining silent about her?

"Some people like the carrot and the stick," Melvin told Razor. "That's how the Enforcers worked Melvin. Promised a lot of cash first. Then told

Melvin how big the stick was if Melvin didn't deliver. Melvin appreciates that. Melvin is a stick and carrot guy too. You just got a taste of how Jimmy does his business. That should be enough to convince you why you should deliver her. But there's a carrot here too. You'll get half of what Melvin gets from the Enforcers. So asking again, where is she?"

Caitlyn waited for Razor to lift his eyes and give away her presence, only a couple of feet above their heads.

"I've got her hidden somewhere else," Razor managed to say. "Give me about an hour. I'll come back with her."

"Again, you're treating Melvin like he's stupid. You really think Melvin's going to let you out this door? Instead, you tell Melvin where to find her. Jimmy will wait here with you. Melvin will go and send someone else to find her. You got five seconds to tell Melvin where she is."

"Then I suggest you close your eyes. Caitlyn," Razor said. With effort.

"Caitlyn?" Melvin's voice rose. "What kind of crap you talking? Jimmy, you're going to have to hit him again. Take a little off it. Melvin don't want his diaphragm ruptured until we find out where she is."

"Wait," Razor said, speaking more clearly as he regained strength.

"Two seconds."

"She's right here."

"Here," Melvin repeated. "You couldn't hide a mouse in here."

"She's here," Razor repeated. "All you need to do is look straight up."

SEVENTEEN

At the end of the hallway in the small apartment, Mason heard the sound of a kitchen drawer opening. And the light clanging of silverware.

Mason grinned. The young woman thought she'd find a weapon good enough to stop him?

A quick glance gave him what he needed. An upright lamp. He ripped the electrical cord loose from the wall, and sprinted into the kitchen with it in both hands.

He'd guessed right. In the dim light of a kitchen without windows, she was looking for a weapon. There was a butcher knife in her hand. Half raised.

Mason had been in plenty of fights. Hurt a lot of people. He knew indecision was their worst enemy. Paired with disbelief and a lack of willingness to inflict pain.

She was still trying to comprehend that this was happening. Didn't know if she should actually use the knife. And wasn't ruthless.

Mason, on the other hand, knew exactly what he wanted to do. And how it needed to be done.

Using the lamp like a bat, he swung it so that the electrical cord lashed across her face. She raised the knife arm in instinctive defense. Then he swung the lamp back the other way, hitting the knife arm with such force that he heard the crack of the forearm.

She screamed. But only for a spit second, because he lunged, falling on her.

The knife bounced off the floor. He rammed the side of his palm into her mouth, cutting the scream short. She was biting, and he enjoyed the sensation of pain in the meat of his hand as he covered her body with his.

With his free hand, he reached past her for the knife. He closed his fingers on the handle and brought the point of it to just below her eyeball.

"You know who I am, don't you?" Mason whispered.

She blinked.

Answer enough.

"I'm not here to take anyone back to Bar Elohim. Blink twice if you agree not to scream."

One blink. Then another. With tears streaming from her eyes.

He pulled his palm away from her mouth, watching for a sudden inhalation that would warn him of a scream.

She was compliant though. He loved it. A knife and a scared, compliant woman. Some things were just like his old life in Appalachia.

"We're going to stand," he whispered. "I'm going to follow you back to the living room. Understand?"

He didn't even have to tell her to blink twice. It came. He knew he owned her.

He kept the knife to her throat and his body close to hers as they made it back out to the living room.

Abe was still on his back. Staring without much comprehension at the ceiling.

"Kneel," Mason told the girl. "Beside him."

When she did, Abe's eyes focused. He tried to croak out some words.

"Do you want the old man to live?" Mason asked her, crouched behind her, one arm around her shoulder, knife still to her throat.

"Yes, yes, yes," she babbled.

"Then you'll tell me everything I need to know about Billy and Theo."

Mason tenderly nicked the skin below her pretty chin.

"Old man," Mason said. "Do you want the girl to live?"

Mason hadn't wanted or planned it this way. He would have preferred a helpful conversation and the chance to leave without worrying that his identity was known. It would have given him time to find a way to get rid of Abe and leave the body hidden for at least a few days.

On the other hand, this wasn't working out so badly either.

"Don't...hurt...her," Abe managed to say. "Whatever you want is fine."

"We'll start with the password to your bank account," Mason said. "Then the information about Billy and Theo."

"Jesus," Abe said.

"No prayers."

"You're not going to hurt us, right?" Abe asked.

"Of course not," Mason said. "Just tell me everything."

"That's the password," Abe gasped. "The word *Jesus*. Five three seven eight seven on the keypad. Jesus."

"Good," Mason said softly. "Keeping going."

EIGHTEEN

Where we at, Holly?" Pierce said. He held a cup of coffee. In a plain white china cup. He liked that; the recycled paper cups in the office always gave a small tang that he hated so much he was tempted to mask with cream.

She was on the leather couch across from him in the hotel suite. After opening the door to let her in, Pierce had returned to the desk near the window, where his laptop was still open, and had swiveled the chair to face her. She knew, of course, that he'd reviewed the footage from the Enforcer monitor, so she knew that he knew what Jeremy had spoken about last night. Best to keep it distant and formal when the two of them were alone.

"Up and running," Holly answered. "Hidden camera installed in the crip's chair. The link is in place op-site so you can watch the action at any time."

Op-site. Operation Web site. She was referring to an NI Web site. With advanced encryption, security wasn't an issue. First thing a team leader did for any new operation was set up an NI-based site. All team members had a code to send in information and reports but could only see their portions of the site. The team leader had the code for the overview and could get all the vital information by jumping on the Internet. Saved a lot of time.

"The crip is Melvin." Pierce finished his coffee, debated pouring more from the carafe delivered by room service. Stainless steel, not plastic. No wonder the coffee tasted so pure at the Pavilion. Pierce decided against the coffee, grabbed nearby notes, but didn't leaf through them. Unlike Wilson, he didn't have to review notes. Details stuck to Pierce like flies on glue paper. Earlier, Jeremy and Holly had spent an hour with Melvin offering encouragement for him to cooperate with them. Of course, the meeting had involved removing Melvin from the wheelchair because that kind of intimidation made encouragement easier. And also allowed for a techie to install the camera. All Pierce had to do was hit the link and he'd have access to the footage, live and archived, of Melvin's activities since they'd released him.

"Melvin," Holly agreed. "Crip's name is Melvin."

She had short hair, dark with gentle curls. She was tall. Willowy, as Pierce had decided was the best way to describe her. She dressed to show it and preferred to go through life straight-faced and serious, as if daring anyone to try to discover there was more to her than that. Pierce liked her attitude. Kind of like a rebel ice princess, she used cursing and crude language once in a while just to shake people up.

"And Jeremy's got the crip covered," Holly said. "Close by. Turns out you're pretty good at choosing a base."

"Just lucky. She couldn't go far on foot from where the Enforcers picked her up. I like this hotel." He arched an eyebrow. "How lucky?"

"Building across the street. It's a combination office tower with residential luxury penthouses. Jeremy's outside it with a couple of low-level op guys for backup. Crip went inside at basement level saying he knows how to find the Illegal but wanted to go in alone."

Pierce said, "Some people might find *crip* an offensive term."

"Do you?"

He wasn't going to give her anything to work with. Instead he asked, "What happened at the hospital?"

"Avery talked to the skinny kid with the big head."

"Theo."

"We had a camera in the room. Avery's already posted the conversation op-site."

"Say I'd rather save some time and just get your impression of what happened," Pierce said mildly. He was team leader, and he liked getting different perspectives. Otherwise it wasn't a team.

"The skinny kid—"

"Theo," Pierce corrected.

"Skinny kid seemed suspicious," she said, making a point that he couldn't correct her. "Kid strikes me as some kind of idiot savant. Fast talker, eyes darting, short attention span. But not stupid. He's got to know this is about Caitlyn. But Avery gave him enough of a song and dance about informers that it might work."

"Probably not."

"Probably not. But the skinny kid and the big one." She stopped, shook her head. "The other one, Billy, just so you don't need to interrupt... They took off from the hospital as soon as Billy woke up. About five minutes after Avery left them unattended. Tracking device has them going outside the city walls. You'll find a link at the op-site that will give you a real-time location whenever you want."

"Fine. Any guesses as to why they came here?"

"Caitlyn's here."

"And what does that tell you?" Pierce asked.

"Does getting this right help me to the next pay grade at NI?"

"People who work for me get stained by my reputation," Pierce said. "Jeremy is our token ladder climber, but I took him on to make Wilson happy. You I picked because I figured you didn't care a lot about rules. Balances Jeremy out."

"What if I just like power?" She studied him for several long moments, letting the tension build. She crossed her legs and leaned back.

"Ever seen an Illegal who didn't know the third rail holds live current?" Pierce said.

"Too many times."

"That should give you an idea what happens to people who don't understand all the implications of power."

"And what if I understand? Completely." She smiled at Pierce, letting more tension build.

The day before, he wouldn't have read anything into it. Now, after Wilson's warning, it was different.

"Billy and Theo are here because they knew Caitlyn would be here," she said, as if deliberately popping the moment to prove she had control of the room. "They're in contact with her somehow. Or she told them ahead of time. Either way, she still wants them in her life. So until we find her, we make sure to keep them under observation. Tracking device has it covered."

"Was finding Caitlyn last night related to what happened with Billy and Theo?"

"Can't be," she answered. "Coincidence. You ready to tell me about the wings?" When the Enforcers used the word, it had triggered software that was monitoring all Enforcer communications and had alerted them to Caitlyn's location.

"Wings? You'd have to be at the next pay grade."

"You want us to find her, but you won't tell us anything about her. Fine. If I were you, I'd be wondering why she's here in DC and not somewhere else."

"Been wondering." Pierce grinned. He liked her attitude. And the implied danger that came with the prospect of getting past the rebel ice princess thing.

She leveled her straight-faced gaze at him. "Last night, just before we tried to take her from the Enforcers. The stuff Jeremy said. It's not true."

"I know," Pierce said. "He's not gay. It's obvious he's interested in you. Just keep it away from work."

"Not that. The part where he said I'm hot for you. If you're not going to bring it up, I think I should. Just to clear the air."

"Consider it cleared," Pierce said. "He was messing with you, knowing it would be there for me to hear."

"I don't think you understand." She was deadpan. "The part that's not true is the thing about you being too old for me."

Pierce didn't look away from her expressionless face. Last thing he wanted to show was a reaction of his own.

"Well," he said. Just as deadpan. "That really clears the air, doesn't it?"

In the silence that followed, she let the tension build again. So quiet that he heard her vidphone buzz. She'd left it on the armrest of the couch. Now she picked it up and read the message.

"It's Jeremy," she said. "Things are about to get interesting."

Pierce remained silent.

"The crip has trapped the Illegal who took away the girl. Might be a good time to link up to the video."

Pierce turned in his chair. Tapped the keyboard. Pulled up the NI site in place for this op and clicked on the link.

The video came from a wide-angle lens that gave a fishbowl look to footage. Holly moved in behind the chair and looked over his shoulder at the screen.

The Illegal was there, looking straight ahead. And speaking to the guy in the wheelchair.

"She's here. All you need to do is look straight up."

NINETEEN

"Then I suggest you close your eyes. Caitlyn."

Barely maintaining her outstretched iron cross between the walls near the ceiling, Caitlyn tensed. Had she understood Razor correctly? Or was she wrong, and he was going to give her up?

"Hold him good," Melvin told Jimmy. "I don't trust him."

Only then did Melvin look up from his wheelchair. Directly into Caitlyn's eyes.

Time paused. His mouth slackened with shock.

Caitlyn had no choice now. She closed her eyes and dropped.

She landed on Jimmy's broad shoulders and desperately tried to wrap her arms around his neck. She bounced against him and ended up halfway down his back, hugging at his windpipe.

Caitlyn kept her eyes closed and squeezed Jimmy's neck as hard as she could manage. He turned and tried slamming her into the wall. But there wasn't room to get momentum to shake her loose.

Eyes still closed, Caitlyn fought to keep her burning arms wrapped in place. She pulled herself up and put her face into his head. Her lips felt his ear, and she bit hard, feeling her teeth go through.

Jimmy yelped.

"Jimmy, Jimmy!" Melvin shouted. "Don't let go of Razor!"

Too late. Jimmy's instincts had taken over, and he reached up to pull her arms free. He found Caitlyn's head with one hand and closed his fingers over her face. His other hand tore her arm away from his neck with as little effort as pulling off a scarf.

"Jimmy, close your eyes!" Melvin screamed. He was finally coming to the conclusion that had guided Caitlyn. He must have remembered the vid of their escape from the police.

A tremendous, searing white flash came through Caitlyn's closed eyelids a split second later. Just like the night before.

Jimmy squealed with the pain of his blinded eyes. He let go of his grip on Caitlyn, and as his massive arms went to his face, she fell away, landing at an angle but managing to keep her balance.

"Outside!" Razor shouted at Caitlyn.

With his knife, Melvin slashed at her upper arm as she swung by. There was a flash of pain. She pushed past the wheelchair, taking the two steps to the open door and the hallway.

Escape. Down the short corridor.

From the night before, she knew the next door led outside to an alley at the rear of an office tower. On the other side of the door was a security pad, where Razor had touched his fingertips to a scanner to let them in.

She flung it open, expecting Razor to be right behind her. Fleeing.

The first shock was three men, standing guard, backs to her, staring at the alley. They whirled, but she reacted first and slammed the door shut again, hoping it locked.

The second shock was the emptiness of the hallway. Razor wasn't behind her.

She darted back to the open door that led into his hideout. A quick glance showed what had happened.

Jimmy, face still contorted in agony, had blindly managed to get hold of Razor's left bicep. Razor was throwing futile punches, with Jimmy holding Razor at arm's length. Melvin had moved in as close as his wheelchair would allow. He slashed out with his knife at Razor's abdomen.

Caitlyn grabbed Melvin's wheelchair handles. She lifted them high, flipping Melvin into a pile on the floor. His knife skidded across the floor when he opened his hands to protect himself against the fall.

"I'm a crip!" Melvin shouted. "You can't do that."

She threw the empty wheelchair into the hallway, where pounding came from the outside door down the hall.

"Jimmy! Jimmy!" Melvin screeched. Not fear. Rage.

Caitlyn grabbed Melvin's ankles and yanked him a few feet away from Jimmy, almost into the hallway. Then she knelt and wrapped her fingers around his neck. In close, she could see little white specks clinging to his hair. The nits of lice.

She gritted her teeth and sucked in air, fighting her revulsion. At the lice, but also at what she had to do next—attack a cripple. But the man was smart. Smart enough to have closed his eyes before Razor's flash burst.

She began to squeeze her fingers around his larynx.

"Tell Jimmy to drop him," Caitlyn said. "I've got nothing to lose here."

"You won't kill Melvin," Melvin croaked.

"Ask the man whose belly I put a knife in last night?"

"That was you?"

Caitlyn responded by tightening so hard that Melvin gagged. She eased off, just enough to let him speak.

"Jimmy!" Now Melvin's strained voice sounded the same as Razor's after Jimmy's blows. "Let him go!"

As if lashed by a whip, Jimmy dropped Razor.

"Melvin?" Jimmy was totally blind, cocking his head to Melvin's voice.

"Find me," Melvin said. "Down here. Grab the girl!"

Razor was already leaping forward, pushing Caitlyn to the hallway.

Melvin was partly in the doorway. Caitlyn was clear now. Razor shoved Melvin deeper into the room, where Jimmy tripped over the man and tumbled toward them with the ponderous weight of a falling tree, hands outstretched.

Razor managed to slam the door shut. But not completely.

A tremendous muffled scream reached them from inside.

Caitlyn pointed at three fingertips extruding from the door frame, just above the floor.

"Can't do it," Razor said. "Can't leave him like that."

He popped open the door and, as the fingers disappeared, slammed it again, as if expecting that Jimmy would try to charge through.

Razor slid the bolt in place. Jimmy thumped the door from the inside, howling in rage and pain. To Caitlyn, the hinges appeared to flinch.

"Your arm," Razor said, pointing.

She looked at it. In the adrenaline rush of the previous minute, she had not felt the pain. Blood dripped from her left elbow, from a slash wound halfway to her shoulder.

Banging from the outside door drew their attention.

"Melvin's men?" Razor asked.

"No," Caitlyn said. "Suits. Like last night. Three of them."

"Crap," Razor said. "They've probably got the building surrounded."

Blood droplets hit the floor from her elbow.

"No place to run outside," Razor said. He pointed at the splatters on the floor. "And that will give them a trail to follow."

He reached for her arm. Instinctively, she pulled away. Nobody touched her. Ever. She was a freak.

"Come on," he snapped. "Don't be stupid. If you had any idea how much I hated blood…"

He reached again, and she let him examine it, aware that her skin was not like other women's.

"Pretty deep," he said, pulling off his outer shirt, leaving him in a black undershirt. He looked at the blood on his fingers, swallowing a look of distaste.

He folded the shirt once, then twice. He applied it like a pad to her arm. "Hold that in place."

"What about you?" she said, looking at his belly, where the black T-shirt was seeping blood.

"Crap," he repeated. He pulled up the T-shirt. With his fingers bloody from Caitlyn's wound, he probed the shallow slash, wincing. Not perhaps in pain, but revulsion, marked by the tone of his voice. "Blood."

He tucked the T-shirt back into place. "It won't leave a trail. Now let's go."

He jogged down the hallway away from the banging of the outer door. He stopped and turned. Caitlyn had not moved.

"Are you insane? You still not convinced that chances are better with me?"

He stretched out his arm, and Caitlyn ran to him.

TWENTY

Pierce was watching the video for the second time. He didn't want to like the kid but couldn't shake off a degree of reluctant admiration for the kid's nonchalance and cockiness.

First impressions. *"Pierce whoever you are, better luck next time. That girlfriend of yours. Hot looking. Slow though. Might want to think about that."*

Pierce had reviewed that a couple of times too, the footage from the monitor of the Enforcer car the night before. The kid should have been running, but took a few seconds to deliver the shot, screening his face with his fingers, but leaving his grin obvious below them.

That had been the night before. This morning was different. The kid hadn't known about a camera in place in the wheelchair. Hadn't been screening his face.

First time Pierce had seen this footage, it had been live, with Holly behind him. But now he'd made operational calls for agents to swarm the inside of the building, agreeing that Holly should go help. She would arrange logistics with Enforcers since NI didn't have to justify or explain any demands they made on local law.

So he was alone in the hotel suite to go over the footage again, watching for any small thing he had missed the first time. It had some grain to it because of the low lighting, and the fishbowl distortion of the wide-angle lens didn't help either. It showed a long, narrow, nearly bare room. Razor—the name Melvin had called the Illegal—was holding himself in pain, face squeezed tight after taking a blow from Melvin's bodyguard, someone named Jimmy. Flowers were scattered on the floor.

But even distorted, the footage would be enough for face recognition software to compensate, especially with a couple frames that showed Razor's face from different angles. Only a matter of minutes had passed since the actual live footage, but agency techies were already working on it. If Razor was anywhere in the system, he would be identified within the hour.

"Hold him good," Melvin now said on the screen, directing his thug. *"I don't trust him."*

Melvin couldn't know, of course, that there was another danger. Directly above. First run-through, Pierce had flinched at the suddenness of what happened next. Even prepared this time, he blinked as a dark figure dropped without warning onto Jimmy's shoulders. Somehow she'd been up on the ceiling.

Caitlyn.

A couple seconds of struggle, with Jimmy trying to slam Caitlyn against the wall without losing his hold on Razor. Then her mouth at the side of Jimmy's head.

Pierce slowed the footage. Saw what he'd missed the first time that made the thug squeal. She was biting through his ear. Pierce grinned in admiration.

"Jimmy, Jimmy! Don't let go of Razor!"

Jimmy was focused on the pain, though, and pulled Caitlyn off him like he was removing a shirt.

"Jimmy, close your eyes!"

Pierce stopped the footage. And stared at the frozen image of Razor pulling away from Jimmy. Pierce knew what was coming next. Another flashball. But how had Melvin guessed in the heat of the action?

Then Pierce understood. Melvin had seen the police footage the night before and had anticipated Razor's flashbomb. Pierce made a note to himself not to underestimate Melvin's intelligence.

Pierce advanced it superslow, watched as Razor reached into a sleeve and threw out a small round object that burst into supernova whiteness.

Another note to himself. Try to find out where Razor could get something this sophisticated. Not many Illegals—correct that—*no* Illegals had those kinds of resources.

"Outside!" Razor shouted.

Pierce watched closely, trying to confirm what he'd guessed as he watched the footage the first time. Yes. Melvin had swiped at her with a knife. Yes, he'd made contact. There was blood.

Then Caitlyn was out the door.

Jimmy still had Razor, by the bicep, with Razor throwing rabbit punches that had no effect. Melvin had moved in close to slash at Razor's belly with the knife he'd used on Caitlyn.

She appeared again. Loomed in close to the wheelchair. And the footage went sideways as she spilled Melvin and flung the wheelchair over.

It was down to audio now, with only shoes showing in the frame.

"I'm a crip! You can't do that."

More blurry footage, the wheelchair spinning into the hallway. The spy cam was at an angle, enough to show only the doorway and Melvin's useless legs partway in the hall. Audio picked up some drumlike pounding in the background.

"Jimmy! Jimmy!"

Slight pause.

"Tell Jimmy to drop him." Caitlyn. *"I've got nothing to lose here."*

"You won't kill me."

"Ask the man whose belly I put a knife in last night."

Caitlyn had been forced to defend herself the night before. Wouldn't hurt to have agents look into it.

"That was you?"

And Melvin knew about it. He'd make sure to interview Melvin later, find out more.

"Jimmy!" Melvin sounded like Caitlyn was throttling him. *"Let him go!"*

"Melvin?"

"Find me. Down here. Grab the girl!"

Then Razor and Caitlyn were back in the frame, Razor pushing Caitlyn out.

Razor shoved Melvin deeper into the room. There was a flash of Jimmy's hands as the big man fell toward the hallway and Razor slammed the door. Followed by screams.

Pierce was using his computer to run the footage. With a few flicks of his keyboard, he zoomed in. Saw fingers protruding from the closed door. Winced.

"Can't leave him like that." On the screen, Razor popped open the door.

Fingers disappeared. Razor slammed it again. Slid the bolt in place.

Pierce stopped the footage again. He frowned. An outside bolt.

Pierce ran the footage to the end for the audio.

"Your arm," Razor said.

The drumlike pounding. Pierce guessed it came from the outside door.

"Melvin's men?" Razor asked.

"No," Caitlyn said. *"Suits. Like last night. Three of them."*

Pierce's men. Outside, getting the video feed and responding.

"Crap. They've probably got the building surrounded. No place to run outside. And that will give them a trail to follow."

But Pierce didn't need a blood trail to finish this. They were in the building. He'd get them.

But Wilson's strict orders had been DOA.

Not dead on arrival, but the agency term.

Dead or alive.

TWENTY-ONE

Who are you?" Caitlyn kept Razor's folded shirt wrapped against the wound on her arm. "You walk in like you own this place. The elevator key…"

Down below, at the end of the hallway, away from the agents banging on the door, there'd been an elevator. He'd used a special key to the penthouse floor. A key he'd presented by pretending to pull it from Caitlyn's ear.

Now he and Caitlyn were in the penthouse office, thirty-five stories above the spartan closet where she'd spent the night. Looking out the window, she recognized the Pavilion, where, until the day before, she'd worked as a maid. Gray sky, with clouds of darker gray sliding past the other buildings. If Caitlyn stared without focusing, it seemed like the buildings themselves were moving and the clouds were stationary. It gave her a brief sense of vertigo.

"Who am I?" He turned to her. "More importantly, who are you?"

Caitlyn looked down at her arm. Razor waited for her answer. When none came, he turned back to the window.

Caitlyn thought about the unmarked vials and the hypodermic needles she'd found in Razor's hideout. Maybe drugs made Razor so difficult to talk to.

"I don't go anywhere unless I have at least two ways out. Three is better. I know this building better than the engineers who designed it."

"What about whoever works here? How can you know they won't walk in any second?"

"Gone. I keep track of his schedule. Besides, I think the NI has likely locked the place down by now."

Caitlyn sat back against the armrest of a couch that was part of a sitting area of a formal office, part of the layout of a luxury apartment suite, with hallways leading away from the main area. By the window was a spotting scope on a tripod.

Razor had moved to it and placed his hand on the dark steel. Half turned away from her, he explained. "Remember the couple of minutes I left you alone down there?"

Just before they'd entered the elevator, he had disappeared into a utility room off the hallway in the depths of the building.

Caitlyn nodded.

"I went to the control room and recoded some security cameras to cover our moves in the hallway. I gave us a couple hours. After that, they'll give up the search."

"So you're going to pretend like you own this place until then? How do you know all this? Are you some kind of flashy thief?"

"I may be a lot of things, but I'm not stupid."

"No, maybe not stupid. But dishonest. And wrong."

"What does wrong have to do with this?" He cast her a look of scorn. "Influentials live in a perfect world. They have money and security. They own the Industrials, like domesticated dogs. Cattle or sheep to be used and abused. And the Illegals are like wild animals, surviving by sneaking around and taking what we can. You think we'd survive if we were obvious? We're foxes, and the Influentials are the farmers. Stealing their chickens would be stupid. They can count those. And they'd set the hounds on us if one was gone. But if we can find a way into the chicken house, we can take eggs now and then. So I leave this coop the way it is."

"Unsecured," Caitlyn said.

"In and out when I want. No traces I was here."

Suddenly, a helicopter appeared and hovered at the giant windows.

Caitlyn dropped to the floor.

"Well, that's not good," Razor said.

"Then move away from the window."

"That's not the problem. These are mirrored windows. The bigger problem is that they've brought in a chopper. How big is this search?"

He leaned in to the spotting scope and pointed it at the streets. He studied in silence for nearly a minute before he spoke again. "Enforcers. They've got cruisers set up as roadblocks. We're trapped. All they have to do is flood the building with Enforcers and start from the bottom up..."

A few seconds of silence as he studied the situation longer. "And they're carrying thermal radar guns. We're dead."

"Thermal radar kills?"

"What world did you come from?" Again, half scorn. "Thermal radar can scan heat signatures through walls and doors. Not too difficult to tell what's human. Which would include us. Only thing we have in our favor is time. They'll move slow, but eventually they'll flush us out."

"What happened to fast and sharp and dangerous and at least two ways out of every situation?"

"You say that like you're happy to see me in trouble."

"I'm angry. I didn't need you to step into my life. I'm here because you got Enforcers involved. I'm here because I was stupid enough to trust that you would take me to a safe place."

"How about you focus on how we get out of here?" Razor snapped. "Worry later about how the entire world has betrayed you."

Razor paced back and forth, staring at the chopper. It hadn't moved from rooftop level. That put it almost directly across from them in the sky, a couple hundred yards away.

"Or better yet," he said. "Let me take you straight outside—up to the roof so the guys on the chopper can wrap you up and take you away. With Melvin out of the loop, I can keep all the money for myself. I mean, you're going to get caught anyway. It might as well do me some good."

"I don't need your help," she said. "Do what you should have done last night. Leave me alone."

"It's a little late for that. If anybody has a way past thermal radar, I haven't heard about it. Short of jumping off the building and—"

He cut himself off, spun, and stared at her. He spoke slowly. "They know you can fly." He nodded emphatically, talking more to himself than to her. "They're watching the roof because they know you can fly."

Silence as he processed his own conclusion. "But we don't hear the chopper. It's a stealth chopper. Not many around. Why would they have that in operation instead of a regular—"

He moved back to the spotting scope and trained it on the chopper. After thirty seconds, he spoke to her. Now disbelief was written across his face.

"Sniper," he said. "They've got a sniper in there."

He walked closer to her, repeating it. "Sniper. And a stealth chopper. They *want* you on the roof. Where they can get a clear shot. What have you done?"

"Nothing," Caitlyn said. She thought of who she used to be. A girl living securely in the love and protection of a daddy she once adored. That Caitlyn—the old Caitlyn—would have been bewildered here. Close to breaking down. Who she was now had learned that if a daddy could betray and hurt, then there was no one in the world to trust. So you got cold and learned to believe in no one but yourself. Or you let self-pity overwhelm you and you gave up. With a cold smile, she drew upon her anger. She was not going to quit, no matter what. If she quit, there was no one to help her find the willpower to continue.

Razor must have misinterpreted her cold smile.

"If you haven't done anything, then what do they want from you?" His face was intense. "Tell me. I'm now part of this."

"Don't be a part of this. Walk away."

"They want you bad. They've got me on police video rescuing you from agents last night. Melvin's going to let them know we're on the run together. If I walk out there, you think they're going to give me a pat on the shoulder and send me on my way? Not if they're willing to shoot you on sight. You and me are stuck together. I need to know what you know."

Caitlyn could not answer. She mutely held the folded shirt across her arm.

He began pacing again. "It's because you can fly." He laughed. "What is it? Some military secret you stole? I mean, flying soldiers? Surely that's pretty valuable." Suddenly he froze, cocked his head as he looked at her. "That's not as stupid as it sounds. How do you fly? It's some kind of trick. Right?"

Caitlyn bit off each word. "Just. Go. Away."

"Not an option."

"Then stop asking questions." Caitlyn should have felt fear. Instead, she was defiant and cold inside. She was a freak. Alone against the world. No choice in how she existed the way she did. No choice even in the fact of her existence. Aloneness was all she knew and understood now. And it would be how she died.

Razor studied her face. "When they step into the room in a few minutes, you plan to just stand and face them and wait for them to start shooting?"

"No. If they make it to that door, that chair is going through a window. With me following it. Remember, one of us can fly."

He walked away, beyond the office area.

Caitlyn didn't bother to turn her head to watch. Maybe he was leaving her. Maybe she should just go to the roof and stand and wait for a sniper's bullet. But no. If this was the end, defiance was all she had left. She would not allow herself to be broken. A race to the roof's edge to beat the sniper, then out into the sky. Free. If only until the first bullets hit her.

She would never give up.

TWENTY-TWO

S he's going to be there next time, right?" Theo asked Billy. "Right?" Billy said, "Maybe we need tattoos."

"Huh?" Theo asked. He stopped, and his shadow appeared on the ground to his right. Billy was big enough to put Theo in shade. Literally. The sun was to the left of Theo, left of Billy. Theo had been playing a game, concentrating on stepping in concert with Billy, making sure none of his own shadow ever showed. "What are you saying? That she won't show up? Ever? That we need to become Industrials?"

Billy stopped too. He ran the top of his forearm across his face, wiping away sweat. "It's not good for you, working the smelter. We could find other things if we were Industrials."

"So that's what you're saying. She won't show up. Ever."

"How many times we been to the meeting place?" Billy asked. "Right time. Right place. How many times?"

"I don't keep track," Theo said. He'd pulled the bandages from his face. Already, dark bruises had given him raccoon eyes. "Not many. Not enough to give up. She said she didn't know how long it would take to get to the surgeon. Or how long she needed to heal before she could travel."

"Theo, tell me how many flies you've killed in the last week. Out of how many tries."

"Don't know what you're talking about."

"Think I don't notice? A fly lands on you, and you do your best to catch it then throw it down on the ground so that it's stunned and you can stomp it."

"Don't know what you're talking about."

"How many steps you manage to stay in my shadow in the last half hour?"

"Huh? You noticed that too?"

"You know numbers and you watch details. Pretending you don't know how many times we've been to the meeting place tells me you know it's too many but you don't want to admit it."

"She'll be there," Theo said. "She promised."

"So why did you ask me?"

A fly landed on Theo's right forearm. He studied its position. The trick was to try not to smash it flat. Theo knew that when you did that, the hand also pushed a small wall of air out in front of your open palm. The air helped propel the fly away. So to catch a fly, you needed to cup your palm and draw the fly up into the wall of air. A better trick was to sweep your hand just above the fly. But you needed to sweep toward its eyes. It would have no choice but to fly forward, and that closed the gap to your hand. If you swept about three inches above the fly, it would reach your hand in the span between detecting the threat and zooming straight into it.

"Theo?"

Theo ignored Billy. He swept his hand forward, anticipating the fly's movement. He caught it in a swift motion. He closed his fist and shook it, feeling it bounce around. He threw it down violently, releasing it only a foot from the ground. The fly hit the ground and spun in a dazed circle.

Theo stepped on it. "Eighty-nine out of one hundred two. Just under ninety percent."

"Uh-huh," Billy said. "How many times we been to the meeting place?"

They went every second day.

"Twenty-four," Theo said, sadly. "She'll be there. I know it."

"If we get tattoos, that won't stop us from going there, same place, same time, every time, until she shows up."

"If we get tattoos, we'll be stuck with them forever. Then what about our dream? West. No cities with walls."

"The smelter is going to kill you, Theo."

"So will living here with tattoos."

"She could have changed her mind. Something could have happened to her. Maybe she got surgery and decided to live normal, the way Jordan wants it. Instead of joining us."

"I don't want to talk about it," Theo said. "She's going to be there. Someday. And if we never stop going, she'll never wonder what happened to us."

TWENTY-THREE

You dropped these," Razor said, stepping out of the kitchen area. "In the elevator."

Caitlyn recognized the folded papers he held in his hand. Letters that she'd kept close to her body, beneath the cloak.

Silently, she took them away, refusing to ask if he'd read them. She was so angry, she didn't care.

He smiled at her obvious anger. "Those flowers that Melvin took from me? I had really gotten them to give to you. Just so you know. Not poisoned. As a peace offering."

He went back into the kitchen.

She heard water running. Razor came back with two glasses of water and a household first-aid kit. He had a couple of small towels tucked under his right arm.

He handed her a glass of water. She took it but did not drink.

He offered her a couple of aspirin. She declined. He popped a few into his mouth, chewed, and swallowed. Then sucked back half a glass of water. He poured the remainder of the water on the corner of one of the towels.

He pulled up a chair and sat facing her, wet towel in his hand.

Caitlyn stared out the window at the chopper outlined against the dark gray clouds, ignoring the water in her hand. Men. In the chopper. Waiting to execute her. This was what Papa had set her free to find? Proof again that she could not trust anybody. Ever.

Razor handed her the clean towel and motioned for her to give him the bloodied shirt. Caitlyn traded shirt for towel, barely registering the act in her conscious thoughts.

"Thermal radar," Razor said. "Last night, regular Enforcers pick you up. Within minutes of sending a video, agents appear. Like they're monitoring communications and waiting for you. Here's what's stranger. Those agents Tasered the Enforcers and didn't even bother to shut off the monitor in the car, like they wanted whoever sent them to know they'd taken you. So I'll ask again. What is it about you that brings on that kind of heat so fast? Who are you? Where'd you come from?"

"You've got your secrets," Caitlyn said. She saw needle tracks on the inside of his elbow. "I've got mine."

"Not ones that have the Influentials sending all their dogs after me. Even if by some miracle the thermal radar misses us, how far are you going to have to run until they stop looking for you?"

When she didn't answer, he opened the first-aid kit and pulled out gauze and a roll of tape.

"Give me your arm," he said. "You can stay and wait for them to knock on the door, but I'm going to patch up these cuts like I actually have a plan to get us out of here."

He didn't give her the option of refusing. He pulled away the towel from her arm before she could react.

He squinted. "A cut like that should still be bleeding. How did—"

He pulled up his shirt and used the towel moistened by her blood to dab at the cut on his belly.

"I'm not bleeding either," he said. Now his face was unreadable. "This can't be coincidence."

TWENTY-FOUR

He sat on a curb by a Dumpster near the loading dock, behind a hotel called the Pavilion. In the shadows, and glad not to be squinting, Mason felt the satisfaction of accomplishment. Only one day Outside, and look at the progress he'd made. From Lynchburg to DC on a high-speed train at a rate that made it seem like only minutes through the countryside. Off the train and a short walk to a hotel where Caitlyn worked. He knew the information had been correct; he'd taken Abe and the woman in the last minutes of their lives to a point where they would utter nothing but truth.

Now all he had to do was wait.

The dock had a surveillance camera trained on the loading area. Mason's theory was simple. The longer it took someone to show up, the sloppier the security.

He'd been prepared to sit idly until that happened. Until he spotted a small rectangular container on the ground against the wall.

Pest control. A rattrap.

He hoped it was a simple trap, not one armed with poison bait.

Mason left the curb and discovered just another portent of good fortune to go with the wad of cash that Abe had conveniently withdrawn just before Mason's own form of withdrawal from Abe. Here, the good fortune was the fact that when Mason squatted, lifted the box, and shook it gently, he felt and heard the light thumping sound inside. He smiled. The rat was alive.

He kept his back to the surveillance camera and reached inside his shirt for the kitchen knife he'd taken from the apartment. He opened the box and deftly skewered the rat with his knife. It squealed briefly but died so quickly he got little satisfaction. He slipped the knife and the rat back into his shirt.

"Hey!" came a voice from the loading dock.

Mason stood and faced a potbellied elderly man in a faux police uniform. By his mental count, it had been about fifteen minutes. That delay plus the fact that the security man was staying up on the dock where it was safe told Mason enough. Not much danger.

"Just waiting for someone," Mason said. He felt some squirming inside his shirt. Apparently the rat wasn't completely dead.

"Not here," the guard answered. He had an earpiece and a small microphone on a headset. "You've got twenty seconds to leave before I call Enforcers."

"It's a girl I'm waiting for," Mason said. He placed his left hand on his belly and felt the shape of the rat. He pinched the rat's neck while its legs futilely scratched at his skin. He felt the rat spasm briefly, and the legs stopped scratching. "She works here."

"We don't have those kinds of girls at this hotel."

"She's a maid," Mason said. The apartment woman had told Mason all about the agency men who came looking for Caitlyn after Billy and Theo left. She'd told Mason a lot more about Caitlyn than she'd told the agency men. But then again, Mason had been able to motivate the apartment woman in a different way. "She looks weird. Almost like she has a hump on her back."

The security guard tilted his head and squinted. "You know her?"

Mason's belly tingled. It wasn't the rat, but his predator's instinct. He *was* close.

"I'm waiting for her," Mason said.

The guard tapped his earpiece. He covered his mouth and spoke into the microphone. Mason tensed, wondering if he'd have to run.

The security guard finished the conversation behind his hand, then spoke to Mason.

"Want to make some easy money?" the guard asked. "Someone wants to ask you about her."

TWENTY-FIVE

Razor had stared at her in silence for a full minute, daring her to explain who she was.

She'd stared back. The entire minute. Thinking about what she had just learned because of the healed wound. As a child, she'd been remarkably insulated. From strangers, from children, from activities that might damage her. She'd never been cut, beyond casual scrapes; never hurt herself badly enough to discover this strange thing about her flesh, unless it had happened when she was too young to remember. Then this was just one more thing that Jordan had kept from her.

Finally, Razor dropped the blood-soaked shirt on the floor, leaving it as a mute accusation. He'd gone back into the kitchen.

Caitlyn sat alone on the couch. She heard strange sounds coming from the kitchen of the luxury suite. Muted clattering. She wasn't in the mood to be curious but walked over anyway and looked around the corner.

Razor was moving contents from the fridge into the oven beside it. To all appearances, inexplicable. Razor glanced at her. Said nothing. As if daring her to ask. So she didn't.

She returned to the couch, wondering again if she should just take her chances on the roof. Maybe if she bolted and threw herself from the roof, she'd make it past the waiting sniper and have a chance to land far enough past the blockade on the ground to find a way to escape. Billy and Theo were at the soovie park. Waiting. Ready to go west. Until this—the helicopter outside—there was only one thing she had to do to reach that dream. Become invisible. Not like the Invisibles. Truly invisible. Through surgery that would remove the outer signs that her DNA had been spliced and manipulated at an embryonic stage by the man who called himself her father.

That was the terrible contradiction she had faced. To become free, she'd have to give up what truly made her feel free. Surgery would be Jordan's redemption. Not hers. It had been easier to make no decision.

She stared at the gray sky. At the chopper. Hovering. Waiting. Holding a sniper in place to execute her. It was no longer just Mason in pursuit, but the power structure of the Outside. She and Billy and Theo had made a plan, had dared to dream. But her darkest secret was as inescapable as the forces pursuing her. If somehow Razor got them out of here, the only way she could live without hunters on her trail was to give up who she was.

Razor grunted as he pushed the fridge on wheels out of the kitchen area. He stopped it just before the door that led to the hallway and elevator.

"Remember the mirror down there?" Razor asked, puffing slightly from the exertion of moving the fridge. "It's where I practice illusions. I like games. I like creating illusions. I like fooling people. That's why I didn't hand you over to Melvin. I thought this was a game I'd enjoy. I thought it was a game I was good enough to win. If it had just been Melvin, I could have."

Leaning against the fridge, Razor looked beyond her at the helicopter. "Believe it or not, I'll get past them. I'll get you out too if you want, but then you're on your own. This is your game, not mine. I want out."

"Maybe you're creating an illusion right now, just to turn me in."

"I'm done playing." The exasperation in his voice told her it was truth. "You said it yourself. I'm worth a lot to them."

"Help me move this fridge. I'll get you out."

"Make me trust you." If they got out of here, she'd find a way to the surgeon.

He paused, searching her face. "I used the computer in the bedroom to access the building's security system. When the fire alarms go off, we have about ten seconds to get this fridge out the door and into the elevator. Stay and you're dead."

"Or go with you and have you turn me in."

He opened the door and pushed the fridge halfway into the hallway. Looked back at her. "You're spooky. You can fly, trick or not. A bleeding knife wound that doesn't even need bandages, and somehow you stop me from bleeding too. They've assembled an army to kill you. And they'll know that I now know these spooky things about you. If you're this valuable to them, there's only one guarantee I can't tell anyone about you. If I'm dead. I need to help you long enough so we can walk away from each other. Alive."

Suddenly the fire alarms began to scream.

TWENTY-SIX

N ot bad." Pierce spoke to himself. He'd walked across the street from the Pavilion and was on level five of the building that Razor and Caitlyn had somehow managed to escape, staring at an empty refrigerator in one of the elevators, the door now kept open by a fire key. "Not bad at all."

His one-sided conversation was cut short by a team leader approaching, his shoes slapping the tile of the hallway.

"Confirmed. Building is clear. Both are gone." Redhead, buzz cut. Maybe five years younger than Pierce.

Pierce didn't know the agent's name. Didn't care. The guy was standing ramrod straight. JAA. Just another agent. Bracing himself for outrage. Or sarcasm. Or however else Pierce was going to vent, given that two Illegals had defeated fifty-plus operatives, thermal imaging, and professional snipers in a stealth chopper.

But Buzz Cut didn't know Pierce.

Pierce pointed at the fridge. "Find out where it came from then."

"We've got over thirty levels in this building. Twenty to forty doors per level. A lot of angry Influentials. That fire alarm—"

Pierce wasn't a screamer. He merely locked his eyes on Buzz Cut, waited for silence.

"Somewhere there's an agency tree chart that illustrates why you shouldn't second-guess me," Pierce said. "Lucky for you, I don't give a crap about tree charts. You don't have much moral high ground here. Not after all the resources you mismanaged in the last half hour."

"Not a person left this building without my men giving a close visual inspection. Even after the fire alarm."

Which is exactly what Razor and Caitlyn would have expected. Attention diverted to everyone leaving the building.

"Open the fridge door," Pierce said. "Tell me what you see."

Sullenly, Buzz Cut reached for the fridge handle.

Pierce slapped it away.

"Fingerprints," Pierce said. "Start thinking."

This was a pain. Now Pierce would have to ask later for Buzz Cut's name. Not to report breach of procedure. That wasn't worth the paperwork. But to make sure to avoid working with the guy on future operations.

Pierce took off his belt, used it to wrap around the top of the fridge handle, and pulled it open it from there. "What do you see?"

"Nothing."

"Not even shelves," Pierce said, sliding his belt back into place. "And what do fridges usually hold?"

"Food."

"Cold food or hot food?"

"I'm not a child."

Pierce stared the man down again. "Cold food or hot food?"

"Cold."

"So get someone on each level with thermal radar again. They don't have to open doors. Have them scan for a pile of something cold inside a room. It won't have warmed to room temperature yet. In ten minutes I want not just the room number; I want to know if it's a personal or a business suite. Who the owner is. How those two Illegals got inside."

Buzz Cut was frowning. A lack of comprehension.

Pierce's vidpod began to vibrate.

Even without the interruption, Pierce wasn't going to explain. Razor and Caitlyn, inside the fridge. Invisible to thermal radar. Riding down the elevator. Parking it here. If Buzz Cut couldn't figure it out, all he was good for was grunt work.

"Just go," Pierce said, reaching in his pocket for the vidpod.

Buzz Cut hit the button for an adjacent elevator.

Pierce walked a few steps down the hallway as he checked out the screen. Incoming message.

POSITIVE MATCH TO FACE STRUCTURE. SUSPECT IDENTIFIED AS TIMOTHY RAY ZORNENBACH. AGE 22. MOTHER DECEASED. LEGAL REGISTRATION AS ADOPTED SON OF FATHER: TIMOTHY RAYMOND ZORNENBACH. AGE 78. REGISTERED STATUS FOR BOTH: ELITE

Pierce let the address of Timothy Ray Zornenbach scroll past without giving it much attention.

His mind was on something else.

Elite.

Interesting, Pierce thought. But made sense. Timothy Ray was an Influential. A rich kid. Explained how he got the magic.

He stopped his thoughts. Tapped on the screen. Reread the address. Called down the hallway just as Buzz Cut was stepping on the elevator.

"Hold your men," Pierce said. "Except for one. Send him to..."

Pierce glanced at the vidpod again. The address belonged to this building.

"Send him to the thirty-fifth level. Tell him to check 3519 first. Then confirm the suite is registered to someone with the surname Zornenbach."

Buzz Cut gave a curt nod before disappearing into the elevator. Pierce hadn't made a new friend.

Pierce studied the information on the vidpod more slowly. That's how he liked to work it. A quick reaction first, going on instinct, then a slow, thorough exam, using intellect. Not always successful, but it had afforded him the luxury of not giving a crap about tree charts.

Timothy Ray Zornenbach. As in Ray Zor. Razor.

Got your real name, Pierce thought, sending that thought out in radar waves to the kid named Razor. *Time you learned mine.*

TWENTY-SEVEN

Y ou can have the knife and the hand," Mason said. "But the rat is mine."
He was in a small, windowless room somewhere in the basement of the
hotel. Not much breathing space. Two well-dressed men, easily years younger
than Mason, and just as easily outweighing Mason by a hundred pounds each,
blocked the door. One had just frisked him while the other had trained a
Taser gun at him. Now the Taser gun was sheathed. They were making a point.
Hands and fists were now enough to contain Mason.

Neither answered. One had taken the knife. The hand in the Ziploc bag
was on the floor.

"I said the rat is mine." Mason stared them down as best he could given
the eye patch and the tendency for his other eye to wander.

"Give him the rat," came a disembodied voice from a speaker built into
the ceiling. Mason glanced upward. Saw the unblinking camera eye beside the
speaker.

This is good, Mason thought. He'd learned they were under observation. It
also established that he had something that the faceless voice wanted badly
enough that he would allow Mason to have the rat. For Mason, now it was a
matter of using the leverage to maximum push.

One of the big men flipped the rat at Mason.

Mason tried to catch it, but he hadn't yet adjusted to his lost depth perception, and the limp rodent bounced off his fingers and fell on the floor.

Both men chuckled as Mason bent over to pick it up.

Mason smiled in return. Straightened and bit the rat's head off and
thoughtfully chewed, knowing the sound of the cracking skull would plainly
reach them in their horrified silence.

Mason swallowed and wiped his bloody mouth with his sleeve.

Both men had pressed away from him.

That's better, Mason thought.

"Lovely," the disembodied voice said. Mason wondered if he detected a
note of sincerity.

"What do you want?" Mason asked.

"Give him the photo," the voice said.

Both big men were still staring in revulsion at Mason.

"Give him the photo!"

One reached into his suit jacket. He held the photo in his fingertips and stretched his arm across to Mason, determined to keep as much distance between them as possible.

Mason studied the photo. It was slightly grainy, obviously a still photo taken from video.

Caitlyn.

She was centered in a hallway, a cart of cleaning supplies behind her. Her expression clearly showed that she was unaware there was any kind of electronic scrutiny.

The outline of her body showed the deformity beneath loose clothing.

"Is that the one you're looking for?" asked the disembodied voice.

Blood dripped down Mason's fingers from the headless rat. He sucked the blood from his fingers, then from the gaping hole at the rat's shoulders.

One of the big men gagged.

"Is that the one you're looking for?" the voice repeated.

"If you're going to puke," Mason told the men, "maybe do it outside. Don't want you spoiling my appetite."

"Sir," one pleaded, "cut us a break here."

"I want to know about the girl," the voice answered.

Mason took his time as he ate the rest of the rat's body. One of the men watched, paralyzed. The other had turned his back.

"She might be the one," Mason finally said. "But I don't say a thing until you and me are face to face. And until I get the money that security guard promised me."

TWENTY-EIGHT

Razor had taken her underground. Literally.

To Caitlyn, the tunnel brought back memories of her escape from Appalachia. The mountain at the border had been honeycombed, a result of generations of coal mining.

The width seemed the same, maybe five paces from side to side. And like the mountain tunnels, the height matched the width. The air too had the cool, wet stillness that seemed like a balm to her lungs.

In the mountain, however, the tunnel walls had been hewn from rock, shored with timbers in places, steel beams in others. Here the walls consisted of concrete blocks, forming a horseshoe arch that extended as far as she could see.

Wires ran along the top of the arch, obviously supplying electricity to the lights that were set apart every twenty paces or so. Many bulbs were dark, however, giving uneven, eerie shadows down the length of the tunnel.

Mossy green gravel formed the floor of the tunnel, except for the center, where a footpath had been worn so that the gravel had the color of sun-dried bone.

The significance of this was not lost on Caitlyn. Nor was the isolation of her circumstances lost on her. She was trapped in a place where Razor, or those who walked these tunnels often enough to keep the moss from closing together in the center, would have the leisure of attacking her without fear of interruption.

She said nothing, however. Expressing fear would make her more vulnerable. Surprisingly, she didn't feel the fear with intensity. It was more like an undercurrent that kept her alert.

Caitlyn gave that some thought. She realized she wasn't too concerned about Razor. Was it because if he did have malevolent intentions, he would have tried earlier, when she was in his room?

No, she decided, that wasn't it. Her instinct told her that she could trust him to a certain degree. But could she trust her instinct?

She thought of the man who had threatened her on the rooftop. Everett.

The one who had smiled hungrily because she was a freak. Then her instinct had shrieked warning.

She would relax around Razor then. And trust he knew what he was doing. It was Razor's careless confidence. This tunnel was his escape hole. He wouldn't have brought her here if it held danger. He walked as if he'd been here before, as if he knew where he was going.

She'd follow because what she now wanted most was to get to a pre-arranged location to meet Theo and Billy.

She carried two folded pieces of paper against her skin, held in place by her microfabric. One was the letter from her father. As a reminder of his betrayal. It fueled her anger. Kept her strong. *We had decided, the woman I loved and I, that as soon as you were born, we would perform an act of decency and mercy, and wrap you in a towel to drown you in a nearby sink of water, like a kitten dropped into a river...*

The other folded paper had directions to the address of a surgeon in the DC area. One of the Influentials. Dr. Hugh Swain.

She'd made her decision. Surgery. There was relief in it and relief that there really hadn't been a choice. She needed the surgery to survive. She'd meet Billy and Theo, let them know she was ready to go to Swain. She'd live with Billy and Theo, protected by Billy among the Industrials and Illegals, until the surgery was arranged. Once finished, all three would take their chances and try to make it beyond, to the freedom of western territories. One freedom would be gone—her wings—and she'd exchange it for another.

It meant if she wanted to get beyond the city walls, to Billy and Theo, she would trust Razor to get her out of this tunnel.

Then she'd be finished with him.

TWENTY-NINE

Leo, the security manager, had an office on the third level. No windows. Just a swivel chair facing a computer screen on a desk, surrounded by an array of half-eaten donuts. A tall filing cabinet, under more half-eaten donuts. And a row of video monitors, too much out of reach to be victimized by food litter.

Pierce had introduced himself, shown identification. Now he was standing behind the swivel chair, focused on the monitors above. Seated in the chair was a large, large man in a security uniform barely able to contain the folds of flesh that spilled over his belt like meat from a sandwich. A guy named Leo. Sweat beads popped through sparse hair. The scramble out of the building during the fire alarm had not been kind to Leo. The forced march back to the office to meet Pierce had exacerbated the man's wheezing.

Pierce breathed through his mouth. Leo needed a few lessons in the basics of personal hygiene, and the large man's body heat radiated not only the day's sweat, but probably leftovers from the entire previous week.

"Go back twenty-four minutes," Pierce said. He'd cross-checked the time against the original footage shot from the wheelchair. That's when Razor and Caitlyn first began running.

"Lot of Influentials from this building going to be making calls about how you disrupted their lives," Leo said smugly.

"Twenty-four minutes." Pierce needed results. Immediately. What he wanted was to see the movements of Razor and Caitlyn. Give him an idea of how and where they'd escaped. "Show the basement camera first."

"Whatever you're looking for," Leo said, "better be worth it."

Pierce dropped his hands on Leo's shoulder. Pierce dug his fingers through a layer of fat and found a loop of muscle and pinched slightly.

Leo spasmed as he screeched.

"Need to see those fingers on the keyboard," Pierce said, no heat.

Leo didn't need another prompt. He clicked at the keyboard, and within seconds the videoscreens went blank.

"Huh?" Leo hunched forward and did some more keyboarding. He tilted his head upward again.

The screens were still dark.

"Explain 'Huh?'" Pierce said.

"Here's a half hour ago," Leo said. More keyboarding. The screens flickered with images again.

"Here's ten minutes ago." Leo's fingers flashed. "Look at the basement hallway. There you are."

Pierce saw an image of himself. Looking into the elevator. With Buzz Cut beside him, arms crossed.

"Now," Leo said. "Here's twenty-four minutes ago. Correct that. Twenty-five minutes ago. The exact time you wanted."

Dark screens again.

"What's happening?"

"Not what's *happening*," Leo said. "It's what *happened*. Someone got into the system and shut everything down. Let me read some code here."

Leo craned his head at the computer screen. "Someone must have hacked in. Put a fifteen-minute timer on the shutdown."

"How?"

Pierce didn't have to ask who. Surveillance shuts down when Razor is trying to escape? Obviously the rich kid had done it. But learning how would tell him more about Razor. "Got a list of people who have access to administration on this?"

"I'm just a flunky."

"A flunky who has access that lets him read code?"

"I can read it. I can't write it."

Fair enough, Pierce thought. "So it's either someone who had access or has managed to hack this."

"Yeah."

"Get me a list of administrators."

"Be a few minutes. I've got to make a call and get authorization."

"As long as you stay in this room," Pierce said. Hopefully he'd start getting used to the smell. "I'll be right beside you."

THIRTY

That's her," Mason said.

He'd been awed by the luxury of the penthouse suite. Fascinated by the urbane smoothness of the man who'd snapped at the bodyguards to stand in the hallway and had closed the door to appraise Mason openly, until introducing himself as Everett Tippler, then walking effeminately across the room to bring Mason to a flat screen that filled an entire wall.

Now, however, Mason's total focus was on the colored images moving across the wide flat screen. The scene was clearly a roof, and long shadows showed it was the end of the day. The man holding a wine glass was Everett, moving toward a girl with her back to him, who turned as if startled, with faint orange light across her face.

Everett held a remote. The image froze.

"An easy face to remember," he said. "You told security she was your friend. I think you're lying."

Mason was a new refugee in the outside world. Except for the cash he'd taken from Abe, he had nothing. Except something that Everett wanted.

"Does it matter?" Mason said.

"Extremely. The wrong answer means you're a dead man."

Mason felt the vibration inside. Everett had killed before. And enjoyed it too.

"Tell me why you think I'm lying," Mason said.

"She doesn't strike me as the type to truly like a man who can eat rats. There's an innocence to her. You, on the other hand..."

"I want to drink her blood," Mason said. "I want it spilling from her veins, and I want her watching me as I drink."

"That was the right answer." Everett flicked the remote again. "Watch."

An unnecessary instruction. Mason absorbed every detail. The images moved soundlessly, although it was obvious that Everett and Caitlyn were carrying on a conversation.

Mason felt more internal vibrations. The body language of each showed

Everett was predator. Caitlyn was prey. The eeriness was in the silence, the silhouettes and shadows.

Then the images slowed, as if their movements were choreographed, with Everett beginning to pull at Caitlyn's clothing, with Caitlyn apparently helpless.

Mason felt a possessiveness and more than a trace of anger. He leaned forward, half in anticipation of where the violence would lead, half wanting to know that she was still alive, that he could still hunt.

The silhouettes broke apart. Everett falling backward. Caitlyn still upright.

Everett stopped the sequencing.

"That was last evening. As you can see, at dusk. If there were more light, you'd also see that she put a knife into my gut. Fortunately for me, it missed anything vital. I released myself from the hospital a few hours ago."

Mason turned slowly and stared at Everett. The man hadn't moved effeminately. Simply gingerly.

"Why would she have a knife?" Everett asked.

Mason didn't answer. He looked back at the flat screen. This told him something new about Caitlyn. She now carried a weapon.

"Who is she?" Everett asked. "For that matter, who are you?"

"What do you want?" Mason countered.

Everett hit the remote. "She moves to the edge of the roof. There. See? Most of the sun is gone, but the roof lights are enough to show the next few seconds."

He stopped it again. "I'm prepared to pay you well to find her. But only if I trust that you know her well enough. Tell me, rat man, before I advance the frames, what happens next?"

Mason only had to remember the last moments he'd spent with Caitlyn before she abandoned him to die in the cave. His disbelief.

He spoke two flat words to Everett.

"She flies."

THIRTY-ONE

"Seventy years ago," Razor said, "this was a subway tunnel. Farther down, you'll see where other tunnels have been carved out over the generations since. This is a city beneath the city."

Caitlyn had been silent ever since dropping down the ladder. That self-possession irritated Razor as much as he found it intriguing. It was like her soul was shrouded in mystery. He wanted to sweep aside the shroud, find a way to make her vulnerable to him, as vulnerable as he wanted to be to her.

After going only about a hundred yards, they had stopped at a gradual bend. Razor didn't explain why. He kept waiting for her to ask why, but she refused.

"Subway," Razor repeated. "Mass transit. Trains. Moving beneath the city. Used to be steel tracks here, on this gravel bed. Been a long time since the steel was scavenged though."

"Somebody keeps the lights on," she said.

Her voice was a deep whisper. From anyone else, it would have seemed an affectation, a clumsy attempt at allure. From her, utterly without pretense, it only added to the mystery of her existence.

"Scavengers," he answered. "That's the entirety of this world. Illegals who scavenge for survival. Everybody knows the stories of life beneath the city. They just haven't seen it for themselves. It's not worth the risk."

He expected a reaction. Of any kind. It didn't come.

"We steal the electricity," he said, choosing *we* over *they*, pushing hard to force her curiosity.

Again, she said nothing. She simply watched her surroundings with an eerie detachment.

He wanted her to want something from him. He should have found the hump on Caitlyn's back repulsive. And her long, unnaturally skinny fingers. Was it the secret behind her appearance that made her so attractive that he looked beyond those superficialities?

No doubt he was fascinated. Caitlyn could fly. He'd seen it. When he'd first witnessed it, he'd believed, naturally, that it was a magic trick he could take for himself. That's why he'd been waiting for her in the alley.

But now, obviously, there was much more to her ability than a complex magic trick. The swiftness of the events of the last twelve hours was enough proof of that.

"You're not afraid?" he finally asked. "You do know what happens to people who go beneath the city. The urban legends are not just legend."

"Pretend I don't," she said.

"You haven't heard about the cannibalism?"

"Cannibals?"

"Some of the Illegals who live down here have never seen sunlight. Some of their parents haven't seen sunlight. Those are the lucky ones. The ones who go to the surface have no legal status. They do what it takes to bring back food and necessities and anything of value they can steal from Influentials, or even the Invisibles, inside the city walls."

"So far you're only telling me about the Illegals down here. What happens to people who go into the tunnels?"

"There are places on the street," Razor said, "where the Illegals from below the city know to go to offer themselves for service. Any service. All service. Influentials pick and choose. Some Influentials prefer..."

Razor spoke more slowly, determined not to let any emotion sneak into his voice. "Some Influentials want children. What they are willing to pay makes it possible for two dozen families of Illegals to survive."

"Parents give up their children."

"The poverty here is desperate. It's how their children can eat well and sleep safely and perhaps someday be permanently lifted out of all of this." Razor snorted. "I read constantly. Knowledge is power. I can tell you it's no different than five hundred years ago, when parents volunteered their boys to the rich, and the rich would make them become castrati in the opera. Then and now, the boys were no more than playthings."

"Castrati?"

"Boys neutered before reaching puberty," he answered. "So their voices would not change. Didn't matter that, without growth hormones, it affected everything else about them. Even the shape of their bones."

Caitlyn had no response and didn't seem to want to discuss it more. As they walked on the chunks of stone that had once served as bedrock for tracks, few stones shifted. Loose stones had found their place a generation earlier.

A low, eerie whistling sound filled the tunnel. It was impossible to determine where it came from—in front or behind.

Razor stopped. "They found us. The Illegals."

He saw that Caitlyn glanced behind, forward, around. Looking for escape.

"No sense running," Razor said. "They know this world. You don't."

"What's going to happen?"

"Listen." The whistling grew in volume. "Up and down the tunnels, they're signaling that we are here. When enough are gathered, they'll appear."

"Then what?" She was standing rigid, unblinking. Her chest rose and fell. Fear, Razor thought, cloaked by a determination to remain dignified.

"Can you understand, even a little, how much it destroys a family when a child among them loses the lottery? How much they all hate Influentials for putting them in that position? How much they hate themselves for choosing survival over the hell a child must go through to pay for it?"

Caitlyn nodded slowly.

"Then you'll understand why they inflict what they do on anyone from above who enters their world. But I promise you'll be safe among them."

"Safe? How do you know? How can you make a promise like that?"

She was looking up and down the tunnel again. The eerie whistling was growing louder.

"Trust me." Razor had been using the conversation to distract her. That was one of an illusionist's foundations.

He allowed a flashball to roll into his palm.

He dropped it.

He was prepared. His eyes were closed and shielded behind his hands.

Hers were not. While she was paralyzed, he knelt down beside her.

From a sealed plastic bag, he pulled out a damp cloth and pressed it against her face. She breathed in the fumes and sagged into unconsciousness.

THIRTY-TWO

"Tell me what you know about Timothy Ray Zornenbach. Penthouse suite. Floor thirty-five."

Leo snorted. "Nut case. Recluse. Rich. Owns the building. Nobody sees him."

"Owns it?" Pierce juxtaposed that thought against the image of Razor's face. "Inheritance from his old man?"

"He is the old man."

"What about his son. Legally adopted. Same name."

"You need me working for NI," Leo said. "Whoever is giving you information is a quack job. If the old man had a son, I'd know. I promise, any boy you'd ever see with the old man is anything but a son."

"Meaning?"

"Just rumor," Leo said. "But we're talking kink."

"What kind of kink?" Pierce asked.

"Hang on," Leo said. Right hand up, cutting Pierce off.

"Not smart." Pierce gently rested his fingers on Leo's shoulder again. He thought the first attitude adjustment had been successful, but maybe not.

"No!" Leo said, jerking his shoulder way. "I meant wait, someone's back in the system again."

"Doing what?"

"If I'm right," Leo said, "it's someone from a remote location. Retrieving surveillance footage from the last half hour. Every hallway. Every entry."

Which meant someone was now in a position to review the entire operation.

"Shut it down," Pierce snapped. "Now."

"Can't," Leo said. "Whoever is in has put the computer on override."

Pierce shoved the swivel chair aside, dropped to his knees, reached for the power bar behind the computer.

"Hey!" Leo said. "Don't you want to be able to backtrack this guy, see where the stuff is headed?"

Pierce now had a choice between looking stupid for unplugging it or looking stupid for not thinking it through. And he'd just lost the moral high ground to Leo, who could have let Pierce make the situation even worse. But Pierce cared more about results than appearance.

Pierce backed out slowly. He stood and dusted his knees.

"Good call," Pierce said. "Going to need your cooperation. I'm going to call in some techies, and they'll need your office for the rest of the day."

"No problem," Leo said. "I got somewhere to go anyway. Lunch break and an important meeting. You cool with that?"

"Go," Pierce said. "Make sure you come back. We'll have questions."

"No problem. I'm good. I can tell you all you need to know." Leo spun around in the swivel chair. "How does someone apply for a job in NI anyway?"

THIRTY-THREE

At his permanent suite in the Pavilion, Razor flipped through images on a computer screen. Using Trojans long in place, he zipped past the firewalls. He was scanning footage from the building's security cameras to see what had happened after their escape.

He was disturbed by how quickly the agency had found the Zornenbach suite. The footage showed that a secondary search had not been random. There had been agents with thermal radar on only one level, not all of them. And in the hallway on level thirty-five, the agents had moved with purpose directly to the suite.

Other footage had shown a muscular blondish-haired agent—no suit, but a black shirt—staring thoughtfully at the refrigerator Razor had left behind on the elevator. It was one thing to deduce how and why Razor and Caitlyn had used it to escape thermal radar. It was another thing to have pinpointed Razor's home base.

Next they'd find out the suite was registered to Timothy Raymond Zornenbach. That, at least, would send them in a different direction. Looking for Timothy Raymond. Excellent distraction.

Razor flipped through more images. His main focus was the calm, black-shirted agent who seemed to be in charge.

Interesting.

Here was some footage of the guy, going directly into the security office. To talk to Leo. The pig.

That made sense. He'd want the same thing Razor found valuable. Access to the security cameras to learn more.

It gave Razor an idea.

He uploaded all the security camera footage to a remote server, knowing he could access it any time from any computer.

Yes, Razor needed to know more. About the agent who seemed so intelligent. And especially about Caitlyn.

It wouldn't hurt to talk to another source.

THIRTY-FOUR

Everett Tippler had genuine curiosity on his face—not disgust or revulsion—as he held up a clear plastic bag with a human hand in it.

"We might be able to work together." He threw the bag to the side. Stared at Mason. "But first explain this."

"Tried using the sensor chips in the fingers at a money machine."

Finally, Everett showed comprehension. "You used it on a bank machine?"

"Doesn't work," Mason said.

"It needs to be attached to an arm. In turn, the arm needs to be attached to a human." Everett smiled. "A living human."

Mason saw no humor in Everett's efforts. "I had his password. Still didn't work. He promised he had money in his account. But nothing."

"And the guy who owned the hand...?"

"Dead. Can't believe he lied to me about the password. The way I had him, he was begging to tell the truth. I've got experience with these things."

"Appalachia, right? It's your accent. Haven't been here long, have you?"

"What does that matter?" Mason said.

"The fingerprint sensor also needs to detect a pulse within a normal range. Anything too fast, machine judges that someone is forcing the person to put his hand there. Heart rate too slow, well"—Everett pointed at the plastic bag—"guards against that too."

Mason glowered at Everett. Mason didn't like any kind of criticism. "I'll survive a lot longer in your world than you would in mine."

"That'd be why you're the person who's going to find her for me."

"I hunt alone," Mason said.

"As long as you bring her in when you find her."

"Not sure I want to."

"In this world, you'll need weapons and cash. I supply that. Name your bounty price."

For the first time since entering the room, Mason smiled.

THIRTY-FIVE

Pierce was at the basement level of the building, still looking for how Cait-lyn and Razor had found a way out.

He'd pictured Caitlyn and Razor, inside the fridge, door cracked open for air, riding the elevator down while the stairs were jammed with people leaving the building during the fire alarm.

Both would know the building exits would be guarded, so once they stepped off the elevator, they'd leave the fridge behind, hit a different button, and let it go to a different level. Make it more difficult to guess which level they'd actually used to escape the elevator.

But they hadn't gone out the top or the sides of the building. They weren't in the building. Jeremy and Holly were confirming that one more time. So the only conclusion was they'd gone out the bottom.

Which sounded like an impossible conclusion. So Pierce had gone down to the room in the original footage, where Razor and Caitlyn had been trapped by the wheelchair guy.

Ignoring a couple of operatives in the basement hallway, Pierce gave the small room a quick glance first, getting the spartan feel. Murphy bed folded up in place on the wall. Bare of decorations. Shelving above a small fridge and office chair. Definitely a hiding hole. Kid had a luxury place to stay upstairs. Didn't need much here. Big question was why a cubby hole?

All Pierce could think of was that rich kid Razor liked slumming it among Illegals. Pretending he was one of them. So if he ever had to show them where he lived, he could give them this instead of the penthouse.

Pierce gave the closet a slow study. He stared at the high ceiling, trying to figure out how Caitlyn had been hidden up there, but couldn't come up with an answer.

Next he stepped into the hallway. There was the outer bolt he'd seen in the video footage. It had bothered him then, and it bothered him now.

Pierce stood still, patiently exploring that gut feeling.

Bed inside. So Razor either used it or intended to use it for longer stays.

Pierce imagined himself on the bed. Imagined whether it would feel safe. Only if it were locked.

Pierce stepped inside, closed the door. Bolts on the inside too. A degree of safety then.

But the outer bolt still bothered him.

He pulled down the bed from the wall. It creaked slightly as he stretched his body across it. In his mind, he closed the door.

That was it. What if he were inside and someone slid the bolt shut on the outside? Now the hiding hole had become a trap. No way out. Razor wasn't stupid enough to allow for that possibility.

So there had to be a way out.

Easy enough to determine. Thermal radar. Scan the room; look for differences in wall temperature.

Pierce slid off the bed, folded it back up into place, stepped into the hallway, and barked for someone to get the thermal radar.

Two minutes later, they found the escape. A portion of the back wall with a large round aura of blue. Pierce didn't waste any niceties looking for a way to slide back a panel.

He kicked through. Yes, he could have had a couple of the operatives behind him do the work, but this was why Pierce liked being in the field. Discovery. Hunt.

He pulled aside the debris. Cool air washed over his face.

There was a steel ladder attached to the wall of a tunnel going straight down.

Pierce would confirm with a map later, but he guessed this fed into one of the ancient subways.

Chances were, this was how they escaped.

Except going into world beneath the city was certain suicide. Illegals in shantytowns were one thing. But the Illegals below had lived there generations already. Like primitive tribes. Pierce doubted he'd get the authorization to send agents down there. Last time the subway had been breached, the city had been shut down for a week, and it had cost twenty lives.

Didn't a rich kid like Razor understand what he faced down there?

THIRTY-SIX

S pears.

When she woke and her vision had cleared and she realized Razor had abandoned her, Caitlyn could hardly believe her eyes, looking at the men who surrounded her. Four ahead of her. Four behind. Men short and wide, wearing ragged black shirts and pants.

White spots had still been floating in her retinas, and it had been difficult to focus. She had no idea where Razor had fled. Only that he'd abandoned her. With these short, wide men advancing to trap her. Nowhere to run. So she'd remained in place, body tense, wondering about Razor's last words to her. *"I promise you'll be safe among them."*

Each man held a spear waist high, pointed at her as they gestured for her to stand. The spears had wooden handles and steel-tipped heads. But the men kept their distance, as if wary of her.

Once on her feet, she fought traces of a headache. Whatever Razor had used on her, it had left a residue of grogginess.

One, with a habit of wiping hair away from his forehead with his free hand, grunted a few words and gestured farther down the tunnel. They herded her in that direction, but not far.

There was a break in the orderliness of the stone blocks that formed the arch of the tunnel. Stones had been pulled out; the hole was the width of a man's outstretched arms.

"In there."

Brief as the sentence was, Caitlyn heard a strange accent, and she barely understood.

Despite her hesitation, they kept their distance.

"Turn in there," the man repeated.

Her eyes had begun to adjust again. The hole no longer seemed like a black vacuum. She could see a glow inside.

Some of Razor's earlier words came back to her. *"You do know what happens to people who go beneath the city. The urban legends are not just legend. . . You haven't heard about the cannibalism?"*

"No," she answered. It was beyond her imagination, what might wait inside that hole. "I will not."

The men withdrew slightly. Conferred in mumbles.

She was much taller than they were and looked down on their broad shoulders. She was tempted to run. But to where?

They straightened. The man who spoke approached her. Now he held his spear sideways, hands close together on the shaft.

Without a word or any passion, he swung the handle hard and upward. The blow caught her beneath the jaw.

She toppled, again unconscious, not even able to feel the hands that caught her before she hit the ground.

THIRTY-SEVEN

Are you insane?" Leo hissed. He was half naked, lying on the bed, covered by only a towel. This was in a room in a cheaper hotel, a couple blocks down from the Pavilion. "You're toxic waste, man. Go away."

In the corner sat a girl dressed in a nanny outfit. *What a cliché.* She was sitting back, legs crossed, kicking an ankle. Bored. But Razor wasn't going to let her out of the room. He didn't want her double-crossing him and putting out a call to Melvin that would give up Razor's location.

"Toxic waste?" Razor said. "Leo, that's harsh."

Leo's hands were tied to the bedposts. Another pitiful cliché.

Razor was grateful the girl had put a towel across Leo's midsection before moving into the corner. Bad enough seeing that massive flabby chest, hairless and sagging in horizontal lines.

"You know how much you're worth if I make a call?" Leo said. "Melvin's put the word out."

"Need your hands free first," Razor said. "Can't see me doing that."

Leo glanced over at the girl in the corner. She smiled coldly. Shook her head no.

"Not curious how I knew I'd find you here?" Razor asked. Leo was clockwork predictability. And this was one of his habits. Accepting a noncash payment for allowing a street girl on his shift to move in and out of the suites when called by any of her client Influentials.

"Toxic waste," Leo said, uselessly pulling at his bonds. "You're cutting into my time with her."

"She can wait, Leo," Razor said. "I need some answers. What happened today?"

"She never waits," Leo said.

"So talk fast. What happened in there?"

"Like I'm stupid? You pretending you don't know they wanted you?"

"Who, Leo? Who wanted me?"

Leo smirked. "The whole world. Melvin. NI. What'd you do?"

"NI," Razor repeated. Made sense. "You're security. Someone interview you?"

"You and me?" Leo said. "We don't have a deal anymore. No way I'm hiding you down there any longer. They found it anyway. Your little cubbyhole."

"Leo, Leo, Leo," Razor said. "You're not in much of a position to call the shots. See, I know where you live. With your mother. Think she's going to like a digital of you tied to the bed? Or a closeup of the diapers you have on under there? That would make for fruitful discussion, wouldn't it? Dear Mommy, how come I still want to be treated like a baby?"

"You'll go away, right?"

"Baby bottle under the bed too."

"You'll go away, right?"

"So someone talked to you."

"From NI," Leo said. "Guy called himself Carson Pierce."

"And?"

"Wanted to review the security camera footage. But the time period he wanted wasn't there. I told him it looked like someone had hacked in. This Pierce guy likes control. Should have seen him flip when someone started downloading all the other footage."

"Someone hacked in to your computer?"

"While we were there. He's got it swarmed with techies. Trying to find out how the system was penetrated."

"Anything else?"

"Nope."

But Leo had shifted.

"You're a bad liar," Razor said. "And I'm a great photographer. You look good in diapers, Leo. What are you hiding?"

"He asked about Timothy Raymond Zornenbach," Leo answered. No hesitation.

"Who's that?" Razor said.

"Old guy. Owns a suite near the top." Leo looked smug again. "Floor thirty-five. Plus he's on the registry as the owner of the corp that holds the building."

"You know this?"

"Hey, I've got a lot of time in that little office. I do my snooping."

"Tell me about Zornenbach. What's he look like?"

"Haven't seen him in a long while. Was old then; must be ancient now."

"You tell this to that guy from the agency?"

"'Course. The guy was NI. He knew it already anyway. But still wasn't that smart. Said the old man had adopted a kid. Right. And I can do a hundred sit-ups."

"Agent have anything else?" Razor asked.

"I told him they needed someone like me in the IT department. He said maybe I should apply. He'd put in a good word for me."

Razor had what he needed. Confirmation of who was after Caitlyn. And he had a bonus. The operative's name. Carson Pierce.

"Leo," Razor said, "you believe too many things."

"Huh?"

"You really think NI is going to make room for you?"

"I helped him."

"And you really thought I wouldn't take a digital to send to your mother?"

"Come on," Leo said. He pulled futilely against his bonds. The towel slipped slightly. "That's low."

"Might be," Razor said. "One last question. How'd Melvin know where to find me in my cubbyhole?"

Leo struggled harder with the bonds.

"That's what I thought," Razor said. "Not sure I'm going to enjoy taking the digital, but I am going to be happy to send it out to your mother."

THIRTY-EIGHT

Mason squirmed as he walked past shanties crowded in crooked lines. Not from sunshine. Clouds had moved in, a mixture of white and gray, nothing that promised rain. But the temperature had dropped, and wind was coming in gusts. Much better than unrelenting brightness.

Mason squirmed with something else. Desire. He was looking for a victim. He needed to test the capabilities of the Taser Everett had given him, promising that although it was unregistered, it didn't have fingerprint controls as a safety device. Only an idiot hunted with a rifle that he hadn't sighted. In the same sense, Mason wasn't going to put himself in a position of relying on a weapon he didn't fully understand.

Some stared at Mason. He knew he was set apart because he didn't have a swirl of tattoos on his face. Set apart because of the eye patch. Set apart because he walked with his shoulders straight and chest out. A confident predator.

He had not been in this setting for long, but he already knew that every person who looked at him was a person trying to decide the answer to an important question based on Mason's lack of facial tattoos. Was Mason an Illegal and thus someone who could be used? Or was Mason an Influential and looking to use someone here?

Mason had only one question in return.

What kind of victim would best serve his need to test the Taser and his need to savor fear? The terror of the weak and old held attractiveness because, the closer to the end of life, the more most clung to it. Yet there was a satisfaction in taking someone young and strong with a false sense of immortality and introducing the taste of what the old and frail lived with every waking moment.

Mason looked around, then realized he was feeling a foundation of buoyancy beneath his desire. This was so strange; he found himself pausing to analyze it in a rare moment of introspection.

It was rare because Mason didn't like introspection. Introspection was a weakness. It led to self-justification.

The people he had hunted in Appalachia always offered reasons for why they had betrayed the government. They were weak.

Mason didn't care whether their reasons for becoming fugitives were right or wrong. Caring was weakness too. He was not a weak man. That's why he was good at what he did. Right or wrong didn't matter to him because he didn't waste time on introspection.

Neither did he waste time on justifying his role as a bounty hunter for Appalachia or why the heretics he had captured needed to be silenced. He was a hunter. They were fugitives.

He enjoyed hunting people. No need for introspection there either. He didn't need to justify his cruelty and coldness, the two qualities that, along with his peculiar skills, made him so successful. With the exception of Caitlyn, nobody in Appalachia had ever escaped him, and his captures, each one, were celebrated on vidpods that every citizen there was forced to watch.

But buoyancy? This was unfamiliar; it was an emotion that needed attention. If it became a distraction, he'd be less effective.

So Mason stopped walking and turned slowly, as if he were a giant cat, sniffing the wind.

He'd been walking away from the city wall and was still close enough that it dominated the horizon behind him, ominous in a straight line low against the sky, serving as a backdrop to the shanties that seemed huddled in its shadows.

Around him, crowds of people moved in all directions. Dirty people. People dressed in rags. Not like the people of Appalachia—fresh faced and smiling to hide their thoughts. Nothing to mark that they served the religious leaders without question.

These people were marked though. Webs of tattoos across their faces, blurring their features, adding a darkness to the setting.

Buoyancy.

As he turned slowly, Mason concentrated on the sounds. The hum of conversations. An occasional shriek. A dull industrial pounding so low and so far away he couldn't choose the direction.

Facing away from the wall again, he noted a smudge of smoke that in the still of the day was an ominous broad stroke that, like the wall, made another backdrop to the shanties, putting them in a flat valley between the wall and the smoke.

Mason stilled himself completely. Whenever possible, back in Appalachia, at the beginning of the pursuit, he'd stand alone in the fugitive's empty house, trying to put himself in the mind of his prey. Invariably, he'd look for soiled laundry. He'd crumple the clothing and push it up against his face, drawing in deeply the smell of the man or the woman he was about to begin hunting. Mason loved the sense of smell.

Here, it was a combination of urine and sweat, an animal smell that gave him shivers of adrenaline. There was more. A vague sense of burning plastic, mixed with foods cooked over open fires.

And hunger. He could smell hunger. Just like he could smell fear.

Buoyancy.

Then he knew.

Around him was freedom. In Appalachia, the people had looked free and happy. But only because the government told them that religion demanded that appearance.

Here, the people were free to be miserable and smelly, free to walk where they chose, even if those choices could only lead to more misery and stench.

Mason drew in a deep lung full. Smiled.

He'd been a bounty hunter in Appalachia. But there'd been no freedom in that. He was sanctioned by the government. His hunting did not involve any risk. It was like penning pigs and setting him loose among them with a rifle. Some pigs ran. Some didn't. But none ever dared attack him.

Here, he had no protection.

It was just the opposite. He'd killed already, the two Christians who believed he needed their help. It was only a matter of time before the government here began hunting him.

He was truly on his own.

He realized he'd been wrong about this unfamiliar emotion. He had not been feeling buoyancy.

After a lifetime in Appalachia, he had just learned the sensation of freedom.

THIRTY-NINE

Cool. Wet.

Caitlyn woke to the sensation of a gentle touch to her face. Someone using a damp cloth. She was on her back.

Instinctively, she flinched and tried to roll away. No one touched her. Ever.

But there was no place to roll. No place to sit.

She realized she was in a horizontal chamber, like a coffin, but open only on the side. Her vision was filled with the outline of a woman, sitting on a chair, level with the chamber. Her chamber, then, was only a few feet off the ground.

"Easy, easy," came a soft voice. "You are safe here. Under my protection."

Caitlyn reached her hand to her jaw. She winced at her own touch.

"The men will apologize," the soft voice said. "But only when you are ready. I sent them away, the idiots. You should rest. Relax."

"I don't know where I am."

"Among us. Beneath the city."

Caitlyn heard a sound she had not heard in a long time. Laughter from a child. It sounded like the child was running. She knew nothing about her surroundings or these people. But how bad could it be where a child's movement and laughter were unhindered and unadmonished?

"I'm thirsty," Caitlyn said.

"Would you like water?"

"Yes."

"Then ask."

I don't like to ask anything of anyone, Caitlyn thought. Then she wondered if that was precisely why this gentle old woman had said this.

"Please," Caitlyn said. "Could I have something to drink?"

The old woman reached down and, when her hand came up, passed across a plastic bottle.

Caitlyn wondered how she would manage to drink it. She was flat on her back. The chamber fit her so well that there was only six inches clearance above her.

Again, the old woman anticipated her thoughts.

"Are you well enough to roll out and sit up?" the old woman asked.

"I am."

The old woman pushed back her chair, but remained sitting.

Caitlyn swung her legs out. With her feet planted, she twisted slightly and turned and stood but was faint headed. She leaned against the wall and breathed deeply.

"Idiots and morons," the old woman muttered. "Trust me, they've heard from me what I think. But they'll hear it again. What were they thinking, hitting you like that? You've been left under our protection."

This room was barely more than a chamber too. Hard-packed dirt floor. A bare light bulb, softly glowing. Caitlyn looked back at where she'd woken. It was a coffin-sized hole cut into the wall. Blankets for a mattress.

It wasn't the only bed space. Beneath that was another horizontal chamber. And above it another. The entire room was cut with these sleeping holes. All of them lined with blankets as mattresses.

The child's laughter came from outside. Joined by another child. It sounded like one was chasing the other.

It was such a natural, joyous sound that it again countered Caitlyn's foreboding at the strangeness of her surroundings. Such a bright sound in such a dark place.

Caitlyn opened the bottle. Clear plastic. In contrast to something as ancient in design as a spear of wood and sharpened metal.

"My name is Emelia."

Caitlyn sipped at the water, then couldn't constrain herself and gulped it until the bottle was empty, aware of the pain in her jaw with each slight movement. She nodded in gratitude as she studied the old woman.

Emelia's stooped back almost brought a bitter smile to Caitlyn. Unlike Caitlyn, the old woman at least had a natural excuse for her hunched back.

Emelia's head had sunk into her shoulders; gravity and age an enemy she could no longer push away. The wrinkles in her face had assembled in an expression of patient endurance. Her hair was held in place by a dark-colored scarf to match the formless dress over a squat body.

Caitlyn noticed, too, the old woman's smell but couldn't decide what it was. Smoke and animal grease?

"For how long?" Caitlyn asked.

"How long?"

"You said I was under your protection."

"You are under Razor's protection."

"Who is he that you listen to him?"

She laughed. "He brings us money. Food. Medicine. He helps people in the shantytowns too. Razor is, well, Razor. Comes and goes. No one owns him. Does as he pleases."

Caitlyn tried to fit this into what she already knew of Razor. It seemed like a contradiction, so she didn't pursue it.

"How long am I here?" Caitlyn asked.

"Until the refuge is no longer needed."

"There it is again. An answer that is not an answer."

The old woman spoke softly. "You're the one who came down here with Razor. He didn't tell us why you need refuge or when he'd be back. You don't know?"

"I don't."

Emelia said, "I want you to kneel beside me."

There was such compassion in the woman's voice that Caitlyn found herself obeying. On her knees, her head level with the older woman's shoulders.

"Tired child," Emelia said. "Whatever has sent you here must be a tremendous burden. I can see you vibrate with the effort to hold yourself together. You can't live like this. You must not live like this. Let me hold you."

No one touched Caitlyn. Ever.

But when the old woman put her arms around Caitlyn, she didn't fight.

She closed her eyes. Breathed in the old woman's smell. Allowed herself to be pulled in close.

And began to sob in great racking spasms.

FORTY

Moving along with the pedestrian flow, Mason was still trying to decide how best to discover the capabilities of a Taser when he felt a tug on the back of his shirt.

"Mister!"

He twisted, glimpsing a waist-high child moving to hide on the other side of him. He felt contact on his rear.

Mason growled and twisted again. This time, because of the patch on his eye, he lost sight of the child. So he swung violently, raking his hands across the air. His fingers made solid contact, and he was able to grab the child's shoulders. He pulled the child in front of him, where he could see.

A girl. Giggling. "Mister, you're fast."

"Go away," Mason said. He pushed the girl backward. He glanced at the passersby, to see if they were going to interfere. They averted their eyes.

"Mister," she said, smiling. Her face was streaked with tattoo lines. She pushed strands of hair away from her forehead. Her hair might have been blond, but it was too dirty to be certain. She was in bare feet. "I bet I can tell you where you got your shoes."

"Bet what?" Mason snorted. She might have been six years old, if that. What would she have of value?

Then he snorted again. At himself. That simple question had trapped him. Now he was in a conversation.

"What do you want to bet?" the girl asked.

"Not interested," he said.

"How about this?" The girl flashed a paper note. Looked new. Looked like one of the bills Everett had given him, Mason thought. He slapped his back pocket. Empty. He kept most of the money inside his shirt but had placed a bill there so, when he needed some, he wouldn't have to pull out an entire roll.

"How about you give it back to me," Mason said. "You don't know who you're messing with."

"My name's Thirsty," she said. "What's yours?"

"Nothing as stupid as Thirsty," Mason said. "I want that money back. Now."

The girl danced backward, frailty making her light on her feet. "Come on, mister. Bet I can tell you where you got your shoes. I'm wrong, you get this back."

"It's mine. I don't need to win a bet to keep it."

"Afraid I might know the answer?"

Mason took pride in his boots. They were the only thing remaining from his life in Appalachia. Black soft boots that were as comfortable as socks. First thing he'd done at Abe's was rework and polish the leather to make them supple again after time in the river. No way the girl could guess he'd taken them from a fugitive he'd been forced to shoot in the back.

"You don't know the answer," he said, realizing he'd made another mistake by dropping the issue of the ownership of the money. But the girl was unafraid enough to be of some amusement value.

"We got a bet? Ready for me to tell you where you got your boots?"

Mason sighed. "It's a bet."

He stuck his hand out to win back his own money.

"Where you got your boots," the girl began, then paused and grinned, "is right on the ground where you're standing. Yup, you got your boots on the ground."

"Very funny," Mason said. He made a flicking motion with his hand. "Give it back."

The girl giggled again and ran, darting between a couple of shanties.

Mason took a step in that direction, irritated. "Come back!"

"Don't do it," a soft female voice advised from the other direction.

Mason glanced over to identify the source. He'd missed her. She was sitting, cross-legged, just off the wide path, well below his eye level. The constant flow of people had obscured her.

"You listening?" The woman's head was tilted slightly. She had long dark hair, brushed back. Her face wasn't conventionally pretty, but seemed pleasant enough beneath the webbing of tattoos. "You hear me?"

"'Course, I'm listening," Mason snapped. "I'm looking right at you."

"Well, don't chase her," she said. "She's looking to get you off the main path. If you go back in those shanties, about ten of them will drop on you. They'll take anything you have of value and then kill and dismember you so that no one will ever know how and where you disappeared."

Mason didn't think about women much, not in the way he knew most men hungered for them. He wasn't wired that way and didn't care. His own hungers were more difficult to satisfy.

But he wasn't blind to a woman's physical attributes either. In Appalachia, women wore modest clothing. Always. This one, web of blue tattoos across her face, sitting cross-legged with a loose skirt, had on some kind of deeply plunging V-neck shirt, and she seemed careless about the exposure.

Mason moved closer, feeling a slight sense of shame for the view that his vantage gave him.

"You still there?" she asked, head tilted.

"'Course I am," he said. "Right in front of you. You blind or something?"

Her chin dropped in a few inches of shame, and the silence was enough of an answer.

Then he saw a bowl beside her. With a few scattered coins in it.

Mason wanted to kick dirt. This was exactly why he avoided conversations. His life as a bounty hunter consisted of listening to lies or confessions or telling people what to do. Or better yet, uttering threats. He didn't have much practice with conversation.

"Look," he said. That led to another moment of awkward silence, this time on his part. He'd just told a blind person to look.

He started over. "It's like this. I've got only one eye myself." When he'd had two eyes, one always wandered and gave people the creeps, but he wasn't going to admit that. "I wasn't trying to insult you."

She turned her face upward, and he noticed her eyes were creamy white.

"You sound like a nice man," she said. "It's all right. And I can tell you're not from here."

"How can you know that? You're..." Mason let his voice trail off, embarrassed again that he couldn't manage this conversation.

"Blind. I know. But Thirsty, she don't try leading anybody back among the shanties unless they're strangers. You don't have a tattoo face mask either, do you? She wouldn't have tried if you were one of us."

"No," Mason said. "I'm here looking for someone. They're supposed to be at the Meltdown. I see smoke. I figure that's where I need to go."

"It's a long ways," she said. "You'll need to pay attention as you go."

"Don't worry," Mason said. "I'm good at paying attention."

Especially right now. Given the V-neck on her dress, he couldn't help his wandering eye from doing a lot of wandering. Most of the time, when he'd actually been with women, they hadn't been too willing, but circumstances as a bounty hunter gave him a large degree of latitude in how he took his pleasure with them. Other times, much more rare, the women had been far too willing, drawn to Mason because of his reputation.

Here, there was something about the combination of the woman's sadness and vulnerability that quickened his heartbeat. But he couldn't take her like he'd taken others, and she wasn't directly offering either. He didn't know how to handle this.

"You seem like a nice man," she said. "And I'm an excellent judge of character." She pulled her bowl onto her lap, and it sagged into the material of her loose skirt. Mason had a flash of imaginary vision of lithe legs hidden.

"I'm not asking," she said in a quiet voice, "but if you could spare a little for the trouble I saved you, I'd be grateful. I'm hungry. Real hungry."

The words came out of Mason's mouth before he fully understood what he was saying. "Are you lonely some too?"

FORTY-ONE

Later Caitlyn would learn that, unconscious, she'd been taken to what the Illegals in the subway called a sleeping chamber, where one or two families would retire each night, with every person allotted one of the coffin-shaped excavations in the side of the wall—like the ancient catacombs beneath Rome, with the difference being that living bodies occupied the resting spots, not corpses that the early Christians were trying to keep from cremation by Roman authorities.

Later, she would learn that the sound of laughing children came from a much larger chamber designated as a general communal living space. And later, she would understand more of the events that had forced the Illegals to literally carve out an existence beneath the city, driven into a life where the old subway tunnels served as thoroughfares to a network of tributaries and small territories of living chambers.

But for now, in Emelia's comforting presence, all that was still a mystery to Caitlyn. Her sobs eventually subsided as the older woman stroked her head and murmured again and again, "Poor child." Caitlyn found herself telling Emelia all that she'd held back and kept inside for as long as she could remember.

She told Emelia she had never gone to her papa—when she thought of her childhood, he was Papa to her, not Jordan—for this kind of comfort. Papa was a caregiver and kept her safe. But Papa wasn't someone she brought her secrets to. All through childhood, isolated in the hills of Appalachia with her papa—Jordan—Caitlyn had always been adoringly shy, content just to be in his presence, so aware that she was different and so convinced that she was a burden to him that she was afraid to complain or even share the constant anguish that came with her deformity. She knew, always, that they were hiding in Appalachia because of who she was.

"He loved you," Emelia said, after giving Caitlyn's confession a long pause of respectful silence.

"He loved me." Caitlyn had straightened by then and was out of Emelia's arms. Kneeling near Emelia's chair. At times looking straight ahead, at times into the old woman's face. She ached for the days when it was that simple, daily life with Papa, just the two of them.

"A child must feel loved," Emelia said after a pause. "Look around here. Humans were not meant to live the way we do. Some of the children haven't seen sunlight. Ever. But you hear laughter. It is good that you were loved. It is better that you knew you were loved."

"Papa loved me. He was willing to give his life for me. In Appalachia, when the bounty hunter and the dogs were close, he left me behind and drew the dogs. Later, he told me he didn't expect to escape."

"There is anger in your voice."

"Jordan also betrayed me. Kept secret what I am. That's why I'm here. Outside of Appalachia. Hunted. Alone."

Emelia spoke softly. "He must have had his reasons."

Caitlyn thought of the letter she carried, rescued from the front seat of the Enforcer car. "He told me that before I was born, he had vowed to perform an act of mercy and decency and drown me like a kitten."

Emelia didn't push Caitlyn to speak, simply waited, as if realizing Caitlyn had never spoken of this to anyone.

Caitlyn closed her eyes, thinking about the nights, in her dreams, that Papa appeared. To rescue her from the destiny he had thrust upon her before she was born. To return to her what he had taken. Her trust and innocence.

When her dreams took her to those childhood days in Appalachia—picnics with Papa, holding his hand, watching the hawks—she woke up happy. Loved. Secure. Just for a moment, until she realized where she was. Outside. Alone. Angry. Needing this anger to force away her fear.

"His secret was my deformity," Caitlyn said. She was tempted to strip down, to spread her wings, to show Emelia what Jordan had done to her. "He was a scientist. Before the war. I was an experiment. He betrayed me before I was born. He betrayed me by keeping it secret from me. He betrayed me by setting me loose."

The old woman made a humming noise as she lost herself in thought.

Caitlyn found the noise comforting, but she found everything about the woman comforting.

"What do they want from you?" Emelia asked. "Those who hunt you?"

"I don't know."

"And your papa—"

"Jordan."

"And Jordan. He helped you escape from Appalachia but stayed behind."

Caitlyn felt her face twist in a bitter smile as she remembered the night of her escape. A clear, moonless night. Wind coming off the slope of the high ridge overlooking the perimeter fencing that imprisoned Appalachia.

She'd been poised to leap into the night sky, to escape. Jordan had reached for her. She'd stepped away, knowing how much her rejection would hurt him. He had spoken, softly. *"I love you as big and forever as the sky."*

They both knew it had been his plea for forgiveness. Since she could remember, that was their game. *"Caitlyn, how much does Papa love you?"* And her answer: *"As big and forever as the sky, Papa."*

That night, on the ridge, with the wind waking her senses, with her arms and wings outstretched, she had simply needed to utter a single word in response. *Papa.* He would have known he was forgiven.

Instead, in cold, blind anger at what she had learned about Jordan, she had leapt into the abyss, determined to reject him. But when her wings had made instinctive adjustments and she'd exulted in her destiny, found joy in flight, she finally called back, not knowing if it had reached him.

"Papa."

It had been a cry of love and of forgiveness to set him free too.

Some nights, waking from childhood dreams, Caitlyn hoped the wind had carried that single word back to him. So that he realized she missed her papa. So that he would always know she was grateful for the chance to flee her pursuers and alter who she was.

Although she had escaped Appalachia, she could not escape her hatred of what he had robbed from her—the trust and innocence that had sustained her all through childhood. To the world she had been a freak, but not to him. His love had been the ultimate shelter. Until discovering why she was a freak and what he had hidden from her. Until understanding that when he made a choice not to drown her, Jordan had thrust upon her this fate. Alone and hunted.

Most nights, then, she hoped he did not hear that last cry. So that, as childish punishment, she could take satisfaction that Jordan believed she was still as cold to him as in their final days together.

She hated that she hated him. And hated that she loved him.

"Your papa," Emelia began, but Caitlyn cut her off again.

"Jordan," Caitlyn corrected her. "Jordan Brown. A scientist."

"He gave you no instructions?" Emelia asked.

Caitlyn thought of the papers she always carried. One was a letter from Jordan to her, just before he'd abandoned her the first time. *We had agreed— the woman I loved and I—that as soon as you were born, we would perform an act of mercy and decency and wrap you in a towel to drown you in a nearby sink of water.*

The other paper was a letter. Given the night she escaped Appalachia. With the name of a surgeon and how to reach him.

"I was to visit a surgeon," Caitlyn answered. "An old friend of his. The surgeon would remove my..." *Wings,* Caitlyn nearly said. But she caught herself in time. "...my deformity."

"Yet you haven't."

"I haven't," Caitlyn said. "But I've decided. It's time."

FORTY-TWO

Razor loved illusion. Razor loved the irony of a truth in illusion and of an illusion in truth.

In the hallway outside the hotel room, he decided he had less than three minutes to complete his next illusion. The street girl he'd left in the corner on a chair in Leo's room was at least in her midtwenties. Easy conclusion: she was a survivor. Illegals didn't live too far into their teens if they were not. Survivors were calculators and highly motivated by self-interest. Much as she might have pretended boredom, she had spent every moment in that chair thinking about the reward Melvin would pay for Razor's capture.

Right now, as Razor moved down the hallway, she was reaching for the phone. How much more ideal could it have been for her?

Razor had left Leo blubbering in his blubber, tied to the bedposts. With Razor gone, Street Girl was in complete control. She'd cash in on the knowledge of Razor's location while Leo shivered in his diapers. A quick call and Melvin would have Illegals on the street, waiting for Razor to step outside the hotel, ready to shepherd him into an alley, totally confident that no Influential would bother interfering.

Razor had less than three minutes, but he only needed forty-five seconds. The time it took to ride the elevator a couple levels higher. He had a hotel card in his back pocket, one for another permanent suite under a different name. All told, Razor had a half dozen residences in the city, each stocked with chemicals of choice. He had plenty of chemicals to aid his illusion. To put together flashballs. To put people to sleep. And more.

His first priority was the single biggest illusion of his life, granted to him by unmarked vials in a drawer in the bathroom alongside unused hypodermic needles and rubber tubing.

Razor locked the door. With expert movements acquired through practice, he one-handedly wrapped the tubing around a bicep and made a knot that would hold. As his veins began to swell, he dipped the hypo into the vial, and sucked up a small portion of the drug. He kept his face blank as he injected it, then drew deep breaths of air into his lungs. He hated blood, even the sight of the tiny drops that would appear on his punctured skin. Or maybe he hated the sight of blood because of those punctures.

He stared at the mirror for a full minute, almost in self-hatred.

Then another deep breath to get ready for his next illusion.

Beneath the sink was a toiletry kit that didn't contain any toiletries. Instead, there was a latex mask with only a straw hole for the mouth. He took a small can of specialty paint from under the sink and set it on the counter. Then a straw. He checked his watch, and set an alarm for ten minutes later.

When he pulled the tight-fitting latex over his head, his nostrils, eyes and mouth would be sealed.

This was a familiar routine, but it still unnerved him, the five minutes of helplessness he would feel with only a straw for air.

Slowly he pulled the tight, dark rubber over his head and onto his face.

His first necessity was the straw. Eyes shut beneath the latex, he groped the counter for it and felt on his face for the hole that led to his mouth. He inserted the straw and sucked in air. The sound of it barely reached him because the latex mask also sealed his ears.

Now that he could breathe, he patted and pulled at the latex to make sure it fit every contour of his face. It was a delicate task because of the pattern of open, curved lines in the mask that left slits on his chin, cheeks, and forehead exposed.

Once he was satisfied that the mask was in place and held no wrinkles, he reached for the paint can and felt the nozzle with his fingertips to make sure it was facing him.

He forced his tongue down on the straw to force it upward at an angle. If he accidentally sprayed paint into the open end, it would clog the straw and risk spraying paint into his mouth.

The paint felt cool against his skin.

With his tongue, he manipulated the straw to point downward and sprayed again, ensuring that there would be no pattern left from the straw at its upward angle.

Razor waited, motionless.

The paint would dry quickly. When the alarm sounded, he knew the paint would be like indelible ink, soaked and sealed into the pores of his skin. Granting him the power of yet another illusion—facial tattoos, with a registered bar code pattern that would make him indistinguishable from any of the Industrials who lived in the shantytown and migrated into the city on a daily basis.

When he had no more need of this illusion, a special chemical solution would dissolve the tattoos and let him return to the illusion he cherished and hated the most.

The person he called Razor.

Fast, sharp, and dangerous.

FORTY-THREE

Outside, gusts of wind rocked the tin-roof shanty. Inside, grateful for the cooler air, bare from the waist up, Mason rolled onto a lumpy, thin mattress, supported a few inches off the floor by a slatted frame. He'd carefully placed his Taser and his shirt directly beneath him, in easy reach.

Mason shivered. Not necessarily from anticipation. From memories of his time in the cave he had just escaped.

Mason was terrified of the dark. Always had been. When he was a boy in Appalachia, his mother had locked him in a root cellar every time she needed to punish him. He never knew what act might deserve punishment. Something she'd laugh at one day would throw her into fits of rage the next. She'd strip him naked, drag him to the root cellar, and throw him down the steps. The door would close, leaving him on a clammy dirt floor, waiting for spiders and centipedes to begin to crawl toward him, and he would feel a scream start to build, knowing she was outside, listening, waiting to punish him further if he made noise, punishing him by adding extra time in the pitch-black root cellar among the molding vegetables and the smell of his own stale urine from the hours and hours he'd spent as prisoner of the hated darkness.

Here, while there were enough cracks in the walls to send sharp beams of light in horizontal lines across the narrow shanty, it was dim enough to trigger that irrational claustrophobic fear, and the slashes of light barely kept those emotions at bay.

His wandering eye was greedy—for the light and for what the woman was about to reveal, for she was still in the loose skirt and the shirt that had drawn him to this moment, and he could see enough to anticipate the next moments.

Slowly and awkwardly, she moved to the bed, reaching out with her hands to find the edge of it.

She sat beside him.

"Can you close your eyes?" she asked. "If you watch me as I undress, it will seem dirty…"

She drew a deep breath. "It's just that I don't do this. Other women take money, and I know you offered me money and I have to take it because that's how my life is. You don't understand how hungry I am and what it does to a person, but I don't do this for money. I have my bowl. I have my spot there, near the path. There's another area, where women stand, to sell themselves. I don't do that."

"I'll close my eye," Mason said. "My other eye, remember, has a patch."

She reached for his face. He took her hand and guided it toward his patch. Her scent was slightly sour, but it made her seem more real. Her fingers touched and explored his face, stopping first at his eyes, then his lips.

On his back, Mason discovered he was holding his breath, hoping she would not stop stroking his face. He realized what it was that had softened him toward her.

Dark was her world. She was blind. She lived his terror.

"How do you do it?" he asked her.

"Maybe this isn't a good idea," she said. "I don't want to talk either."

"No, no, no," Mason said. Why did he expect her to read his mind? "Living without sight, I mean. No light. Ever."

She didn't answer.

Mason felt a need to fill the silence. "I couldn't. I've got this eye. I lose it, and I lose everything. I don't believe in God, and I don't believe in mercy. But if something were to take away my eye, I'd be in hell. I'd beg for mercy." Mason hadn't ever confessed a weakness to anyone. There was a certain buoyancy now, like the sensation of freedom.

"I guess you live blind," she said. "Or you decide not to live. What other choices are there?"

"You asked if I was lonely," she murmured. "Yes. Hold me first. Just for a little while."

He did, mentally exploring what tenderness was like. Maybe it was all right. Maybe it was a way to push back the dark. He closed his eye. He didn't count the seconds.

When she shifted and pulled away, it didn't seem to break the spell.

She stood and moved away from the bed. He was holding his breath again, waiting for the sound of her clothing falling softly from her body. Ridiculous, he knew, because she was blind, unable to know if he was, but he was keeping his promise. He did have his eye closed.

But the sound he heard was the creaking of the shanty door.

There was brightness against his eyelid.

He turned his head, looking now, opening his eye, and saw silhouettes in the doorway, moving toward him. Lightning fast, because he was still a hunter, he twisted on the bed and reached down for his Taser.

And couldn't find it.

Frantic, he swept his hand in all directions.

Too late.

Bodies fell upon him. Hands dragged him from the bed. Other hands rose, and against the light, he saw the outline of clubs. Now coming down.

The blows, across his chest and head, drove the air from his lungs. Instead of fighting, he slumped. Didn't resist.

More hands against him, like the crawling of spiders long ago in the root cellar. The roughness of hemp. Until his hands and feet were bound. He kept his head down, letting it loll against his chest. Anything to give him an edge. And if it arrived, he'd erupt. Savage. Hateful.

"It's all under the bed," he heard the woman say. "I pushed it back. Out of his reach."

"Lots, you think? I found a good one, didn't I, Mommy?"

Mason recognized the voice immediately. The little girl. They'd been working together. And the woman wasn't blind. Not if she'd seen where he'd placed the Taser.

"Whore!" Mason shouted. "Whore!"

His anger wasn't at her. But at himself.

Nothing he could do. She'd warned him earlier that if he had anything of value, he'd be dead.

Eye open, he counted five of them. Sunlight from the door was too bright a backdrop to make out any features.

"He's afraid of blindness," she told them. "Take out his good eye. Let him live. Thinking he can come into our world and buy what he wants."

Snickering from the men who had him surrounded. One brandished a short knife and reached toward his face.

Mason bucked against his bonds. A wild animal in a frenzy. He was fighting so hard that it took him a few seconds to comprehend that not all the screaming was his. And a few more seconds to realize he was no longer fighting anyone, only the bonds.

He stopped his useless flailing and sat back, heaving for breath.

The five men were on the floor. The woman and the girl gone.

And someone tall and large standing above him with a Taser in one hand.

The large man picked up the knife that had fallen from the hands of one of the attackers.

"Let me cut the rope," the large man said. "I'm here to help."

Mason rolled back, not trusting.

"Everett sent me to follow you," he said. "Told me to watch your back. Looks like you needed it. What were you thinking? Letting yourself get trapped like this? No tattoos on your face. There's places you just don't go out here."

Mason relaxed. Everett. This man wouldn't know Everett's name unless he was telling the truth.

"I smell burning," Mason said. "That was a Taser?"

"When the setting is strong enough, it'll torch hair," the man said. "Might need a solar recharge after zapping all of them. A couple hours should do it. Not a lot of electrical outlets out here."

Mason accepted the man's help with the bonds. When the rope was cut, he rolled over and searched under the bed. Found his shirt and wallet. Found his Taser.

When he stood, the man Everett had sent was shaking his head. "They'd have cut you up and cooked the choice pieces by midnight. Old trick out here, putting in contacts that make it look like cataracts. I can see I'm going to have to stay pretty close."

Mason's response was simple. He flicked the switch on his own Taser as he shoved it into the man's chest.

The crackling result was instantaneous.

Mason had shot plenty of men before, and more often as not, it would take a couple of seconds for the body to fall. He'd see it in their eyes. A split second before comprehension, then another couple of heartbeats as the brain tried to fight the body, until shock overwhelmed the nervous system and the body collapsed.

Here, the electrical charge exploded through the synapses, and the man in front of him had become nothing but meat, unguided by any thoughts or impulses.

The man simply dropped.

Nice weapon, Mason thought. And it had been a good situation to test it.

Mason leaned down and tapped the man's chest. Everett's man was far beyond hearing, but Mason spoke anyway.

"I hunt alone," Mason said.

He scooped up the knife as he left the shanty. After he'd found Caitlyn, who'd made him lose one eye, he'd come back and look for the whore who'd wanted to take the other and leave him blind.

This knife, he vowed, would cut out both of her eyes. But not until the same knife had worked its way across her body and delivered the justified punishment for fooling him into a weakness that would never occur again.

FORTY-FOUR

Caitlyn climbed a short ladder that ended at a trapdoor, following two of the men with spears. A couple were below her, in case she tried to turn around.

One of the men above her banged on the bottom of the trapdoor, a complicated code of raps and pauses. Seconds later, the door creaked open above her, and weak sunlight made it to Caitlyn's eyes.

The men above her climbed upward and into the room above. The men below her pushed her upward into the light.

She had no idea, of course, where she was. The interior of the room above her gave no clues either. Tin-sheet walls, no windows, low, exposed roof made of the same stuff, where a hole had been cut to allow sunshine inside.

Then she was blindfolded. She had to trust that if they were going to harm her, they would have done so by now.

One of the men gently took her by the elbow. She heard the door open. The man led her outside, where the warmth of the sun hit her face.

The man spun her several times clockwise, then several times counter-clockwise.

She began to count paces as they led her away. Began to smell the aroma of human waste and smoke.

At the hundred twenty mark, the man stopped her and pulled off her blindfold.

She was now out of the tunnels beneath the city, well beyond the city walls, in the center of a shantytown with no landmarks to guide her as to which one. Clouds had darkened the sky, spatters of rain finally coming down.

Six men still surrounded her, making it clear she was under their guard. As prisoner. And as protectors.

Walking went faster now that she could see.

Five minutes later, they stopped at a shanty, indistinguishable from any others. One stepped over a small muddy stream to open the makeshift door and pointed. There was a table inside. A chair. And a basket with a loaf of bread and a big chunk of cheese. Jar of water beside.

Despite the quickening of rain drops, the others remained in position outside.

She understood clearly. The shanty was hers. And she wasn't going to be allowed to leave.

Razor was on a trolley with other Industrials, headed toward the address he'd secured earlier. Windows were open, despite the light rain. Windows were never closed in a trolly. Too much smell.

The car wasn't full yet, as it was making a pass from the inner city to the outer wall and was collecting more passengers at each stop.

The street was essentially a canyon with high walls on each side—not as high as the city wall, nor patrolled by soldiers—and only the tracks for electric trains down the center. No sidewalks. Cameras with motion-detector software monitored the street. The software was set up to detect biped motion. The silent trains that whisked past every fifteen minutes did not trigger alarms. Only pedestrians came to the attention of Enforcers. Since it was impossible to scale the walls—strung with barbed wire and electrical zappers—anyone stupid enough to walk the streets was immediately put into custody.

It was a good system for the Influentials, as the entrances through the walls to their neighborhood consisted of two types. The first was for Influentials. Large, clear acrylic bubbles extended from the wall out to their trolley stops. Inside those bubbles, they were protected. From weather. From any interaction with Industrials. Their trolleys were air-conditioned, seats with leather trim, smoked glass windows. No chance for an Industrial to enter these trolleys. Transportation for Influentials only stopped at the bubbles, and access to the bubbles from the neighborhood needed a password and retina scan.

In contrast, the Industrials had to pass through a guarded checkpoint in and out of the neighborhood. Going in, they faced metal detectors and body-scanning devices. Suicidal as it was for an Industrial to attack an employer, the safeguard still existed. Going out, they faced the same scanners—this was protection against petty theft.

Their trolley stops—for trains without air conditioning and without any seating—had no protection. When Industrials were finished with their jobs for the day, they would each pass through the wall, then wait in clusters for the trolley that would take them to the outer city wall, where they would walk to the shanties and soovie camps.

Industrials around Razor ignored him. He was tattooed again. One of them.

As the trolley whisked down the street, he saw the trees and rooftops of the houses behind the walls. Each house would have wonderfully tended gardens—attended to by Industrials happy for labor-intensive employment. Other Industrials cleaned and cooked. Some even provided tutoring for the children of Influentials. Households might have eight to twenty Industrials at work during the day. But at dusk, the neighborhoods emptied, and only Influentials remained in the houses.

Razor became more alert as the trolley slowed for the stop he needed. Not to disembark, but to wait for new passengers.

The trolley door slid open, and ten Industrials stepped aboard. They had passed through the checkpoint and were now bound for a checkpoint at the outer wall. There was the usual jostling for position. These ten were no different than the other assortments the trolley had been collecting. Some young, some old. Some with defeated posture. Others not so bowed. All with the spider-webbed tattooing across their faces.

Razor didn't hesitate and didn't care who heard him ask.

"Any of you bondaged to the Swain household?"

Eyes swiveled his way. Then a woman—stout, old, hair bound beneath a handkerchief—quickly looked away.

But nobody answered.

Razor shrugged. Looked back out at the high, thick brick walls that passed in a blur. He swayed with the rhythm of the trolley. He waited until after the next stop, when another dozen Industrials boarded and pushed all the passengers in tighter.

Razor shifted, and it didn't take much for him to get near the old woman.

When the trolley picked up speed and the murmuring of conversations began again, he leaned closer and spoke into her ear. He smelled bleach, knowing the scent came from her hands. She was a domestic cleaner then.

"I know someone who wants to ask questions about the doctor," Razor said in a low voice. "You will be well paid for your answers."

He knew he would learn a lot from how she responded. In households where Influentials treated Industrials with respect and decency, the ties became almost familial, with a shared loyalty. Influentials who abused their Industrials, however, were betrayed in as many unseen ways as possible.

The old woman gave no reaction. Her silence could have been loyalty. Or fear. It confirmed for Razor, however, that he'd guessed correctly. She was bondaged to the Swain household. Otherwise she would have denied it immediately.

The trolley windows were open, and air blew an assortment of passenger smells across Razor's face. If it had been hotter, like the day before, the smells would have been worse. He was patient; there was no place to go anyway. He couldn't exit at any of the stops. If he actually stepped off the trolley, he would have only two choices. Walk down the empty tracks and face immediate arrest. Or approach a gate, where the guards would likely deny him access, and possibly find out he was wanted by Enforcers.

He had to ride to the end of the line, something he had expected.

The old woman must have known it too.

She remained silent and ignored him until that final stop, just short of the city's outer wall.

As the Industrials unpacked themselves from the trolley and began trudging to the outer gate, she discreetly tugged on Razor's shirt.

"What is it you want to know?" she asked in a voice much softer than her appearance. "And how much is it worth?"

FORTY-FIVE

Rain had quit, barely minutes after starting, and the shifting clouds left receding gray to be replaced by patches of white. Mason found a vantage point on a hill of discarded computer monitors. Billy and Theo might be somewhere in visual range, but he wasn't worried that they might see him.

Back in Appalachia, where hawks soared in clear blue skies, the predator birds would often screech from the air, knowing that the sound would startle small animals and send them scurrying. The hawks did this because when their prey flinched or started scurrying, the frightened movement gave away their hiding spots, and the hawks would swoop down and strike in savage satisfaction.

With the oily smoke of burning plastic swirling around him here, Mason looked for the same advantage.

If Billy or Theo recognized him from when he'd almost killed them in Appalachia, their reaction would set them apart in the pattern of activity among the dozens and dozens of scavengers searching among the acres and acres of debris—dismembered car engines long pulled from the corpses of soovies, rusted bicycle frames, video game consoles, and the hazardous electronic waste of the rich.

This was the Meltdown, set farthest away from the city wall that encased the Influentials, a distance measured in miles, ensuring the acrid smoke never wafted into their manicured gardens.

On his journey here, Mason had noted the progression, or rather regression, of status in loosely defined layers. Closest to the city walls, the Industrials and Illegals with the most status lived in sturdy shacks, with the least walking distance between them and the checkpoints at the city walls. Many of them had large dogs chained nearby for protection; the Influentials never allowed weapons more sophisticated than knives among any of them, so the dogs were essentially enough to keep a shanty safe if the owner could afford the resources it took to feed the animal.

Each successive layer outward from the wall held populations that were poorer and had more distance to walk the dangerous and unpoliced trails from where they lived to reach inner-city, near-slavery employment among the Influentials. Nearly an hour by foot from the checkpoint at the city walls, the final outer layers consisted of the soovie parks, and beyond was the Meltdown, where Mason now stood. Here, the poorest and the most desperate spent all their daylight hours trying to glean copper, brass, and other metals for sale at stalls closer to the city wall.

The noise was as horrendous as the smell of burning plastic, with relentless scavengers tearing apart computers and other electronics with hammers and pliers, many of their faces pitted with tiny scars from exploding glass.

On his hillside of computer monitors, Mason enjoyed the sensation of being above it, surveying the scavengers from his precarious perch.

He had his left hand in his pocket, fondling the fur of a freshly killed rat, when someone finally challenged him.

Short of spotting Billy and Theo, he'd been hoping for this. It would have been simpler to walk up to a scavenger and start asking questions, but not near as enjoyable.

The challenge came in the form of a rock that bounced off a computer monitor at Mason's feet. He looked for the source and saw four of them, young men in grimy jeans, shirtless. They wore soot-stained kerchiefs across the bottom half of their faces. Not for disguise, but to filter out the noxious fumes.

Three held rocks poised to throw. The fourth was gesturing for Mason to move down the pile of monitors toward them.

Mason shrugged. It took him a few minutes to pick his way among the monitors.

"We got rules here," the one without a rock said. "Simple rules. You don't work alone. Half of what you find goes to us."

"Screw your rules," Mason said. Offering to pay them for information was undoubtedly a mistake. It would only mark him as prey to be robbed.

The leader stepped forward, his face twisted with a threatening leer.

Mason was expecting it and closed the distance instead of retreating. At the same time, he kicked upward and outward, striking the center of the man's groin. As the man fell forward, Mason grabbed his hair, spun him around, and put him in a chokehold.

That kept the rocks at bay.

Then, with his other hand, Mason Tasered his victim in the back. Not at full stun. He didn't want jellied meat. He wanted a man in agony.

The leader shrieked and sagged to his knees.

"Tell them to go away," Mason said. "I want to talk."

"Get him!" the man shouted instead.

The other three rushed Mason, who dropped his human shield and swung his Taser in an arc. Two fell instantly, still conscious but partially paralyzed. The third hesitated in disbelief, and Mason swiped him with the Taser too. Same result.

He adjusted the weapon to a higher power, and just like stabbing them with an ice pick, punched each of the three in the throat with his Taser.

None of them even managed a croak as each collapsed completely.

Mason turned back to their leader.

"Hope you're ready to talk now," Mason said. "I'm not bad with a knife either."

FORTY-SIX

The old woman didn't have to instruct Razor to walk with her through the main checkpoint at the outer wall. Both knew that if they stopped walking, it would draw the attention of Enforcers. The rules of departure were very simple—three lines of single-file pedestrians.

Given that Industrials were already screened for theft at the secondary walls that surrounded each neighborhood, the departure checkpoint was not as carefully guarded as the entrance checkpoint the old woman would have used at the beginning of the day to get inside the city wall for a trolley to take her to the Swain neighborhood. Here the point was simply to get the Industrials out of the city as efficiently as possible. If they wanted to loiter and form groups beyond the city wall, that was not a concern for the Influentials. Because they were weaponless—death to any Industrial and the entire family if anything beyond a knife was found during a random raid—they were no threat with a guarded wall to scale to reach the inner core.

Razor stayed in line, face straight ahead for the cameras, silent like everyone in front of and behind him. He passed through the checkpoint with no incident, nor did he expect any. His face was tattooed like all the rest.

The checkpoint gate had a turnstile where the cameras scanned the bar code tattoos for each of the three lanes of pedestrians. Computers tallied the number of Industrials who had entered the city at the beginning of the day and compared it to the number who left. There was an allowable variance because, unofficially, some Industrials, especially the young and attractive, stayed behind at the whims, or abuses, of Influentials. But the comparison number—just like the difference between the in and out for each neighborhood—was still watched closely for any large difference that might indicate that Industrials were staying inside the city for a possible nighttime revolt.

Finally past the outer wall—which was thirty feet tall and wide enough for the two-soldier patrol at the top—the old woman turned to Razor.

"Food." She nodded her head toward a street vendor, who had a cart with strips of fly-specked cooked chicken hanging from wires.

Razor bought two pieces, using crumpled bills of small denominations. Only idiots allowed themselves to look wealthy outside the walls.

He returned to her, keeping one of the pieces for himself. He ripped off a piece of chicken with his teeth and deliberately chewed with his mouth open, essentially mimicking the way she attacked her chicken. She said nothing until all of the greasy meat was gone.

Then she spoke with weary hatred. "That man, the doctor, he keeps my daughter behind two or three nights a week. Who can stand against it?"

Razor nodded. He understood with far more clarity than he would ever share with anyone. Images tumbled through his mind, the images of his nightmares, and he took a deep breath to clear his emotions.

Because of those images, Razor understood hatred too. And how it could be used. This woman would not protect Swain. Chances were, no Industrial in the household would.

"How long have you been in his service?" Razor asked.

"Five weeks. Maybe six."

"He is a surgeon?"

"Yes. But no one visits him for surgery. He doesn't leave the house."

"Old? Young?" Razor wanted a picture of the man in his head.

"Early fifties. Beyond that, I know nothing. No one in the household does."

"No one?" Razor said it with disbelief. In most households, Industrials were given no more attention than an appliance. Valued as little as any slave. As a consequence, most Influentials talked or acted around them like they didn't exist.

"We're all new to the household. All of us joined when I did."

"Why were the previous household Industrials all dismissed before you got there?"

"Maybe they knew too much. This man, none of us like him. We all fear him. He is abusive." She spat on the ground.

"Still, I can't believe in six weeks you know nothing beyond his occupation."

"My daughter says he occasionally has a visitor. Late at night. A military man. And sometimes a woman, who comes there with the military man."

Razor nodded. The old woman didn't need much encouragement.

"My daughter is locked up when the woman comes and is not released until she goes. Like he doesn't want her to know about my daughter."

Razor shrugged.

"There's nothing else I can tell you," the old woman said. "Really."

"If I need to find you again?" Razor asked.

"Do I look young enough to live near the city wall?"

He knew what she was implying. Industrials with the most status lived close to the gate that let them into the city to work during the day. The walk was shorter. She was too old to have status.

"How far do you walk?" he asked.

"Almost to the soovie camps," she said. "And soon I'll have to move there."

Poverty slowly drove them outward, with the weakest and poorest at the fringes, to be preyed upon by the gangs that ruled the soovie camps.

"I have money for you," Razor said. "From the person who wanted to ask about Swain."

"No." The old woman tightened her lips. "If I spend it, those around me will wonder where it came from and if I have any more. I don't need that kind of danger. I don't want money. But if what I told you harms this surgeon in any way, I'll take my satisfaction there."

FORTY-SEVEN

Billy said, "Do you believe what they said?"

On foot, they were well past the city wall, halfway through the shanty-town buffer that led to the collection of soovie parks at the outer rings of DC. Orchestrated by wind that stayed as an aftermath of a rainstorm too brief to conquer the dust that rose and fell in small funnels, small pieces of litter danced with the same rhythm.

"Have to believe. Phoenix will be safe as long as we report to them from the soovie park. He gave me a phone that only calls to one number. We see or hear anything about people getting together to fight Influentials, we're supposed to call."

"Influentials or government people don't kill little girls," Billy said. "They'll find a place for her."

"I'm not worried about that," Theo said. "I just pretended to believe his threat. So we could get out of there."

"Still want to go west?"

"Yeah," Theo said, indignant. "As soon as Caitlyn meets us."

"Could be an easy job, helping the government, protection and all."

"You don't mean it."

"No," Billy said. "Just making sure you still want what I want."

"Freedom for Caitlyn."

"That's something else," Billy said. "The government finding us. Don't you find it strange? Think of all the places we could have gone from Lynch-burg. All the hundreds and hundreds of shantytowns and soovie parks."

"Almost like they tracked us," Theo said. "Remember the Factory in Appalachia? How they put chips in each person?"

"I remember you dug it out of your arm. With a knife. But when the gov-ernment talked to us in Lynchburg, those guys didn't do anything to you or me."

"I'd have fought them," Theo said. "Couple quick kicks in the tender parts, and down they go."

Billy smiled. "You did wrestle the one guy." Billy's smiled faded, to be replaced by a look of concentration. "Theo, remember? The one guy started shaking you for no reason. You fought back. Your glasses fell off."

"He was sorry he messed with me. Apologized like crazy. The other guy made sure..."

Billy nodded. "Made sure to check out your glasses, like he was sorry he might have broken something."

"...and could have easily tagged my glasses with a tracking device."

Billy continued to nod. "You'd never notice because when you take your glasses off, you see like a bat. And I'd never have a reason to check your glasses because they're on your face."

Theo had already taken off his glasses. He held them out for Billy to take. It took Billy only a couple of seconds to find the tracking device.

"Theo," Billy said. "They know exactly where we are. Right now."

"Sneaks," Theo said. "Now I sure wish I would have kicked them in the—"

"No," Billy said. As always, he spoke slowly, allowing time to be thorough as he thought. "This is good. Really good."

From a chair in the corner of the penthouse of the Pavilion, holding coffee he'd poured univited from a nearby carafe, Pierce watched Holly and Everett interact. It was as if Everett considered her about as interesting as an old piece of furniture.

Maybe that was Everett's style. Boredom.

Maybe he simply never had any interest in a hot-looking woman in her late twenties to early thirties. Wearing a dark shirt and dark skirt.

Either way, Holly wasn't cracking him with her questions. Pierce wasn't going to step in either. That would make it look like the boss was tired of the underling doing a bad job. Short term, in this room, he doubted that would get results with Everett. Long term, it would hurt the team. Pierce did have confidence in Holly and wanted her to know it.

Besides, she hadn't yet asked Everett about the knife wound.

"Just to clarify," Holly said. "You have no knowledge about the girl in the photograph."

From the Enforcer video and the video shot from the hidden camera in

Melvin's wheelchair, they'd been able to come up with several good choices for a closeup of Caitlyn's face.

"I'll have to take your word for it that she worked here."

Holly had already confirmed this with the head of staff at the Pavilion. "How about your health?"

Everett showed no reaction to the sudden change in questioning tactics. "You're in the medical field too?"

"Knife wound," she said. "In the belly. Let's talk."

"Sure." Utterly nothing changed on his face. "If you start making sense."

"In general," Holly said. "I imagine something like that would hurt."

"What?"

"A knife wound in the belly."

"I imagine it would."

Holly glanced at Pierce. "I'm done. Anything for you?"

"Nope," Pierce said. As he stood, he knocked his coffee over. Shrugged at the sight of it ebbing into expensive carpet. Didn't get much petty pleasure from it, as Everett's face remained bored. "Lunch sounds good."

Holly stood.

Everett remained seated. In keeping with his style, he didn't bother to wave or acknowledge their good-byes.

In the elevator, Holly said to Pierce, "That went well."

"Not really. That coffee was the best I've had in months. He'll snap his fingers. Carpet will be scrubbed clean in the time it takes me to get another cup."

"My sarcasm was directed toward the lack of information we possess. Not at your pitiful attempt to be the alpha dog by knocking coffee on his floor."

"What do you expect?"

"That's exactly what I'd expect from you."

"From Everett. He's a lawyered-up Influential."

"Maybe you should have been asking the questions."

"Wouldn't have been near as pleasant for all involved, me showing the amount of leg that you felt necessary to put on display."

"Accident, skirt riding up like that when I sat."

"My conclusion too," Pierce said. "And note my skill with sarcasm."

"Really," she said, irritated. "It was an accident. I don't need to show leg to make a good impression. I don't stoop to that."

"My apologies. By the way, nothing I could have done would have had a different outcome in there. And I liked the way you ended, not pressing him further on the knife wound thing. You got it across that we know about it. Maybe it will make him nervous."

"Probably not," she said. "But it was all I had."

"Not quite all you had. Accident or not, your legs did make a good impression."

Against agency policy, this kind of talk. But Pierce had a good defense. She'd started it.

FORTY-EIGHT

W hen he finds out you didn't call," Razor said with a shrug to the guard at the checkpoint into Dr. Hugh Swain's neighborhood, "it'll be your job to lose."

Late as it was in the afternoon, it had been no problem getting back inside through the gate at the outer wall. Because of the number of Industrials streaming out of the city, security there, except for a weapons search by body scan, was usually minimal, based on the reliance on tighter screening into individual neighborhoods.

Razor had fully expected this resistance at the checkpoint.

"Stand here," the guard at the neighborhood gate said. "Try to run, and I'll Taser you. And if Dr. Swain doesn't want to see you, I'm calling in Enforcers. You can explain to them why you've got no authorization for this neighborhood."

He was a small man, trying to look larger in his uniform. By the tightened features in his face, he was obviously pleased to have a reason for his tough-guy look combined with holding a Taser in two hands in the ready position. The pleasure diminished as he gingerly removed one hand from the Taser and reached for the keypad with his free hand. It diminished more as he struggled to lock eye contact with Razor while he felt for the keypad entries.

"Keypad it yourself," the guard finally said, resuming his two-handed grip on the Taser. "95863. And face the camera directly."

Razor memorized the number as he punched the keypad buttons, using the knuckle of his forefinger to avoid leaving a fingerprint. No doubt there was a surveillance camera recording this, but that didn't matter to him. Although, by necessity for banking purposes, he was in the facial-recognition database, he was confident it wouldn't set off any alerts here. This surveillance system was set up to look for faces with criminal records. His didn't have one. Nor did his facial profile have any other kind of alert on it. And his facial tattoo pattern would scan him as an Industrial.

Within seconds, a voice responded. But the chest-high videoscreen in front of Razor remained dark. The videophone was set on one-way. Images from the gate reached Swain, but no image was returned.

"What is it?" the voice snapped. "I'm not expecting visitors."

Razor was here to learn as much as possible about Swain. Even this short statement—tone and content—told him something.

"Apologies for disturbing you, Dr. Swain," the guard said, "but this Industrial says it's so important, you'll want to see him. I've got him at Taser point, and I'll disable him if you say so."

"I'm not expecting visitors." The voice had an even, low timbre. Entitled authority.

"I'm sorry, sir. You're expecting the daughter of a old friend," Razor said. He kept his head down. With tattoos webbed across his face, his role here was that of an Industrial. While Razor wasn't afraid of Swain, any Industrial would be. Projecting a degree of confidence would ring false.

"I'm not expecting visitors."

"Name of Jordan Brown," Razor said, head still down. "His daughter, Caitlyn, sent me to ask you something."

Silence. It was so long that Razor wondered if he'd gambled incorrectly. If Swain refused and called for Enforcers, Razor would be looking at a far different and far less favorable outcome.

"Give him directions to the rear entrance of my house," Swain finally told the guard from the anonymity of the speaker.

"No escort?" the guard said.

"You stay there. And don't sign him in."

Razor knew all too well that Influentials indulged in tastes that remained unofficial and unrecorded. A nonescort wasn't that unusual. But if Swain wanted to keep this unrecorded, Razor was fully aware of the situation; because there wouldn't be a record, Razor would be at his complete mercy. As Razor also knew far too well, Industrials who entered Influentials' homes without a record sometimes didn't make it back outside the gates alive.

FORTY-NINE

Caitlyn's guards—or protectors—had agreed to Caitlyn's request for her to sit outside the shanty in the late afternoon sun. Sky had nearly cleared again, and wind was dying. It signaled the imminent return of heat. Which might make a night in the shanty more comfortable.

It didn't take her long to realize that the grouping of shanties in this area was deliberate, housing a close-knit family unit with a small common center area.

Nor did it take her long to realize that the few children playing on the dusty ground in the tiny open area inside this circle of shanties were forbidden to leave the common area. These children were Industrials, marked by facial tattoos, showing that their parents had been given permission by the government to have the children.

Influentials had learned from how the Muslims had toppled Europe a generation earlier, not through war but through population growth. Originally, Europeans had welcomed immigration as cheap labor, expecting the predominantly Muslim immigrants to integrate. Instead, Muslims had remained in cloistered communities, raising families, on average, of eight children. Within seventy years, the Muslim population numbers had so dominated the Europeans' that Muslims were able to easily outvote any opposition, and in effect, the countries had become theirs, including the imposition of sharia laws that reduced rights for women.

Here, in the shantytowns, Influentials weren't going to let that mistake be repeated. Industrials, the descendants of illegal immigrants who had once flooded America from Mexico and south to take the jobs citizens didn't want, were limited to two children. Both would be registered and tattooed with a distinctive bar code pattern needed for access through all checkpoints. Any other children would be Illegals, allowed to mingle with Industrials in the shantytowns and soovies but barred from the city core and any official employment, forced to live with all the perils that came with it.

Caitlyn watched one girl in particular, maybe three years old. She didn't join in the vigorous games, and all the other children seemed solicitous of her well-being.

Caitlyn walked up to one of the men and asked.

He shrugged, but it wasn't a shrug of indifference.

"She's sick. Something inside eating at her. We don't know. She cries a lot at night. When she falls, she cuts easy. Takes weeks for the wound to heal. We're careful with her."

"I'm sorry to hear that."

"It's life," he said. "You take it as it is."

"Timothy Raymond Zornenbach?" Melvin said. Then cackled. "Good luck, man. The old dude is sick, like twisted sick. Talks to nobody. Has a dozen different places to live. Makes it so no one ever sees him."

"He's got a son," Holly said. "Legally adopted. Named Timothy Ray. Have you met the kid?"

"The son is news to Melvin," Melvin said.

Again, Pierce had let Holly take this one. They were in a crowded coffee shop just down the street from the Pavilion. Melvin called it his office, refused to speak unless Jimmy was allowed to stay beside him. The big man was mute, cradling a bandaged hand in his good one. Pierce glanced at the big man's ears, looking for where Caitlyn had bit him after dropping from the ceiling.

Melvin's background was similar to men like him in other quadrants. A nonvoter, he had citizenship papers that allowed him residence inside the city walls, and as a person with vocational education, he fell into the invisible gray area between Influentials at the top and the uneducated Industrials and Illegals at the bottom. Unofficially, he knew what he was. An Invisible. Officially, he was registered as a custodial technician, employed, in theory, at various buildings to monitor and fix the heating and cooling systems. Officially, that's what provided his income.

Unofficially, however, his income depended on how well he controlled the Illegals who found gaps in the system. Like rats, Illegals were impossible to eradicate, in part because Influentials wanted some of what the Illegals could provide—drugs, prostitutes. As a result, unofficially, Enforcers allowed men like Melvin a degree of power based on their abilities to keep the seamier parts concealed from official notice.

"No son," Holly said in response to Melvin's comment. Pierce observed that Melvin, unlike Everett, showed intense interest in Holly's appearance. Almost to the point of lasciviousness. And Pierce noticed that Holly seemed impervious to Melvin's wandering eyes.

"No son," Melvin said. "But the dude loves sewer kids. Buys them. Makes them pretty. Gets rid of them after a few years."

Melvin cackled. "Guess it means he's had lots of sons."

"Buys them from you?" Holly said.

Melvin slammed his right hand on the arm of his wheelchair. "Not a chance. Melvin don't traffic in that. Never."

"Who's the old man go to to get the kids?" Holly asked.

"Told you. Direct to the sewer. Spreads the cash, so I hear."

"How about Melvin finds the old man for us?"

Melvin smiled. "Cash delivery." And he named a price.

"Not a chance," Holly said. Smiling. Mimicking Melvin's cadence of speech. "Holly don't traffic in that. Never."

"Then don't expect help from Melvin," Melvin said.

"No problem," Holly said. "Did I forget to mention this?"

She leaned forward and tapped the front handle of Melvin's wheelchair. "Later, when Melvin gets a chance, Melvin should take a close look here."

"Why?" Melvin was grinning. He'd copped a look at Holly's cleavage as she leaned forward. Obviously wanted the grin to let her know it too.

"Melvin will find a hidden camera there."

His grin ended abruptly.

Holly's smile was sweet, like little-girl innocence. "Melvin's going to help us, or Melvin's going to have to deal with what happens when Melvin's private life hits the streets."

Jimmy looked at the floor.

Holly continued smiling. "What does Melvin think about that?"

Pierce hid his admiration. He sure liked her style.

FIFTY

Two miles away, beyond the outer city wall, were the shacks with tin roofs, crowded in rows between open sewers. Here, in contrast, the houses were three stories tall, with large landscaped yards as buffers between each residence. During the day, Industrials would labor to maintain the landscaping and clean the interiors of the homes. Now, with dusk approaching, the yards were empty, with a whispered breeze bringing hinted scents of tree blossoms and flower beds.

The brick walk to the rear entrance of the house took Razor beneath a canopy of lush oak trees with squirrels scampering up the bark. Razor climbed the steps, pushed a button, and announced himself. The door buzzed as it unlocked.

He pushed it open, entering a tiny square room with hooks on the wall and several sets of ragged clothing. As he stepped inside, the door locked behind him. He gave it an experimental tug, but it wouldn't open. The interior door was locked too.

Razor was effectively trapped in the small, bare room.

"Strip down," Swain's voice commanded from a hidden speaker. "Leave your clothes behind."

Razor hesitated.

"There will be clothes waiting for you on the other side," the voice said.

Yes, Swain was observing him.

Razor saw no choice. As he hung up the final piece of clothing, the inner door buzzed. He pushed through it to a second and equally small room with tiled walls and a tiled floor. In the center was a drainpipe. On the other side, a third door.

He waited for it to be unlocked.

Instead, there was hissing. Razor glanced upward at the sound, and saw mist released from a series of nozzles. It was acrid, the first touches of it burning his eyeballs. He lowered his head and covered his mouth with a hand, coughing.

"We don't talk until you're disinfected." Swain's voice again.

It had been hot outside, but this chamber was chilled. The mist fell long enough for Razor to begin to shiver as he hacked for breath, still shielding his mouth from pesticide. Razor wasn't worried about his tattoo bleeding away from the chemical, just about getting any into his bloodstream. His blood was whacked out plenty, and he didn't want to invite more of a cocktail swirling through his veins. Finally the mist stopped. Then began again, with more force. It was cold water. When this stopped, the inner door buzzed and opened automatically. The backside had a set of hooks. On one hook was a towel. On another hook, disposable brown paper clothing and paper slippers.

Razor dressed quickly. The fibrous paper soaked up the water he'd missed with the towel. It was a familiar feeling, that of being a commodity, and his anger steeled him. It took effort to hang his head and slump his shoulders as he finally left the disinfecting room. It could have been worse; some Influentials only allowed Industrials into the house if all their head and body hair was shaved.

On the other side was a larger hallway, where a man with silver hair sat in a chair, about four paces away. Beyond, the hallway led to living areas, with walls decorated with large framed paintings and hardwood floors with luxury rugs. Razor doubted he'd be invited there; the silver-haired man held the leashes to two Rottweilers panting on their haunches, staring intensely at Razor.

"Far enough." The voice identified the man as Swain. It wasn't enough that he was an Influential and Razor the Industrial. Or that he'd forced Razor to strip and endure a disinfectant mist. Or that Swain was restraining two attack dogs. Swain underscored the lopsided power balance by wearing immaculately tailored clothes and sitting with one knee over the other. He appeared fit, his face handsome with lines softened by expert plastic surgery. "Don't move. Talk."

"She says you are a friend of her father, Jordan. She says you are expecting her. To help her. With surgery. She has a letter from her father to you."

"The letter. It's in your clothing outside?"

Razor kept his head bowed, aware of the breathing of the Rottweilers. "She made me memorize it."

"I want to hear it then." Swain leaned forward. Razor was acutely aware of the shift in the man's body language. The intense interest in what Razor had to say.

"Hugh, I trust you now as I did then," Razor said in a monotone. "She's not a number now. She's my daughter. Arrange the surgery that will let her live a normal life. Help her escape. When she's free, I'll send you the code to the funds we diverted. The money will be all yours. Signed Jordan Brown."

Swain took a deep breath and let it out slowly. He absently patted the head of the closest Rottweiler. A man who cared for his animals but saw Industrials as commodities.

"Why did she send you?" he asked.

"Before she puts herself in your hands, she needs to know if she can trust you."

"Tell her she can," Swain said. "Her father believed in me. She can too."

Sure, Razor thought. *A man who keeps Industrials home at night to suit his needs.* Again he fought a shiver against the images that threatened to overwhelm him.

"She has questions," Razor said.

"Tell her I will answer them. For her. Not for you or anyone else."

"Until she trusts you, she wants me to ask them."

Swain blinked a few times, assessing Razor. "What questions?"

Here was Razor's opportunity. Caitlyn, of course, had not sent him here, nor did she even know he was intent on learning all he could about her. But Swain had no way of finding out that Razor was running a bluff. As long as Razor's questions were ambiguous instead of specific, the bluff could continue.

"She wants to know about her past," Razor said. He'd given thought to his questions. "Things that her father wouldn't tell her."

"Like what?" Swain was immediately impatient. "I'm not going to spend hours explaining things to you."

This was another tipping point. Razor had taken this chance under a couple of assumptions. The first was that Caitlyn's value—obvious by government pursuit—would also have value to Swain. His gut told him that Jordan's trust in Hugh Swain, implied in the letter he'd read before returning it to Caitlyn, was misplaced. He doubted that Swain would be motivated to answer Razor's questions out of wanting to help Jordan or Caitlyn. He assumed Caitlyn would be a prize of some kind to Swain, either because he knew enough about Caitlyn to understand her value to the government, or as the letter implied, the code, whatever it was, would be enough reward.

"Caitlyn says she wants to know why the government wants her so bad."

Swain scowled. "Does she know why Jordan fled to Appalachia?"

Someone who was fast and sharp and dangerous would have no problem dealing with a question like that. Razor hid his confidence though. "I don't know what she knows. She sent me with questions, not answers."

Swain made his irritation obvious. "I hope you're not as stupid as you look. I'll start from the beginning. You tell her every single word. And in a safer place than this. Understood?"

His gamble that Caitlyn was irresistible bait had just succeeded. For Razor, it was the sensation of feeling the final tumblers click into place.

Razor kept his face blank and nodded. "Understood."

"And one more thing," Swain said. "I'm going to tell you where she can meet me. If you can bring her, I'll make sure you are well rewarded."

Razor, for the first time, looked directly at Swain. Like he was a greedy Industrial, finally comprehending something. "Maybe you'd better explain exactly how much reward you mean."

FIFTY-ONE

S ince perching on the hill of computer monitors, Mason Lee had adjusted his approach.

Thanks to the information he'd enjoyed forcing out of the young thugs, Mason now knew that Billy and Theo usually worked at the far end of the Meltdown, at the lowest status place possible. Given that, he no longer thought of himself as a soaring hawk needing to startle them into movement. Now he was a stalking mountain panther. Mason was very familiar with the animals of Appalachia and had a memory of a mountain cat that never failed to stir him. The cat had sprung out of deep grass, pouncing on a deer from behind, raking its front claws across the hind end as the deer tried to flee, pulling the deer down and snapping its neck with powerful jaws.

To stalk properly meant to blend in to the background. Mason realized his white face was a liability. So, walking away from the four shirtless men he'd left nearly dead at the pile of monitors, Mason had reached into a mound of cooled dark ashes and used his fingers to smear black lines like swirls of blurred tattoos across his cheeks and forehead. He'd also taken a kerchief from one of the fallen men and tied it across the bottom of his face.

Weaving among the piles of the Meltdown to his destination, he drew far fewer glances from the hordes of scavengers and guessed the attention he did get came because of the eye patch.

He didn't mind.

Like deer unaware of an upwind mountain panther, Billy and Theo, first of all, had no way of knowing that the great Mason Lee had departed from Appalachia and was on their trail. If they did spot him, he was wearing the kerchief like any other scavenger, and it would be next to impossible to link his smudged face to that of the famous bounty hunter who had nearly eviscerated Billy and Caitlyn in a barn. The eye patch was something they had not seen on him before either. No, when he'd been hunting them, Mason had had use of both eyes.

The thought quickened his pulse with a stab of renewed anger. If they hadn't helped Caitlyn, she never would have escaped, nor left him to die—in hated darkness—where a rat could puncture his eyeball. Billy and Theo were just as responsible as she was for blinding him. No doubt they'd share in her punishment. No doubt at all. Mason had a knife in his pocket, the one he was saving to slice the eyes of the whore. Maybe he'd use it on their eyes too. Taser them at moderate strength, just enough to paralyze. Then describe what he was doing as he ran the blade. Be good if their eyes were closed as he did it. He'd be able to cut through their eyelids at the same time, maybe even peel the eyelids off like the skin of a pearl onion. But it was important to let them live. Blind. That was worse than death.

These were his thoughts as he reached a mound of glass bottles as high as a three-story building. When he rounded the base of it, the sight of the scavengers feeding the glass smelter broke him out of his pleasant reverie of revenge.

This was a bootleg operation on a large scale. Dozens of boys and men were working. Some to tear wooden skids apart as fuel for the smelter. Some to smash bottles. Others to shovel the shattered glass in.

Mason stood sideways and pretended to be examining some of the bottles nearby. He made sure he stood so that his good eye was nearest the operation and scanned back and forth between the bottles and the scavengers.

He saw Billy first. Large. So large he was unmistakable. He had stripped down too, his massive upper body shining with sweat. Billy didn't have the type of build that showed muscle definition, but Mason had learned that his hand was strong enough to knock down a horse with a single punch. Mason would have to be careful. Billy wouldn't stand against the Taser, but there were too many others around for Mason to make a bold, open move.

He saw Theo next, rummaging through a bottle pile, sorting clear glass from green bottles. Beneath his kerchief, Mason smiled coldly. Theo was small enough; maybe Mason could pull an arm off him like a wing off a fly.

This is good, Mason thought. These two would give him Caitlyn.

All he had to do was keep stalking.

In his memory, Mason saw the mountain cat, nearly hidden in tall grass. He knew he could do the same.

Mason moved forward and found a makeshift shovel.

He stepped among the men, picked up a length of dirty cardboard, and began scooping up broken glass to feed the smelter with them.

FIFTY-TWO

Wednesday night

At first, because of the tattoos on his face, Caitlyn didn't recognize Razor. When he'd stepped into the shanty, she thought he was just another Industrial. Until he spoke.

"Not surprised," she said.

"To see me again?"

"That you look the way you do. You must live and breathe deception."

"You learn fast," he said, grinning, his teeth white against the dark tattoos of his face. "Not even interested in how I manage this?"

"Don't care," Caitlyn said in a flat voice. "I just want out of this prison."

"Think of it as protective custody." The web of tattoos on his face blended into the shadows, and Caitlyn couldn't read any expression there.

"What gives you the right to decide I need protection?" Caitlyn exploded. "And if I did, what right do you have to decide you're in control of it?"

"Those questions prove how much you need my help. Outside the city wall, nobody is given rights. Not to air, water, shelter, or even life. Outside the city wall, all rights belong to the strong and the smart." His voice, in contrast, was mild. Almost amused. And certainly smug.

This angered her even more. "Get it into your head. I didn't ask for your help. I don't want your help."

"You'd rather be dead?"

"I'd rather be free."

"Then you will be dead. I suppose that's a form of freedom."

"I'm a survivor."

"Tell me what you know about life outside Appalachia."

Caitlyn had been ready to stand and leave. That one word froze her. *Appalachia.* She'd never told him about Appalachia. Had she been betrayed by Emelia? She didn't want to believe that. Not betrayed. Again.

Razor continued. "Don't be so shocked. It makes sense. The missteps, the odd questions or statements. You don't understand this culture. You haven't lived in it. And because you haven't lived in it, chances are it will kill you."

"I'll learn." This was an admission of sorts. But would it do any good to deny her background?

"Here's some history for you. Generations ago, when America was flooded with illegal immigrants, the lawmakers at best ignored them. At worst, they persecuted and killed them. Hundreds of thousands of families essentially lived underground, out of sight. But not without value to the established. Those illegals needed to live. From my great-grandparents down, to survive we've had to perform menial tasks for little pay. We became too important to the economy. As much as politicians postured, getting rid of the people without citizenship became unthinkable. Making them legal wouldn't work either, because then they'd have rights too. Persecution, however, played well for the economy. The fewer rights, the more those illegal immigrants became commodities. Powerless people are worth a lot to people with power. And lawmakers, the early Influentials, only reflected the will of the people. All the people. Because to remain silent in the face of injustice is to be part of the injustice."

Razor sneered. "Your Appalachia? The religious freaks? Those who tried to rule people in the name of Jesus? Where were they to help the so-called downtrodden? Just as silent."

Caitlyn had no answer. Jordan had never talked to her about this.

"Then came the Wars," Razor said. "America needed water. Canada refused to sell. America took water. Countries chose sides. America turned to their illegals for help as soldiers. But the illegals, for the most part, refused. They weren't citizens. Think that created more of a barrier between the haves and the have-nots? At the same time, the government used the war as an excuse to erode civil liberties, promising to return them at the end of the war. They didn't. When the war was over, this is what evolved from the anarchy: Influentials at the top. Descendants of illegal migrants at the bottom, without citizenship but willing to accept cheap labor like their parents and grandparents to survive. Industrials. Marked by tattoos. Those who refused tattoos became the bottom-of-the-bottom, the Illegals. But that far down, you're free again. Unlike the Industrials, who became slaves."

He paused. "It's become ancient Rome."

Caitlyn cocked her head. "Ancient Rome? How do you know all this? You're an..."

She caught herself, but too late.

"An Industrial?" he said. "A brainless hive worker bred to serve Influentials? Or an Illegal who paints himself like an Industrial when it suits his purpose? And someone who reads voraciously because knowledge is power and knowledge gives the power to sustain illusions?"

When she didn't answer, he continued, smiling coldly. "Or am I truly the lowest of low? One of the Illegals who lives beneath the city."

Caitlyn smiled just as coldly. "Illusion is your life. Maybe you don't even know who you are."

"Influentials leave us to feed ourselves, shelter ourselves, and govern ourselves. They only care about us in terms of preventing revolt. Heard of Spartacus?"

"No."

"Invisibles don't fight for power. They are laptops to the Influentials, protected by them. In the other three worlds—Influentials and Industrials and Illegals—the strong rule. Survival of the fittest. It's that simple. If you don't understand, when you leave here, you'll be eaten."

"So your lecture is over? I can go?"

"Why are you so determined to refuse help?"

"Your lecture isn't over. But still, I go."

Caitlyn stood. She stepped toward the entrance.

"I know what your father did to you," Razor said, stopping her. "I know how you got your wings."

FIFTY-THREE

As he walked through the well-lit common area of his apartment complex, Tim Merritt patted his back pocket. He had a wad of cash there and liked the sense of power it gave him.

His Industrials, the ones who came through his gate into the Swain neighborhood, all expected to pay the daily toll he charged to let them through without hassle. He kept it affordable—no sense killing the goose to get the golden egg—and didn't care about their openly hostile resentment. What could they do? That's what gave him just as much satisfaction as the cash. His power; their powerlessness.

Yeah, he lived in an apartment complex. But it was inside the city wall. Influentials had their world. Industrials and Illegals had theirs. Merritt didn't mind at all living somewhere in the middle.

There was always the cash. And what it could buy.

Long hours of boredom as guard were lessened by the fantasies he let drift through his mind. Fantasies he was able to purchase.

One of the Industrials who passed through his checkpoint was a chubby one, a little old, but desperate. She'd be waiting at his apartment as instructed, willing to do all that he instructed, just for a portion of the cash he'd already taken from her and the rest of them.

Merritt ran through the fantasy one more time, careful to construct it just so, imagining the sequence of events that was waiting for him once he opened the door. He'd instructed her to leave the lights off. In the dark, he could fool himself into believing she wasn't quite that old.

He sauntered up the two flights of steps to his door, forcing himself to walk slowly, his mouth dry in anticipation.

The power.

That's what it was all about.

He pushed open the door. Grinned in the darkness.

He shut the door behind him. The apartment door opened immediately into a kitchen area. Beyond that was the living room. Where she was waiting.

He started to unbutton his shirt. He stepped forward, whistling. Stopped. Did he smell fresh-brewed coffee?

Then something, someone, grabbed him around his neck.

He gave a gargled shout of outraged surprise. This wasn't part of the game he'd told her to play.

He pulled at the arm around his neck, trying to loosen it. He half registered that the arm wasn't soft flesh, but rock-hard muscle.

The kitchen lights went on.

At the cheap table, pushed up against the wall to make as much space as possible in the cramped quarters, sat a man with sandy-colored hair, black shirt, black jeans, holding a cup of coffee in one hand, a cordless power drill in the other, staring expressionlessly at Merritt.

Merritt's first thought was indignation. That was his cordless drill. He never loaned it out, and he'd painted it fluorescent yellow to identify it.

"First things first," the man said. The man poured out his cup and dropped it, letting it break on the floor. "Your coffee is crap. Heard of roasted beans?"

"You got no right to be here," Merritt tried as a bluff. But something about the man's confidence told him otherwise.

"You don't believe that," the man said in a quiet voice. "We're going to talk. Unless you want to find out exactly how many holes I can make in your body before you bleed out."

A tall woman—younger, dark clothing, slender—stepped into the kitchen from the living room area. She carried duct tape. The invisible man holding Merritt by the neck maintained the chokehold while he shoved Merritt forward, spun him around, and forced him to sit in the other chair at the table.

In silence that was as terrifying as the suddenness of this, the woman with duct tape strapped Merritt's ankles to the chair legs. This was too real and too scary to be anything like a fantasy. She taped each of his upper calves to a chair leg, forcing Merritt to sit with his legs apart with not-so-symbolic vulnerability. Next Merritt's wrists. Taped behind his back to the upper part of the chair.

The woman and the man with solid arms stepped outside the apartment.

That left the man in black with the power drill staring thoughtfully at Merritt.

"What's going on?" Merritt squeaked. "You can't do this."

The man smiled humorlessly. Revved the drill.

"Think I'll start with a kneecap," the man said. "Ever smelled bone when it burns?"

That's when Merritt wet himself.

Pierce detested bullies. He was also aware of the hypocrisy of bullying a bully. Especially when unnecessary. Chances were, Merritt would talk without the psycho-drama threat that came with the borrowed power drill that Pierce had no intention of using past a prop. It's the way Pierce had expected to handle it, coming to Merritt's apartment with Holly and Jeremy.

But earlier Pierce had spent a few quiet minutes talking to an obviously exhausted Industrial they'd found waiting on a couch in Merritt's apartment, shivering in ridiculously small fishnet lingerie. She'd probably been up well before dawn to make the trek to the city wall and through the outer gate. She'd already spent a full day in the walled community where Merritt worked security. Then, as Pierce had learned while she spoke, wrapped in a blanket Pierce had found for her, Merritt demanded most of the evening with her but intended to send her out into the night when he was finished with her, expecting her to hide someplace as she waited for dawn, when curfew ended and Industrials were allowed to move through the city again.

Would be good, Pierce thought, *to change the man's view of Industrials.*

"There's a chance you can keep your body parts," Pierce told Merritt. "Even a chance you won't be reported for extorting tolls from Industrials."

"I don't extort—"

Pierce cut him off by revving the power drill. "Think when we ask every one of them who passes through your gate that all of them will support your claim?"

"Everyone does it, takes money from them," Merritt said. "Come on. They're Industrials."

Pierce seriously thought of running the quarter-inch drill bit through one of the guy's earlobes. Knew he wouldn't like himself for it. *Earlobes.* That triggered a half thought he couldn't quite grasp.

"Despite the mess in your crotch," Pierce said, "after the kneecap, we'll move there."

"You can't do this," Merritt said.

Pierce went to the man's fridge. He found some grapes inside. Perfect.

He returned to the table with a grape. "What I've learned is that eyeballs kind of pop. Hydrostatic pressure."

Pierce held the grape between the thumb and forefinger of his left hand. Drilled into it with his right. He squeezed at the same time to ensure a satisfying pop of the grape. He licked his fingers as he stared at Merritt.

Yeah, he was bullying a bully. He could just as easily have invited Merritt in a friendly voice to sit. Showed him the NI identity badge. Taken him through a couple of questions. No doubt the guy was a common type. A wannabe Enforcer. He'd love to feel important by helping Pierce.

"I'm going to ask questions," Pierce said. "I already know some of the answers. So I'm testing you to see if you're going to tell the truth. If you don't, you'll lose an eyeball too."

Another rev of the drill.

Merritt licked his lips and swallowed hard, eyes focused on the drill.

"You let an Industrial into the neighborhood today," Pierce said. "He wasn't registered to the neighborhood. What time was that?"

Merritt answered. Quickly. With the right time.

Pierce knew it because that's how they'd spotted Razor. Influentials didn't allow surveillance cameras anywhere that affected them but fully supported the cameras anywhere it helped control Industrials. Face identification software wasn't perfect and didn't always deliver immediate results. But it had pinpointed Razor to Merritt's gate about a half hour after Razor had arrived. It had taken another fifteen minutes for the information to reach Pierce. Too late to get to the gate before Razor left the neighborhood. But not too late for him to follow up with Merritt.

"We also know who he visited," Pierce said. This was not true. It was much easier to find out this way than begin asking the Influentials of that neighborhood. One, Influentials had lots of friends who could make life difficult for Pierce. But two, and much more importantly, Pierce wanted to know who Razor had visited without alerting that Influential. "Tell me."

"Hugh Swain," Merritt answered without hesitation. "Now *there* is a man who keeps Industrials in his house after curfew."

"Really," Pierce said. "You admire him?"

Merritt turned stone faced.

"You're doing fine so far," Pierce said. "Don't stop now. How'd the unregistered Industrial get in? Did Swain let you know ahead of time that he was expecting him?"

Merritt shook his head no. He spoke fast as he described the entire conversation. "Swain didn't want to see him. The Industrial said Swain would want to see him. Said there was a friend named Jordan. Had a daughter that Swain was expecting."

Pierce kept a bored expression on his face. But, for the first time, he felt close. *Jordan Brown.* The fugitive he'd failed to get in Appalachia. And Caitlyn, who'd somehow managed to escape too.

Pierce set the drill on the table. Merritt watched every move as Pierce stepped to the outer door. He spoke to Holly outside.

"We'll need everything you can get on an Influential named Hugh Swain."

Then back inside, where he grilled and regrilled Merritt, punctuating his questions with the power drill, occasionally putting holes in the kitchen table.

When Pierce was satisfied he had as much information as possible, he ripped loose the duct tape from Merritt's left wrist.

"Do the rest yourself," Pierce said.

Pierce pointed at the neatly drilled holes and small piles of sawdust on the surface of the table.

"Your guard booth is going to be under 24/7 surveillance from here on in. A couple of warnings: none of this gets back to Swain."

Merritt nodded. Eagerly.

"And you take any money from Industrials or force any of them to visit you after hours, we'll be back. Middle of the night, when you least expect it."

Some bluffs were more satisfying than others.

FIFTY-FOUR

Was it Emelia?" Caitlyn asked softly. "Did she tell you?"

"Listen to me and you decide," Razor said. "More than two decades ago, before the Wars, Jordan was head scientist in a military lab. Genetic experiments. Women served as surrogate mothers."

Caitlyn clenched her jaw. That's who she was. A genetic experiment. Named after the woman who died giving birth to her. Jordan had told her this, but not at any time while raising her in Appalachia. Only in their last moments together. After he'd betrayed her.

"Jordan wanted out," Razor said. "He wanted to help one of the women out too. He had a colleague and close friend who agreed to help. Hugh Swain."

Swain! Caitlyn hadn't told Emelia about the letter. There was only one way Razor could have known. The letters he'd found in the elevator. That he'd handed her walking out of the kitchen, up in the highrise."

"You read the letter Jordan gave me."

He nodded.

"And his instructions on how to find a surgeon I could trust. Hugh Swain."

"Think of my point of view. What I needed to know."

"What do you want from me?" she asked, using coldness to contain her rage.

He must have understood the intensity of her question. He blinked. Hesitated nearly thirty seconds before answering. "At first I thought I wanted your magic trick. How to soar. How to hide the wings. But now I know it's not a trick."

"What. Do you want. From me."

"It's obvious now that whatever this is, it's so big that I'm going to be on the run for the rest of my life unless you get out of this," Razor said, still choosing his words with care. "I don't know how to do it, but I want—no, I need—to figure a way out. And I can't do it without knowing as much as possible about the situation. So what do I want? Help. Answers."

Caitlyn concentrated on controlling her breathing. Slow and deep. Since fleeing Appalachia, she'd been on hair-trigger rage. "What you're telling me was not in either letter."

"I visited the surgeon," Razor said. Razor described how he'd done it. "Swain. He was expecting you. He got me instead."

Caitlyn wanted to flail out, but curiosity held her in check. Jordan had promised her that Swain was a surgeon she could trust. Who would finally make her normal. Sure, by cutting through tissue and muscle and sawing through bone. Removing her wings. "Swain. And he gave you answers?"

"I told him that you wouldn't visit unless you trusted him. And that you wouldn't trust him unless I had answers to bring back to you."

"You didn't ask my permission for that."

"You wouldn't have given it to me."

It was Caitlyn's turn for silence.

Why was she so determined not to accept help from Razor? Because he was cocky to the point of arrogance?

No. It was something else. Something she didn't want to admit to herself. But she couldn't keep fighting it. If she allowed herself to be truthful, there was something more about him that bothered her. Yes, he was deeply attractive. But for all the wrong reasons. He wasn't strong and gentle, like Billy in her memory. He wasn't deep and consistent, someone who would carry her through all storms. Still, if she let herself, she could sense an excitement that would make the risk of danger so worthwhile. Or maybe it was the risk of danger that would lead to excitement.

Yes. It was time to admit instead that she didn't want help from anybody. If she were to be truthful, that's why she wasn't with Billy and Theo. She'd found a reason to abandon them, not even wanting to place any faith in the strong yet gentle, even the total acceptance that Billy offered. Maybe Emelia's comfort had opened her eyes to this. Jordan, the rock of her entire life, had proven to be nothing more than shale, easily shattered. The lesson she had learned was trust nobody, trust no illusions, fight for herself, and protect herself with the satisfying yet paradoxically empty rage that came with distrust.

Time to admit that she needed help. This was a strange, strange world. Razor was correct. She didn't understand it, and sooner or later, even without pursuers, it would end her. Her pursuer was no longer Mason, but an enemy with unlimited power. And she only increased that enemy's power by remaining ignorant. What hope did she have alone?

But did she have any hope with Razor?

"What did Swain say?" she asked. Curiosity had won over anger and caution. She sat back, no longer on the edge, ready to fight or flee.

"That you shouldn't have lived," Razor said. "They'd been running the program for five years. Hundreds of pregnancies had ended in deformities, often didn't make it to the third term or never lived more than minutes beyond birth. It was one of the reasons Jordan wanted out and one of the reasons Swain agreed to help. It came to a point, before you were born, where it was too monstrous for them."

Monstrous. Caitlyn felt the full implication of the word. But she'd felt it her entire life.

If Razor understood the pain he'd inflicted, he didn't show it as he continued. "Jordan and Swain planned it carefully. They found a way to hack the computers, to steal and hide all the research data. In effect, it would end the experiments. But there was only a small window of time before it would be discovered. Jordan agreed he would take the blame because he was fleeing to Appalachia anyway. Swain, who would be left behind, would appear innocent."

The words from Jordan's letter of confession to her echoed in her head.

We had agreed—the woman I loved and I—that as soon as you were born, we would perform an act of mercy and decency and wrap you in a towel to drown you in a nearby sink of water.

Since the shock of reading the letter weeks earlier, Caitlyn had consoled herself that, at the least, Jordan's actions in protecting her had been motivated by a father's love for his daughter. Decimated as her soul had been to discover it was Jordan's genetic manipulation that had created her as a freak, she still clung to the hope of his love.

Now she had to wonder.

When she was born, did Jordan clean and dry her for a reason other than overwhelming love? Did he choose to spare her life because of scientific curiosity, because she was the first experimental fetus, among hundreds of failures, to live?

Cold anger once again strengthened her resolve to survive, to fight.

"Jordan raised me in Appalachia," Caitlyn said. She wanted to speak in short, clipped sentences that would hide her emotions. "I knew nothing about this until an agent from Outside began to hunt us in Appalachia. Jordan helped me escape. He'd found a way to reach his old friend Swain, to arrange surgery. He promised it would allow me to live invisible and unhunted."

"How long since you escaped?"

"Six weeks. Seven. Eight. Not sure."

"But you didn't go to Swain for the operation."

It was an unspoken question. The answer was that Caitlyn couldn't choose between freedom and flight. That, in a way, she was defiantly proud of what made her different. It wasn't the answer she would give Razor though.

"I have friends," she said. "We were going to find a way out."

"Where?"

"Parts of the world where the government wouldn't look for us." Vague but true. She didn't have to tell Razor the specifics of her plan with Billy and Theo.

"You do know what the government wants, right?"

This was another tipping point. The angry and defiant Caitlyn would not admit ignorance. But she could not survive this alone.

"What I do know is that the government wants me because they can unlock the genetic research from my body."

From her eggs. Another thing so hideous she couldn't say it aloud.

"There's more," Razor said.

"The funding that that was diverted when they hacked the computers?"

"More." Razor paused. "Swain wouldn't tell me. He said only you could know."

FIFTY-FIVE

Back in the Pavilion, Pierce was exhausted. Too much made little sense. The NI had power, but so did Influentials. Whatever they might get from Everett about the knife attack Melvin had mentioned to Caitlyn, would take days if not weeks. Even answers about the hospital records. All Everett would do if pushed would be to get a team of lawyers as a buffer.

Pierce couldn't make sense of Razor, either, or the kid's motives. Pierce's first hunch said he was the adopted son named Timothy Ray, a rich kid slumming it, using his power and money to give him an advantage while he posed as just another Illegal. But a search of all official records showed only T. R. Zornenbach, the Elite in his late seventies. Except for the notes on official adoption and the required photograph that went with it for facial recognition software, the son of the same name was like an erased ghost nowhere in the system. Holly was working on banks to release some records, including the facial ID attached to those records, but given the system and privacy accorded to Influentials, that was still a couple of days away.

Maybe Pierce could learn something helpful from what Holly and Jeremy had pulled up on Hugh Swain and downloaded to the op-site.

Pierce sat in front of a laptop screen at the small office desk in the corner of the room, pot of room service coffee beside him, and began to review it.

He made it through two cups of coffee before realizing what bothered him about the report. That there was nothing to bother him.

Not only had Hugh Swain had an entirely bland life, but there were no chronological gaps of missing information. All bank accounts were displayed, with no unusual deposits or withdrawals. His occupation was listed as accountant. Marital status single, no dependents. Military record showed five years as desk jockey overseeing supplies issues. The list went on and on. Normally it would take days to compile everything in front of Pierce. He'd received it in less than two hours.

As if the information had been packaged and waiting for the day government intelligence might come looking.

He knew what it suggested.

Some sort of witness protection. A relocation. New identity.

But the guy was tied to this.

Easy enough to guess that Caitlyn had sent Razor to Swain. But why?

Pierce knew himself well enough to realize that if he tried to sleep, no matter how tired he was, he'd stare at a dark ceiling and futilely try to come up with answers.

He also knew that waking someone else from sleep for questions would catch them at their most vulnerable.

So he made a team decision.

Without the team.

And was out the door in less than a minute.

FIFTY-SIX

In the dark, safely hidden, Mason watched the soovie shell that contained Billy and Theo. Waiting patiently for the time to strike.

His thoughts took him to earlier in the day, back to the whore who'd pretended to be blind.

What had been important to her was stripping him of his Taser.

It was as Everett had warned him before sending him out into the shanty-towns to look for Caitlyn: weaponry was what preserved the lifestyle and culture of the Influentials.

A hundred years earlier, Everett had said, America had been based on principles of fairness and equality, something he believed had almost brought it to ruin. America had essentially neutered itself, listened to liberal softies who didn't allow America to use its full power in international conflict. Then, Everett had said, America worried about the body count—not its own, but of its enemies. America held back, and because of it, America's enemies thought America was soft.

Everett had then outlined the military strategy of ancient Rome. Offer a carrot, but have no hesitation using a big stick. City-states were offered citizenship to join the empire, but those who opposed Rome were annihilated in the worst possible way—women and children included. It sent a strong message to other city-states.

America, on the other hand, had been so worried about world opinion that country after country defied it, until the great Water Wars almost destroyed it.

Influentials had learned and had applied their lesson to all aspects of culture. Murders and violent crimes were punished swiftly and decisively.

Weapons ruled. And those with the weapons maintained control.

Technology was on the side of the Influentials. Weapons were matched to owners by fingerprints. Weapons didn't fire unless fingerprints matched.

There was more to it, Everett had explained.

Those who defied Influentials paid a price far out of proportion to their defiance. Again, Everett had referred to the ancient Romans. If a slave assaulted or murdered his master, not only was the slave tortured and executed, but his entire family as well.

If any Industrial or Illegal in a shantytown was found with a weapon, all shacks within a hundred yards were destroyed, and the families in those shacks were executed. This same drastic reprisal applied even if that Industrial or Illegal tried to obtain a weapon.

Everett had smirked at that point, saying it had been a decade since the punishment had been necessary. As a result, Influentials were able to maintain control of a population base much larger than themselves, much like the Romans had controlled their slaves.

Mason liked this, of course, especially as he was one of the weapon holders. In the animal world, the strong ruled and the weak paid the price. It was natural. It belonged in the human world too.

Settled back against a wall that overlooked the soovie camp, Mason let his thoughts drift to the whore who had not been punished. Yet.

From the Meltdown, he'd followed Billy and Theo here and settled in as dusk, then night, cloaked all of them. There hadn't been any good chances to isolate them and learn what they knew about Caitlyn. He'd remain a mountain panther. Stalking them patiently until the right opportunity. If he was lucky, they'd lead him to Caitlyn.

It meant in the morning, he'd have to stay on their trail. All day. Even if it meant another exhausting day at the Meltdown. That wouldn't give him an opportunity to punish the whore.

On the other hand, it wasn't very likely that Billy and Theo would leave the safety of their soovie during the night.

Too dangerous.

They didn't have any weapons.

Mason, of course, did. He never slept much anyway.

He decided as long as he returned in a few hours, it was unlikely he'd lose Billy and Theo. Even if he did, he'd be able to find them. As a pair, they were distinctive enough that someone, somewhere, would be able to give him information. All Mason would do was ask about a kid with raccoon eyes.

Not worried about losing Billy or Theo, Mason rolled softly onto his feet.

Time for some retribution.

FIFTY-SEVEN

Y ou know what I miss about Appalachia?" Theo whispered to Billy.
"Nothing?" Billy asked. He set aside a carrot he'd been eating as slowly
as possible, deciding to save what remained for a day or two later. Carrots
were a luxury, but Billy hated going a week without some kind of vegetable.

"Almost." Theo was sitting up in the dark in the soovie. "I miss the quiet.
Before our family was sent to the Factory, we'd sit outside. Just listening. All
we heard were crickets and frogs. I liked that. And once in a while, something
in the night would scare them all. And then we'd hear nothing. I liked that."

Billy knew Theo's story, how he'd escaped the Factory. His parents and
sister dead. Theo didn't talk much about those days, so he guessed Theo had
a reason for it now.

"Out west," Theo said, bringing his knees toward his chest and holding
them with both arms, "think it will be quiet?"

"Not many people out there from what I hear," Billy said. "It's people
noise that seems loud."

"She's going with us, right? She hasn't changed her mind."

"She wants freedom too," Billy answered.

"What if she finds a way to get it without our help?"

"Then we should be happy for her."

Theo hummed for a few minutes. That told Billy that Theo was thinking.

"You would think people could be happy living in cages," Theo finally
said. "That all we would need is to eat and sleep and be safe. But I remember the Factory. If you did your work and obeyed the rules, they took care of
you. A person should be happy with that. Should. But it's not like that. You
can only keep people in captivity so long. Then they'll fight until they are
free. Or dead. It's like humans would rather be dead if they can't be free."

"God made us that way?"

"Maybe. But I don't like that answer," Theo said. "That can be the answer
for anything. It doesn't explain it."

"I know," Billy said. "Remember the rich man who asked Jesus how to
get to heaven? When Jesus told him, the rich man walked away. I think about

that a lot. Why didn't Jesus run after him and stop him? He could have done a miracle or something to change the guy's mind. But Jesus let him walk away."

"He didn't want to force him."

"Right," Billy said. "Like in the garden, when God let Adam and Eve choose. He could have forced them to stay away from the forbidden fruit. But he didn't. He wanted us free, like that's just as important as air and food and water."

"If Caitlyn doesn't show up, will you and me go west without her?"

Now it was Billy's turn for silence. This was his biggest worry. How long to wait until they gave up. Caitlyn had said she was going to get surgery so that she would be normal and it would be easier to go out west. They couldn't know if something had gone wrong or if she had changed her mind. All they could do was wait.

"Theo," Billy said, "here's something you need to think about. The government is still trying to track us. That's because they don't have Caitlyn yet. We have to make sure we survive because, someday, she's going to need us."

FIFTY-EIGHT

Pierce had just shown his NI badge to Hugh Swain and tucked it back in his pocket.

Pierce had a good idea of how it looked to Swain, who had opened his front door with the usual type of indignation an Influential would have at this time of night when all that should be waiting outside on an evening like this is warm air and the sound of crickets.

Behind Pierce, on the street, beneath a light, was a standard issue Enforcer car. One of the perks of his government rank was the right to flag that kind of vehicle and use it as a taxi. More importantly, because of layers of bureaucracy, nobody in Pierce's division would be alerted to his movement for hours, if not days, if ever. And right now, given the Swain dossier, Pierce didn't want anyone else in the agency knowing what Pierce was doing.

"If you have an issue with this, take it up with them," Pierce said to Swain, wearily waving a hand back toward the Enforcers. "I'll get them to turn the flashers and siren on for the neighbors while we talk in the backseat."

"You can't intimidate me like that," Swain said. His silver hair wasn't even rumpled. He was in pants and dress shirt, carefully buttoned. Pierce hadn't pulled him from sleep. "If this is government business, come back during the day. Your lawyer can speak to my lawyer."

Pierce lifted his hand. Made a circle.

Immediately, the red and blues started flashing.

"Siren next," Pierce said. "Long enough to get the neighbors looking out their windows. Then I'll make sure you're in handcuffs while I lead you to the car."

"Fine," Swain said, teeth gritted. "You'll pay for this tomorrow, I promise."

Pierce made another lazy circle with a raised hand. The lights stopped flashing.

"How about I come inside?" Pierce asked.

The front room was as luxuriously equipped as Pierce had expected for a house in this neighborhood. Dark leather furniture, flat-screen television that covered an entire wall, oil paintings on the other walls, thick rugs on hardwood.

What Pierce hadn't expected was the woman, sitting back in a love seat, legs crossed, drinking what looked like water from a plain glass. Auburn hair, wearing a tan cashmere sweater and jeans. High cheekbones, expert makeup, and eyes too green to be anything but colored contacts. Exquisite confidence. She was late forties, he guessed, but that was only because of some tightness around the sides of her eyes. Trim, attractive, and that said something about the work she put into it. Twenties to thirties, it didn't take that kind of work.

She didn't get up when Swain brought him into the room, but merely assessed Pierce as she sipped from the glass. Exquisitely.

Swain said nothing. He crossed his arms and glared at Pierce.

If this had been a social situation, the silence would have been awkward.

"Who are you?" Pierce said to the woman. Niceties didn't seem like they'd make a difference.

"She's not going to tell you," Swain answered.

"Too bad." Pierce moved closer to the woman. She had a small, expensive black handbag on the table beside her. Pierce lifted it.

"Put that down," Swain said. "We're not Industrials or Illegals. You have no right to anything in this house without a warrant."

"You're correct," Pierce said. "But I do have a right to reasonable expectation for identification."

He started to open the handbag.

"Her name is Jenny Owen," Swain snapped. "Put the bag down."

"Sure." Pierce opened the bag. "But it would be good to confirm that."

All he saw inside were blood vials and syringes.

"Interesting," Pierce said.

"She's my nurse," Swain answered. "Satisfied?"

Which told Pierce that Swain knew what was in the purse. That was interesting too.

Pierce put the bag back down. Nurses couldn't afford the kind of exquisiteness this woman projected, nor the cashmere draping that exquisiteness. His eyes met the woman's. She still had not moved.

"Interesting hours for a medical call," Pierce said, turning to Swain.

"My private life is not your business. Nor the business of the government. I will be taking action on this."

Pierce took a chair, sat, and crossed his legs too. "Tell me about a visitor you had today. An Industrial. Late afternoon. He told you that someone named Jordan sent him."

"No," Swain said.

"No? We've got witnesses that say otherwise."

"I mean no, I won't tell you about it. Or anything else. The only reason I invited you inside was to be spared telling you the same thing in the backseat of that car."

Approaching headlights out the front window caught Pierce's peripheral vision. Was it his imagination, or had Swain straightened slightly?

"Expecting someone?" Pierce asked. "This late?"

"Our conversation is over. Unless it involves my repeating that our conversation is over."

The headlights came to a stop beside the Enforcer car. A few seconds later, the headlights moved forward again. As the body of the car cleared, Pierce saw it was a private vehicle. Very few of those.

"How long have you lived here?" Pierce asked.

"Our conversation is over."

Pierce stood again. He wasn't in a position where any kinds of threats were going to leverage answers. But maybe he'd learned enough.

And maybe he could learn more.

Pierce dug his NI badge out of his pocket. He tossed it gently onto the woman's lap. "How about Jenny photocopies this, just so you'll have a record of who I am. Your lawyer can call my lawyer."

"Our conversation is over," Swain said. "You are leaving."

Pierce shrugged. He held out his hand for the badge, and Jenny took it from her lap and handed it back to him. Pierce was careful to hold it by the edges as he slipped it back into his pocket.

At least now he had the woman's fingerprints.

FIFTY-NINE

Mason took the girl first. The one named Thirsty. He took her from her bed at the side of the shanty where the whore had trapped him earlier in the day.

He was impressed the girl didn't shriek. It's what saved her life.

Mason wasn't stupid. He assumed that among the shantytown people, there was a common loyalty. They'd fight each other but would join forces against outsiders. That's why when, in the dark, he'd been approached by a boy offering any kind of service, he'd made sure the boy didn't run away after Mason's bribe to learn where Thirsty and her mother lived. He'd stayed right beside the boy all the way up to the shanty, not trusting that the boy wouldn't look for friends to interfere with his plans for the whore. The boy had knocked on the door—a familiar voice, saying he had a message. Mason had pushed his way inside when the whore opened the door. That boy was unconscious now, dragged inside the whore's shanty, his body blocking the closed door. Mason had dropped him after Tasering him, ignoring the whore and going straight to the bed for her daughter.

Yeah. Mason loved his rechargeable Taser.

Now Mason had Thirsty by the hair, knife to her throat. The shanty walls were thin enough that noise would likely carry to other shanties in this crowded area. Yup. Good thing she was smart enough to stay quiet.

"You got some light?" Mason asked in a conversational tone. "Let's brighten this place up."

"Who are you?" the woman asked.

"Get some light. And don't think about yelling for help. Your little girl won't live but a second or two if you do that."

Rustling. Then the strike of a match, the flame touching a small oil lamp.

"Make yourself comfortable," Mason said. He pulled back on the little girl's hair, exposing her throat even more. "I'm sure you can see this knife. If you're smart, she'll live. I like her."

"You," the woman said. Horror and shock. Mason liked that.

"Me," Mason answered. "I had a few hours to kill, thought I'd spend them killing. Didn't like the way we were interrupted the last time we were together. Thought I'd make up for it."

"It wasn't me," the woman said. "I have no choice. Working for those men."

"I've been giving it thought," Mason said. "The last thing you said. Something like, 'Take out his good eye. Let him live.'"

He paused to enjoy the sight of the woman biting the inside of her cheek. Mason had no doubt that he looked like a nightmare to her. His face still dirty with the smudged soot. And his stitched-shut blind eye no longer hidden by the patch. He'd put that in his pocket, wanting her to see it in all its rat-bitten glory.

"You want me scared, don't you?" she said.

"I usually don't think ahead when I do something like this. I like to go with the flow."

"I'm scared," she said. "Don't hurt her."

"Thought she was your weakness."

"Take from me what you want."

"Maybe I want to take her," Mason said, stroking the knife against the girl's throat. "You were going to let me live without sight. How about I let you live without her?"

He expected a big reaction from the whore, but instead she grew very still as she dropped her voice to near silence.

"I named her Thirsty," the woman said. "Because that's what it took to have her. Drinking hardly any water. What they put in it keeps a woman sterile. Controls the population. Unless you want to apply for a child; then you get some chemical that balances out what's in the water. But once you apply for a child, you lose freedom. So I went thirsty until she came along. Then my husband died, and I ran out of choices. Please don't hurt my little girl."

Mason wasn't against the begging that came with terror. He waited to see if she'd say anything else.

"What do you want?" she whispered. "Anything you want that I can give, it's yours."

Mason felt something warm on his fingers. For a couple of moments, he wondered if he'd pressed the knife too hard against Thirsty's thin little throat. He glanced down, expecting blood. Instead, he saw tears that had streamed down the girl's face, down her chin and onto his fingers.

"Anything?" Mason said.

"Anything."

He smiled. "I came in here to cut your eyes. Make you blind the way you wanted me to be blind. But I've changed my mind."

"Not her," the woman said. "Whatever it is, put it on me."

"I didn't change my mind about leaving you blind," Mason said. "Just how it'll get done. You want this girl alive bad enough, then all you need to do is cut your eyes instead of me doing it. Then I'll go."

"What?"

Mason truly was enjoying this. "Remember when I asked what it was like? You're the one who told me that you live blind or you die. So that's your choice. Live blind. Or die. Along with your girl."

SIXTY

Thursday morning

Pierce was having coffee at the pool in a hotel robe and a swimsuit he'd picked up in the souvenir shop for triple what it would cost anywhere else.

Early, but already hot. The brief weather front that had passed through was obviously not going to circle back.

Carson Pierce had had about three hours sleep but wanted a private place for the conversation he was waiting for. He figured it was going to be a long day. An hour in the sun was an investment in relaxation to keep his batteries charged.

Waiting for Holly, he was thinking about the genetic makeup of the male species.

Other side of the pool was a blonde in a matching hotel robe, leaving enough of it open to show a bikini beneath. Just that phrase, *blonde in a bikini*, should have been offensive. She was a woman, another human being, with thoughts and feelings, but male genetics compelled him to reduce her to categorized object. He could blame his chromosomes for that rather than take personal responsibility.

She was maybe five years younger than he was and had just looked over at him. A second time. He was thinking he should walk over and ask her name. Otherwise it was dehumanizing just to think of her as a blonde. *See*, he told himself, *a male person could and should fight the Y chromosome.*

The importance of that fight was underscored when Holly walked into the pool area, dark pants and shirt, dark sunglasses. *Fortunate*, Pierce thought, *that she's not here to swim. Easier to keep it professional when a willowy and sassy brunette isn't in a hotel robe.*

"Morning," Pierce said when Holly sat in the chair beside him. It gave her the same view of that blonde on the other side of the pool. "Coffee?"

"Sorry to interrupt your daydreaming. Surprised you're not wearing mirrored sunglasses. Most guys do when they want to check out poolside babes."

"*Babe* is a dehumanizing term," Pierce said. "Besides, the point of not wearing dark sunglasses is that it lets you make eye contact. Shows confidence. Shows you're not like other guys. And it's part of my long-term goal of reducing said dehumanization. Making the world a better place."

"Don't let me cramp your style."

"Hang around. It's actually helpful. A babe like her sees a single guy by himself at the pool, she starts wondering what's wrong with him. A drop-dead gorgeous woman like you shows up, and now she begins to speculate at all I have going for me. Especially with you dressed like you are. Makes you an accessory."

"Accessory?"

"I'm in a robe. I'm the power guy here. Can't hang out in a robe otherwise. So now she's wondering if you work for me or are just coming by to say good-bye before you do something reasonably glamorous out there while I'm entitled to remain languid across the pool. Either way, in her eyes, I'm a winner."

"Languid?"

"Languid."

"This fantasy life ever work out for you?"

"Ask me again if you make the next pay grade. You can access a different level of intel at that point."

"Not if," Holly said. "When. You might want to remember it was 4 a.m. when you knocked on my door and wanted fingerprints off the badge you put in my hand."

"Not to be dehumanizing, but you looked okay for that time of morning."

"Well, not so much anymore. I'm not wearing these sunglasses to check you out. These bags under my eyes are part of the reason my next pay grade isn't an 'if.'"

"Was doing you a favor," Pierce said. "Knew you'd appreciate all the extra time I was giving you to get answers by now. Besides, you had full authorization to put Jeremy to work too."

"I want all the glory to myself."

"And?"

"I learned something about you. Only two sets of prints on your badge. Yours and hers. Was wondering if there'd be other women to find."

"Discipline. I only have time for work."

"The prints not yours belong to Jessica Charmaine. Forty-nine years old. Scientist, cleared for level-four military work."

"Good work."

"You might want to note 4 a.m. is when you handed me the badge."

"You're trying to make a point about not waking you up in the future."

"Which you'll ignore."

"What kind of science?" Pierce asked, thinking of the blood vials and syringes in the woman's purse.

"Genetic."

"You've got her file?"

"Posted on the op-site. Your eyes only."

"Let me try a long shot here," Pierce said. If Charmaine was forty-nine, she would have been late twenties when Jordan Brown pulled the plug by destroying everything and leaving for Appalachia. "Before the Wars, she was part of the Genesis lab."

"Yup. How'd you know?"

"Tut, tut," Pierce said. This knowledge finally gave him a good indication why Caitlyn had come to DC. "Wrong pay grade. Not going to share."

"Suddenly, old isn't that attractive to me anymore. What I said yesterday? Forget it."

"That's fine. Makes room for the blonde across the pool. What did you learn about Swain?"

"Same thing. Former genetics scientist. Genesis lab."

"You're getting closer to the next pay grade," Pierce said.

"Blonde in a bikini couldn't come close to what I'm capable of."

Pierce was glad his cell phone buzzed. He held up a hand of apology to Holly and answered. "Pierce."

"Tell me again why I keep doing you favors." Wilson's voice.

"I've saved your life three times." Pierce said from his lounge chair.

Wilson had not confirmed whether Pierce's cell was crypt protected from electronic eavesdropping. Nor did Pierce ask Wilson. It was a given since both were in flagrant violation of agency policy. Given the subject, Wilson's call to Pierce was definitely beyond authorization.

"Want to tell me why you asked for this favor?" Wilson asked. "You're trying to pull something together, and it can't be good."

"How much deniability do you want to lose here?" Pierce had asked to make an unauthorized location check of private vehicles to find the one that fit the specific time and location of the car that had pulled up to Swain's house the night before.

"Granted. But I don't like what I found."

"Spill."

"How high in the World United can you go?"

World United. The replacement for United Nations.

"You're talking the top?" Pierce asked. "Like the very top?"

"Richard Dawkins. We both know his military background."

"Yeah." Pierce was quiet for a few seconds, giving it some thought. Then, "Run a cross-check and see if there's any connection to Swain. Anytime. Anywhere."

"Pierce."

"Sorry. *Please* run a cross-check and—"

"No. I did it already. And what I got there is even worse. It's the Genesis Project. He was on the committee that oversaw the budget and operations. You should walk away from this. Now. If that was Dawkins and he was visiting Swain, he's going to know it was you inside when he passed by. Someone like him has a lot of juice. Like, unlimited."

Pierce didn't answer. The blonde in the bikini had just given him a third glance. More than a glance. A long look. Which was bold considering Holly was right beside him. It was more than bold. It was an open invitation. Did Pierce really want to leave the sun for a journey into the swamp of agency politics? Maybe he'd be better off poolside for the rest of the day. Or month.

"Pierce? You there?"

"I'm here," Pierce said.

"You hear me?"

"Yeah," Pierce said. "Thanks for your help."

He snapped the phone shut.

"You should have worn mirrored sunglasses," Holly said pertly. "She's acting like I'm not even here."

Pierce smiled back at the blonde, knowing that Holly was watching.

SIXTY-ONE

I've had time to think about this," Caitlyn told Razor. "There's more you should know. About the escape from Appalachia."

Breakfast had been more bread. More cheese. More unfiltered water.

She had folded herself into a corner of the room so that the walls hid the hunch of her back. She sat with her knees up, arms across her legs.

"A week before, others made it outside. Friends who had helped me make it to the border. I was supposed to meet them at a safe house."

"Stop," Razor said. "Safe house?"

"There's a network inside Appalachia. Working with the network here. Like a church, but without rules of religion. They help newcomers, get them work permits, find them a place to stay once they escape the official church of Appalachia. We were sent to Lynchburg."

"They still there?"

"When I made it over the wall, a guy named Johnny brought me to Lynchburg. I was supposed to go to a place the next morning where a network person was waiting for me. But Billy and Theo found me first and—"

"Your friends."

Caitlyn nodded. "Billy and Theo said the government had been asking questions."

"NI."

"NI. I decided to get out as fast as possible. Billy and Theo and I agreed to meet after I had my surgery, when we wouldn't have to worry about my wings giving me away. But to do that, I needed to come here to DC. They said they'd go too, even if it meant living in a soovie park. We went at different times. Our go-between was the network woman who secretly helped us. I got her a message that I was working at the Pavilion. They got her a message that she passed on to me. Every two days, at noon, they would wait for me outside the city wall at the farthest east checkpoint."

"You're telling me this because that's in a couple of hours, right?"

"Yesterday, I was trying to escape so I could meet them today. Billy and Theo. But your people turned me around."

"Too dangerous," Razor said. "Word is out. You're worth a lot of money. You start moving around, it's going to get someone's attention. No way can you go out there and look for them."

"I know," she said. "But you seem to be able to go anywhere you want."

SIXTY-TWO

Mason was in a bad mood as he followed Billy and Theo. Not just because of the sunshine that he was learning to hate.

They'd chosen not to return to the Meltdown, but were traveling down the paths as if on a mission. That should have put him in a good mood. Especially because Theo didn't have his glasses and was stumbling so badly that Billy needed to guide him. That made both easier prey.

But something was wrong with Mason, and he was disgusted with his own weakness.

The night before, just as the whore had begun to press a knife against one closed eye with a trembling hand, Mason had ordered her to stop. He was still trying to figure out why he'd walked away from the woman and the girl, leaving both of them physically unhurt, clinging to each other and weeping with relief.

He was in a bad mood because, once again, he was indulging in introspection. And in a bad mood because he'd actually shown mercy to someone. Introspection was weakness. Mercy was weakness. The weak did not survive.

Had he shown this mercy because he'd been so affected that someone could love enough not only to face the terror of a lifetime of blindness, but also to cut her own eyeballs as a sacrifice of love?

Or was Mason so utterly terrified of the dark that he couldn't handle inflicting blindness even on someone else?

Either way, he didn't like the internal shift that seemed to be happening. Weak. Weak. Weak. Maybe his time of hell in the black of the cave and the near-death experience had not been good for him at all.

As he gnawed at those thoughts, he was maybe fifty yards behind Billy and Theo, blending in easily among the strays and scavengers that infested this seemingly endless shantytown.

Mason wasn't worried about them noticing him, let alone recognizing him, so that gave him plenty of time to be alone with his loop of thoughts. Hunters didn't think, he told himself. Hunters didn't feel. Hunters hunted.

He tested himself by speculating about what he'd do to Caitlyn once he found her. No amount of begging for mercy would impact his actions there. He savored the emotions that came with his speculations and satisfied himself that he was still a hunter.

It cheered him slightly.

But not near as much as discovering, a few minutes later, near a checkpoint at the city wall, that Billy and Theo had left the Meltdown to meet with someone.

Following all three, no matter how long it took to find the perfect moment to strike, was going to be simple. Enjoyable. And rewarding.

SIXTY-THREE

Near the checkpoint, outside the city wall, Razor had no trouble identifying the two Caitlyn had described.

He sidled up behind them. The big one was really big. Twice as wide as Razor. A head taller.

The little one stood in front of Billy, in a protective stance. Neither bore face tattoos but were poorly dressed and did not have bodyguards, so they were obviously not Influentials. Or even Invisibles. The little one had huge bruises around his eyes.

The clear and correct assumption, then, was that they were Illegals, and this made them targets for vendors who would never dare to draw the attention of Influentials.

"No," Theo said in squeaky, high voice, shifting to stay between each new proposition and Billy. "Not interested. Not interested. Not interested."

Razor stepped to their side.

"How about a woman?" Razor said. He was enjoying this, messing with them as he tried to get a sense of who they were.

Billy ignored Razor, turning his head in different directions. Easy to guess he was looking around for Caitlyn.

Theo, however, frowned and squinted at Razor with full attention.

"Let me guess," Theo said. "A woman who is pure and very athletic."

"I suspect both," Razor said.

"And what does that mean?" Theo was blinking hard. "Just once I'd like someone to explain exactly why that should be of interest, instead of laughing when I ask."

His innocent seriousness was so intent that Razor understood why the question would be greeted with laughter.

Billy still ignored Razor. Among the people streaming past them, he was like a large boulder, impervious to water.

"No one ever offers me a woman," Theo said. "Always him. I'd like to know why."

"If you don't understand, you won't understand."

"Then the answer is no. He is not interested. No matter how pure and athletic. He is waiting for someone and nobody else."

"Would her name be Caitlyn?" Razor asked.

Razor had been focused on Theo, enjoying the boy's naiveté. His peripheral vision caught movement, but before Razor could react, his world shifted. He was off his feet, shoulders firmly in Billy's grasp, facing Billy directly, face to face.

"Where is she?" Billy said. No anger. But no mildness either.

"Put me down," Razor said.

"Where is she?" Billy repeated.

Razor knew he could end the confrontation with a few reassuring words, but he'd survived as long as he had by never appearing weak. He'd answer Billy's question, but only after dealing with Billy.

Billy's legs were together, his groin protected, so Razor brought his knee up hard, into Billy's stomach.

The big man barely grunted.

Theo, however, reacted by grabbing both of Razor's legs.

Razor tried to kick him free. He noticed that he didn't waver in Billy's grasp, even with his struggle with Theo.

"Where is she?" Billy repeated.

"Tell the terrier to let go, and you put me down," Razor said.

"Where is she?" Billy repeated. "I don't like hurting people."

"We'll talk when I'm on the ground."

Billy began squeezing Razor's shoulders. It felt like his fingers had penetrated through layers of muscle to the bone.

"This is stupid," Razor said, his eyes inches away from Billy's direct stare. "All it would take is a head butt to break your nose."

Billy pushed him away, moving Razor out to arm's length. Although the additional strain to do this must have been tremendous, Billy held Razor totally motionless. And still those fingers dug deeper and deeper.

"She sent me to find you," Razor told Billy. With the pain of Billy's grip, only pride kept Razor from squeaking like Theo. "It's not safe for her to come here herself."

Billy slowly set Razor down.

Theo backed away, glaring at Razor. The effect, however, lost any potency because of his height and because of his squinting and because of the bruises that made him look like a raccoon. "Next time I'll bite you," Theo said. "Where's Caitlyn?"

"You'll have to come with me," Razor answered. Nobody nearby had paid any attention to the small drama. In the world of Industrials and Illegals, people minded their own business.

"Nice try," Theo said. "We don't trust anybody."

"Don't be stupid," Razor said.

"Theo is not stupid," Billy said.

"What I mean, is how else would I know to look here for you unless she sent me?"

"You could be someone from the government." Theo said. "Tracking us down."

"She told me to tell you the last thing she said to you," Razor said to Billy, "beside the river, where you rescued her from drowning. If I'm right, you know she sent me."

Billy's eyebrows furrowed.

"She said she would look for you on the Outside," Razor said. "And she called you William."

SIXTY-FOUR

"Caitlyn! Caitlyn!"

From two steps away, Theo threw his little body as fast and as hard as he could at Caitlyn, and she rocked backward with the impact.

Caitlyn had been standing outside the shanty. Razor had made it clear that her safety here, unlike in the tunnels, depended on anonymity among the thousands of Industrials and Illegals. As long as she stayed in one spot and didn't draw attention, no one would find her. There were men around who listened to Razor. Not too many, otherwise it would have been noticeable. Enough to handle most trouble. Enough to make sure Caitlyn didn't leave.

As Razor had led Theo to this spot, he'd watched Caitlyn grin as Theo got so close he almost ran into her before he recognized her.

Theo continued to clutch Caitlyn.

She smiled as she looked down on his thatched hair, and Razor realized it was the first time he'd seen her smile with this kind of warmth. All he'd ever been given was the cold, tight version.

"What happened to your eyes, Theo?" Caitlyn asked.

"Nothing important," Theo said.

Billy stood nearby in the classic shy stance. Head down, his toes suddenly far more interesting than Caitlyn.

"William," she said softly. "Come here."

He loomed over her, but she drew him in, and for a moment, they were a joyful family.

"Got to keep moving," Razor said, more gruffly than he expected. Yeah, he felt jealous but didn't want to sort out why. Not now. Probably not later.

Theo was the first to break the embrace, squeezing out from between Billy and Caitlyn.

"Hey," he said to Caitlyn, pointing at Razor. "Who is this guy? Wouldn't answer any of my questions. Wouldn't even tell me his name."

"Hundred and two questions," Razor said. "I counted."

"Some were repeats," Billy said.

Razor couldn't tell if Billy was being sardonic. His speed of talk matched his size. Either the guy was brilliant and hid it well. Or he was transparently not so brilliant.

Caitlyn began to speak. "His name is—"

"T. R.," Razor jumped in before Caitlyn could finish. He was beginning to figure out the chemistry between Billy and Caitlyn. Irrationally, he didn't want Billy even knowing his nickname. "T. R. Zornenbach. We've got to keep moving; we've got to keep safe."

"Great," Theo said. Heavy sarcasm.

"We can trust him," Caitlyn admonished Theo.

"No," Theo said. "Great. My glasses. We're not going back to the soovie park, and that's where I left them."

"You can't see much without them," Caitlyn said. "How would you manage to forget to wear them?"

"We were at a soovie camp." Theo spoke in his usual hyper rush. "Strange there. Real strange. Then a death doctor came and Billy tried to stop him from killing the mother. Made people mad. My glasses got broken when Billy was fighting one of the soovie gang guys. Thought we were dead. Then government came in with a helicopter and pulled us out of there. Billy almost didn't make it. We were in the hospital all night. Government asked us to go back to the soovie park and spy for them. But we knew that was a lie. Billy said they must be tracking us, otherwise how could they know we left Lynchburg? Billy said it was strange they made sure to fix my glasses and give them back to me. Sure enough, that's how they found us. So when we don't want to be tracked, we leave the glasses behind. Right, Billy?"

Theo looked to Billy for confirmation, a satisfied look on his face that indicated he'd told the entire story, or at least the important parts of it.

"You need glasses bad?" Razor asked.

"Real bad," Theo said. "Once, before I had them, I tried to eat a skunk. Really. Ask Caitlyn."

"I'll get you a new pair," Razor said. "But I need to go back and get the old pair. Tell me how to find them."

"Why?" Billy asked.

"He won't answer," Caitlyn said. "But you can trust him."

Billy was shaking his head. Not to trust Razor.

Caitlyn put a hand on his arm. "Really. The same way you can trust me."

SIXTY-FIVE

P ierce stood in a hallway facing a closed door. Avery and Holly behind him. They were in an apartment block in one of the low-income quadrants. In theory, only work permit holders were licensed to occupy the units. In his rookie days, when he was JAA—just another agent, like the two behind him— he'd been to places like this enough times to know that a large percentage of wealthier Illegals found places inside the city. In situations like this, he wondered what it would have been like before thermal imaging and before technology made it possible to restrict firearms. He hoped he would still put himself in front, when a closed door would have ratcheted the tension exponentially, agents wondering what weaponry was waiting on the other side, how many people waiting and their positions in the room. When bursting into a room meant adrenaline-filled suspense before kicking the door down and instant decisions that determined life or death in the microseconds after.

Nothing like that now.

Pierce knew from thermal imaging that it was a one-room unit. Kitchen, bedroom, and living room all in an open floor plan.

Thermal imaging also showed one person inside. Small. On a bed. No objects in hand. Which meant no weapons.

Pierce even knew the kid's identity. Theo. Via a tracking chip in the kid's glasses, they'd had tabs on him since releasing him and Billy from the hospital. The two were rarely separated. But thermal didn't show anyone else. So Billy wasn't here. Something Pierce would deal with later.

Unlike pre-thermal days, they wouldn't have to kick open the door either. The agent behind Pierce had just used a laser drill to silently take out the door lock. Wisps of smoke were all the warning that the kid inside would get.

Pierce nodded at his two agents, then pushed open the door.

Squeaky hinges.

The kid looked up, either at the noise or at the movement. It wasn't Theo. Some other kid about the same size. Who didn't seem too concerned about three strangers pushing their way into the apartment.

"Nice," Pierce said. Meaning the opposite.

Pierce stepped inside, but waved the two agents back into the hallway.

The unit had about as much ambiance as a warehouse office. Just the bed. Plain table. Nothing on the walls.

Pierce saw Theo's glasses sitting on the table. That's where a tracking device had been imbedded. Since it was next to impossible to successfully send surveillance agents into a soovie park, they'd been relying on the glasses to track Theo's movements and confirm the whereabouts of Billy and Theo when they wandered away from the agent mole inside the camp. When GPS had shown movement outside the park and back into the city, they'd picked up surveillance again. When Pierce had heard Billy was absent and there was no sign of Caitlyn, he'd decided to have a talk with Theo.

"Kid, you steal those glasses?" Pierce asked. He'd prefer that to be the answer. Pierce had gambled two things. That the kids from Appalachia were too new to this world to suspect a tracking device and that Theo needed the glasses almost as much as he needed oxygen.

"Razor gave them to me," the kid answered.

Pierce didn't have to give that much thought before asking his next question. "He told you to tell me that?"

"Yup."

"What else?" Pierce asked in a resigned voice.

"It don't make sense to me, but what he said is, if you want the flying girl, follow these directions to where you're supposed to go and wait for Razor."

In the crowded coffee shop, Pierce thought about how technology would always take second place to organics.

The last hundred years had gone from rotary dial to vidphone, dial-up Internet to broadnet, pirated movies to interactive pirate movies. But coffee beans were still coffee beans, and the satisfaction of taking that first sip of a dark, rich beverage was probably just as good now as it had been five hundred years earlier.

This was the place of Razor's choice. Downtown core, near the Pavilion. Pierce anticipated that Razor had information to sell or negotiate, so Pierce had delayed getting here long enough to have agents set up in place for a quick swoop. Razor was going to lose a lot of leverage once he was in custody.

Pierce was halfway through the first cup of coffee when an Illegal sat down beside him. She was tarted up, and her profession was obvious. The days of pimps were long gone. Handlers were instead Enforcers who had the local power to decide when and where they could operate.

"First thing," she said, leaning forward and setting her elbows on the table, "is I got something for you from Razor, and it's going to cost you one hundred even. This is a cash transaction."

Holly was across the coffee shop. Pretending to read an e-book. Pierce didn't want to think what Holly would have to say about this later.

Pierce found a bank note. She held her hand out for it, nail polish as uneven as her penciled-in eyebrows.

Pierce extended the bank note but didn't let go as she gripped it. With a quick twist of his wrist, he ripped it in half, leaving each of them with a portion.

"That's cold," she said. "You don't trust me?"

"Payment on delivery."

"First thing, then, you put your vidphone on the table. And leave it there." Pierce did.

"Now I check you out for wires. Best is in a bathroom. But I'm fine here too."

Sure, Pierce was going to step into a bathroom with an Illegal dressed like her. With Holly watching.

"I'm not wired," Pierce said.

"I trust you like you trust me."

She reached under the table and ran her hands up and down his legs. Then she stood behind him, lifted his shirt. She reached around and ran her fingers up his belly and chest.

"Get a room," Pierce heard someone say. It was Holly. The café laughter that followed was probably more enjoyable to her than it was to Pierce.

"Like I said, not wired," Pierce told the Illegal. "Satisfied?"

"Usually that's my question," she said.

"Funny. Now what."

"How do you take your coffee?" she asked.

"Black," Pierce said.

"Good. Leave it for me. Across the street is public transport. Next high-speed to New York arrives in one minute. You get on it. Alone."

SIXTY-SIX

There's something I need to tell you," Billy said to Caitlyn. "Before Theo gets back. I don't want you to hate me for it."

Billy was hunched on a chair that he'd backed into the corner of the shack, obviously uncomfortable.

"I couldn't hate you," Caitlyn said softly. "Not ever."

The softness around the edges of Billy's face was gone. He'd begun to lose his boyishness. Caitlyn couldn't help but compare her feelings in Billy's presence to the attraction she had to the edgy darkness of Razor. Billy was a man. Big and solid in more than body. Someone who would comfort and protect, give her a safeness she'd never have with Razor. Billy would stop the trembling; Razor would cause it.

"You're beautiful," Billy blurted. "I thought of you every day since Appalachia. I wished I wasn't so big and stupid. You know, like some giant that would accidentally crush a beautiful bird."

Caitlyn had no experience with men, except for the instinct that told her how amazing it would be to hold and kiss and lose herself in an embrace. Kneeling close, she put her hand on Billy's arm, thinking if he reached for her, put his arms around her horrible hunch, she'd find a way never to think about Razor again.

Billy looked down at her hand and smiled sadly. "I can't bear to talk about it, but I have to. But you need to know that there's no one more beautiful, no matter what Swain told me."

She recoiled slightly. "Swain?"

"He told me what I had to tell you about being..."

Billy put his head straight down so that she was looking at the top of his short hair. Then he rose again, finding the courage to look her in the eyes. "About being different."

She had no reply.

"I know you're different. You know I know it. That's why you got to believe I think you're the most beautiful woman. Not that I'm thinking you'd ever look at me the way I look at you. But if I got to tell you what Swain said, then I got to tell you how I feel, no matter how much you might laugh at me or feel sorry for me for saying it."

"William," Caitlyn said. With Razor in her mind, not wanting to step forward and betray both Billy and Razor. "I think about you too. A lot."

Then more quietly, she said. "You visited Swain?"

"In Appalachia, before Jordan put me into the river, he asked me to protect you. He told me what he wanted for you. He wanted you to live normal so you wouldn't have to hide your whole life. He said when you were little, surgery wouldn't have helped. That he had to wait until you were grown up, but once you were grown up, if you had surgery in Appalachia, you'd get caught. He said only one person would be able to help you. Swain. Outside. He made me promise I'd help you get to Swain, told me how to find him and what to say. But when you and me didn't meet in that first week, I thought maybe you went to Swain, so I went there to look for you. And Swain, he told me stuff. About you. That you would need to know before you made your choice. Then I went back to Lynchburg to Theo and waited for you."

"You couldn't tell me about it when we met in Lynchburg?"

"We were in a hurry because we were afraid government might find you. And once you found us I knew you were going to Swain anyway, so I didn't have to tell you. I thought all we'd have to do is wait for you to meet us. After the surgery."

"I kept trying to find the courage to do it," she told Billy. Which was almost a lie. The truth was she thought she'd made her choice. To live as an outcast and freak, to angrily revel in her solitude, to hold on to her wings, to reject what Jordan had wanted for her, a punishment for his betrayal, a refusal to give him a chance for redemption.

"I thought for a while I might want to keep my wings," Caitlyn said, easing the lie. "But now it looks like I'll be hunted forever. If I don't lose my wings, I'm dead. And probably anyone who hides me."

Or loves me, she thought.

"There's more," Billy said. "It's not your wings. It's about your blood."

SIXTY-SEVEN

O*kay,* Pierce told himself as he stepped onto the train, trailed by a couple of women, *the kid isn't stupid.*

In contrast to the previous generation's inspections, which had been limited to airports, body-scanning technology no longer relied on metal detectors and human inspectors. Passengers stepped through a portal that blended thermal imaging and x-ray; software analyzed the result within microseconds. The convenience had extended inspections to all public transport.

It meant the kid would be assured that Pierce had no weapon.

More importantly, by sending a message to get on the train in under a minute, it gave Pierce no time to set up a plan or have agents remain in surveillance position. The train car was set up so that passengers departed from the opposite-side door new passengers entered from. From inside, the kid would be able to watch Pierce's approach and decide between staying on the train or leaving in a crowd going the opposite direction.

But it wasn't foolproof. The train was on a track, going in a predictable direction at a predictable speed. With Pierce on the train, he expected that Holly was smart enough to make some calls and have people in place at every stop ahead.

Pierce found a place to sit.

Five stops later, with no contact made, it occurred to him that maybe the kid had bolted.

Ten stops later, with the train thinning of passengers, he was almost sure of it. The train was well outside the city and headed north to the New York stops.

He was just about to exit at the next stop when he realized there might not be any agents in place. Impossible to spread out agents at every stop on a trip of hundreds of miles and dozens of stops.

That's when he realized he'd probably been outsmarted again.

And he settled back to wait a while longer. It would be interesting to see how Razor intended to play this out.

❖

The corridor train hummed at near maximum velocity, cushioned on air less than half an inch above a magnetic rail. At three hundred miles an hour, the light poles along the tracks seemed to pass Carson Pierce in silent swooshes, leaving comet tails on his retinas as he stared without focus at the blurred background.

The compartment was nearly empty, and the sleek bullet train had almost lulled Pierce to sleep when he felt something flick at his hair. Like the fluttering of a moth. Then a light touch on his nose. Before he could reach up with his hand to get rid of it, however, something bit fiercely at the skin of the front of his neck and pulled him backward to the headrest behind him.

"That's fishing line," a voice whispered from behind him. "I've made it into a garrote. You'll be all right if you don't move. Hands on your lap and stay relaxed."

Pierce kept his head very still. He'd learned to coldly assess situations under pressure. Because of the agency's training in all weapons, Pierce knew the effectiveness of a garrote, especially if the assassin used a stick to tighten the ligature like a tourniquet. The nylon would be strong enough to partially decapitate him before it snapped. At the very least, once it started cutting through skin and muscle, it would be no different than a knife across his throat, and it would be a race to see if he died from blood loss or strangulation.

Brilliant.

Thin nylon line and a stick. A few feet of fishing line. A thin rod of some kind, maybe even a pen. Easy enough to move undetected through the security portals at the train station.

Ahead, the compartment door opened. One of the train's stewards entered, a thin, stooped man in black trousers and a badly fitting red vest, pushing a drink trolley, head down.

"Don't ask for help," the low soft voice warned Pierce. "You're going to want to hear what I have to say."

Because there were so few passengers this far into the run, the steward reached them almost immediately. Pierce had no intention of asking for help. The steward stopped beside them. "Refreshments?"

"Nothing, thanks," Pierce said, head upright, expecting that the nylon line around his neck would be invisible. Stupid thought crossed his mind. He'd been hoping to buy coffee. Even if it did come in a cup of recycled paper. Now he'd have to wait for the steward to come back.

The steward pushed on.

"Refreshments?" the steward asked the person behind him.

Only silence. The reply must have simply been a negative head shake, the turning stick of the garrote undoubtedly shielded in some manner.

The trolley creaked as the steward moved through the rest of the compartment, then exited.

"All right, Timothy Ray Zornenbach," Pierce said. "How about less pressure with the garrote, and we get right to your questions."

SIXTY-EIGHT

S wain said you were a number." Billy closed his eyes in concentration, making sure he would get it right. Slow was better than fast. If given a choice, Billy would rather remain silent than make a mistake. "CZ8513. They had embryos. One-cell embryos. All with numbers."

It was worse because now Billy would be talking about Caitlyn. "You know about cells, right? They didn't teach us about cells in school in Appalachia."

"Jordan talked about it with me at times," Caitlyn said. "But he was a scientist from Outside."

This was why this conversation was worse. Each of them knew that Jordan had done something to Caitlyn that made her the way she was.

"So you know about genes too?"

"The DNA information inside each cell," Caitlyn said. "It programs how the cell works in the body."

She was making it easier on him, talking like it didn't matter. Like this was about someone else or something else.

But it did matter. Billy knew. And she had to know.

"If a change is made to the genes in a skin cell," Billy said, hearing Swain's patient explanation in his memory, "those changes aren't passed on to other cells."

He felt embarrassment at what he had to explain next. "But we all start as one cell. And when the egg cell is, you know…"

Part of Billy's embarrassment was the memory of what he'd learned from Swain about human reproduction. In Appalachia, that subject was only for married people.

"Fertilized," Caitlyn said. "It becomes an embryo."

"Yes," Billy said quickly. He didn't want those pictures in his head. Not with Caitlyn right here. He focused instead on the memory of Swain drawing a circle. Then splitting it into two. And four. "One cell divides into two. Into four. Into eight. And it copies the gene with the same information. Then the cells specialize, and they only use a short piece of the information. A skin cell uses the skin information. But the cell doesn't specialize until after it's divided into four. So once it got to four, the scientists would pull them all apart, so those four cells each started over like the original embryo and began to divide again. Doing this again and again gave them hundreds of single-cell embryos, all identical."

Caitlyn smiled encouragement at Billy. But she didn't want to interrupt him.

"If a change in the thread of genes is made in the very first cell, every cell after that will keep the change." Billy lowered his voice. "That's what happened to you, Caitlyn. Some DNA was inserted into the first embryo cell so that you were programmed for..."

"Wings."

"That's not what I was going to say. But that's part of it. Some of your cells that would specialize and grow into muscles had a change in the gene threads. To make them stronger." Billy went through his mind and patiently waited until he was sure he remembered correctly. "Swain said the gene change blocked myostatins. Myostatins keep muscle to a certain size so they don't grow too big. You don't have blockers. You're as strong as someone twice your size."

"To support my wings." Caitlyn paused. "I don't need to know how. Tell me what Jordan wouldn't tell me. Why they did this in the first place. Why they made me like I am."

Billy's temples hurt. He rubbed them.

"William," she said. "Tell me."

"Swain said the scientists were experimenting. To see what would happen if they tried making a hybrid human. They used the gene thread from the embryo of a giant eagle on you."

"What?"

"Not Jordan," Billy said, reading her reaction of outrage. "And Swain said he wasn't part of it either. He said they both worked at a place where other scientists could splice the gene threads into embryos at the one-cell stage. They had thousands and tried lots of things. They'd see if the embryos survived in a test tube. And if one lived long enough, then it would go into a woman to keep growing. See if it could come to term naturally."

"Experimenting," Caitlyn repeated coldly. "More like playing God."

"Swain called it a gene map. They have the gene maps of all kinds of animals. Swain said little changes to gene threads could make big changes in animals and humans. That's why there are so many different species. He said they were playing with it like clay but using proteins instead."

"Stop," Caitlyn said, more forcefully than she'd intended. "I'm sorry. I don't want to hear any more."

Billy looked at her and was silent for a moment. "He said the agency wants to find why your gene map is different, what let you survive when all those other embryos didn't."

"So they can experiment more?" Caitlyn spat. "What do they want, an army of flying soldiers?"

"No," Billy said. "It's your blood. It carries some cells that are like the opposite of cancer cells. Healing cells."

She swallowed and closed her eyes. "Go on."

Billy paused to make sure he'd been correct about that too, then repeated it. "Embryonic stem cells. Cells that haven't specialized yet. They can become any kind of cell. Repair any kind of cell. Swain said your gene thread must produce stem cells that float in your blood. That maybe that's what keeps you alive and feeds your muscles. He doesn't know. But the government wants to know, and that's why he told me to tell you everything. He's worried something might happen to him now that you're Outside."

Billy rubbed his temples again, speaking without looking up. "There's more. You won't like it."

"Tell me."

"When they made changes to the gene map…"

"Yes?"

Hayflick Limit. It was the last term he had to tell her. He thought slowly. He'd gone to a lot of effort to listen carefully to Swain because of the importance of this. And every day, he'd found a quiet spot to repeat everything in his mind so he'd be sure not to forget. "They wanted to see if they could eliminate the Hayflick Limit. The amount of times a cell can divide before the copies of the gene thread break down. If the Hayflick Limit is gone, and if cells could always replace themselves…"

"People wouldn't get older."

Caitlyn was silent. Billy thought he understood her silence. She was trying to absorb this, just as he had barely been able to comprehend.

"Swain said that when Jordan found out the scientists went past experiments with the Hayflick Limit and started trying to make animal hybrids, he didn't want to be part of it anymore. He decided to get out."

Now Billy couldn't read Caitlyn's continued silence, especially since she'd looked away.

"The government doesn't want you because of your wings," Billy said. "They want you because your wings didn't destroy you. Because your blood and muscles let you survive the gene thread experiment. And it's all related to something in your genetics that has stopped the Hayflick Limit. Swain told me you might be able to live a hundred years longer than anyone because of all this. Like some of the people in the Bible."

He wished he didn't have to tell her anything else. But he couldn't lie to her. Even if it was holding something back.

"There's one other thing," Billy said. "Gene-line therapy. That's when a change is made to a fertilized egg that can be passed on to the next generation."

She turned her eyes back on him.

"Your...differences," Billy said carefully. "They'd be passed on to your children. And to their children. For generations. Until there is a new race of humans who are twice as strong and live twice as long."

SIXTY-NINE

Call Wilson," the soft voice said from behind Pierce.

Pierce blinked a few times. How had the kid learned enough about the agency to know about Wilson?

The invisible noose tightened, and the voice behind him became more insistent. "Call Wilson. He's waiting for it."

Pierce used his phone, knowing the call would be encrypted automatically. Wilson answered in one ring.

"It's Pierce." He had the phone to his ear, opting out of visual contact on the screen.

"They said you'd call," Wilson said. "I need your help. Bad."

"They?"

"Someone has Luke," Wilson said. "All they ask is why NI is tracking the head of World United. I don't have a clue because my calls to you don't make it through. They tell me you're going to call and I'm supposed to get the code to the op-site. I'm supposed to wipe out the site and all the intel. Or my boy comes back to me in little pieces."

Strict NI policy meant only the op leader had full op-site authorization. Part of checks and balances. Once Pierce gave Wilson the code, both were breaking national security laws.

"There's more," Wilson said. "I need to deliver the girl. Not to the agency. To them. It's my boy on the line. Anything else, I wouldn't be asking."

Wilson was speaking slowly. Pierce doubted anyone else knew Wilson enough to understand that's what he did under stress.

"I'm in," Pierce said. Pierce knew that it wasn't T. R. Zornenbach behind him. Whatever calls Holly had made earlier had triggered something. Wouldn't have been difficult to set this up. Take out Theo and move the glasses to a place where Pierce would believe Razor had been. Make it look like Razor was setting up a meet. Pull Pierce into it step by step, get him into a position with no backup agents and no weapons. Have someone waiting on the train from a few stops before it reached Pierce.

The garrote was classic. Few defenses against it. None, in Pierce's situation. The fishing line was in place; the seat back was protecting his attacker. No way to get his fingers beneath the line. He didn't have a knife to cut it—the weapon would have been detected at the body-scanning portal.

"I need the op-site access now," Wilson said. "They said if I don't get it, I hang up the phone and my son's dead. No negotiations."

The ten-digit password would give Wilson access to all the files of a specific operation, plus computer contact with all the field agents, in effect letting him run the operation. Or wipe out all intel completely.

Pierce wondered if Wilson knew that as soon as Pierce gave it, Pierce was dead. If Pierce was reading this right, once Pierce gave up op authorization, all Pierce's leverage was gone. Wilson had been put in a position of choosing his son over his friend.

What choice was there? For either of them?

Pierce gave him the password. Twice. Speaking slowly.

"Get to my office as soon as you can," Wilson said. "I've got a way we can move forward under the radar."

Hope sprung eternal. Even an agent as experienced as Wilson wanted the illusion. That he'd get his boy back. That Pierce would return. Unless Wilson knew there was no hope and wanted to leave Pierce with some.

"Yeah," Pierce said. "Be a couple of hours."

Wilson hung up. Pierce didn't. He left the phone in place against his ear.

"Got to tell you a couple more things about the operation that aren't on file," Pierce said into the silent phone. He kept speaking, outlining the situation.

Pierce couldn't think of any way out. He couldn't stand. Even if he managed to turn sideways, it wouldn't take the pressure off his neck.

All he could hope for was that someone else would enter the compartment and he could wave for help.

"You got any guarantees you'll get the boy back?" Pierce asked the silent phone. "Any indication where we can make a trade once we get the girl?"

This was too cute. Once he was dead, the person behind him could walk away, leave the ligature in place, holding Pierce upright by the neck, bound to the headrest, fishing line invisible in the folds of skin. It would look like Pierce was asleep. Might not be until the last stop that anyone noticed he wasn't. By then, the assassin would be long off the train.

"Your wife know anything about this?" Pierce asked the phone.

Why was he fighting for extra time? He was going to be killed once he hung up the phone. Or he'd read it completely wrong, and he wouldn't be killed. Either way, what did a few more seconds matter?

The compartment door opened. A woman entered. Jeans. Loose black jacket. Looked young, but hard to tell because her head was down. Dark hair covered most of her face.

Now Pierce had another decision.

Person behind him was a killer. If Pierce waved for help, just the three of them in the compartment, might also guarantee the death of the woman. The garrote would kill Pierce in a few tight twists, leaving the assassin plenty of time to deal with the witness.

Pierce kept talking into the phone, letting the woman pass.

He heard the door at the back of the compartment open and close.

"You're done," the whispering voice behind him said. "Drop the phone."

Irrational as it was, Pierce began to turn. It wouldn't help him; he had no chance. But he couldn't just let it happen without a fight.

That's when the noose tightened, delivering a horrible thin bracelet of liquid pain. Instinctively, Pierce brought his hands up to pull. Another futile effort. His fingers were useless claws, scrabbling against his skin.

His scream of frustration and rage came out as a gasp.

In that moment, there was a muffled thud. The noose slackened.

Pierce wedged the phone between the fishing line and his neck, used it to leverage more slack. Panting, he pulled it away. Spun to see what was happening behind him.

It was the woman. Wig askew. Rubbing her elbow.

"Don't know if she's okay," the woman in the loose black jacket said, only it was a man's voice, and the hand pointed in the seat, where another woman was slumped sideways. "I had to hit as hard as I could. Didn't see much choice though."

Pierce remembered the voice. From surveillance tapes yesterday.

It meant the woman in the skewed wig and the loose black jacket had been the one to set up this meet.

"Razor," Pierce said.

"Yeah," he answered. "Good move, wasn't it? Walking past, opening and shutting the door and sneaking back. It's why they call me Razor. Fast. Sharp. Dangerous."

Razor pointed at the unconscious woman lying across the seat, blood seeping from her jaw. The barely visible fishing line in a long, loose thread. "Want to explain what's happening?"

SEVENTY

Caitlyn was half asleep, sitting upright against the outside wall of the shanty, when a high-pitched wail snapped her out of the pleasantness of warm sunlight and emptied thought.

It only took her seconds to understand what had happened.

A couple of the older children had been playing with Jasmine, the sickly three-year-old girl. Jasmine had tripped, skinning her knees. It was probably the shock of falling; she seemed inconsolable, her face contorted as she wept.

Caitlyn had never thought of herself as motherly, but then again, she'd never been around children much. Although it was just skinned knees, and rationally Caitlyn knew it was a minor issue, she couldn't help feeling a rush of compassion at the girl's sorrow.

The older children crouched over her, but Jasmine brushed away their attempts at comfort.

Caitlyn rolled to her feet and scooped up the little girl, who clung to her neck.

No one had ever depended on her like this, trusted her so completely, and Caitlyn clung back, startled at how good it felt to hold a child like this.

Jasmine's sobs began to subside as Caitlyn rocked her.

But it didn't help the little girl's scraped knees.

As Caitlyn stroked Jasmine's hair and soothed her with a low humming noise, Caitlyn had a thought that she tried to dismiss. But couldn't.

The three had led him to Caitlyn, where Mason's viewpoint of the shanty allowed him a clear view of Caitlyn as she slept. He was tempted to rush in and brush past the children playing tag on the hard-packed dirt.

But watching Caitlyn and daydreaming about the ways he would make her scream provided a nice diversion as he waited, and he was also aware that taking Caitlyn by force right now might have complications. Short of killing her, he'd have to fight her the entire distance he'd need to go to be alone with her. He didn't want to kill her. At least not quickly.

So he continued to wait and watch.

One of the smaller girls fell and began to shriek. For Mason, it was a sound like nails against a chalkboard.

When Caitlyn picked the girl up and stroked her hair, Mason relaxed, but didn't lose his focus on Caitlyn and continued to stare at her with his one eye.

Then she did something that puzzled him.

She brought the girl back to the wall of the shanty and held the girl in her lap with one arm.

With her other arm, Caitlyn reached behind her and pulled out a short dagger.

That wasn't what puzzled him, however. He'd already known about the knife from Everett.

It was what she did with the knife.

Caitlyn punctured one of her fingertips. Then smeared her blood across the little girl's bloody knee.

To Caitlyn, within minutes after spreading her own blood across Jasmine's knees, it seemed like a thin, pink fabric slowly grew across the edges of the bleeding scrapes. Before the advancing fabric had fully knitted into a scab, a second layer began to spread across the first, gradually began to cover the thin layer of pink. This new layer was light-colored marble skin. As it advanced, it looked like new skin had been grafted into place.

Caitlyn was mesmerized.

And terrified.

SEVENTY-ONE

The train was slowing for its next scheduled stop when Pierce opened the bathroom door and backed into the swaying corridor.

Razor had been standing in front, as if waiting to use it, ensuring no one would enter while Pierce bound the woman who had been using the fishing line garrote. He caught a glimpse of the woman curled up inside on the floor. Just above a swatch of hair that covered her lower face like a beard, her eyes were wide—fury, maybe, or fear—but it looked like Pierce had done a good enough job binding her using the fishing line, shoelaces, and lengths of cloth ripped from the loose black jacket Razor had been wearing earlier.

"Nice touch," Razor said. It wasn't necessary to mention what Razor meant. Pierce had stuffed the wig deep inside the woman's mouth, wrapping it in place with a strip of ripped cloth, hair sticking in all directions.

Pierce shrugged. "She can breathe."

Razor was trying to put this together. He had painstakingly thought through every detail to set up a meeting with Pierce without risking his own capture. Getting Illegals—the kid and the hooker—to deliver his messages had been simple. Timing the train was a little more complicated, but worth it; if Pierce had tried to take other agents onto the train, Razor could have escaped easily, and he'd been watching Pierce's approach from the train window to ensure Pierce was alone.

Razor had seen two women get on the train with Pierce and had waited stop after stop, trying to decide if either was connected with him or to him. When Razor had made the final approach, in his simple disguise, he'd seen the woman behind Pierce. Thinking trap, he'd noticed something much different instead.

But why had Pierce been a target?

"May be better if she can't breathe," Razor said. Throwing it out there to see what he could learn from the answer.

"Be my guest," Pierce said, hand on the door, ready to open it. "All you'll need to do is pinch her nostrils. She's not in a position to stop you."

The answer had given him nothing.

Didn't matter too much, Razor thought. He still had the leverage he'd planned to use with Pierce before this complication.

Razor had Caitlyn.

Pierce didn't.

"Killing's not my style," Razor said.

"Mine either," Pierce said. He rubbed his neck. Gingerly. The fishing line had cut through in a few places, and when he pulled his hand away, his fingers were smeared with blood. "But I was tempted."

Pierce gave the door handle a quick twist, breaking it off.

Razor noticed that Pierce tucked the handle in his pocket instead of dropping it. That did tell him something. Pierce was careful. And smart.

"An old move," Pierce said. "But effective. It'll give us a couple hours. Enough that we can make it back on the train in the opposite direction."

He paused before asking Razor, "You like coffee?"

Five minutes later, they'd crossed the platform and caught the inbound train. They found the restaurant compartment, where Pierce had ordered coffee.

What Pierce hadn't told Razor was that while he was tying up the assassin in the bathroom, he'd made a call behind the closed door. There'd be someone in New York to collect her. He also hadn't mentioned that if Razor had called his bluff and tried to kill the woman, Pierce would have stepped in to stop it. Dead women can't talk; Pierce wanted her alive and held because what she knew would be helpful, sooner or later.

He'd called in a few favors to his New York contacts. They came from the rough side of town, and they'd get answers from her. First thing Pierce wanted to know was if the kill attempt had been authorized by the agency or the military. That would make a big difference to Pierce's long-term future. Short term, though, he had an unlikely partner.

Pierce looked over his cup at this new partner, who'd chosen cola, on ice, wedge of lemon.

"How old are you?" Pierce asked. It was more a rhetorical question. As a lead in. Pierce already knew the kid was twenty-two.

"Not ancient." Leaving it unsaid. *Like you.*

"When you're ancient," Pierce said, "you know that a couple of colas a day adds up to a lot of sugar. Keep doing this, by the time you get to my age, you'll weigh double."

"You pick your poison. I'll pick mine."

"Fair enough." Pierce sipped at his coffee, waiting. Razor had been the one to make the move for them to get together.

"I can't see you having any reason to trust me," Razor said.

"Which is another way of saying you're not going to trust anything I say. How about let's get straight to it. What do you want?"

"Let me ask first. That woman who tried to kill you, it have anything to do with Caitlyn?"

Pierce continued sipping his coffee. He was confident his face wouldn't reveal any answers.

"I doubt someone from the agency wants you dead," Razor said. "You were on the train to make contact with me. Why get rid of you before getting me? So it had to be someone outside the agency. If it was about Caitlyn, who else knows what's happening? And how do they know? It wasn't until night before last that the Enforcers picked her up."

Same questions Pierce wanted answered. Or rather confirmed. His guess was the military, stirred up after Wilson tracked down who had been at Swain's the night before.

"What do you want?" Pierce asked Razor.

"Maybe we should be working together," Razor said. "I can keep you in safe places over the next few days."

"We're opposite sides of the table here," Pierce said. "My job is to put you in custody. Not look for sanctuary."

"Because you want Caitlyn. I got that figured out."

"Yet here you are."

"And here you are. Haven't tried anything to put me in custody. Like pulling an emergency cord, stopping the train, and getting it put in lockdown. Or taking me down right now and getting someone on the train to call in that you've got me captured."

"Maybe I made a call while I was tying up the woman. Maybe agents will swarm us at the next stop."

"You're not that stupid," Razor said. He hadn't touched his soda yet. The glass was sweating slightly, bubbles still accelerating up the sides. "Can't be coincidence that someone tried to take you out. It's possible that it's unrelated, but come on. What are the chances that with all that's happening, there's some other factor involved?"

"Tell me why you wanted to meet," Pierce said. "Or are you too stupid to figure out I'm not interested in talking? Just listening."

"I've lost a lot of motivation to talk," Razor said. "I've just learned that someone wants you dead, and it's got to be someone well connected. Until I know who and why, I'm going to wonder if you're still in a position to help me."

"Depends what you want."

Razor finally picked up his soda. He drank through the straw, keeping an eye on Pierce. He drank all of it. Slowly. Like he was taking time to think.

"Here's my bet," Razor finally said, setting the glass aside. "Whoever wants you dead is outside the agency, and the reason is because this 'whoever' also wants Caitlyn. That means whoever it is doesn't have any fear of the agency or doesn't expect the agency can help you. So you're going to need Caitlyn, either to save your own life or to give the agency some leverage. I bet we end up on the same side of the table."

Pierce had to admit, only to himself, that the kid was sharp.

"That would mean you'd have to trust me," Pierce said. "I don't see that happening."

"As long as I hold on to what you want until I can get away safe, I'll be fine."

"Fair enough." Pierce felt the coffee kick in. Or maybe it was a delayed buzz from his near death. It had been like this a few other times. In the moment, all you can do is react. Later, when it was safe, the shakes would start.

But it wasn't safe yet. Wilson and his son were in danger. Pierce needed more information to decide if he and Wilson had been given up by the agency.

"That mean I won my bet?" Razor asked.

"I don't make bets I'd lose," Pierce said. "And yes, I might need a safe place for the next couple days."

"Then I'll go first," Razor said. "There's a guy named Swain. He thinks I'm going to deliver Caitlyn this afternoon to an address of his choice. An old-fashioned exchange. The girl for money."

"You're not going to deliver?"

"Depends on who will give me more for her," Razor said. "My plan was for this to be a negotiating session. Highest bidder wins. You need to prove to me you're in a position to deliver whatever you promise to get her first. So start by telling me why the agency wants her so bad."

SEVENTY-TWO

I was sent into Appalachia not long ago," Pierce told Razor. He was going to play this cautiously, give out as little as he could. If it turned out the agency had nothing to do with the assassin on the outbound, he still had his duty. On the other hand, if the agency had cut him loose, he couldn't afford to give up all his knowledge on this. It was becoming obvious that secrets were leverage and that Razor had more than a few himself.

"Our government worked out a deal with the Appalachians," Pierce continued. "My job was to bring back a scientist who'd fled there before the Wars."

"Jordan Brown," Razor said. "Destroyed the genetic research, took a surrogate mother with him, the woman pregnant with Caitlyn. Jordan left Swain behind to play the straight man. You missed catching him, and Jordan sent Caitlyn Outside to go to Swain."

"You know so much, why bother asking me about it? Or you just like showing off?"

"Letting you understand that if you start lying to me, chances are I'll figure it out. Then you and me are done. I'll just deliver her to Swain without you."

"Or I make sure you don't leave this train unless you're in custody."

"You already told me you want a place to hide. That doesn't sound like someone who can take me in and expect either of us to survive. I love games, but here's the time and place it makes sense to come at you straight."

Razor leaned back and lifted his shirt. "See this scar? Guy named Melvin cut me good. I know you know that. You saw it on tape."

Pierce raised an eyebrow.

"Yeah," Razor said. "That surprises you too. But I had a good talk with Leo. You'll remember him from security. Not so skinny. Not so smart. Smells bad."

"I'm on board," Pierce said quietly. "No games."

"What's significant here," Razor said, "is that you're looking at a scar. Not a day-old cut that's barely had time to scab."

Razor dropped his shirt.

Pierce leaned forward. "Show me that again."

Earlobes. That was it. Jimmy's ear. There had not been much of a scab.

Razor obliged. Pierce looked closely. Razor had the flat belly of youth. The scar wasn't even pink anymore. Pierce couldn't think of any way that Razor had faked this. It had been clear on the video review that Melvin had hit Razor with the knife. Pierce had seen blood splatters on the floor.

"He slashed Caitlyn too," Pierce said.

"She stopped bleeding by the time we were in the penthouse suite. Something like that shouldn't happen. You're telling me you didn't know about this?"

"My job was to find Jordan and Caitlyn. I'd been briefed on why he was a fugitive and likely places to find him. Later, what they told me about the girl was the genetic altering. We knew it was wings. We'd seen copies of the x-rays."

"You had no idea about the blood?"

"Here's me coming at you straight," Pierce said. "I knew it involved genetics. That's all, not the specifics. Our goal was simple. Bring her in. Best case, we wanted her alive. Worst case, we were told that her body had enough genetic information to meet the agency objectives."

"That's cold."

"I had to stop thinking about what was cold and what wasn't a long time ago. I don't make moral decisions."

"What happened was her fingers were smeared with her blood," Razor said. "I touched my cut after my fingers were smeared with her blood, and a couple minutes later my belly is warm and I look down and the bleeding's stopped. Two hours later, it's a fresh scar. Today, looks like I've had this scar all my life. Is that as scary to you as it is to me?"

"Yeah," Pierce said. *Blood.* Pierce thought of the vials he'd seen in the woman's purse.

"I don't make moral decisions either," Razor said. "Chances are I'm colder than you've ever been. Selling her to the highest bidder is going to be what keeps me alive. Whoever gets her can do what they want with the miracle properties of her blood. Help the human race or sell it for a million dollars an ounce. Doesn't matter to me. Reason I'm coming at you straight is because it's going to be helpful to both of us to understand how much is at stake here."

"You know all I know so far," Pierce said. "I wasn't able to get either of them in Appalachia. Agency mounted a priority hunt for her Outside."

"Including a search for Billy and Theo."

"Want to tell me how you got the glasses with the tracking device?"

"So far," Razor said. "I've told you a lot more than I've heard. I'd like to listen."

"They weren't difficult to find. Appalachian refugees are given work permits, allowed a chance to integrate. We had them followed, kept close surveillance on them, hoping they'd make contact with the girl. I got all the reports. Agency was watching them close and had to rescue them from a soovie camp. We decided at that point it would be easier to track them by GPS and we let them go. About the same time, our computers tracked that she'd been picked up by Enforcers. You know the timeline from there. Video from Melvin's wheelchair gave us enough of a face profile that we found you when you made a visit to Swain. Caitlyn sent you to him, right? Why?"

"You don't get that information yet. Let me ask you again. Who tried killing you?"

"Don't know," Pierce said. "Someone in New York—someone I can trust—is going to find out from her. That's why I dumped her where she could be found when the train gets there."

"The assassin's worth more to you alive than dead. Cold. I like that."

"There's more," Pierce said. "I turned over the operation files to someone inside the agency. It means nobody's going to give up hunting you just because I'm out of it. My guys know I went on the train to meet with you. Whether or not the agency set up the kill attempt, with me missing, they're going to throw ten times the manpower at this to find you."

"I appreciate the warning."

"Isn't you I'm worried about," Pierce said. "The longer you stay alive, the longer I stay alive. So make sure you're just as good against them as you were against me."

Pierce gave Razor a tight smile. "Like you said. Cold."

SEVENTY-THREE

Pierce glanced at Razor as Wilson answered. Pierce put it on speaker.

"What did you find out?" Pierce asked. "Did the agency send the woman killer after me?"

"No," came the answer. "Definitely not. You don't have to worry about anyone inside the agency. It's an outside source. My guess would be your guess. You triggered something by asking about the visitor last night."

"That something won't be going away. I want to play this safe."

"Safe?"

"I've got a source that can lead me to her," Pierce said. Another glance at Razor.

"Who? Where?"

"Not so fast," Pierce said. "I trust you. Let's be clear on a plan of action. I'm thinking if the agency gets her and protects her, she's important enough that nothing is going to happen to your son while we hold her. Stalemate. We have her. They have your son. Gives you time to negotiate for your son. Time to find him."

"Then we protect her with everything the agency can throw at this," Wilson said. "It also protects you. Once we have her, you can come in."

"Good. We're clear. To make it happen, we're going to have to deliver on protecting someone else. You've got the authorization to make it happen."

"I'm listening," Wilson said. "It sounds like you've got me on speaker. So I guess that person is also listening."

"Yeah," Pierce said. "It's the kid who snatched her from us in the first place. Calls himself Razor."

"The one we got on the wheelchair cam? What's he want?"

"Protection. Physical first, immunity second. And some money. Then he'll give her up."

There was no hesitation from Wilson on the other end. "Done."

Razor finally broke into the conversation. "I'll need to see the money in an account. I'll give you the number. You've got five minutes for it to show up."

"And how do we know you can deliver?"

Pierce said. "He's got them in protection himself. In a shanty, guarded by Illegals. He'll take me to them if we have a deal."

"Them?"

"The girl and her two friends. Billy. Theo."

"Only half the money up front. The other half on delivery. And you keep Razor in custody the entire time."

Pierce gave Razor an inquiring glance.

Razor nodded.

Pierce said, "Wilson, at the same time, I want an electronic letter of immunity sent to my attorney. One for the kid. One for me. Signed by you."

"Also done."

"You're the only guy I trust at this point," Pierce said. "Once the agency has her, I become her protection. Short term and long term. We work together to get your son back. Got that?"

"Got it. Back to you in five minutes with confirmation of funds."

Pierce hung up and looked at Razor. "Satisfied?"

Wilson set his phone down on the burnished walnut desk and looked without emotion at the man across from him.

"You heard the entire conversation," Wilson said. "She's with the others from Appalachia. We'll need a stealth chopper. You're military. You authorize it. Come up with whatever reason you need. I haven't been out of the field so long that I can't do this myself. We've got a short window here. We need to be in the air before Pierce realizes the money is not showing up in that account."

"It's not enough that we get the girl," the man said. "I need to know Pierce's location. He's one of two people who can link this to me."

Wilson knew the man's dossier. General Richard Dawkins. Head of World United. Seventy-five years old. Looked barely a day over fifty.

Wilson also knew where the man had been the night before. In the backseat of a private vehicle Pierce had spotted while visiting the scientist.

"You don't get Pierce," Wilson said. "If I could kill you for sending someone after him today, I would."

Dawkins opened his desk drawer. He pulled out a Taser and pointed it with a steady hand at Wilson. "You're the other weak link."

"Please," Wilson said, more in mockery than protest. "Think I'd go into this without my own backup? I've been documenting this from the beginning. I've got something set up in cyberspace, ready to go out if I don't plug in a password once a day. If I'm dead, I don't care who knows about this. But you'll care. Because it will go to the agency. To the military. You won't be safe anywhere."

Dawkins kept the Taser trained on Wilson. His knuckle on the trigger slackened.

Wilson continued to speak calmly. "I'm not a weak link. I've got as much to lose as you do."

Dawkins set the Taser down. "Pierce has to go. He doesn't have anything to lose. If he's not gone, your son is. It's that simple. You choose between the two."

Wilson stared at the ceiling for a long time. He kept staring at it when he finally spoke.

"We know where Pierce is headed," Wilson said. "Same place we are. Only we'll be in and out before he gets there."

Again, a long, long pause. Again, eyes locked on the ceiling.

"Put a couple of snipers on the chopper," Wilson said. "We'll leave them in place to wait for him."

SEVENTY-FOUR

Thursday evening

The skinny one, Theo, had just stepped back into the shanty. There were a half dozen men still outside. Guards.

Still, it was time to move. Mason had decided on dusk. Just as the eastern sky shifted into purples and the western horizon glowed orange. The black of night would be too risky. Too many people around Caitlyn, too many unknown factors. It had been different with the whore and her daughter, Thirsty; in that situation, Mason had been led by a local boy and knew that the two were alone.

Mason didn't want to wait until daylight the next day either. First, his patience was ebbing as his rage was building. All he needed to do was rub his destroyed eye to be reminded of what he wanted to do to her. Second, he didn't know what the new day would bring. Caitlyn had spent time with Billy and Theo and the other one. Discussing what plans?

No, Mason had to act before then.

Dusk was his best option. He'd wait until the light had almost faded, then spring. Like the panther he was. He'd use the Taser to take out as many guards as he could and rely on his knife if the Taser ran short of power.

Mason crept away from the wall that had shielded him during his observations. Waiting for the perfect moment to pounce.

"I need your help," Caitlyn said to Billy.

"I'll do it." Billy had been sitting against the shanty wall. Now he stood. He exhaled, looked toward the door, as if she were calling him to action.

"Listen to me, okay?" Caitlyn hardly spoke above a whisper. "I just want you to listen to me."

He nodded.

"Then sit," she said.

Awkwardly, he found a position near her.

Caitlyn found his presence comforting. She knew he wouldn't have resisted if she reached for one of his hands to hold, but she didn't want the intimacy of contact. She wanted to be in a bubble because it felt like the words were coming out of someone else, not her.

"You were the first to see my wings," she said. "Remember? At the river?"

She'd almost drowned. Billy had waded into the raging water, fought the current, and borne her weight as he pulled her from death. She'd spread her wings to dry, bewildered and terrified and exhilarated. Only moments before, she had soared into space and discovered the mystery of her body's deformity.

"You don't know it," she said, "but I think if you had reacted differently, I would have hated myself. Instead, and I know because I was watching you so closely, you smiled. It was a beautiful smile, William."

Then, even though she wanted to be in a bubble, alone and yet not alone, the memory compelled her to touch his hand. "In that moment, you made me feel just as beautiful. I will always be grateful to you for that."

He kept his head bowed, staring at her long, almost unnatural fingers. She left her hand there.

"William," she said, "I'm not sure I can ever explain to you what it's like to be in the air. The freedom. The first time, it was like getting to a place you never knew existed, until you got there and then realized your entire life you were longing for it, and you also suddenly realize the certainty that it was waiting, like the blood in your veins, something you'd be aware of only when you began to lose it."

"You told me to listen," Billy said. "But I got to say something. Or I'll never find the right time or place to say it. I know what you mean."

He lifted his head. His face was strange mixture of determination and fear. "That's what it was like for me. Meeting you. Not knowing a person could have the feelings I had, but then understanding that's what a person is made for."

Caitlyn touched his face, gently. And was betrayed by wondering what it would be like to touch Razor's face in the same way.

He misinterpreted her slight frown and pulled away. "I'm sorry."

"No," she said. Feeling horrible. Billy was the right one for her. Why did she want Razor? "It's me. That's why you need to listen. Who could ever be with me? The way I am?"

"Caitlyn," Billy began to protest. "Don't you know how beautiful you are?"

"I need you to listen."

He gave a slow and reluctant nod.

"If you gave me the choice, today," she said, "I would say yes to my wings. Yes to being a freak. I would say all that hurt along the way was worth it for what it feels like when I fly. That's why I never went to Swain. I wanted to be me. I didn't want to lose my wings."

She blew air from her lungs in a long, quiet sigh. "The way I am, right now, I will always be hunted. No one around me would be safe. Ever. And when I'm caught..."

She knew it was going to be a struggle to articulate this. She didn't have the medical knowledge. But Billy had told her enough that she could guess at the future.

"When I'm caught, it'll be because they want to make more like me. Experiments. I'll be the one responsible for inflicting this deformity on the babies that are born. They'll be kept prisoners, like me."

She had it now, knew what she was trying to say. "Will they be given a chance to fly, given a chance to find the place that is waiting for them? No. Never."

She didn't have to tell Billy to keep listening. He soaked in her sadness.

"To stay the way I am," she said, "would be selfish. I can't do that. You and Theo, you know where Swain is. Let's call Theo. Then both of you, take me there. For surgery."

"Caitlyn?"

"William, I have to lose my wings. There is no other way."

SEVENTY-FIVE

In a crowded alley, two nondescript men blended in with the Industrials and Illegals around them. Both were armed with agency air pistols. There wouldn't be enough noise to draw any attention when they fired the weapons. The poisoned pellets only had a range of about ten feet and had just enough velocity to break skin.

They were waiting to step in behind their target and shoot him in the back of the neck. The target would feel little more than a vicious wasp sting, but the poison would send him to his knees in seconds, to his death in seconds more.

"There he is," the first one said, pulling his partner's elbow.

"Yup," the second one said. "Rogue agent."

Their target, Carson Pierce, was about ten paces away. He had no chance of realizing anything was wrong. Not in this crowd.

"You got it," the first one said. "No mercy."

Pierce followed Razor through the crowd in the shadows between the shanties. As Pierce stepped around two little girls, one grabbed for his hand. They were five years old, maybe six. Ragged hair and face tattoos, indistinguishable from any other children who'd circled him and begged for money.

Anyone else and Pierce's reaction would have been a counterattack. Here, Pierce simply tried pull away, to disengage without hurting the girl, who laughed and giggled and held on like it was a game. Her friend, too, grabbed Pierce's other hand. She turned her face upward with a big smile and laughed.

Pierce tugged harder and the girls laughed harder. They held tight and dragged their feet.

The crowd's current seemed to shift. Then Pierce realized it wasn't an illusion. Women and other children cleared. He saw men, their tattoos making their expressions inscrutable, moving in quickly. Pierce needed his Taser to defend himself, but the girls were still clinging.

A defensive move would have been simple. The girls were rag dolls. He just needed to jerk them toward his body, into an upraised knee. But something like that was capable of shattering a nose, breaking a jaw. Given enough time to appraise the situation intellectually, maybe Pierce could have forced himself to do it. Maybe not. The girls knew exactly what they were doing. The choice was him or them.

Emotionally, it was certain he couldn't react with that kind of violence against little girls. He made a desperate ineffectual shake of his hands. That was all he had time to do before the men were on him, fingers like talons on his biceps. Arms from behind him, around his neck. He was swarmed and taken down in seconds.

He fought hard to keep his hands in front of him, but there were too many, and in seconds more, he was on his belly, knees on his back, a body across his head, his face pressed into the ground.

They were too smart to disarm him. His gun was programmed to send in a silent alarm if it was moved more than six inches from his body, and it wouldn't fire without recognizing his fingerprints.

Instead, they tied his hands behind his back.

He wondered what would be next. A knife to his throat? A homemade shiv between the ribs?

But all the attackers moved away.

Pierce waited before rolling onto his back and exposing his belly. A second later, he told himself that was stupid. If they meant to hurt him, it would have already happened.

Slowly, he maneuvered himself onto his feet.

Razor was waiting, facing him.

"Don't remember this as part of our discussion," Pierce said. It was obvious that Razor had set up this trap.

"Would have been stupid to bring it up," Razor said. "I need you out of the way."

"No," Pierce said. "You need me."

"Maybe later," Razor said.

"Somebody should explain to you how a deal works. You got your money. And your letter."

"I'll let you in on a secret," Razor said. "I asked for double what I really wanted. The first half of that money is all I need. That letter puts me home free. Gives me a chance to see what I can get from the other side. If they're stupid enough to pay half up front before delivery, then I'll come back to you and we'll do a little more negotiating. See?"

Razor grinned.

He pointed at a nearby shanty, and a half dozen of the Industrials pushed Pierce toward it.

Pierce lost sight of Razor, and seconds later he was inside. Trapped and well guarded. Looking at hours ahead in the heat and smell with his hands already numb from how tightly the rope around his wrists bit into the skin.

SEVENTY-SIX

How do we get out of here?" Caitlyn asked Billy and Theo.

"You can take them," Theo said. "In a fight. There's only five. You can take them."

"I don't like to fight." Billy looked at Theo, then at Caitlyn. "Both of you know that. I don't like hurting people."

Caitlyn didn't want to force Billy to do anything.

"We don't trust Razor," Theo told Billy. "If we could trust him, why would he keep her and us here like this? Why not let us do what we want?"

"He said it was protection," Billy answered.

"Right," Theo said. "Protection for himself."

Theo didn't hide his exasperation and pleaded for help from a higher source. "Caitlyn. Do you trust Razor?"

That was the big question, wasn't it? She didn't know. And she didn't know if that's why she found Razor so exciting. She trusted Billy. But didn't feel the same excitement around him, the almost delicious uncertainty that came with the mystery that cloaked Razor.

Did she want to wait until Razor returned? Or should she try to escape again, relying on Billy?

Billy took the decision away from her.

He stepped over to the wall of the shanty, where the framing was exposed.

"Maybe we don't need to fight," Billy said. He grabbed one of the beams with both hands. He leaned back, lifted one foot, and pushed it against another beam.

Billy was deceptively soft in appearance for such a big man. No definition of muscles when his body was at rest.

Here, with full exertion, his arms seemed to grow. His biceps bulged, and Caitlyn realized Billy's arms were thicker than Theo's legs.

It wasn't just the framework that he needed to break, but the metal sheeting that formed the exterior wall and the assortment of nails and rivets and screws that held the sheeting to the framework.

He was fighting more than that; Billy was fighting his own strength, pulling his arms in one direction, against the push of his legs in another. Another man might have grunted. Billy's face, however, settled into serenity as he focused all his strength on prying apart the frame. It wasn't Billy who eventually groaned, but the framework. The popping wasn't gristle or muscle or tendons, but the screws and nails and rivets that could no longer endure the forces against them. And finally, the opposite beam snapped, where Billy was putting all his pressure against the wood with one foot.

Billy half staggered but managed to keep his balance.

The wall had literally separated. Outside, the dusk of sky and the outlines of other shanties.

Billy breathed heavily but said nothing. Didn't even look to Caitlyn for praise.

Theo skipped to the wall, examined the broken metal sheeting, skipped back to Caitlyn.

"Like Samson!" Theo said. "Just like Samson. Except *I'm* blind and Billy's not. Nobody can stop us!"

Billy managed a bashful grin at Theo's exuberance. "I think we only need a few minutes head start. They won't know what direction we went. Plus it's getting dark. They shouldn't be able to find us out there."

"Thank you," Caitlyn said. She pushed thoughts of Razor out of her mind. She didn't need him, and Razor was only trouble. Just like her wings. "Let's go."

Mason saw the wall of the shanty burst. Then saw the three of them. Coming out the back.

Perfect!

As that thought crossed his mind, Mason felt a sound. That was the best way to describe it. There was noise, but it didn't quite reach his ears. At least not for a few moments.

Helicopter?

Mason hesitated, looked upward.

At that moment, the sky pierced him. Except it wasn't the sky. It wasn't the light from the chopper that tore through him.

It was unreasoning terror that collapsed him as surely as if he'd Tasered himself.

❖

"Billy," Theo said. He pointed upward at the dusk of the sky. "It's the sound again."

"What sound?" Impatience rarely bothered Billy. But they were on the run. Billy didn't feel smart enough to judge whether the three of them were sufficiently clear to have the luxury to stop. Especially because Theo's keen sense of hearing, combined with his usual nervousness and a vast imagination, meant the sound could have been anything.

"The night we went into the hospital. When everyone freaked out. You know, in the soovie camp."

Just the memory of the overwhelming dread was enough to stop Billy cold. "You sure?"

"Not sure." Theo cocked his head. "Now I'm sure. It's closer."

"What are you talking about?" Caitlyn asked.

"Can't explain," Theo said. "Just that all of a sudden it felt like a room-ful of monsters were going to rip me apart and that they were backing me into a corner. I couldn't move. The monsters weren't like anything you could explain. More like roaring demons, smoke and fire. It's the freakiest thing ever."

"Where do we go?" Billy asked. "Where do we go?"

Billy wished he was better at thinking. With the shanties in all directions, there seemed like no clear path in any direction, especially with people in clusters along the paths. Until now, all the people around them had provided a perfect screen from any pursuers. Now the memory of that overwhelming dread already made him feel trapped.

"We keep walking," Caitlyn said. "We don't run. That's what's going to draw attention."

Billy imagined he felt a breeze, then realized it wasn't his imagination. The *thump-thump* sound followed. His first instinct was to pull Caitlyn close.

That's how the spotlight pinned them.

Caitlyn in Billy's arms. Theo, half turned, looking upward, shielding his eyes with his arms against the piercing white glare.

Something bounced off Billy's shoulder. A small canister.

"Theo!" Billy shouted.

Theo saw it too. Theo dove on it.

It didn't matter.

A split second later, panic overwhelmed Billy. He staggered in his desperation to pull Caitlyn out of the spotlight. But she was in a panic, flailing and screaming, and a part of his consciousness realized that to hold her, he'd have to apply so much force it would crush her.

Billy fell to his knees, dimly aware of the sounds of screams from the paths between the shanties beyond Caitlyn.

The spotlight that kept them in a circle didn't move.

It was difficult for Billy to keep his thoughts coherent. Fear had buckled him, wrapped him so deep into himself that his leg muscles were cramping and his face hurt from the rictus of terror. Yet much as he wanted to close his eyes and wait to die, he was driven by a need to protect Caitlyn.

Too frozen to help, he kept her in his vision.

It seemed like a monster had descended from the sky, the black-masked figure swaying in midair, hanging from a shiny cable that glinted in the spotlight.

Then the figure dropped and knelt over Caitlyn, whose flailing had diminished to shuddering spasms.

Above the roaring of the machine above them and the roaring in his mind, Billy yelled in futile rage, on his side, curled in agony, unable to move.

Billy was incapable of pegging movement to time, and he swirled through a vortex of altered consciousness as he vainly tried to force his arm to reach out for Caitlyn.

The black-masked figure stood again. The cable seemed attached to Caitlyn's body. The black figure sprang upward with distorted slow motion in Billy's perception. It seemed like the black figure hung in the air again.

Until he was gone.

And, as if pulled by gravity, Caitlyn's body rose upward in pursuit.

SEVENTY-SEVEN

Caitlyn was on her back, on a table, hands bound. In a room, but she didn't know where. A hood had been placed over her head.

She heard footsteps. Soft footsteps. Someone creeping up to where she was strapped helplessly to the table.

Caitlyn didn't breathe. Couldn't breathe.

Worse than the sound of footsteps was the silence when the footsteps stopped.

Caitlyn knew someone was standing beside her. Examining her body. She tried to put herself in another world. She tried to remember the sensation of flying, tried, in her mind, to be soaring over a valley in Appalachia, wind in her face, a different kind of silence that came with that exquisite solitude. Not this tortured, silent prison.

But she couldn't remove herself. Someone was beside her. Waiting. For what?

Then a feathery sensation on her face. Fingers on the hood over her head. And slowly, the hood began to be lifted.

Razor stepped into the shanty with Billy and Theo. Pierce was on his feet, watching.

They looked at him with coldness.

Razor spoke with savage anger. "Tell him."

"Gone," Theo said. "She's gone. They took her. Helicopter. Just like the time before when they came for me and Billy and took us to the hospital."

Billy said nothing. Pierce noticed a trail of blood coming from a bandage on Billy's right bicep.

"You mean like a panic attack?" Pierce asked.

"Panic?" Theo said. "I couldn't think. Like a hundred lions were roaring at me from two feet away."

"Fear pheromones," Pierce said. "Something only the agency has. But that's impossible. It wasn't Wilson."

Pierce directed his next words at Razor. "The leak is from your side."

Razor pointed at Billy. "He was still in panic. It took seven guys to hold him down. We dug out a bug. Tracking device. From inside one of his injuries you guys had fixed at the hospital."

"I didn't know about it," Pierce said. "Only the one in Theo's glasses."

Razor said. "I got some kid to swallow the bug. He's headed back to the soovie camps. In case they're still tracking."

Pierce spoke again, more to himself. "I didn't know about it."

"Still trust Wilson with your life?" Razor asked. "Or want to check my account information for the money that never showed up?"

SEVENTY-EIGHT

When the hood was pulled away, Caitlyn saw a woman's face. High cheekbones, green eyes. Auburn hair. She was midforties, maybe older. The light came from across her shoulders, softening her face with shadow. She wore a long, dark skirt and cashmere sweater that exhibited how trim she was. A waft of perfume hit Caitlyn.

Caitlyn lifted her cuffed wrists. "You have a key?"

The woman shook her head.

"I need to undress you," the woman said. "Only briefly. If you fight, I'll need help. If you don't, we'll have privacy. I'd rather we began our relationship with cooperation. It will be better for you. I promise."

"Who are you?" Caitlyn asked in a monotone. She saw no sense in fighting something that was inevitable, as dictated by the cuffs. Even if she overcame that handicap to fight this woman, the men who had taken her into the chopper were probably in the other room nearby.

"Jessica Charmaine."

"You're government."

The woman ignored her statement and moved behind her, unzipping the microfabric Jordan had given Caitlyn. In Appalachia. In another lifetime. When Caitlyn's world was simple. She and a father whom she adored.

Caitlyn kept her back muscles tight and her wings furled.

"Amazing," the woman whispered. "For a gene code sequence like this to work. Just amazing. The intertwining of muscle and bone and nerves and blood. It's like adding extra arms to a body."

"It's like making someone a freak," Caitlyn said. "Without their permission."

"No one gives permission to be born," the woman said. "You are a unique testament to survival. Tens of thousands of embryos didn't make it past the sixteen-cell stage. The hundreds that did gestated less than a month. Barely a dozen made it to late term. You are the lottery winner. The only one to live. Can you open your wings for me?"

"Open the cuffs."

"He wouldn't let me."

"Don't tell him. Whoever he is."

"Please don't be difficult. Neither of us has a choice in this. We're going to be together a long time. When you have babies, I'll be the only one here for you."

Caitlyn didn't want to give herself any silence to think through the implications. Anger and pride, that's what she needed to use as a shield.

"You're a midwife," Caitlyn said, scornfully. Still, she couldn't escape a sensation of cold. Babies. Not baby. Babies. As in year after year. Her life as an experiment was going to continue. Suicide flashed through her mind. Not driven by hopelessness. But by the core of her anger. Suicide to thwart the experiment of people she hated.

"I'm a scientist. One of the best. Can you open your wings for me? I'd like to see the structure."

"They are not like bird wings." Caitlyn snapped out the words. "My arms work with the wings. I can soar, like a glider. If you want the wings open, I need my wrists free so I can support them with my arms."

From behind, Charmaine didn't reply. Instead, the woman scientist continued to remove all of Caitlyn's microfabric. The folded letters fell on the ground. Charmaine ignored them.

Standing rigid, eyes shut in anger and humiliation, Caitlyn willed herself not to shed a single tear. She drew deep breaths, imagining each sucking in anger. She would not succumb to self-pity.

She felt the woman's hand on different places of her body. Gentle poking. Squeezing.

Caitlyn remained a statue. There were men outside the room. If she fought now, they would enter and exponentially increase her humiliation.

I'm a zoo animal, Caitlyn thought. *She's my keeper.*

When Charmaine had finished the examination and dressed her, she stepped in front of Caitlyn again. "You've begun your menstrual cycles?"

Caitlyn couldn't help herself. She spat in Charmaine's face.

Charmaine shook her head sadly and wiped her face with the sleeve of her cashmere sweater. "I have to ask these questions. Or would you prefer a complete exam? One way or another, the general is going to find out if you carry eggs."

"You make me feel so much better about myself," Caitlyn said. "Thank you."

"You're welcome. I don't see any sense in euphemisms or dancing around issues. I find life is easier when you are realistic about any situation."

"That's not why I feel better," Caitlyn said. "I've always believed it's how you look that makes you a monster. But now that I've met you, I see it's not true. Monsters don't have to look like monsters."

"You want me to react," Charmaine answered. "But you're not going to be able to manipulate me like that. I can see a bigger picture. You can't. Have you begun your cycles?"

Caitlyn set her jaws tight. Until she found a way to escape or kill herself, she would not give any cooperation.

"I've seen that stubbornness before," Charmaine said. "Jordan passed it on to you, didn't he?"

Caitlyn felt herself flinch. She desperately wanted to ask what that meant, but then her sullen anger would be gone, and she'd be in a position of weakness.

"I really want to be your friend," Charmaine said. "And we'll have lots and lots of time to talk. Your father and I were very close once. But he couldn't see the big picture. When he found out he had fertilized some of the eggs, including the one that developed into you..."

Caitlyn turned her head toward Charmaine. Staring. This was an admission of curiosity, and they both knew it.

"Don't be so stubborn," Charmaine said. Smiling. "We've shared him. At different times in our lives. We can start with that as a bond."

Caitlyn blinked. Jordan was her biological father? Like she'd believed all her life until the last few months?

"Don't look at me like I seduced him," Charmaine said. "Believe me, I tried. He was speaking out in meetings, against some of the, um, advanced experiments. I thought if I could have him, he'd stop. Apparently he was more tempting to me than I was to him."

She sighed theatrically. "I became a woman scorned. But also a woman with access to drugs to knock him out, and the knowledge of how to medically collect what I needed him to contribute to fertilizing eggs. For him, it was like falling asleep after a late meal at the lab. He didn't discover I'd collected what I needed until long after, when he learned his paternity of some of the developing embryos. I thought it would be enough for him to finally go along with our experiments."

"You were wrong about him," Caitlyn said. She thought of the pieces of the story that she knew about Jordan's defiance. How he and Swain had sabotaged the program beyond repair. How Jordan had fled with the surrogate mother who carried Caitlyn. How Jordan had taken Caitlyn into Appalachia to escape the agency. And she thought of the letter Jordan had given her.

. . .holding you in the first moments outside the womb, I was overwhelmed by protective love.

He was her father after all.

"But I was right about the new gene sequence techniques," Charmaine said. "You are living proof. He was a whistle-blower, and we turned it on him. He became the fugitive, not us. It's delayed everything twenty years, but in a month, with what I learn from your gene code, I'll be on track again."

Charmaine smiled again, wiping hair away from her own face. "What's truly amazing about you is that your blood is going to give me that twenty years back. And then some."

"Monster."

"Come on," Charmaine said, ignoring the venom in Caitlyn's voice. "We'll get you back in that tight fabric. Time to meet the man who made all of this possible. He's not in the mood to wait."

SEVENTY-NINE

To get back into the city core, Pierce had to show his NI identification to the guard at the outer wall checkpoint, knowing it was a gamble.

If Wilson was acting on behalf of the agency, Pierce would already be tagged on the computer system and be held for immediate arrest. If Wilson was acting alone, chances were Wilson wouldn't want to alert the agency by taking overt steps against Pierce.

The guard, pimply faced and badly in need of extra testosterone to fill in his attempt at a goatee, handed back the identification with a bored expression but looked past Pierce at Razor, Billy, and Theo.

"With me. Custody," Pierce said. Then, throwing in jargon he guessed the kid would like, "It's a need-to-know basis."

"No handcuffs?"

"Death chips," Pierce answered. He leaned forward. "Keep it secret. Agency's just come up with them. We inject the chips into the thigh. They try to escape, *bam*. Remote control activates the cyanide."

"Cool," the kid said, waving all of them through.

Pierce didn't allow himself to relax, however, as they stepped onto the next train into the depths of the city.

Since Wilson had already lied, there was one other possibility. That Pierce had been tagged by the agency. Not for custody at a checkpoint, but to leave an alert in the agency system, to be tracked for another kill attempt as soon as logistics made it possible.

"Wow!" Theo chortled inside Razor's suite at the Pavilion. "People actually live like this?"

He was twirling in a circle, arms spread, taking in the luxury of the hotel room.

"Pick up the phone," Razor told Theo. He'd already moved to the desk in the corner, racing his fingers over the touchscreen computer.

"Huh?"

The computer screen came to life.

"Pick up the phone," Razor repeated. "Dial seven eight. Trust me."

Theo tiptoed to the phone, as if afraid to wake himself up from a dream. He dialed and waited for an answer. Then he straightened and froze. He covered the mouthpiece and whispered to Razor. "They asked what I want to eat."

"Tell them," Razor said. "Anything you want."

Theo looked to Billy, his hand still over the mouthpiece. "He's kidding, right?"

Billy shook his head, negative.

"Milkshakes," Theo said into the phone. "One of each flavor. Three cheeseburgers. Three fries. A pizza. No, two pizzas."

Hand over the phone again, speaking to Billy. "Anything for you?"

"We'll share," Billy said. "Don't want you to bust."

"Couple of steaks, medium rare," Pierce said, pulling up a chair beside Razor.

"Steaks?" Theo said. "Didn't know we could have steaks."

Back into the phone, Theo said. "Change the cheeseburgers to steaks. Add two more. Medium rare. One other thing. Do you bring up dessert with it, or should I order that later?"

Pause. "Okay. Chocolate cake."

Another pause. "No. A chocolate cake. The whole thing."

Theo hung up the phone. "Very nice."

"Into the bathroom," Razor said without looking back. "Shower. With soap. Stay in until the food arrives. You need it bad. Then Billy's turn."

Theo zipped into the bathroom. As he closed the door, his admiring voice drifted outward. "You have got to be kidding!"

Billy stood with his hands in his pockets. Unsure where to look.

"We're going to find her," Razor said.

Billy nodded, didn't smile.

"Check this," Pierce announced from the chair at his computer. "Check this out. Holly came through with a few requests."

The screen had about a half dozen icons in a horizontal row, each a thumbnail of a photo.

Pierce touched the first one, and it zoomed open, showing the head and shoulders shot of a woman with straight auburn hair.

"Jessica Charmaine," the computer announced in monotone.

Pierce brought up the computer menu and silenced the speak-aloud feature. He could read much faster than listen.

Jessica Charmaine. The file information was minimal. It reported that she had a PhD and was a scientist in the now-defunct Genesis Project. Personal information was brief too.

Razor reached past Pierce, double-tapping the font with Charmaine's address. It expanded to twenty-four-point size.

"That's where Swain told me to bring Caitlyn," Razor said. "How much you want to bet that's where Caitlyn is?"

Pierce's hands were fluid on the touchscreen, bringing up a map with a satellite view. "Not long to get there. We should have access to the neighborhood. But if they're inside, I doubt we're going to be able to just march in."

"Getting there is a start," Razor said.

Pierce leaned back, obviously in thought. His head brushed against Billy, who had moved in closer.

"There's the man I met once when I came into DC from Lynchburg," Billy said pointing over Pierce's shoulder at unlabeled photos of the scientists from the Genesis Project. "Swain."

"Don't see him," Razor said.

"Can I touch?" Billy asked.

"Knock yourself out."

Billy's big hand reached out. He found an icon and gingerly pressed it. The photo opened.

"There," Billy said. "Swain."

Razor squinted. "That's not the Swain I met."

Pierce looked at Billy. "Me neither," he said.

EIGHTY

Wilson was standing at the glass wall that divided the large room in half. Behind him, it was set up like a combination of science lab and operating room. He gave that little thought. He was mesmerized by horrid fascination, staring at the two hybrids behind the glass. Like a pair of half-formed cave men.

They were standing over a severely mangled human body.

Both hybrids were turned toward Wilson, heads cocked at an angle that suggested, despite their obvious blindness, that they were aware of his presence.

Wilson had seen a lot of violent death in his three decades at the agency. But he was having difficulty with the body on the other side of the glass. He was compelled to ask the obvious question.

"Who was that?"

"An actor." As Dawkins spoke, the hybrids, in sync, lurched toward the glass. "Once we discovered that Jordan Brown had been living in Appalachia with the third embryo still alive, the real Swain was helpful in giving us all the information we needed. Let's just say pain strongly motivated Swain. We removed Swain. Actually, gave him to the hybrids. Then we hired the actor to pose as Swain and live in Swain's house to wait for Jordan or the girl. Gave him alot of background to be able to play the part. Where else would Jordan go for help? With good reason, as you can see, I couldn't trust that the agency would find her. We pulled all the long-time Industrials from Swain's household and replaced them with new ones who believed the actor was Swain. His job was to keep us informed if Caitlyn ever showed up. Now his job is no longer necessary, and we don't want any leaks of any kind. So the phony Swain had a chance to spend time—short and brutal as it was—with the hybrids."

"But—"

"Throwing him to the hybrids?" Dawkins anticipated. "He knew too much background. When they can eat human protein, it makes their blood more potent."

Wilson failed to keep the repugnant expression off his face.

"Spare the moral outrage," Dawkins said. "Those two are keeping your son alive."

The angle of the light gave a reflection of Dawkins's face. Wilson didn't have to turn his head much to glance at the man.

Dawkins was shoulder high to Wilson. No word suited him better than *dapper*. Lightly graying, trim hair. Lightly graying, trim mustache. Trim, compact body in a trim, compact suit. Hands behind his back, surveying the hybrids too.

"Charmaine says they're deaf," Dawkins said. "She thinks they can feel the vibration of sounds, which alerts them to us. My voice makes the glass wall move slightly, and they know it. They have an incredible sense of smell. She thinks they're psychic too; you know, the way pets are waiting at the door when owners come home. I think she makes too much of it. She's fonder of them than she should be. And she's the only person they don't attack. I think they think she's their mother." He laughed softly. "And given her role in producing them, it's more true than not."

"Their blood...," Wilson said.

"These came from a pool of embryos with a gene change to overcome the limits of how many times a cell can divide without corrupting its DNA. The Hayflick Limit. That's why we die, you know. Eventually our DNA just wears out. When these two made it to term, Charmaine quickly discovered a couple of things. First, their myostatin blockers were altered. There are no limits on their muscle growth."

Dawkins gestured over his shoulder. "Every six to eight weeks, we have to pare their muscles. These hybrids are strong beyond imagination. We have to send in a gas to paralyze them when we need to operate. If we don't cut back the muscles, they literally begin to squeeze themselves to death. And second, and more importantly, the cell growth in their muscles is tied into the unique qualities of their blood."

Dawkins paused. "Look at me."

Wilson did.

"A little over twenty years ago, doctors informed me about my death sentence. They gave me six months, tops. Leukemia. Just like your son. I get dosed by their blood once a week. Don't ask me for the scientific details; Charmaine can tell you. But it knocks out the leukemia."

Thinking of how the blood vials kept his son alive, Wilson said with accusation, "Twenty years. Think of everyone you could have helped with this."

"How old do I look?" Dawkins asked.

Wilson knew the man's age. It was in the files. "You're seventy-three."

"I didn't ask how old I am," Dawkins snapped. "How old do I look?"

"Maybe fifty."

"Most people assume it's plastic surgery," Dawkins said. "It's not. I don't have an aging portrait hidden somewhere either."

Wilson was puzzled. It must have shown.

"Dorian Gray." Dawkins sighed.

It still didn't make sense to Wilson, but he had more important questions. "You're saying..."

"Their blood has basically stopped the aging process for me. Instead of suggesting I should share, tell me what would happen if that got out as public knowledge. Presidents and generals, the people with the most power, would demand to be given a lease on life. Then celebrities. Everyone would make a case for why they deserve it. And when they don't get the blood, then what? War. Really. People are too afraid of death, too desperate to live. These two hybrids can only give a limited amount of their blood. And they are incapable of reproduction."

"Find funding to research what it takes to replicate this blood."

"Think it through." Dawkins was exasperated. "That wouldn't solve the first problem. Men with armies demanding vials of blood from the hybrids. The hybrids wouldn't live long enough for the research to come up with answers."

"Make the research secret."

"Only three people know. Me. Charmaine. Now you. Think a lab with dozens of scientists would keep this secret? It would be hell again—the scientists themselves would be stealing blood. It's a fountain of youth."

Dawkins smoothed his mustache. "Besides, I've been funding this research in secret. Charmaine has spent the last twenty years in this hidden lab trying to recover the data that was lost when Jordan Brown destroyed the Genesis Project. Now we've got the girl. Her eggs. We have a creature that can reproduce. Once Charmaine maps her genetic code and once we harvest the eggs, we'll be much closer to the secret."

Dawkins abruptly smiled. But it was a cold smile. "You tell me. Say we manage to replicate this. Make it widely available. Who gets to live longer and who doesn't? People with money to buy it? Or people with special abilities, like top scientists or engineers? Or does everyone get it?"

Wilson thought of the decision he'd made. Choosing his son, discarding Pierce.

"What happens to the world's population?" Dawkins asked. "What happens by doubling the human life span? This is something to keep under the lid of Pandora's box. Do I need to explain that common literary allusion too?"

Wilson didn't answer.

"I've only told you this," Dawkins said, "because you have a gun pointed at my head."

Wilson held up his empty hands.

"Your clever little password bomb." Dawkins spoke with intellectual assurance that matched his dapper appearance, waving his hands in elegant, tight circles. "It makes you part of the team. We can't get rid of you, but you depend on us too much to explode your bomb. You need your son to live. We need you."

Dawkins continued, and Wilson realized the man liked the center stage.

"Charmaine and I have maintained this basement lab since before the Wars. Just the two of us. For her, it's been a lonely life. I don't pretend that our affair is anything but convenient for her. It will be nice to have someone in your position to lean on when we need more help. It's a Faustian deal—hope you catch that one—and like me, you'll learn to love it. Our will to live is so strong it overcomes most of what you once thought repugnant. Choose your metaphor when it comes to survival. The ends justify the means. Drowning men grasping at straws. Etcetera. Etcetera."

The outer door opened. Dawkins turned as Charmaine pushed Caitlyn into the room, almost shiny in the black microfabric that clothed her.

"Here it is," Dawkins told Wilson. "Our basket of eggs."

EIGHTY-ONE

Tell me how you see the situation," Pierce said to Razor. "Let's strip this down to the simplest terms."

"I'm not in on this anymore," Razor said. "Yeah, I want to help her, but not that badly."

Billy was in the shower. Room service food had arrived, and Theo had a milkshake in one hand and a steak in the other. Holding the steak like a sandwich, he bit into it. Razor and Pierce, sitting on chairs pushed away from the computer's touchscreen, were ignoring the trays, which were on the bed in the hotel room.

"Hypothetically then. You're sharp. I could use your help."

"She's at the house," Razor said. "Charmaine's house. That's how we have to proceed. I was supposed to deliver her there. They could move her after that, but why take the risk? Once she's hidden, she's safe. Swain—the guy staying in Swain's house to pretend he was Swain—has no idea I'm working with you. He'll have no idea I told you where to look. Besides, what else do you have?"

"Okay."

"So we need to decide who is going. And what to do once we're there."

"What's our goal?" Pierce asked.

"To get Caitlyn."

"Why?"

"Protecting her protects us," Razor said. "You and I are loose ends otherwise. Only way for them to clean us up is to get rid of us. Unless we break this loose first."

"Who goes? And how do we get her?"

"One determines the other."

"Yeah," Pierce said. "Two options for who goes. Us. Or the agency. We go, it's a longer shot that we get her out. Fewer resources."

"You're not making a call to the agency," Razor said.

"You telling me not to call?"

"Predicting. Otherwise you would have made the call already. You still don't know who to trust."

"Wish it was different," Pierce said. "But that's true too."

"So it's down to us," Razor said. "Logistically, we're close enough to get there fast. You've got identification to get us through any gates."

"And when we get there?" Pierce was grilling Razor the same way he grilled the agents on his team. Giving them a chance to come up with the solution. Giving them a vested interest in making the solution work.

"House will have security cameras," Razor said. "If she's there, no way the house is unprotected."

"I can get around that," Pierce said. "Computer geek. Owes me big-time. He won't try to block the system. He can get into a residential system and reroute any alarms. People inside won't know a thing."

Temporary silence. Then, from Razor. "They going to have anyone else with them? Soldiers? Agency enforcers?"

"The more people they bring in, the tougher it is to keep everything secret. So, no."

"I've got a knife," Razor said. "You've got an agency weapon, right?"

"Doesn't get us inside."

This time, the silence was longer, except for Theo's determined slurping of his second milkshake.

"Smoke them out?" Razor asked.

"If you mean that literally, it's going to bring in the fire department. Remember, we need Caitlyn. We can't get anyone official involved here."

Theo burped. Then spoke four words. "I've got an idea."

He blurted it out. Razor and Pierce exchanged thoughtful glances.

"Remember," Razor said. "I was just in on the discussion on a theoretical level."

"Meaning?" Pierce asked.

"You figure out how to do it from here," Razor said. "I'm not a team person. Count me out."

"T. R. Zornenbach is a sick kid," Holly said. "Has an ongoing prescription for HRT."

She'd just finished showering when Pierce knocked on her hotel room door. She'd cracked the door open and told him he had to wait in the hallway until she threw something on. Her hair was wet and she had a towel in her hand. Barefoot, she was in jeans and a loose blue sweatshirt with the sleeves cut off. She sat on the small couch along the wall. No luxury suite for her.

"HRT." For obvious reasons, Pierce hadn't given much thought to this thread of the investigation.

"Hormone replacement therapy. In dosages that suggest without it he'd be like a woman; he's injecting a mixture of testosterone and human chorionic gonadotropin." Tight smile. "You should be impressed I can repeat that without referring to my notes."

"Very."

"That's assuming I still care about impressing you." Long pause, the significant type of pause that Pierce recognized as universal when a woman was about to skewer a man. "Want to tell me why I can't upload that information or anything else to the op-site? It's just gone."

"Things are shifting fast," Pierce said.

"So fast that lower-level ops who don't know why we're chasing Caitlyn now don't get to know why the op-site is gone."

Keeping her eyes locked on Pierce, she began to dry her hair, using both hands on the towel, rubbing it back and forth with vigor. Shapely, muscular arms. And a glare on her face that was a clear indication for Pierce that this was not a good time to admire her arms or get caught admiring her arms, even if he'd been in a mood to let that distract him.

"Things are shifting fast."

"Razor meet you on the train?" She stopped toweling her hair and threw the towel to the side of the room. Ice princess gone. Happy to let Pierce know she was more than irritated. "Perhaps you could have informed the low-level ops of that at some point during the day instead of disappearing?"

"Things are shifting fast." He was watching her face, trying to read whether she knew what had happened in the last few hours. He decided if she did, she was very capable of hiding it.

"How fast?" Her hair was now spiky.

"I know where Caitlyn is. A private residence in one of the Influential quarters. I've called in a favor and had the home security rerouted. I'm going in to get her."

"With me, of course."

"No," Pierce said. "This goes wrong, it's a career killer to whoever goes to the house. The residence belongs to an Influential. I don't have a warrant."

"You just told me home security will be down," she said. "It goes right, it's a career maker."

"It goes right, and I'm going to remember who had my back. I need you in a safe place to call in support."

Which was true. And false. If it went right, Holly would get the next pay grade. But the lie was that Pierce intended to call in support. He still couldn't believe Wilson had turned and wasn't going to do anything that would show up in a file until he'd resolved that.

"How about giving Jeremy the backup role? I want in on this." She ran her fingers through her hair. Pierce was human enough to want to be able to trust her. She looked good in the sweatshirt.

"I've got him on something else," Pierce said. "And now is about the time I mention we're not think-tanking this. I've just given you an order."

While Pierce liked team members who weren't afraid of challenging him or his ideas, to her credit, Holly blinked a few times and simply said, "Jessica Charmaine's address?"

Holly was sharp, and Pierce had anticipated it, so his reply was smooth and not a lie. "She was helpful in providing the true location."

Pierce had given a lot of thought to the woman assassin who'd followed him onto the train. She hadn't been an NI agent. Chances were, she'd been reporting to Dawkins. But she couldn't have gotten close to Pierce unless someone on Pierce's team had been updating Pierce's location. For someone outside the agency.

Pierce gave Holly an address about four blocks away from the address he had for the scientist Charmaine. Close enough that if Holly was in on the betrayal, the chopper searchlights would tell him. Far enough away, he'd be safe from the distraction.

"Just so I understand," Holly said. "You're going in. Alone."

Before he could answer, his phone vibrated. He glanced at a text on the screen. PACKAGE AT LOBBY DESK UNDER NAME U. O. MEE.

Pierce smiled. He had called in another favor for a priority unofficial delivery of agency material that regulations demanded go through a tight official-supply chain. And now Pierce owed the guy. Big-time.

"The less you know right now," Pierce told Holly, "the better for you. Really."

He didn't spell it out further. NI regulations were such that if an agent knew of another agent breaching regulations and didn't report the breach, both agents were equally guilty.

"I don't care about me," she snapped. "I care that you make it back safe. I can help make sure it happens."

"I go in alone, there's a chance I'll find out a lot more than I would by sending in choppers and searchlights and a SWAT team."

She let out a deep breath. "Get this done, Pierce. Just know that after you're back, I'll be putting in a request for a transfer from your little unit."

"Not a problem," he said, thinking of what he'd once told Wilson about Holly. *That'll change. She doesn't know me yet.* "Like I said before, not everyone likes the lone wolf thing."

EIGHTY-TWO

S he is remarkable in more ways than you can imagine," Charmaine told Dawkins and Wilson, as if Caitlyn wasn't standing there. "As far as I can tell, her skeletal structure is human, but the bones are stronger and lighter. Only x-rays will confirm. Her muscles are stronger, pound for pound, than human muscles. And shortly I'll be able to confirm blood content."

"Eggs?" Dawkins asked.

"That's next," Charmaine said, pointing at a surgery table in the corner of the room. "We've got what we need to check. No sense wasting time."

It was surreal to Caitlyn. The large room was divided down the center by a floor-to-ceiling glass wall. The lighting on her half was subdued, except for lamps hanging directly above some operating beds, casting a harsh, sharp light on the sheets.

Despite the implied threat of the assorted medical apparatus, Caitlyn could not help but stare at the other side of the glass, where two large, hairy, humanlike creatures were upright on two legs, with stumps for arms. Both had the sides of their heads pressed against the glass. Behind them, a mangled body.

"They're curious," Charmaine told Caitlyn, noticing her gaze. "They can't hear, but the vibrations on the glass tell them they are not alone."

"They?" Caitlyn was shrinking away.

"Your cousins," Dawkins snapped. "Let's get things started."

Charmaine snapped back at Dawkins. "It's natural that she has questions. I promised her I'd be open with her."

"You don't need that kind of emotional engagement," Dawkins said.

"She's going to be stressed enough as it is. If she knows what's happening, it will make things easier on all of us."

"Just get it done," Dawkins said. "Confirm we've got eggs. Confirm her blood has what we need."

Caitlyn was still reeling inside. Those hideous creatures were her cousins? Her focus changed, however, when she saw Charmaine grab a syringe from a nearby table. It would have been easier to give up. What hope was there?

But she charged forward, bringing her shackled wrists upward to strike down on the smug man who so casually ordered Charmaine. The other man, the stocky square-headed one with the short, graying red hair, stepped in front of her and swung an arm around her chest and pulled her in close.

She tried kicking at him, but it was futile.

His restraint was gentle.

"I hate this," he said softly. "But you are saving my son."

She tried biting his arm. Then felt the needle jab her thigh.

"Don't let her fall," Charmaine said to the big man. "It's going to hit her quick."

They'd crossed the expansive lawn through shadows of large oaks, the sound of their footsteps cushioned by the thick grass, the sound of cicadas in the heat of the night and, most importantly, protected by the hum of the HVAC unit at the rear of the house.

With Billy and Theo standing nearby, Pierce knelt beside the HVAC. He had a small flashlight with an intense beam and immediately found both intake vents. The one to the left was for combustion and drew air only when the HVAC needed to pump heat. The other was for fresh air and drew outside air into the house when the interior fans or air conditioning was on. Pierce was not a heating technician; this knowledge was agency 101, as Theo and Billy were about to find out.

The HVAC's hum told him the air-conditioning unit had kicked in and was fighting summer heat. Pierce confirmed it by turning his palm upward. He held it close to the intake and felt the sucking motion as it drew exterior air into the unit to be cooled and moved through the house. Pierce pulled open the NI pouch that had been in the U. O. MEE package at the hotel front desk. It was a big lead-lined pouch used specifically for hiding the contents from scanners. Getting it past the checkpoint had been as simple as showing his NI badge and pointing at the NI logo on the side of the pouch.

Pierce handed out the gas masks—carbon filters that covered the nose and mouth, strapped into place with a couple of elastic bands around the back of the head.

They'd reviewed how to handle this at the hotel. He wasn't going to repeat it here.

All three put the masks into place.

"Safety off," Pierce told Billy in a voice muffled by the carbon filters. He handed Billy a dart pistol from the bag and another for himself.

The big kid checked the mechanism. Pierce did the same. Each pistol had twenty darts for rapid-fire action, each dart with fast-acting tranquilizers. Used when agents wanted to do more than disperse a crowd.

"Ready for countdown?" Pierce asked Theo.

The skinny kid's instructions were to mentally count to sixty. Nothing as complicated as coordinating watches, which neither Billy or Theo had anyway. All Pierce and Billy needed was enough time to get into position. Billy at the rear door. Pierce at the front.

"Ready," Theo said, nodding in his gas mask.

That's when Pierce pulled the remaining item out of the NI pouch.

A canister of fear pheromones. Large enough to completely infiltrate a four-story hotel. With all the chances Pierce was taking here, at least he could guarantee saturation of every single cubic inch of the interior of the house.

"You'll feel no pain," Charmaine said, as she leaned over Caitlyn. "It will take about twenty minutes. But you won't notice any time passing either."

It had taken a couple of minutes to get Caitlyn into place. She was strapped to one of the operating tables. Arms at her side. Legs apart. Gagged. Charmaine held up another syringe. "This is a hormone that will encourage your body to produce extra eggs over the next months. There will be few if any side effects. I promise."

She patted Caitlyn's upper thigh, then injected.

Under the influence of narcotics, Caitlyn felt euphoric, barely noticed the jab.

"As for getting some eggs now," Charmaine explained. "I'll be using an ultrasound guide. It's small and accurate. I use it to drain the follicles that contain your eggs. You won't feel much. Most of the eggs will be frozen for our research, but some will be fertilized in a test tube. We'll implant one of them into you and let the others divide."

The two men were still in the room. Caitlyn was dimly aware that she should have felt some kind of resistance to a procedure so intimate in their presence, but the drugs made her beyond caring.

Out of focus, Charmaine's face was still looming above her. Smiling, as if Caitlyn were a child in a dentist chair. Charmaine held up the tubelike instrument that she was about to use to violate Caitlyn.

Then came blackness. The sensation of cloth on her face. They had hooded her again.

Caitlyn heard the tube drop and clatter on the floor. In her drug haze, to Caitlyn it seemed like Charmaine's scream was delayed, the way thunder rolls a few seconds after a lightning strike. And the scream, distorted in Caitlyn's perception, seemed low and rumbling too, as if the sound were slowed down.

In the blindness of her hood, Caitlyn's mind was too altered to completely understand what was happening, and this realization terrified her, washing away whatever euphoria had helped her float along.

She heard other screaming too. Realized it was coming from her own mouth.

And her frenzied panic flung her body from side to side against the straps.

Then the mercy of total unconsciousness.

EIGHTY-THREE

Pierce stood beside the front door, out of sight. Hiding was unnecessary though. Pheromone-induced panic attacks left the victim incapable of coherent thoughts. Pierce could have been waiting in full view, holding a large and bloody butcher knife, and it wouldn't stop anyone inside from fleeing through the opening.

His own mental count put it at three minutes. Which meant that two minutes had passed since Theo would have activated the canister at the intake vent. About enough time for the system to draw that air all through the house.

Pierce heard the screams. Prepared himself.

The front door crashed open.

After that, it truly was like shooting fish in a barrel.

He waited until the man had passed him and given him a large target. *Thh-httt!* He fired a dart into the back of the first person who had flailed out through the doorway.

Then a second. A third.

All three managed to stagger almost to the bushes at the edge of the property before falling.

Pierce stayed in position at the doorway. The tranks would keep those three down for at least five minutes.

Pierce left his gas mask in place. Just a whiff of pheromones from the interior of the house would send him into a panic too.

He listened for screams. Heard only silence.

Counted to another sixty.

Agency procedure 101.

House was clear.

He jogged around the side of the house and found Billy.

"Anyone come out your way?" Pierce asked.

"No sir," Billy said from behind his face mask.

"Then let's get Theo," Pierce said. He had plastic tie handcuffs ready in his back pocket. "Three came out my side. And all of them are down."

❖

Totally without any sense of reason, Caitlyn's mind surged back to consciousness. She screamed and bucked and flailed uselessly against the straps
that held her in place on the table, oblivious to pain as the edges of the straps
cut through the skin of her wrists and ankles.

She was also oblivious to the sound of great thumps as the hybrids, in
equally blind unreasoning, battered against the glass barrier that held them
prisoners, their panic and intense muscular power outweighing the disadvan-
tage of their shortened limbs.

Caitlyn continued her epilepsy of terror until the pheromones, drugs,
sheer exhaustion, and stress forced her back into unconsciousness.

She didn't hear the sound of shattering glass.

EIGHTY-FOUR

Choppers," Theo said.

Pierce and Theo and Billy had just reached the bodies at the edge of the yard, slumped figures facedown beneath the trees with decorative floodlights throwing shadows behind them. Pierce had been prepared for up to a dozen people, had plenty of plastic handcuff ties in his back pocket.

Pierce looked up.

"He hears them," Billy said.

Pierce removed his gas mask. They were far enough away from the house and upwind of it. Seconds later, he heard the choppers too. Pierce followed the noise with his ears, and then that became unnecessary as searchlights opened up from the darkness of the sky. Four blocks away. East. Close enough to understand that backup had betrayed him. Far enough away, he'd be safe from the distraction. Once the SWAT team discovered there was no threat at the false address, no way would they dare incur more wrath of Influentials by sweeping the entire neighborhood.

As Theo and Billy removed their own gas masks, Pierce yanked the darts loose from the backs of the three from the house, expertly handcuffed their hands behind them with plastic ties, rolled them over, and used his flashlight to confirm their identities. Wilson. Dawkins. Charmaine.

No Caitlyn.

He felt the blackness of failure. The only way this op would have been justified is if he'd found them with Caitlyn. Wilson would have been exposed for unauthorized abduction of an agency target; that would have tied it to Dawkins and Charmaine and a widening investigation that would clear Pierce's rogue actions.

Unless Caitlyn was dead and he could find her body in the house.

Pierce slapped Wilson's face. Patty-cake. Fast, light slaps, designed to deliver as much stimulus as possible.

From his days as a field op, Pierce was familiar with the regressive stages of a fear pheromone blast. During the panic scatter and subsequent fetal ball, targets were incapable of coherent thought. This lasted roughly ten minutes, with about a five-minute lag before regaining motor skills. During that stage, casualties felt a mild euphoria of relief combined with thought process recovery. Many spoke freely, and a majority would confess intimate and inane details of their lives in rapid-fire, often to comical effect. Despite the agency's best efforts, many of these confessions had become lore among field ops.

Pierce knelt beside Wilson. When Wilson's breathing shifted from ragged to even, Pierce spoke in a friendly tone. "Hey, buddy," Pierce said. "Wilson. You all right?"

"Yeah, yeah, yeah," Wilson said. "Wow, the stuff hits you, doesn't it? Remember our training, when each of us got blasted with it? There was that blonde, she had a lot to say about you, didn't she, when she came out of it? Like truth serum. Would have been okay, except her friend had your name on her lips too. Those were the days, weren't they, Pierce? Before crap like this, when all you had to worry about was how you spent your weekends."

"Different times," Pierce said, knowing he had a short window to get Wilson to spill in the same way. "Makes me wonder how we got here. Never guessed you'd flip me like this. Thought we were friends."

"Crap, crap, crap," Wilson said. He began to sob. "Hated doing it. Anyone else might have been okay. But not you."

"Give me a reason," Pierce said. "Let me believe."

"Reason, reason, reason. Yeah, reason. You can kill me now, bud, but if I had to do it all over, even knowing it would end like this, I'd still do it."

"How's it going to end?"

"Already ending. Thrown away my career. Thrown away your trust. Thrown away your respect. Had to do it. Would do it over. Yup, would do it over. Hate me for it, but I can't change it."

"Why?" Pierce asked.

"Why, why, why. Guys like you and me, what we've seen over the years, watching someone else's pain is like water off a duck's back. Right? Until it's your own kid. Pierce, I had to do it. Little Luke. Needed the blood. It's a choice that's no choice, between him and you. You can take care of yourself. He can't. He's dying. This blood, this magic blood, it's what's keeping him alive. I did what I could to protect you all along, but in the end, knowing if it came down to Luke or you, I had to go with Luke. Someday, if you have kids of your own, maybe you'd understand. Put me in jail; take away my career;

don't let me see Luke again; even shoot me. It's all worth it, the price to keep him alive. Oh, hell, look at me. Bawling my eyes out."

"See any agency people around?" Pierce asked.

"No, I don't," Wilson said. "Nope. None."

"Didn't want this going down officially until I had a chance to hear you out. Decided I'd be judge and jury. Hoped there was a way I'd understand."

"Can't tell you I'm sorry for what I did," Wilson said. "I'm not. Just sorry for how it turned out."

"It's what I needed to hear," Pierce said. Maybe there was a way to rescue all of this in the next few minutes.

Good hunters prepared for the moment. Prepared thoroughly. Mason knew that and enjoyed the painstaking pursuit of details it demanded. It was what had made him legendary as a bounty hunter.

It was a testament to this that he was here, now knowing that Caitlyn was trapped inside the house, with Billy and Theo and the uppity jerk from the agency in his sights.

But preparation wasn't everything. Good hunters also needed luck.

Mason's luck was that Pierce's pursuit of the man he'd called Wilson had taken them to the edge of the property, almost to the landscaped bushes that hid Mason.

Not only had it given Mason the perfect place to overhear what he needed to learn, but there was little open ground he'd have to cover to pounce.

The big stupid one had eluded him once, so he shouldn't underestimate him again. Same with the pesky little one.

Still, the situation demanded that he first take out Pierce. Pierce was the most dangerous. And he owed Pierce. Pierce was the one who'd broken his arm back in Appalachia. Mason hated Pierce almost as much as he hated Caitlyn.

Mason took a moment to visualize how he was going to do it. He had a couple of weapons to choose from, but what gave him satisfaction was his knife. Mason loved knife work, and before this one began, he knew how it was going to end.

When he was ready, he crept a couple of steps to a small opening between the bushes. He'd be invisible, but even if he wasn't, their attention was on the people on the ground.

No hesitation now.

Mason started from a squat, pushed upward and outward, and covered the distance between him and Pierce in three large, quiet steps on the soft grass.

Pierce reached for Wilson's wrists, intending to free his friend.

Something in his subconscious gave him a twinge. A primordial warning of danger. Could have been a sound, could have been a vibration; it was nothing he'd be able to articulate, even given time.

He began to shift in response, then caught a blur of motion.

Pierce always had fast reactions. He slid his head away from the motion, but that was all he was able to do in defense.

Then he was engulfed in a tornado of rage.

Pierce had heard or sensed something and began to move sideways.

Mason was prepared. He swung hard and viciously with a short piece of wood, bouncing it off Pierce's skull.

Mason expected Pierce to topple, but Pierce had managed to slide his head fractionally sideways, enough that the massive blow deflected instead of hitting square. Pierce had been rising. Didn't get to his feet. Somehow stayed vertical, on his knees.

But Mason let his momentum carry him and with a spinning move, wrapped an arm around Pierce's neck. Then pulled and lifted and arched backward so that Pierce's full body weight sagged on the cartilage of his throat.

Then came the knife.

Mason reached around and slashed horizontally across Pierce's forehead, cutting a line left to right about an inch above Pierce's eyes. It wasn't anything life threatening. All it would take was a cloth held in place to staunch the bleeding.

Mason knew, though, that a wound like this inflicted psychological terror that few of his victims could handle. More importantly, the forehead was a part of the anatomy rich with blood. A gash like this generated an instant fountain that streamed into the victim's eyes, blinding the victim, allowing Mason the luxury of toying with his victim until the end of the massacre.

Billy and Theo had finally begun to react.

"Don't move," Mason commanded them, using Pierce as a shield. He placed the tip of his knife blade against Pierce's temple. It would be a shame if he had to kill Pierce this way, this quickly. But Mason needed to immobilize all of three of them.

Billy and Theo obeyed instantly, freezing in awkward positions only a couple of feet apart.

In the decorative floodlights, the blood must have terrified them too. Mason yanked Pierce's head back with his free hand. It briefly showed Pierce's face. It was a red mask, dripping down his chin, onto Mason's forearm in the chokehold position.

"Tie each other up," Mason told them. "Use those extra plastic cuffs."

"Don't," Pierce said. "Whoever it is, take him now, or he'll kill both of you."

The logic was impeccable. Another part of what made Mason a great hunter was the knowledge of his prey. Humans usually made emotional decisions, even when logical decisions were necessary.

Billy and Theo had ignored Pierce's command.

"I'm dead anyway," Pierce said. "Do what you need to do to save yourselves."

"Billy," Mason said. Billy and Theo were paralyzed by the conflicting orders. "On the ground now. On your bellies. Hands behind your back."

He pushed the knife into Pierce's temple hard enough to draw a gasp of pain. It was what he needed to topple them out of paralysis.

Billy fell forward, then onto his stomach.

"Theo," Mason ordered. "Plastic cuffs. Billy's wrists. Then Pierce's ankles."

It all fell into place for Mason. Once Billy's hands were tied, Theo obeyed and cuffed Pierce's ankles. Mason shoved Pierce forward and placed a knee on Pierce's back, pinning him on the ground, keeping the knife in place until Theo had cuffed Pierce's wrists.

"Now Billy's ankles," Mason said. "Then your own."

Mason watched approvingly. Billy was bound, wrists and ankles. Same with Pierce. And now Theo's ankles. The two major threats were neutralized, and Theo, not much of a threat, was hobbled.

Mason dropped Pierce and kicked Theo hard, knocking the skinny kid on the ground.

"Hands out," Mason ordered Theo. Mason finished Theo's wrists.

Excellent. All three of them on the ground.

Mason evaluated the other three, who had come screaming out of the house. Now conveniently cuffed by Pierce.

Mason decided the second agency guy might be a threat. Mason quickly and brutally kicked the bound man in the head. He didn't bother to check if it had knocked him out. There was no doubt. Might have killed him. Mason didn't care.

He didn't care about the smaller man, dressed nicely but groaning badly. The woman, though, might have some use for him.

Tempting to kill Billy and Theo. But this was more than business. Each of the three of them had done something to Mason to demand special vengeance.

Killing Billy and Theo wouldn't be good enough. Let them live with Mason in their nightmares, let them live knowing they were responsible for what was going to happen next to Pierce.

Mason stepped on Pierce's elbow. Grabbed the lower part of Pierce's arm. Pulled upward, like he was breaking a dry sapling. The crack of bone was the same.

Theo screamed.

"Enjoy that?" Mason said to Theo. "You're next, for dropping that rock on my head in Appalachia. But first, something for you to think about for a long, long time. Understand? I'm going to snap each of your arms like I did his. But there's something I need to do first."

Mason rolled Pierce over. He wiped away the blood off Pierce's forehead so that Pierce could see again.

Mason grinned. The low floodlights gave enough illumination. Let Pierce have that grin in his memory for the next half hour as his life slowly bled away.

"Breaking my arm in the restaurant in Appalachia," Mason said, "was a stupid, stupid thing to do. Understand? I've broken your arm, but that's not enough. Not close to enough. Gut wound is one of the worst ways to die. I've been waiting awhile to tell you that."

Mason smiled again. Then plunged his knife into Pierce's belly, twisting the blade as he pulled it loose.

EIGHTY-FIVE

Mason entered the house through the front doors that had been left wide open, carrying the woman limp over his shoulders, ready to drop her at the first sign of danger.

Mason needed to hurt people. It was his nature, simple as that. The need would ebb and swell. He knew his own moods, and if the woman couldn't or wouldn't lead him to Caitlyn, he still had her to give him temporary relief to quell the urge.

Lights were on in the house. Insects had swarmed through the open door from the night air, and moth shadows flickered behind lampshades.

There were photos on the wall at the entry, and Mason saw the face of the woman he was carrying.

Good. She lived here.

"Where is she?" Mason asked. "The bird girl."

No answer. But the woman had shifted several times, and Mason knew she was conscious. She was on the shoulder above his good arm, so he was able to reach opposite with his recently healed arm, holding his knife. He pushed the tip into the skin just below one of her eyeballs.

She gasped.

"The bird girl," Mason repeated. "Tell me. It's you or her."

It was going to get worse for this woman, Mason thought, swallowing down the beginnings of excitement, but no point in telling her.

"I'll tell you," the woman said. "She's at the other end of the house. Down some stairs. In a hidden place in the basement. Please, please don't hurt me."

She used the exact tone of voice that Mason had learned to cherish. He decided he would wait until she had guided him as far as he needed, then Taser her into unconsciousness and leave her in a convenient heap for later use.

Halfway down a hallway, Mason heard a mewling sound behind him. From around the corner where he'd just dumped the woman's body.

He shifted, hand on his Taser. Cautiously, he returned and peeked around the corner.

Then he blinked his good eye, hardly able to believe what he was seeing coming down the hallway. There were two of them. Some kind of naked, dark, hairy creatures with short legs, stump arms, and monstrous faces.

They were bent over the unconscious woman, making pitiful crying sounds.

Both straightened and turned their heads toward Mason. One balanced awkwardly as it tried to make its way toward Mason on half-formed feet.

What kind of zoo is this house? Mason wondered. *A girl with wings. And these things?*

Mason backed up to where the hallway opened into another room. If these monsters were going to attack, Mason wanted space to maneuver.

There was something strange about the way the closer of the monsters was focused on Mason. As if it was listening instead of watching.

Mason bumped into a table, and the extra sound turned the monster's head sharply. One hand on the Taser, Mason felt behind him on the table. His fingers closed on a flower vase. He tossed it toward the monster.

It didn't react. Not until the vase crashed, then the monster grunted and flinched.

How easy could this be? A blind and handless cripple thing.

Mason set his Taser on full charge, warily closed the distance between himself and the monster, and before it could react, Tasered it.

It didn't utter a sound as it collapsed. The other one tried to charge, but the half-formed feet and its lack of visual context made it an easy target for a second Taser shot. It too fell.

For satisfaction, he slashed both deeply and repeatedly with his knife, making sure both were totally beyond ever getting up.

Mason left Jessica behind. He knew where Caitlyn was. In the basement.

Seconds later, as promised by the woman who lived in the house, he found the top of the stairs.

Caitlyn's return to awareness was pain, bands of fire around her wrists and ankles.

She was blind and was bewildered by it. Until she remembered the hood that had been put over her head. Pulling the events together in her memory seemed as though she was assembling shards of glass by sweeping them into a pile with her bare hands.

It slowly came together. The vision of Charmaine's cold, certain smile. The lashing out of rage. Her struggle against the gag around her mouth and the shackles that held her in place for what Charmaine had explained would happen. Then the unreasoning terror just after the hood had been placed over her head, taking away all rational thought.

She could not guess how much time had passed.

Now there was a residue of dread, like a taste in her mouth. Uneasiness that should have rationally been explained by circumstances but felt deeper and more instinctive.

And except for her own breathing beneath the hood—shallow and dry, hot against her face—there was silence.

She tried an experimental tug with her arms, exacerbating the band of fire against her wrist.

More of the shards of memory; how, in the first few seconds beneath the blindfold, she'd flailed in panic far out of proportion to any reaction she should have had to Charmaine's threats.

This was the pain then. Where she'd cut her skin against the bonds in the horror and dread that screamed at her to flee in any way possible.

Silence.

This was frightening too. Not like before, in a way that defied reason and washed her away like a giant wave crashing her against rocks. Her fear now was based on understanding.

She couldn't see. She was helplessly bound. And the silence told her she was alone.

Why? What had happened to Charmaine? to Dawkins? Had they left her here? Why? When would they return?

To call out, though, would be a sign of weakness. She was weak and would admit that to herself. Pride and anger—which outweighed her weakness—would not allow her to speak out into the silence.

She waited.

And listened, forcing herself beneath the hood to draw air in and out of her lungs so slowly that the sound of her breath did not fill her ears.

She heard her own pulse, faintly. She could imagine the flow of blood, constricted by a vein, pushing against her skin in the soft of her throat, like an animal struggling to escape.

Then came a scrape of footsteps. The first scrape might have been her imagination. But not the second or third.

She was no longer alone in the room.

Now she stopped breathing, her entire focus on the direction of sound. Totally motionless, it seemed like the pulse in her throat would give her away.

But that was ridiculous.

She could not see, but it didn't mean she was hidden. She felt like a rabbit in a hawk's dark shadow. But the instinct to freeze would not protect her. Whoever had just entered the room had total control of her destiny. She couldn't even fight against a palm placed over her mouth and nose to suffocate her.

Then the slightest of touches, almost like a caress against the fabric of the hood.

She almost screamed into the gag, but drew upon her anger and rage. She would not give satisfaction to whoever it was above her, the person who had begun to peel back her mask.

The first of the room's soft light reached her eyes.

She closed her eyes. Then commanded herself to face her fear. Whatever happened next, she would not give up her dignity.

The hood continued to peel back. After blinking a few times, she recognized the person above her. His appearance had been altered subtly. Cheeks padded. Eye color changed. Hair dyed.

"Told you," Razor said, his skin now clear of tattoos. He was dressed in a way she hadn't seen before. As an Influential. "Fast. Sharp. Dangerous."

"Told you. Fast. Sharp. Dangerous."

Mason chuckled softly as he took his first steps into the basement room with shattered glass on the floor. The reunion he'd just witnessed from the doorway was ever so touching, the words he'd just heard ever so ridiculous.

"Told you. Fast. Sharp. Dangerous."

The kid, whoever he was, was about to learn who truly was fast, sharp, and dangerous.

EIGHTY-SIX

Caitlyn had moved into a sitting position on the operating table, rubbing her wrists where the shackles had bit into the skin. Razor was bent over. He'd already freed one of her ankles and had begun on the other.

Caitlyn saw movement over Razor's shoulder.

Fast movement.

For a split second, as she recognized the man rushing into the room, Caitlyn couldn't reconcile reality. She'd always dismissed her gnawing fear of Mason as the material of nightmares, part of her horror based on how she'd left him to die.

As the synapses of her neurons raced to match his face to her memories, there was an extra nanobeat of hesitation because of his eye patch. So when she finally reacted, all she could blurt out was a half scream.

"Razor! Behind you!"

Mason was in full stride, arm fully extended with a gunlike object.

Still, Razor lived up to his name. His reactions were so fast that with only two strides left before his attacker reached him, Razor was beginning to fling his arm forward to drop a flashball.

But Mason was too fast.

There was a horrible crackle and an arc of blue light as Mason jolted Razor with a full Taser charge. Razor fell backward, landing hard, and the flashball rolled harmlessly away without enough impact to generate the instant chemical reaction of exploding magnesium. The ball stopped among the shattered pieces of glass where the dividing wall had stood until the hybrids crashed through.

Razor moaned as his body shuddered.

The sound snapped Caitlyn out of paralysis. Frantically, she tried to release the final shackle, leaning forward and scrambling to get the strap's end in her fingers.

"Let me help you with that," Mason said. His leer was far worse than anything she'd seen in her nightmares. "More fun for me if you have a fighting chance."

He slipped his Taser into his back pocket. Then he pushed aside her hand and used his own fingers until the strap fell away.

"Here I am. One good eye. It's all I'm going to need." He leered again. "Nice that you're not wearing much."

Caitlyn tried to punch him in the face. He swatted her hand away.

"I like that," he said. "Keep going. Makes all this fun."

The roof of Caitlyn's mouth was dry copper. She tried to swallow, to add moisture. But she didn't punch again.

"There's a man out in the city," Mason said. "Everett's his name. You might remember him. From a rooftop where you put a knife in his belly. He's got something he wants to finish with you. He made a promise that I could watch if I brought you back to him. But there's nothing that says I have to bring you back right away, if you catch my drift."

Mason reached into his shirt and pulled out a dead rat.

Caitlyn gagged.

"Don't be like that," Mason said. "Thanks to you, I learned to get a taste for this."

He lifted the rat to his mouth.

Caitlyn was still facing the doorway, and more movement caught her attention. This time, the movement was slower. This time, her recognition wasn't delayed. This time, she didn't shout a warning.

She brought her eyes back to Mason.

"You eat rats?" she asked, trying to keep her voice steady. If she could hold Mason's attention for the next few seconds, maybe there would be enough of a distraction to escape.

In the doorway was one of the hybrids.

But Mason had caught her slight shift in attention. He grabbed her hair with his good hand and spun behind her to face whatever she'd seen, using her as a screen.

Then he laughed.

"Another one of them," he said. "How many they got in this house? Slower and stupider than a half-dead monkey. Blind too. And no arms. It's hardly a fair fight, but then, I like it that way."

The hybrid mewled as it moved into the room, sniffing and casting its head as if trying to get the scent of Mason.

Mason yanked Caitlyn's hair, pulling her off the table, then threw her against the far wall. He glanced at her, satisfied that she was immobilized, then turned his attention on the hybrid.

"I'm right here, stupid," Mason called to the hybrid. He brandished his knife and advanced on the hybrid. "I'm the one that got your brother."

The hybrid mewled once again, in a higher pitch.

From the floor, Caitlyn was stunned but was still able to focus on Mason. The second hybrid moved into her vision.

"Hey," Mason said. "Didn't I just…"

In the light, it was clear that both hybrids had slash wounds. But their blood had already congealed.

"You know anything about this?" Mason called to Caitlyn, keeping his attention on both hybrids. "These are the two I left for dead. How'd they get up again?"

Caitlyn found the strength to get on her hands and knees. She wobbled from dizziness and shock.

Mason danced past the hybrids, and Caitlyn understood Mason's plan when Mason reached the doorway.

"Thought you'd get away, bird girl?" Mason said. "Now you got to get past them and me."

The hybrids lumbered in a half circle to follow Mason's voice.

"Come on then," Mason said. "If knife don't do it, I've got my nice little electric surprise for you."

Caitlyn saw past Razor's motionless body on the floor, between the two bodies of the hybrids, as Mason tucked his knife behind his belt and pulled out the Taser.

She also saw something round and smooth lying among the shattered glass pieces. With the two hybrids blocking Mason from a direct route to stop her.

On her feet now, Caitlyn lunged forward and grabbed the flashball. Like Mason had just done, she moved around the hybrids to get a clear view of Mason in the doorway.

"Still here," he cackled, waving the Taser. "One on three, but I like my odds."

Caitlyn lifted her right hand, ensuring that Mason had to keep his eye on it. She threw her hand forward and down, closing her eyes and averting her head as she released the flashball onto the floor at Mason's feet.

Even with her eyes squinted shut, the sudden light was bright enough to hurt.

Mason screamed with the agony of that same mini-nova burning his vision.

Eyes open now after a couple seconds of waiting, Caitlyn saw that Mason had dropped the Taser. He was on his knees, blindly reaching for it. There was still a large gap between Mason and the hybrids. Caitlyn darted forward and kicked the Taser away.

The clattering of the Taser across the floor was enough for Mason to realize what had happened.

"Bird girl, you're dead," he shouted in rage. Standing again, he brandished the knife he pulled from behind his back. It was obvious he couldn't see.

Caitlyn thought about trying to fight him, but the hybrids, mewling back and forth, had shuffled even closer. That's when she realized that the flashball would not have affected them. They were blind anyway, their faces a horrible grimace of rage and exposed canines as they waved their flipper arms and closed in on Mason.

At first contact, Mason slashed out with his knife, stabbing the closest hybrid in the shoulder. But the second one lunged, knocking Mason away from the doorway and into the wall. Mason slid sideways and onto his knees. The first hybrid fell on him with a guttural roar.

Mason screamed as those massive canines found the bicep of his once-casted arm. Mason tried to stand and run, but he couldn't escape those teeth. With his good hand, he tried to plunge the knife into the hybrid's back, but the second one managed to find his other shoulder with its face and buried teeth deep into the muscle.

Mason went down, with both hybrids on him like the Rottweilers that Mason had many times before released on trapped men.

And like those same men before, Mason's screams became gargles of desperation as he stabbed and stabbed in an effort to protect himself.

The doorway was open.

If Caitlyn could drag Razor clear, they'd both have a chance of escape.

As she tried to lift Razor by the shoulders, she was desperately afraid that Dawkins or Charmaine would appear at any moment.

"Come on," she pleaded to Razor. "Come on."

She was able to pull him up to his knees, but she couldn't get the leverage to put him in a position to drag him.

From the doorway came a single word.

"Caitlyn."

It wasn't Charmaine or Dawkins. But Billy, with a twisted expression of relief and pain, one arm hanging awkwardly at his side.

EIGHTY-SEVEN

"Open his shirt," Caitlyn instructed Razor..

When he hesitated, she snapped, "Do it. Billy can't. Theo can't."

Razor knelt above Pierce's prone body and reached down, keeping his own body as far from Pierce as he could, using his fingertips to delicately touch the shirt.

"No," Caitlyn said. "That's not going to work. I can't get to the wound. Get behind him, cradle him upright. Reach around with both hands."

"I can't. I already told you I'm freaked out by blood."

"Watch this," Caitlyn said. She held Mason's knife in her right hand. She pressed the blade diagonally across her left palm. With a swift motion of both hands, she applied pressure and pulled the left away from the right. She opened her left palm to show a blossoming gash.

It shocked Razor into continued silence.

"If I can do that," she told Razor, "you can hold him."

Blood began to drip down Caitlyn's wrist. Instead of letting it splatter on the ground, she held her palm over Pierce's forehead, streaming her blood into the knife gash that Mason had left behind.

"Do it!" Caitlyn said. "Or he's dead."

Her willpower was so intense that Razor nodded. He reached under Pierce's neck and lifted. Pierce was too far gone to resist. Razor pushed more and managed to get Pierce into an upright position. Then, as instructed, he reached around and lifted and held Pierce's blood-soaked shirt away from the wound.

Caitlyn pressed her bleeding palm directly onto Pierce's belly and held it in place.

For Pierce, the first sensation was reluctance. He was in a deep, dark peace. Now, pulled upward and outward, his peace and surrender were replaced by cold, shivering, and the consciousness of renewed pain. His belly. His arm.

Then came the sensation of pressure. Soft pressure. Against the wound.

He opened his eyes.

There she was. Caitlyn. The young woman he'd hunted for months. Her eyes open. Staring at him.

He glanced down. Her hand was on his belly.

Back at her eyes. Intensity. Compassion. Determination.

He was shaking. So cold. Arms around him from behind. He closed his eyes. He wanted to go back to the warmth. The calm. The cessation of everything.

"Don't go back," she said. "Stay with me."

Pierce's eyelids were sticky. But the blood flow from his forehead had stopped. He reached up and touched it with his fingers, expecting more stickiness. Instead, he discovered it had hardened into a scab.

"You?"

She nodded.

"And down there?" he asked.

She lifted her hand off his belly, showing a diagonal gash in her palm. "It stopped bleeding. I had to cut it again to get you more blood."

With her hand removed and the pressure relieved, Pierce felt warmth where Mason had plunged the knife.

"The pain," Pierce said. "It's going away."

This was true. Except for his arm, where Mason had snapped the bone.

Caitlyn opened and closed her palm. "Mine too. Don't ask me how. But that's the way it is."

Then Pierce completely understood all that was at stake. Her blood was capable of this. Caitlyn had the gift of life. Hers to bestow. Or withhold. Unless she was a prisoner, giving her captor the same gift. And if the secret to this could be genetically unraveled...

"Mason...," he said. Slowly. His lips were losing the numbness of cold as his shock receded.

She jerked her head toward the house. "Still in there. But it's over."

"No," Pierce said. "It's not."

The immensity of the blessing and the curse of her gift was like a deep, black chasm in front of him. Free, she would live with it all her life, government always searching. Held by the government, the power of life and death would be taken from her, owned by the rich and powerful and the too often corrupt.

"Yes. Mason's dead," she said. "And some others. Like me but not like me. It's over."

Arm limp at his side, Pierce now had the strength to sit upright without help. That's when he discovered Razor behind him.

"You're here," he said to Razor. Pierce was coherent, his pain was fading, and the concerns of the world were back on his shoulders. He was also aware that the warmth in his belly was growing more intense, and he wondered if that was part of the healing process.

"You're surprised?" Razor asked.

Pierce rolled forward to his knees, a movement that suddenly shot stabbing pain from his broken arm. He'd broken bones before and expected the pain should have been worse. What was the extent of the healing powers of Caitlyn's blood?

"No longer surprised when you surprise me," Pierce answered. "Tell me what was inside."

With Billy and Theo standing silently in the background, Razor described it with succinct and efficient detail. It wasn't difficult for Pierce to make solid conclusions. A scaled-down genetic program needing Caitlyn or her DNA for the final pieces.

"You've got to run," Pierce said. "All of you."

If they didn't, Caitlyn would be in agency hands. But how long before they found her?

Pierce glanced at Wilson's motionless body. If his friend was dead, there would be less to cover up. If Wilson survived, he still wouldn't know what was going to happen in the next minutes. And later, Pierce would be in a good position to negotiate with Wilson.

"Run?" Razor echoed.

"Get them safe," Pierce said, nodding his head at Caitlyn and Billy and Theo. "Keep them safe. Later, get to me. We'll talk. But I don't ever want to know where they are."

"We want to go west," Theo said. "Across the Mississippi."

"I'll help Razor make it happen," Pierce said. "Go."

"You want them free?" Razor asked. Near disbelief.

Free. And with no pursuit from the agency again. He needed to get into the house and clean things up. Before he called in the agency. Maybe there was a way to stop anyone looking for her again.

"How much clearer do I have to be?" Pierce got to his feet. "And I want to recruit you for the agency after that. You'll get immunity for killing Timothy Raymond Zornenbach."

"What?" Razor said. "How did you figure it—"

"That was a bluff," Pierce said. "Thanks for confirmation. If the rest of my guess is correct, you had good reason for it. My offer stands. Join the agency. Get immunity. But I can't make any of this happen unless you go."

"Thought you didn't make moral decisions," Razor said.

"I lied." Pierce grinned. Incredibly, except for his broken arm, he was feeling close to one hundred percent. "But obviously, so did you."

EIGHTY-EIGHT

Pierce had dragged Charmaine outside after finding her unconscious in the hallway of her home. The homeowner's gender didn't necessarily mean the house had to have candles, he figured, but given how obvious it was that she pampered her looks, he decided in this case it was a sure bet.

Pierce found them in the first place he looked. The master bathroom. Cinnamon candles, big round block candles perched on the counter nearest the tub. The wicks were blackened, with dried puddles of wax.

Pierce briefly wondered about the nights Charmaine spent alone in the house. Reclining in a hot bath in the candlelight, with the hybrids imprisoned below in the lab, hidden away from the world.

She would have needed something to light the candles.

Pierce hoped it wasn't matches. It would be hell to try to strike matches one-handed. Ignoring the pain in his broken arm, Pierce threw open drawers, scattered various toiletries as he pulled out the contents and flung them on the floor. His second break—he found a lighter, not matches. He shoved it into his pocket and dropped the candles down the front of his shirt to carry them kangaroo style while he went to look for the hidden lab in the basement.

Conscious of the pain that throbbed through his broken arm, Pierce never thought he'd see any circumstance where he might feel pity for Mason Lee. Until this.

Blood. On the walls, on the floor.

With the bodies of two beasts beside a motionless Mason Lee. The man's face had been ravaged, almost torn off. A knife to the hilt in the chest of one of the hybrids and the throat slashed on the other. Giant pools of blood. They were beyond recovery.

No time to study the scene here. Too much to do.

Pierce scanned the rest of the room. There was shattered glass on the floor. Operating table. Different medical machines. A small white refrigerator across the room.

He found the canister inside.

When Pierce leaned forward to grab it, the candles inside his shirt rolled forward and mildly bumped at the bottom of his tucked in shirt. He took the canister and added it to the pouch.

Wilson's son would live.

Pierce moved out of the room again. The next step was to get rid of all of this permanently. He'd make sure that later Mason's body would be identified as Caitlyn's.

Mason should have been dead, but some of the blood that had drenched him from the hybrids had begun a viral healing action that kept him alive and barely conscious.

Dimly, Mason was aware that someone else was in the room. There were footsteps, crunching of glass. The sucking sound of a refrigerator door opening. Closing. Retreating footsteps.

In the silence that followed, he found the strength to roll over. He bumped into the bodies of the hybrids. It was dark, and Mason wished he could walk over to the wall and switch on the lights. He felt around until he found his knife, still in the chest of one of the hybrids. Mason twisted the knife loose and tucked it into the back of his pants.

When he tried to sit, it took so much effort that he began to pant, but he was resolute. He wanted light.

He refused to let pain overwhelm him. He managed to crawl until he bumped into a wall. He blindly followed the walls, on his hands and knees, until he found the doorway. With a groan, he pulled himself up to a standing position. He fumbled for the light switch.

He clicked it, expecting light to flood the room.

It didn't.

Disbelieving, he brought his hands to his face and explored the wreckage.

And with a guttural moan of rage, he realized his worst nightmare had come true.

❖

The water heater was in a utility room in the center of the house. Copper pipe entered the bottom of the tank, where it fed natural gas to the heater.

On his knees, Pierce shut off the pilot light. He wanted charred bodies left in the house. But didn't want one of them to be his.

He stood again, lifted one foot, and smashed his heel down on the copper pipe at the base of the heater, again and again and again until it broke free.

He knew he imagined the hissing of natural gas from the jagged end of the badly bent pipe—the system ensured it was a low-pressure feed—but the rotten-egg smell of the odorant added to the gas was not his imagination.

At a fast pace, but not in panic, he backed away and shut the door to the room. He needed for it to fill with the methane of the natural gas, and estimated he had about five minutes.

Outside the door, he retrieved a candle from his shirt. He'd pulled a chair up earlier, and he set the candle on the chair. Then the second candle. Eventually, the gas would escape the utility room and lick outward until reaching open flame. And the ignition would follow that first small stream of gas back into the huge pocket waiting to explode. Putting the candles on the chair instead of at floor level would buy a little extra time.

Pierce pulled out the lighter and hesitated.

It was one thing to intellectually believe that the natural gas wouldn't seep out from under the door until it had filled the utility room. It was another thing to test it while standing there.

He didn't have a choice, however. And the longer he hesitated, the greater the chances of a finger of that gas reaching for the flame.

He flicked the lighter. Found himself still alive.

He lit both candles. He touched the front of his shirt to make sure he still had the canister in a safe place.

Then he spun and ran.

A monstrous figure loomed in front of Pierce, blocking the hallway.

It took Pierce a second to realize it was Mason, knife extended, lurching toward him.

Pierce backed up slowly, swallowing horror at the damage inflicted on Mason.

"I know you're there," Mason said, stabbing at air. "Who are you?"

"Drop the knife," Pierce said. "We've got to clear the house."

"You? I killed you. I'll do it again."

More pathetic stabs into the air.

The man was blind; Pierce knew in a flash.

"Drop it," Pierce said. "I'll help you out. The house is about to explode."

"Explode." Mason seemed to savor the word.

Pierce was expecting a forward lunge or some other form of attack. Instead, Mason dropped to his knees, then sat.

"Come on," Pierce urged. The natural gas was pooling. When it seeped out from under the door...

"I'm staying," Mason said.

"That would make you a dead man."

"I guess you live blind." Mason's head was tilted, and he seemed to be speaking to someone else. "Or you decide not to live. What other choices are there?"

"No choice," Pierce said. "I'll drag you."

Seated, Mason lurched his upper body forward and started stabbing at the air again. "Try. I'll fight until we both die."

Every second counted. Pierce needed to be well clear of the house. He didn't know that he had much choice. He could disarm Mason, but if the man was intent on staying, the fight truly would kill both of them.

Pierce made his decision. He edged past the injured man, staying well clear of any lunges in case Mason heard his footsteps.

Pierce got past him, turned. "Last chance."

Mason's face gaped open. A twisted, macabre smile. "Better dead than blind."

EIGHTY-NINE

Illusion. All that was needed was money. Something Razor had in abundance, thanks to the man who had once tormented him for years, T. R. Zornenbach.

After he'd walked away from Pierce and Theo, Razor had gone to another one of his hideout hotel rooms. He'd dyed his hair, popped in contact lenses to change his eye color, put padding inside his upper cheeks to alter the dimension of his face.

But the biggest illusion was clothing. His sleek new clothing clearly marked him as an Upper Influential. That alone guaranteed him immunity. Not only as he moved through various strata of Influentials, but also preventing any hassle by Illegals.

In less than ten minutes, dressed in the expensive silks and cashmeres that gave Influentials the illusion of beauty and self-importance and entitlement, he had transformed himself. His sleek wallet held false identification.

He had walked without fear back into the hallway and to the elevator and through the checkpoint into Charmaine's neighborhood, telling the guard he was looking for some entertainment at a friend's house.

On the way out of Charmaine's neighborhood, clearing the gate at the neighborhood checkpoint would be just as easy; a trolley would take them to the inner core of the city. Back to one of Razor's permanent hotel rooms, where they'd be safe until Pierce arranged for their escape to the west.

Just before the checkpoint, Razor drew Caitlyn to the side and spoke softly, making it clear the conversation wasn't meant for Billy and Theo.

"You can't stay here very long, near this city or any other city, with your wings and expect your secret to be safe," Razor said. "Too many people."

"That's the reason for going west."

"Yeah," Razor said, "Pierce told me he meant his promise. He'll make sure you reach the west. The three of you."

Billy looked back once, briefly, but must have understood the intensity of their conversation because he looked away immediately.

Billy was the right one for her, Caitlyn thought. Why did she want Razor?

"Pierce offered you a job as an agent," Caitlyn said. "You'd be a good one."

"I'd go west," Razor said. "If you asked me."

This was a big moment. She knew it. Beside her was fast and sharp and dangerous. Ahead was Billy's large silhouette, his broken arm against his side. A man who loved her without reserve. Who had filled the doorway when she most needed it. Who played no games.

Billy was the right one for her.

But in his own way, Razor had not abandoned her either.

As a girl, even in her solitude in the mountains with Jordan, Caitlyn had wondered if she would ever find someone who would look past her freakishness and want to kiss her. She had wondered what it would be like to be kissed, how a girl could know a kiss was coming, how to respond.

Here it was. Certainty. If she leaned forward, turned her head in invitation, Razor would close the gap. He was holding his breath, waiting. So simple.

So complicated.

A kiss. What would it tell Razor? And if Billy looked back, what would it tell Billy?

She ached to kiss Razor but couldn't trust whether it was simply a physical desire or something deeper. West was the best option, especially with Pierce's promise to help. Could she accept the responsibility for taking Razor away from the setting where he was most alive? Fast, sharp, and dangerous, able to move through all the levels of this world. Or perhaps she could accept surgery to stay here and, in so doing, change who she was? Either way, one of them would sacrifice.

This man did make her feel alive. Perhaps that sensation could make up for losing her wings.

But did she have a right to think only of herself? It flashed into her mind, the image of the little girl she'd held in the shanty, and how Caitlyn had helped the girl with a smudge of blood.

In that moment, Caitlyn realized what she had to do. That her own wishes mattered little compared to the responsibility that came with the powers woven into her genetic code.

If she were choosing between Billy and Razor, and this was the moment it had to be done, the most important question was simple.

Who would be the better father?

It meant there was something she had to know about Razor.

"Back there, Pierce offered you immunity," Caitlyn said. "Is it true? You killed someone and took his name?"

"Holly," Pierce said on the phone, well down the street from the house where Mason had chosen to die. Wilson beside him, helping keep Dawkins on his feet, was still cuffed. Charmaine now conscious, hobbling along. "I'm calling in backup. There's a hostage situation in the house. Two genetic freaks called hybrids. Holding Caitlyn. I've been able to clear two others—Dawkins and Charmaine—from the house. Wilson's with me. We need a team to take out the hybrids. Be better if we kept Caitlyn alive, but remember Wilson's orders. Dead or alive, we want her body."

That should cover it, Pierce thought. Three charred bodies would be found in the house, and this phone conversation had established that Caitlyn was one of them. Government didn't have a DNA sample to prove otherwise. Dawkins and Charmaine didn't know Mason had stayed in the house; they too would believe the three bodies were two hybrids and Caitlyn. Once it was established that Caitlyn was dead, her burned body beyond any genetic use, the hunt for her would be over.

"Sure." The tone of Holly's voice was unreadable. She could have taken this moment to remind Pierce that obviously it had been a mistake to go in alone. She didn't.

"But don't send SWAT to the address I left with you," Pierce said. "Instead, we're four blocks away."

Pierce gave her the accurate address. Of Jessica Charmaine's house. Or what would be left of her house.

"I don't understand," she said. "You said that Caitlyn wasn't at Charmaine's address."

"I lied to you earlier," he said. "There was a leak in our team. Someone reporting to Dawkins. I didn't know if it was you or Jeremy or Avery. I gave each of you a different address. Wanted to see what would happen."

Silence. Pierce thought of the three locations. One east, one west, and one north. He'd given her north. Avery west. Choppers and floodlights had descended on the fake address to the east.

"After you call in for SWAT," Pierce said, thinking of the choppers that had swarmed a place four blocks east, "take Avery, and the two of you put Jeremy in lockdown. He's our leak."

"Must be lonely not trusting anyone."

"You get used to it," Pierce said. "Don't worry. I'll approve the transfer and put in a good word. You'll be at the next pay grade by tomorrow noon."

"You're an idiot."

"But at this point, still team leader. Send out the SWAT team."

"I'm not transferring to get away from you," she said. "I want in another unit so that when we go to a beach in Cuba together, it doesn't break any regulations. And so you won't be so lonely."

"Didn't know anything about Cuba."

"Now you do. I want the transfer tomorrow by noon. And you'd better not have any plans for tomorrow night. Cuba will follow. When I say the time is right."

Pierce started to grin. That's when the explosion from a block away staggered him with a blast of noise and heated air.

"Zornenbach was an old man," Razor told Caitlyn. "He took boys from the subways, kept them a few years at a time. I was one of those boys. The last of those boys."

He let her absorb this, then continued. "He was a rich, rich Influential. He taught his pet boys manners, gave them an education, and made them squeaky clean and refined. Transformed them from sewer rats into something he could enjoy. Until they started to hit puberty. Then he'd get rid of them. When I figured it out, I got rid of him first. Otherwise he would have killed me like all the others and gone back into the subway tunnels for another victim."

No way was he going to tell her the rest of it. That the old man

Zornenbach had decided Razor was special enough to keep longer than he'd kept the others. Nor was he going to tell Caitlyn what steps the old man had taken to ensure Razor's body remained at a prepuberty stage. Steps the old man had taken satisfaction in doing himself. There was a reason Razor's limbs were slightly longer and thinner than normal; a lack of testosterone for a few crucial years in his early teens had meant his bone's joints had not hardened in a normal manner. His rib bones were longer too, giving him greater lung power and breath capacity. These were traits, as he knew from his thorough research on the subject, that made the castrati so valuable in operas.

Razor. Not just because he was fast, sharp, and dangerous. But also because self-irony was necessary to keep him from morbid self-pity. *Razor.* Because of how he'd been altered beyond repair—by the straight razor blade that the old man had used one night after drugging him, leaving him to wake in blood and horror.

"I was smarter with computers than the old man realized," Razor said, pushing aside the memory. "I found ways to hack into his systems and continue his business and banking as if he were still alive. I set it up so that it appeared he had legally adopted me. He tended to be a recluse anyway. No one gave it any thought when they didn't see him for months on end. It worked. All that was his became mine. You've seen how I live my life. Illusion."

His greatest illusion was keeping from the world that he was a freak, dependent on hormone replacement therapy to maintain the illusion. He'd watched Caitlyn enough to know she was a freak too. That's one of the things that had drawn him to her. Made him want to protect her.

"Illusion?" Caitlyn looked directly at him. "When I needed you, you were solid."

"It wasn't an accident I was there when the Illegals had you pinned in the alley," he said. "Remember the telescope on the thirty-fifth floor, across from the hotel? From there, I used to watch you on the roof. I saw what happened the night you jumped. I watched you, in the near dark, soaring down to the alley. And I went looking for you."

"Without you, I wouldn't be alive."

"What do you want now?" he asked.

"You were born for the cities and shanties," Caitlyn said. A slow smile. "Fast, sharp, dangerous. Remember? You sure you would want to leave?"

"I want to know what you want. Not what you think I want."

Would she choose him? Or Billy? He saw Billy staring at them, wondering about the conversation.

"What I want," Caitlyn said, "is a father for my children. A good father. And a place to raise them safely."

Razor drew a deep, deep breath into the lungs beneath his unnaturally long rib bones. Before he could decide how to respond, the sky bloomed bright orange behind Caitlyn, briefly lighting the street in front of her and the others. The tremendous boom of an explosion came as she turned, and then a slight trembling of the ground.

Silence followed. But not darkness. The glow merely diminished, and he could see her face clearly. She closed her eyes, opened them. She put her hand up, between her face and Razor's. She brushed Razor's lips with her palm.

"Thank you," she said, "for those flowers. Seems like a lifetime ago, but it was just yesterday. The ones that you had hidden in your sleeve when we escaped the wheelchair guy."

"That sounds like a good-bye." He knew that wasn't true. It might not have been a good-bye. It could just as easily have been a beginning. But Razor didn't want to find out. And wouldn't give her a chance to tell. Better to always believe she might have chosen him.

He kissed her palm, dropped her hand, and stepped back.

"I'm not the kind of guy who would make a good father," he said. "So Caitlyn, I think that's what it should be. Good-bye."

The Arizona sunset was spectacular but so routine that only the stranger among the other four men was looking sideways from his saddle to absorb the oranges and reds that spread from thin cloud cover to the razor-sharp mountaintops jagged on the western horizon.

All of the men, including the stranger, who'd been given an elderly mare, were on horses, walking a slow pace in the heat that was oppressive even at the approach of dusk. Unlike the others, however, he was not equipped with holstered pistol or a rifle in a saddle scabbard. Neither had they given him a canteen full of water—instead, they gave him water when he needed it. He was further set apart from the men by the cracking skin on his forehead and the back of his neck, where sunburn had peeled away. Of more significance, his hands were bound in front of him. And his feet were bare, except for socks. Without water or shoes, he depended on them totally for his survival.

The lead man stopped the group, pulling the stranger away from his thoughts. They'd reached a sheer rock wall. Hours earlier, the low mountain face had appeared only a couple of miles across the flat desert valley from the town where he'd met the guides.

Both were shimmering illusions. The distance. And the flatness. The sand and cactus hid sudden drops into ancient gullies that might roar with a flash flood only every ten years. Time and again, the horses had been forced to pick their way down in the gullies and back out again, and the rock face had, at times, seemed to recede during the slow progress.

Now the men on the horses were at the base of the steep rock wall, where another gully led outward from the rock face, revealing a narrow canyon entrance that hadn't been visible until less than five hundred yards away. Behind them, the desert flats were clear of any rising dust that would indicate they'd been followed. That was a minimal chance anyway. The group had originally been ten, but every few miles, a man had dropped out to guard the path by hiding in a sniper's position.

"It's time for the hood." The lead man hadn't given his name. He had a square face beneath his brimmed hat and neatly trimmed dark beard. Midforties. Not much fat. A working man on a working horse. "Last chance to turn back."

"I didn't come this far to turn back," the stranger said. He paused and fought the horrible liquid coughs that had slowly been draining his life over the previous year. "And what I've told you is the truth."

"We can hear by your cough how badly you need the Healer. For those with nothing to lose, that's enough reason to lie. Just for the hope that she'll overlook the lie to listen to them plead."

"I understand."

"You're keeping in mind all the warnings. First thing a vulture does is tear out your eyes."

The stranger nodded. Along the way, these men—the Protectors—had pointed out human skeletons stretched out on the sand, wrist bones still attached by nylon rope to stakes in the ground. This is what happens, they'd explained, to anyone who tried to deceive the Protectors. There had been other skeletons picked clean too, but still ragged with clothing. Those did not belong to someone who had been left naked on the sand, but to those who had followed and had fallen where a sniper's bullet had shattered their skulls.

After listening to the stranger's story, they'd made no promises. Sometimes she was in the camp. Sometimes she wasn't. And when she wasn't, there was no telling where she might be or what she might look like. The times she traveled, she was invisible, like an angel in disguise among the people of the territory.

Those who guarded her were invisible too; each of them had in common that she'd saved a child in their family, and in gratitude, they formed a small secret society and called themselves the Protectors.

When she touched and healed, she'd disappear again, changing her appearance, moving on to another town, where she would depend on the kindness of strangers. Her existence had already begun to gentle the lawlessness of the dusty and isolated towns. It hadn't taken long for word to spread—someone among them could perform miracles, but only for people she caught treating others with kindness. As a result, most tended to be conscientious about their behavior, in case she was among them, watching. There had been a revival of faith, too, in the territory, for many, believed she truly was an angel. Some because of the healing and others because of the rumors that she could fly. It had only been a year since she'd first brought someone back from a deathbed, but already, she was approaching mythical status.

"I didn't come this far to turn back," the stranger repeated. "It's all or nothing for me."

The stranger accepted the hood. He didn't need his vision. He had his hands on the horn of the saddle, and he was comfortable with the rhythm of the horse's motion.

Shortly after, he felt the air become cooler, and he knew they had entered the deep shadows of the canyon. A few minutes later, the horses stopped and he heard a man dismount. Now, after all the months to get here, was it the time?

No. He heard light swishing sounds, and it puzzled him, until he decided that the Protector who had dismounted behind them was sweeping the sand clean of the hoofprints of the horses.

The rocking motion of a moving horse began again, and they traveled in silence. The stranger did not count to mark time. He had no need to try to map in his head the route they were taking. He was well aware that the canyon led to a labyrinth of natural stone. And well aware that escape would be impossible.

They'd promised him that if he was telling the truth about his unique claim, when the hood came off to prove it, he would live. Just as they'd described how vultures and desert rats and insects would leave his skeleton dry on the sand for the centuries ahead if he had lied in desperation to be led to the one who could heal.

Despite a range of emotions swirling through him, the stranger felt oddly calm. Almost like an out-of-body experience. He'd lived with memories and hopes, regret and satisfaction. His biggest fear, his only fear, was that the Healer would not be in the canyon sanctuary. The stranger did not have long to live. If she was here, she could heal him. If she wasn't, he doubted he'd be able to survive until she returned.

To him, breathing the stale air that he coughed out from his own lungs under the hood, seconds felt like minutes. And minutes like seconds. He passed the time by visualizing the Healer as she'd been described in the rumors. An angel's shadow. In flight.

Then came the sound that thrilled him with hope. The distant greeting whinny of another horse. Ahead and to the right.

Moments later, he smelled the smoke of burning mesquite. A campfire.

Did it mean she was there? Or was it a camp empty except for other Protectors?

The horses stopped.

"It's your time," the lead Protector said.

His hood was pulled. Ignoring the rifles leveled at him, the stranger sucked in clear, fresh air and drew in the details of the scene in front of him.

Tethered horses. A large canvas tent. A fire with a pot sitting on a grill atop the embers.

A big, big man smiling at him. A kid, older than the stranger remembered, with big glasses and an equally big grin.

"They did it!" Theo shouted. "Razor and Pierce made good on the promise!"

"You know this man?" came the question from the lead Protector.

"He's the one we were waiting for," Billy said. "Jordan Brown."

Billy stepped toward Jordan's horse to help him down. "Welcome home."

Words failed Jordan because a fit of coughing stole from him whatever he might have said.

As Billy took his elbow and guided him toward the tent, Jordan Brown looked around for Caitlyn. He was overwhelmed by emotion now, no longer calm, wondering if he could find the strength to overcome his cough and the discipline to speak without weeping with joy.

He rubbed his wrists absently, barely aware that the bonds had been cut away and the rifles lowered.

An image came to him from years ago, of kneeling beside his little girl, the one the other children had called ugly because of her hunched back and who had retreated alone into a corner of a church they'd visited in Appalachia. Of whispering the words that had taken away the tears from the little girl. *"I love you as big and forever as the sky."*

As he relived that image, she stepped outside the tent, no longer his little girl, but a woman in jeans and a shirt, her belly tight and swollen.

Caitlyn. Arms opening wide as she began to rush toward him. That was the moment when she cried out a single word. The word that always filled him with joy.

"Papa!"

As speculative fiction, like the prequel, *Broken Angel*, *Flight of Shadows* takes place in settings where I've wondered what society might be like at the extremes.

In *Broken Angel*, the religious theocracy of Appalachia is based on what could happen if religious extremists in America managed total political control over society. (Centuries ago, at its most successful and powerful, it was called the Inquisition.)

Flight of Shadows examines the world outside Appalachia. My speculation comes from a mishmash of ancient history and current events. My hope is that the novel's fictional setting will remind you that the real America, with all its imperfections and infighting, is still a glorious democracy and a unique bastion of freedom, a legacy built by the women and men who have sacrificed for it over the last few centuries.

To those familiar with the sources I drew upon, it will be immediately obvious that the story is based on the city-states of ancient Greece and on the walled cities built for defense against primitive weaponry. The "Industrials" are intended to bring to mind a similar slave-based society and the correspondingly low value of life in cultures before Jesus Christ and the impact his teachings had on Western civilization.

It might seem far-fetched that in a few generations America could find itself in a city-state society like the one in *Flight of Shadows*, one of degraded freedoms and stability. Yet several factors indicate that the laws currently protecting human rights based on a Judeo-Christian value system are under attack. Without reform to the immigration system, we may not be far from the stratified societies so recently escaped in America and Europe. In less than fifty years, Europe's social landscape has shifted tremendously and become increasingly polarized due to legal immigration intended to facilitate cheap labor. And in America, can illegal immigration not have far-reaching effects over the next few generations? These illegals live in secret and in fear in America, willing to trade cheap labor and their human rights for the chance at a better life for their children, while politicians accept the inconvenience and posture against such realities until jobs become scarce. I believe the religious right in America, as an organized political force, must lead the efforts to help these desperate immigrant families.

The social strata of *Flight of Shadows* is like that of many developing countries. A tiny percentage of extremely wealthy live as kings among the majority of extremely impoverished.

Yet even democracies can disintegrate, as in Germany, which radically changed under Nazi rule. A country once called Rhodesia, only one generation ago, was a prosperous country in the south of Africa. But political instability due to racial inequalities radically changed the way of life there. And under a dictator who slipped into power through a majority vote, Zimbabwe's economy has now become tatters. By squandering the checks and balances of democracy that currently protect America, the Rhodesian farmers have seen their economy and average life span halved in less than twenty years. The skilled and educated have fled the country, and it is no coincidence that there, too, a small minority of the very wealthy live in comfort among the majority whose hopes of freedom are now withering in shanties. These tragedies were not far from my mind as I wrote.

Other existing conditions across the world influenced the novel. Palestinians travel for hours in darkness to wait outside checkpoints for just a chance to work inside Israel and spend hours in darkness traveling back at the end of the day to the poverty of the Gaza Strip. Like illegal immigrants in America, these men and women are driven by helplessness, working any way possible to feed their children, politically hampered by the extremists among them who turn to terrorism.

Water shortages could completely disfigure our governing system and our nation's economy. Interstate squabbles over water rights have taken place in the southwest and southeast United States, and mass shortages are predicted over the next few decades. Wars have been fought for much less.

As for the decline of civil liberties during and after war, all we need do is examine the headlines about the many challenges to civil rights laws since the war in Iraq to see what can happen if citizens aren't vigilant about the dangers of allowing power to be concentrated at the top.

Could we come to the point where genetic science is capable of what the novel presents? DNA manipulation has already produced insects growing legs out of their mouths and paleontologists modifying chicken embryos to hatch living dinosaurs.

As much as the novel is politically or scientifically speculative, however, my hope is that you might remember it most as a story of a father who loved his daughter, who, like each of us, was born to be free.

As a best-selling author, Sigmund Brouwer has written eighteen novels and also several series of children's books. His novel *The Last Disciple* was featured in *Time* magazine and on ABC's *Good Morning America*. His most recent novel is *Broken Angel*. A champion of literacy, he teaches writing workshops for students in schools from the Arctic Circle to inner-city Los Angeles. Sigmund is married to Christian recording artist Cindy Morgan and, with their two daughters, they divide their time between homes in Red Deer, Alberta, Canada, and Nashville, Tennessee. He can be found online at www.sigmundbrouwer.com.

Her birth was shrouded in mystery and tragedy.
Her destiny is beyond comprehension.
Her pursuers long to see her broken.

She fights to soar.

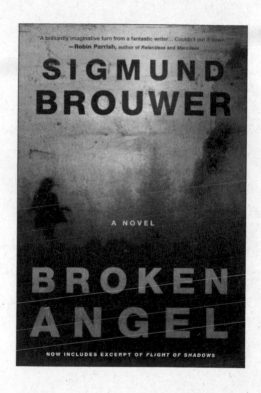

In this engrossing, fast-paced story with a post-apocalyptic edge, best-selling author Sigmund Brouwer weaves a heroic, harrowing journey through the path of a treacherous culture only one or two steps removed from our own.